When they say th[...] they're being euphemistic. War makes a man insane by civilian standards. When the man comes back, he may return to civilian norms again. After a while.

I'm not proud of many of the things that happened in Nam. I'm not proud of some of the things I did myself. But the men I served with were, for the most part, doing the best job they could with the cards they'd been dealt. I'm proud of *them*, and I'm proud to have been among them.

Anybody's got a right to criticize the things that happened. But don't criticize the men who did them unless you've been in their shoes. Ever since I came back, the object of my military fiction has been to put somebody as normal as you, or as I was, into a war zone.

And I hope to God neither you nor your son ever has an opportunity to compare my fiction with the real thing.

A shorter edition of this book
was published under the title
The Military Dimension.

THE MILITARY DIMENSION MARK II

DAVID DRAKE

MARK II: THE MILITARY DIMENSION

Copyright © 1995 by David Drake

A Baen Books Original. (A shorter edition of this book was published under the title *The Military Dimension*.)

Baen Publishing Enterprises
P.O. Box 1403
Riverdale, N.Y. 10471

ISBN: 0-671-87697-X

Cover art by Newell Convers and John Pierrard

First printing, December 1995

Distributed by
SIMON & SCHUSTER
1230 Avenue of the Americas
New York, N.Y. 10020

Printed in the United States of America

DEDICATION

To Mr. Eugene Olson
Who taught by example and enthusiasm
As well as by the book.

ACKNOWLEDGMENTS

"Rescue Mission," copyright © 1988 by David Drake for *The Fleet*, ed. David Drake and Bill Fawcett.

"The Dancer in the Flames," copyright © 1982 by Stuart David Schiff for Whispers *(magazine) #17–18, ed. Stuart David Schiff.*

"Arclight," *copyright © 1973 by Mercury Press Inc. for F&SF*, April 1973, ed. Edward L. Ferman.

"Band of Brothers," copyright © 1990 by David Drake for *The Far Stars War*, ed. Bill Fawcett.

"Firefight," copyright © 1976 by Kirby McCauley for *Frights*, ed. Kirby McCauley.

"Contact!" copyright © 1974 by The Conde Nast Publications Inc. for *Analog*, October 1974, ed. Ben Bova.

"As Our Strength Lessens," copyright © 1993 by David Drake for *Bolos: The Honor of the Regiment*, September 1993, created by Keith Laumer, ed. Bill Fawcett.

"Best of Luck," copyright © 1978 by David Drake for *The Year's Best Horror Stories, Series VI*, ed. Gerald W. Page.

"The Guardroom," copyright © 1985 by David Drake for *Afterwar*, ed. Janet Morris.

"The Last Battalion," copyright © 1977 by The Conde Nast Publications Inc. for *Analog*, September 1977, ed. Ben Bova.

"Something Had to be Done," copyright © 1975 by Mercury Press for *The Magazine of Fantasy & Science Fiction*, February 1975, ed. Edward L. Ferman.

"The Tank Lords," copyright © 1986 by Baen Publishing Enterprises for *Far Frontiers, Vol. VI*, ed. Jerry Pournelle and Jim Baen.

"The End," copyright © 1990 by David Drake for *Sworn Allies: Volume 4 of The Fleet*, March 1990, created by David Drake & Bill Fawcett.

"The Way We Die," written in 1971, copyright © 1991 by David Drake.

I was pleased to note when I put together these acknowledgments that most of the editors cited have remained over these many years personal friends of mine. May it always be so.

CONTENTS

WELCOME TO THE WAR ZONE

I started writing when I was an undergraduate at Iowa, majoring in history and Latin. My first sale (in 1966) was a Lovecraft pastiche. More accurately, it was a pastiche of very bad Lovecraft pastiches by August Derleth; and I can't really understate the story's quality.

I entered Duke Law School and, after I'd completed half the three-year course, I was drafted. The Army offered me a number of choices, all but one of which involved me signing up for more time than the two years to which the draft committed me. I took the remaining option: entry into an accelerated Vietnamese language course, which would be followed by interrogation school.

There wasn't much doubt where I'd be sent after interrogation school; but there wasn't much doubt anyway. At that time (1968) every draftee who'd been to college, and who didn't sign up for a special school, went to Nam with an 11 Bravo Military Occupational Specialty.

Infantry.

So I learned Vietnamese and studied interrogation techniques; and, in 1970, I was assigned to the Military Intelligence Detachment of the 11th Armored Cavalry Regiment as an enlisted interrogator.

In general, MI personnel were rear-echelon types. Most of our people stayed in the 11th Cav's base camp at Di An (which was universally pronounced Zee An by Americans. I don't know why; in Vietnamese the pronunciation was Yee An).

If there was a safer place in Viet Nam at the time, I haven't heard of it. Di An was rocketed exactly once while I was there, and the guys in the field wouldn't believe even that.

The 11th Cav was unusual in that it did keep small units of interrogation and order of battle specialists in the field with each of the three squadrons (a squadron is the cavalry equivalent of a battalion). After a week with the detachment, I volunteered for field duty.

Not because I'm any kind of a hero. I hated the army, but most of all I hated the army's rear-echelon bullshit. It seemed to me that I'd get into less difficulty in the field.

It took a couple weeks before my request was processed, so I was sent to 2nd Squadron just *after* it had spearheaded the invasion of Cambodia. Two of the 12.7 mm machine guns captured at Snuol were set up as trophies in front of the Tactical Operations Center; but the remainder of the months in Cambodia were relatively quiet, as were the months after we crossed back into Viet Nam. I was moved from 2nd Squadron to 1st, but 1st was having a mostly quiet time also.

And then I was transferred back to Di An for the damnedest reason I ever heard of. An MI unit doesn't get many people who know anything about firearms. There was an Inspector General's inspection coming up, and I was the only person in the detachment who knew how to strip the officers' .45 automatics down to the bare frames and clean them.

I spent the last half of my tour in Di An as unit armorer and mail clerk. I was a very good mail clerk, and a good enough armorer for the purpose. I survived.

So. . . . I didn't have a bad war. I wasn't shot; I was almost never shot *at*; and so far as I know, I didn't shoot anybody else.

But I spent my whole tour believing that I was going to die. Not fearing it, exactly. Just the sort of belief you have as you watch the sky cloud up and know it's going to rain.

It could've happened easily enough. I could've been on the track that flipped over after hitting a 20-pound mine. I could've gotten my leg caught in a tank's treads the way an order of battle specialist did. The flame track I was riding could've been struck by lightning and blown up with all the fury of 200 gallons of napalm—to this day, I don't understand why we *weren't* struck by lightning that afternoon.

But where I live now, a woman was killed when a bicycle ran into her. Life has risks.

The difference is that normally you ignore those risks. I spent my tour believing during every waking moment in the imminence of my death. I think that was pretty common among the people I knew.

You can't live that way and stay sane.

I came back saying that I was fine. I finished law school, got a job as an attorney; and wrote, because now I had something to write about besides Lovecraft's fantasy horrors.

For the most part, I still used fantasy and SF conventions. That was easier to sell . . . and maybe easier for me to handle than the unvarnished realities of where I'd been.

Apart from the genre trappings, I didn't make up

very much in my early stories (or, for that matter, in many of the later ones). I used a lot of jargon, simply because the jargon had been so much a part of my life that it didn't occur to me that it wasn't a part of other people's reality also. (An acquaintance remarked that "Contact!" read as though I thought everybody had been to Nam. I suppose I did.)

It was a couple years before it occurred to me that I didn't need to set stories in Nam in order to tell about things that had happened in-country. For the troops at the sharp end, wars had remained more similar than different over the past several millennia. That trend could be expected to continue.

I created a future armored regiment called Hammer's Slammers.

My shorthand description of Hammer's Slammers is the 11th Cav with ray guns. Early on, I tried to hide the fact that I was writing about Nam. It wasn't, some of you will remember, a popular war; and it was still going on when I started doing Hammer stories.

I said that almost all my fiction has been in the SF or fantasy genres. The one exception, "The Way We Die," is included in this volume as a new story. I wrote it within a few months of getting back to the World in 1971, and I couldn't sell it to save my life.

Both the major incidents in "The Way We Die" are true. That isn't important. What *is* important is that the mindset of the narrator (the psychotic mindset of the narrator) is real; and is normal under the stresses of the situation.

When they say that war changes a man, they're being euphemistic. War makes a man insane by civilian standards. When the man comes back, he may return to civilian norms again. After a while.

I'm not proud of many of the things that happened in Nam. I'm not proud of some of the things I did myself. But the men I served with were, for the most part, doing the best job they could with the cards they'd been dealt. I'm proud of *them*, and I'm proud to have been among them.

Anybody's got a right to criticize the things that happened. But don't criticize the men who did them unless you've been in their shoes. Ever since I came back, the object of my military fiction has been to put somebody as normal as you, or as I was, into a war zone.

And I hope to God neither you nor your son ever has a opportunity to compare my fiction with the real thing.

RESCUE MISSION

"Is it true," demanded one of the First Platoon corporals in a voice that filled the echoing bay of the landing craft, "that this whole operation is so we can rescue Admiral Mayne's nephew from the Khalia?"

Captain Kowacs looked at the man. The corporal stared back at the company commander with a jaunty arrogance that said, *Whatcha gonna do? Put me on point?*

Which of course was the corporal's normal patrol position.

Kowacs took a deep breath, but you learned real fast in a Marine Reaction Company that you couldn't scare your troops with rear-echelon discipline. Trying to do that would guarantee you were the first casualty of the next firefight.

"No, Corporal Dodd," said Kowacs. "Admiral Mayne is planning coordinator for this mission, but neither he nor any nephews of his have anything behind-the-scenes to do with it."

He glared at his assembled company.

The behind-the-scenes order had come from Star

7

Admiral Forberry; and it was Forberry's son, not a nephew, who'd been snatched—no body recovered, at any rate—when the Khalia raided the Pleasure Dome on Iknaton five years before.

Nobody else spoke up; even Dodd looked abashed.

Kowacs gazed at the hundred and three pairs of waiting eyes—wondered how many of them would have any life behind them in twenty-four hours. . . .

Sighed and thumbed the handset controlling the holo projector.

The image that formed above Kowacs' head was fuzzy. The unit was intended for use in a shielded environment, while the bay of the landing ship *Bonnie Parker* was alive with circuits and charged metal.

No matter: this was the 121st Marine Reaction Company, the Headhunters, not an architectural congress. The projector would do for the job.

"Fleet Intelligence believes this site to be the Khalia's major holding facility for human prisoners on Target," Kowacs said, referencing the hologram with a nod. "Their slave pen. Reconnaissance indicates that slave ships land at a pad three kilometers distant—"

A second hologram bloomed briefly, the scale of distance merging it with one wall of the big room.

"—and their cargoes are carried to the holding facility by air trucks which touch down on the roof of the Administration Building," Kowacs continued as the image of the outlying spaceport disappeared. The building in the center of the main hologram brightened and began to rotate in three dimensions while the Marines squinted.

"Based on analysis of captured Khalian structures," Kowacs said, "Intelligence believes the building is an integral polyborate casting, probably of two aboveground levels—"

"That high and the Weasels only got two floors?" demanded a sergeant from the Heavy Weapons platoon.

She was concerned, not gibing like Dodd earlier. "Them little bastards, they *like* low ceilings."

"Good point, Sergeant Rozelle," Kowacs said, as if he liked to be interrupted . . . but soldiers who were too dumb to think for themselves were too dumb to trust with your life in a reaction company. "Intelligence believes the building is scaled to the needs of human—slave—intake. But there aren't any windows, and there may well be a third level inside."

Kowacs cleared his throat. Before any of the half dozen Marines poised with further questions could interrupt again, he continued, "The walls and roof are rigid enough to withstand considerable stress, but they're apt to shatter once their integrity is breached. Intelligence believes that strip charges will hole them and that plasma bolts should crumble sections large enough for easy entry."

Almost the entire complement of the 121st was veteran. Even the scattering of newbies was aware that Fleet Intelligence believed a lot of things—but all Fleet Intelligence knew for sure was that no analyst's butt was going to be on the line if his beliefs were false.

"The admin building is separated from the camp proper by double fences with fifteen meters between them," Kowacs continued as the hologram of the building froze and that of the fenced area brightened in turn. "The intermediate separation is believed to be mined and is swept by automatic weapons sited on the building's roof coping. The fence may be electrified."

Marines nodded, easy in the knowledge that barriers impassable to a bunch of unarmed civilians were going to be a piece of cake to *them*.

The forty-eight buildings splayed like a double row of spokes around the hub of the admin building, twelve and thirty-six, brightened as the hologram fence dimmed.

"Beyond that are the slave pens and workshops themselves," Kowacs said.

Just for a moment he paused, his mouth half open—prepared speech interrupted by memories of Khalia and slaves, . . . Memories of his father and mother, dead on Gravely, and his sister's body left behind two weeks later on LaFarge when the same raider landed to replenish its stock.

Its larder.

"Intelligence doesn't even guess at the structure within the compound." Kowacs forced his tongue to continue, though it was several moments more before his eyes were focusing again on the Marines. They were draped over folded bunks and the equipment crated to deploy with them. Some of them looked back at their captain with vacant expressions that Kowacs knew must mirror his of a moment before.

"There may be guards in the barracks, there may not," he continued thickly, damning the emotion that clogged his throat and made him less able to do his job—

Of erasing every living Weasel from the universe.

"If there are guards, they probably don't have weapons; but most of you know an unarmed Khalian can still be a dangerous opponent."

"It's still a fucking pelt, too," growled someone from a corner of the bay.

"Yeah, it's that too," Kowacs said in a voice with an edge. "And any Marine taking trophies while there's still a job to do, I'll take his ears myself. Do you understand?"

The newbies thought that was a threat. The veterans knew it was a promise.

Kowacs took a deep breath and, fully in control of himself and the situation again, continued as the hologram changed. "The outer perimeter is a double fence again, but with guard towers on the exterior."

The tower images glowed like strung jewels.

"Most of them are automatic weapons," Kowacs said without expression, "but there are rapid-firing plasma guns—"

Six of the jewels stood out from the rest.

"—for anti-vehicle defense; and there are a pair of missile batteries. Ship-killers."

"Fuckin' A," said Dodd. He wasn't interrupting, just vocalizing what all the Marines in the bay were thinking right now.

Kowacs included.

"Sir?" asked Sergeant Atwater of third Platoon, a black Terran who was in line for a slot in the Officer Training Unit. "What forces are being committed to this assault?"

"Right," said Kowacs. "The *Carol Ann Fugate* and the *Ladybird Johnson* will land as close to the perimeter as they can. The One-Twenty-second is responsible for the west half—"

That portion of the hologram brightened.

"—and the One-Twenty-third handles the rest. Kamens and Eckland think their companies are nearly as good as mine—"

The back of Kowacs' mind wore a smile at the scene in Admiral Mayne's office, when he and his fellow company commanders had been told their assignments.

"—so I guess they'll be able to take care of the job."

"Ah, sir?" said Atwater, his eyes narrowed on the completely highlighted perimeter of the slave compound. "Ah—where will *we* be?"

"The *Bonnie Parker* sets down on the roof of the admin building," Kowacs said quietly.

He didn't bother to change the hologram; everyone else in the bay was staring at the face of their commander, including the platoon leaders who'd already been briefed on the plan. "You're the best there is in the Fleet, Headhunters. Anybody doubts you, tell him suck on *that*."

Nobody said anything at all.

"Yeah, well," Kowacs continued after a moment. "Your platoon leaders will give you your individual assignments in a moment. Ah—"

He looked out over his company. "Ah, I have been ordered to, ah, emphasize to you that the high command considers Khalian prisoners to be a first priority of all the Target landings, this one included."

He cleared his throat. "Any questions before I turn you over to your platoon leaders?".

"You mean you want us to bring in Weasels *alive*, Cap'n?" Dodd blurted in amazement.

Beside Dodd sat Sergeant Bradley, who acted as Kowacs' field first—company headquarters, headed by the Table of Organization "First Sergeant," was back on Port Tau Ceti, forwarding supplies, mail, and replacements to the company. Bradley was a man of middle height; his flesh was drawn so tightly over his bones that the pink keloid, replacing his hair since a too-near plasma burst, did not appear unusual.

Now he turned to Dodd, lifted the junior non-com's chin between his thumb and forefinger, and said very distinctly, "Did he *say* that, dickhead?"

"No, Sergeant," Dodd whispered.

Bradley faced front with the disdain of a fisherman releasing an undersized catch.

"Any other—"

"Sir?" said Atwater crisply. His arm was lifted but only the index finger was raised, a compromise between courtesy and honor. "Will there be some feints to draw off Khalian forces in the area before we go in?"

Kowacs nodded, but that was a comment on the cogency of the question, not a response to it.

"There's concern," he said carefully, "that when the Khalia realize that we've landed on their home world, their first reaction will be to execute their slaves. Therefore—"

He paused, too clearly aware of the Marines he was leading. This would be a suicide mission if the general invasion timing were off by an hour, maybe even by a few minutes.

"Therefore," Kowacs continued, "a ground-attack ship will go in ahead of us to prep the defenses. We—the assault component—will follow at a three-second interval. No other Alliance forces will be committed to Target until we're on the ground."

"Fuckin' A," somebody repeated in a whisper that echoed throughout the bay.

Commodore Herennis stood as stiff as if a Weasel were buggering him in Kowacs' tiny office—a cubicle separated from the landing bay by walls of film which blurred light and sound into a semblance of privacy. Anger wasn't the only emotion holding Grand Admiral Forberry's military secretary rigid—but it was one of the emotions.

"I told you," said Kowacs from the room's only chair—Herennis had refused it, and there wasn't floor space for both men to stand—"that while I didn't care to leave my men just now, I would of course obey a direct order to report to you on the flagship."

He was holding his combat knife toward the striplight in the ceiling; its wire edge was too fine for his eyes to focus on it, no matter how hard he squinted.

"You *knew* I couldn't formally give an order like that!" Herennis snapped.

Kowacs looked up at the smartly uniformed staff

officer—his social, military, and (no doubt) intellectual superior.

"Yes, Commodore," said the Marine captain softly. "I suppose I did. Now, if you care to state your business, I'll take care of it the best way I can."

"Yes, I . . .," Herennis said. His body quivered as embarrassment replaced anger as his ruling emotion. "Here is the, the chip that was discussed."

The hologram would take up only a corner of the data capacity in the Marines' helmets, nestled among the sensors and recorders that let the high command look over each man's shoulder after the action.

From a safe distance.

Kowacs set his knife on the fold-down desk that doubled as a keypad when he chose to power up his computer terminal. He took the holochip from the commodore and inserted it into the bulkhead projector. The unit was balky; he had to jiggle the handset several times before there was a hum and a face appeared in the air near the filmy opposite wall.

"That's the boy?" Kowacs said. "Well, I'll have it down-loaded into the men's helmets before we go in."

The Honorable Thomas Forberry wasn't a boy, not really. His image looked to be mid-forties, and that was at least five years back. Blue eyes, a ruddy complexion—dark blond hair with curls as perfect as an angel's tits.

For all its pampering, the face was hard and competent. Young Thomas hadn't followed his father into the Fleet, but he ran the family's business concerns, and the Forberrys would have been rich even without the opportunities a grand admiral has of profitably anticipating economic changes.

Used to run the family business.

"Ah, five years could . . .," Kowacs began, letting his voice trail off because he didn't choose to emphasize the changes five years as a Weasel slave could make in a man—even if he survived.

"Yes, he's aware—" Herennis said, then caught himself. "Ah, I'm aware of that. I'm, ah, not expecting. . . . I know you must think—"

Kowacs waved his hand to cut off the staff officer's words, his embarrassment.

"Look, Commodore," he said gently. "Nobody in my outfit's got a problem about releasing Khalian prisoners. If it takes something, whatever, *personal* to give the high command the balls to cut the orders—okay, that's what it takes. Tell your friend not to worry about it."

"Thank you, Captain," Herennis said, sounding as if he meant it. He wasn't done speaking, but he met the Marine's eyes before he went on with, "The unofficial reward, ah, I've promised you is considerable in money terms. But I want you to realize that neither I nor—anyone else—believes that money can recompense the risk you and your men are running."

"Commodore . . .," Kowacs said. His hand was reaching for the leather-wrapped hilt of his knife, but he restrained the motion because Herennis might have misunderstood. "I lost my family in the Gravely Incident."

"I'm sor—"

The Marine's hand moved very sharply to chop off the interruption.

"About half my team could tell you their own version of the same story."

Kowacs saw the doubt in his visitor's eyes and smiled. "Yeah, that high a percentage. Not in the Marines in general, and sure as *hell* not in the whole Fleet. But you check the stats on the reaction companies, not just mine, and see what you find."

Herennis nodded and touched his tongue to his lips.

"Besides that," Kowacs went on with the same tight, worn smile—a smile like the hilt of the knife his hand was, after all, caressing, "we're the ones that hit dirt first after the raids. We've seen everything the Weasels can do to human beings. Do you understand?"

Herennis nodded again. He was staring at Kowacs as if the Marine were a cobra on the other side of a pane of glass.

Kowacs shut off the holo projector. "You're right, Commodore," he said. "None of my team does this for the money, yours or the regular five percent danger allowance.

"But you couldn't pay us *not* to take this mission, either."

The *Bonnie Parker*'s thunderous vibration was bad enough on any insertion, but this time they were going down in daylight. The bay was brightly illuminated, so you could look at the faces of the Marines beside you—blank with fear that was physical and instinctive.

Or you could watch the landing vessel's wiring and structural panels quiver centimeters under the stress—far beyond their designed limits—and wonder whether this time the old girl was going to come apart with no help from the Weasel defense batteries at all.

A shock lifted all the Marines squatting on the deck.

Kowacs, gripping a stanchion with one hand and his rifle with the other, swore; but the word caught in his throat and it wasn't a missile, just the shock wave of the the ground-attack ship that had plunged down ahead of them in a shallow dive that would carry it clear of the landing zone—

If its ordnance had taken out the missile batteries as planned.

Kowacs wanted to piss. He did what he had learned to do in the moments before hitting hot LZs in the past.

Pissed down his trouser leg.

Three plasma bolts hit the *Bonnie Parker* with the soggy impact of medicine balls against the hull. The ship rocked.

The magnetic screens spread the bursts of charged particles, but the bay lights went off momentarily and the center bank stayed dark even after the rest had flickered into life again.

"About *now*—," said Corporal Sienkiewicz, two meters tall and beside Kowacs in the bay because so far as the Table of Organization was concerned, she was his clerk.

Kowacs and Bradley could file their own data. There was no one in the company they thought could do a better job of covering their asses in a firefight.

Sienkiewicz's timing was flawless, as usual. The *Bonnie Parker's* five-g braking drove the squatting Marines hard against the deck plates.

Automatic weapons, unaffected by the screens, played against the hull like sleet. The landing vessel's own suppression clusters deployed with a whoomp-whoompwhoompwhoomp noticeable over the general stress and racket only by those who knew it was coming.

The *Bonnie Parker* was small for a starship but impressive by comparison with most other engines of human transportation. She slowed to a halt, then lurched upward minusculely before her artificial intelligence pilot caught her and brought her to hover. The landing bay doors began to lift on both sides of the hull while the last bomblets of the suppression clusters were still exploding with the snarl and glare of a titanic arclight.

"Get 'em!" Kowacs roared needlessly over his helmet's

clear channel as he and the rest of the company leaped under the rising doors in two lines, one to either side of the landing vessel.

Thrust vectored from the *Bonnie Parker*'s lift engines punched their legs, spilling some of the Marines on the roof's smooth surface. Normally the vessel would have grounded, but the weight of a starship was almost certain to collapse a pad intended for surface-effect trucks. The old girl's power supply would allow her to hover all day.

Unless the Weasels managed to shoot her down, in which case she'd crumple the building on top of the Marines she'd just delivered.

Well, nobody in the 121st was likely to die of ulcers from worry.

There were half a dozen dead Khalia sprawled on the part of the roof Kowacs could see. Their teeth were bared, and all of them clutched the weapons they'd been firing at the landing vessel when the suppression clusters had flayed everything living into bloody ruin.

There was a sharp *bang* and a scream. Halfway down the line on Kowacs' side of the vessel, Corporal Dodd up-ended. One of his feet was high and the other was missing, blown off by the bomblet unexploded until he'd managed to step on it.

"Watch the—," called one of the platoon leaders on the command channel.

At least one plasma gun on the perimeter had survived the ground attack ship. The Weasel crew turned their weapon inward and ripped a three-round burst into the *Bonnie Parker* and the deploying Marines.

One bolt hit the waist-high roof coping—Intelligence was right; the polyborate shattered like a bomb, gouging a two-meter scallop from the building. Kowacs was pushed backward by the blast, and half a dozen of the Marines near him went down.

The other bolts skimmed the coping and diffused against the landing vessel's screen with whiplash cracks and a coruscance that threw hard shadows across the roof. Kowacs' faceshield saved his eyes, but ozone burned the back of his throat and he wasn't sure that anyone could hear him order, "Delta Six, get that f—"

Before anyone in Heavy Weapons, Delta Platoon, could respond to the order with their tripod-mounted guns, Corporal Sienkiewicz leaned over the coping and triggered her own shoulder-carried plasma weapon.

The weapon was a meter-long tube holding a three-round magazine of miniature thermonuclear devices. The deuterium pellets were set off and directed by a laser array, part of the ammunition, and consumed by the blast it contained.

The crack of the out-going plasma jet was sharp and loud even to ears stunned by the bolts that had struck nearby. Downrange, all the ready munitions in the guard tower blew up simultaneously. The blast across the dull beige roofs of the slave barracks was earth-shaking.

"Assigned positions," Kowacs ordered, looking around desperately to make sure that his troops weren't bunching, huddling. Because of the *Bonnie Parker*, he had only half a field of view. Maybe all the Marines who'd jumped from the port side were dead and—

"Move it, Marines! Move it!" he shouted, finding the stairhead that was the only normal entrance on the building's roof.

"Fire in the hole!" warned the First Platoon demo team that had laid a rectangle of strip charges near one end of the flat expanse. The nearest Marines—except the assault squad in full battle suits—hunched away. Everyone else at least turned their faces.

"Fire in the hole!" echoed Third Platoon at the opposite side of the roof—so much for everybody being dead, not that—

The entry charges detonated with snaps that were more jarring to the optic nerves than to the ears. Each was a strip of adhesive containing a filament of PDM explosive—which propagated at a measurable fraction of light speed. The filament charges were too minute to have significant effect even a meter or two from the strip, but the shattering force they imparted on contact was immense.

A door-sized rectangle of the roof dropped into the building interior. Marines in battle suits, their armor protecting them against the glassy needles of polyborate, shrieking and spinning from the blast, crisscrossed the opened room with fire from their automatic rifles. Their helmet sensors gave them targets—or their nervousness squeezed the triggers without targets, and either way it gave the Weasels more to think about.

Similar bursts crackled from the other end of the roof, hidden by the *Bonnie Parker* and attenuated by the howl of her lift engines.

"Alpha ready!" on the command channel, First Platoon reporting. Kowacs could see the Marines poised to enter the hole they'd just blown in the roof.

"Beta ready!" The two squads of Second Platoon under their lieutenant, detailed to rappel down the sides of the windowless building and secure the exits so that the Weasels couldn't get out among the helpless slaves in a last orgy of destruction.

"Kappa ready!" Third Platoon, whose strip charges had blown them an entrance like the one Kowacs could see First clustered around.

"Delta ready!" Heavy Weapons, now with a tripod-mounted plasma gun on each side of the roof. One of the weapons was crashing out bolts to support the units securing the perimeter.

"Gamma ready!" said Sergeant Bradley with a skull-faced grin at Kowacs from the stairhead where he waited with Sienkiewicz and the two remaining squads of Second Platoon.

"All units, *go!*" Kowacs ordered as he jogged toward the stairhead and Bradley blew its door with the strip charges placed but not detonated until this moment.

Three of Second's assault squad hosed the opening. Return fire or a ricochet blasted sparks from the center Marine's ceramic armor. He staggered but didn't go down, and his two fellows lurched in sequence down the stairs their bulky gear filled.

"Ditch that!" Kowacs snarled to Sienkiewicz as she slung the plasma gun and cocked her automatic rifle.

"It's my back," she said with a nonchalance that was no way to refuse a direct order—

But which would do for now, because Kowacs was already hunching through the doorway, and she was right behind him. The air was bitter with residues of the explosive, but that was only spice for the stench of musk and human filth within.

You could make a case for the company commander staying on the roof instead of ducking into a building where he'd lose contact with supporting units and the high command in orbit.

Rank hath its privileges. For twelve years, the only privilege Kowacs had asked for was the chance to be where he had the most opportunity to kill Weasels.

The stairs were almost ladder-steep and the treads were set for the Khalia's short legs. One of the clumsily armored Marines ahead of Kowacs sprawled onto all fours in the corridor, but there were no living Weasels in sight to take advantage of the situation.

Half a dozen of them were dead, ripped by the rifle fire that caught them with no cover and no hope. One furry body still squirmed. Reflex or intent caused the creature to clash its teeth vainly against the boot of the leading Marine as he crushed its skull in passing.

The area at the bottom of the short staircase was broken into a corridor with a wire-mesh cage to either side. The cage material was nothing fancier than hog-fencing—these were very short-term facilities. The one on the left was empty.

The cage on the right had room for forty humans and held maybe half a dozen, all of them squeezed into a puling mass in one corner from fear of gunfire and the immediate future.

The prisoners were naked except for a coating of filth so thick that their sexes were uncertain even after they crawled apart to greet the Marines. There was a drain in one corner of the cage, but many of the human slaves received here in past years had been too terrified to use it. The Weasels didn't care.

Neither did Kowacs just now.

"Find the stairs down—," he was shouting when something plucked his arm and he spun, his rifle-stock lifting to smash the Weasel away before worrying about how he'd kill it, they were death if you let 'em touch you—

And it wasn't a Khalian but a woman with auburn hair. She'd reached through the fencing that saved her life when it absorbed the reflexive buttstroke that would have crushed her sternum.

"Bitch!" Kowacs snarled, more jarred by his mistake than by the shock through his weapon that made his hands tingle.

"Please," the woman insisted with a throaty determination that overrode all the levels of fear that she must be feeling. "My brother, Alton Dinneen—don't trust him. On your *lives*, don't trust him!"

"Weasel bunkroom!" called one of the armored Marines who'd clumped down the corridor to the doorways beyond the cages. "Empty, though."

"Watch for—" Kowacs said as he jogged toward them. Bradley and Sienkiewicz were to either side and a half step behind him.

The Khalian that leaped from the 'empty' room was exactly what he'd meant to watch for.

A Marine screamed instinctively. There were four of them, all members of the assault squad burdened by their armor. The Weasel had no gun, just a pair of knives in his forepaws. Their edges sparkled against the ceramic armor—and bit through the joints.

Two of the Marines were down in seconds that blurred into eternity before Sergeant Bradley settled matters with a blast from his shotgun. The Marines' armor glittered like starlit snow under the impact of Bradley's airfoil charge. The Khalian, his knives lifted to scissor through a third victim, collapsed instead as a rug of blood-matted fur.

Cursing because it was his fault, he shouldn't have let Marines manacled by twenty kilos of armor lead after the initial entry, Kowacs ran to the room in which the Weasel had hidden.

It was a typical Khalian nest. There was a false ceiling to lower the dimensions to Weasel comfort and a heap of bedding which his sensors, like those of the first Marine, indicated were still warm with the body heat of the Khalia who'd rushed into the corridor to be cut down in the first exchange of fire.

Except that one of the cunning little bastards had hidden *under* the bedding and waited. . . .

You couldn't trust your sensors, and you couldn't trust your eyes—but you could usually trust a long burst of fire like the one with which Sienkiewicz now hosed the bedding. Fluff and wood chips fountained away from the bullets.

"Hey!" cried one of the assault squad who was still standing. Kowacs spun.

An elevator door was opening across the hall.

The startled figure in the elevator car was bare-chested but wore a red sleeve that covered his right arm wrist to shoulder. The Khalian machine-pistol he pointed might not penetrate assault-squad armor, but it would have stitched through Kowacs' chest with lethal certainty if the captain hadn't fired first. Kowacs' bullets flung his target backward into the bloody elevator.

"Sir!" cried the Marine who hadn't fired. "That was a friendly! A man!"

"Nobody's friendly when they point a gun at you!" Kowacs said. "Demo team! Blow me a hole in this fucking floor!"

Two Marines sprinted over, holding out the partial spools of strip-charge that remained after they blew down the door.

"How big—" one started to ask, but Kowacs was already anticipating the question with, "One by two—no, *two* by two!"

Kowacs needed a hole that wasn't a suicidally small choke point when he and his troops jumped through it—but the floor here had been cast in the same operation as the roof and exterior walls. He was uneasily aware that the battering which gunfire and explosives were giving the structure would eventually disturb its integrity to the point that the whole thing collapsed.

Still, he needed a hole in the floor, because the only way down from here seemed to be the elevator which—

"Should I take the elevator, sir?" asked an armored Marine, anonymous behind his airfoil-scarred face shield.

"No, dammit!" Kowacs said, half inclined to let the damn fool get killed making a diversion for the rest of them. But the kid was *his* damn fool, and —

"Only young once," muttered Sergeant Bradley in a mixture of wonder and disdain.

"Fire in the hole!" cried one of the Demolition Team.

Kowacs squeezed back from the doorway to give the demo team room to jump clear, but the pair were too blasé about their duties to bother. They twisted around and knelt with their hands over their ears before the strips blew and four square meters of flooring shuddered, tilted down—

And stuck. The area below was divided into rooms off-set from those of the upper floor. The thick slab of polyborate caught at a skewed angle, half in place and half in the room beneath.

An automatic weapon in that room fired two short bursts. A bullet ricocheted harmlessly up between the slab and the floor from which it had been blasted.

"Watch it!" said Sienkiewicz, unlimbering the plasma gun again. She aimed toward the narrow wedge that was all the opening there was into the lower room.

It was damned dangerous. If she missed, the bolt would liberate all its energy in the nest room, and the interior walls might not be refractory enough to protect Gamma.

But Sienkiewicz was good; and among other things, this would be a real fast way to silence the guns beneath before the Marines followed the plasma bolt.

The demo team sprinted into the corridor; Kowacs flattened himself against the wall he hoped would hold for the next microsecond; and the big weapon crashed a dazzling line through the hole and into the building's lower story.

Air fluoresced at the point of impact and lifted the slab before dropping it as a load of rubble. Kowacs and Bradley shouldered one another in their mutual haste to be first through the opening. Sienkiewicz used their collision to lead them both by a half step, the plasma gun for the moment cradled in her capable arms.

It wasn't the weapon for a point-blank firefight; but nothing close to where the bolt struck was going to be alive, much less dangerous.

Kowacs dropped through the haze and hit in a crouch on something that squashed under his boots. The atmosphere was so foul in the bolt's aftermath that the helmet filters slapped across his mouth and nose in a hard wedge.

The Marines were in a good-sized—human-scale—room with a cavity in the floor. There was nothing beneath the cavity except earth glazed by the plasma bolt that had excavated it.

This was a briefing room or something of the sort; but it was a recreation room as well, for the chairs had been stacked along the walls before the blast disarrayed them, and two humans were being tortured on a vertical grid. The victims had been naked before the gush of sun-hot ions scoured the room, flensing to heat-cracked bones the side of their bodies turned toward the blast.

But the plasma gun hadn't killed them. The victims' skulls had been shattered by bullets, the bursts the Marines had heard the moment before Sienkiewicz blew them entry.

Several of the chairs were burning. They were wooden, handmade, and intended for humans. On the wall behind the grid was a name list on polished wood, protected from the plasma flux by the torture victims and a cover sheet of now bubbled glassine. The list was headed DUTY ROSTER.

In English, not the tooth-mark wedges of Khalian script.

Each of the six other bodies the blast had caught wore a red right sleeve—or traces of red fabric where it had been shielded from the plasma. They had all been humans, including the female Kowacs was standing on. She still held the Khalian machine-pistol she had used to silence the torture victims.

"*Renegades,*" Sergeant Bradley snarled. He would have spat on a body, but his filters were in place.

"Trustees," Kowacs said in something approaching calm. "The Weasels don't run the interior of the compound. They pick slaves of the right sort to do it. Let's—"

He was looking at the door and about to point to it. More Marines were tumbling through the hole in the ceiling, searching for targets. The air had cleared enough now that Kowacs noticed details of the body flung into the doorway by the blast. Its arms and legs had been charred to stumps, and its neck was seared through to the point that its head flopped loose.

But the face was unmarked, and the features were recognizable in their family relationship to those of the woman caged upstairs.

Nobody had to worry about treachery by Alton Dinneen anymore.

"—*go*, Marines!" Kowacs completed. Because he'd hesitated momentarily, Bradley and Sienkiewicz were already ahead of him.

They were in a long hallway whose opposite wall was broken with doorways at short intervals. Somebody ducked out of one, saw the Marines, and ducked back in.

Bradley and Sienkiewicz flanked the panel in a practiced maneuver while Kowacs aimed down the corridor in case another target appeared. He hoped their backs were being covered by the Second Platoon Marines who'd been able to follow him. The survivors of the assault squad couldn't jump through the ceiling unless they stripped off their battle suits first.

"Go!"

Sienkiewicz fired her rifle through the door panel

and kicked the latch plate. As the door bounced open, Bradley tossed in a grenade with his left hand.

The man inside jumped out screaming an instant before the grenade exploded; Bradley's shotgun disembowelled him.

They'd all seen the flash of a red sleeve when the target first appeared.

The trustee's room had space for a chair, a desk, and a bed whose mattress had ignited into smoldering fire when the explosion lifted it.

He'd also had a collection of sorts hanging from cords above the bed. Human skin is hard to flay neatly, especially when it's already been stretched by the weight of mammary glands, so the grenade fragments had only finished what ineptitude had begun.

Short bursts of rifle fire and the thump of grenades echoed up the corridor from where it kinked toward Third Platoon's end of the building. Nobody'd had to draw those Marines a picture either.

First and Third would work in from the ends, but Kowacs didn't have enough men under his direct command to clear many of the small individual rooms. He'd expected Weasel nests. . . .

But there were only two more doors, spaced wide apart, beside the briefing room in the visible portion of the hall.

"Cover us!" Kowacs ordered the squad leader from Second Platoon. "Both ways, and *don't* shoot any Marines."

In another setting, he'd have said "friendlies." Here it might have been misconstrued.

His non-coms had already figured this one, flattening themselves to either side of the next door down from the briefing room. Kowacs' fire and Sienkiewicz' crisscrossed, stitching bright yellow splinters from the soft wood of the panel. Bradley kicked, and all three of them tossed grenades as the door swung.

There was no latch. The panel's sprung hinges let the explosions bounce it open into the corridor with its inner face scarred by the shrapnel.

Kowacs and his team fanned through the door, looking for targets. Nothing was moving except smoke and platters jouncing to the floor from the pegs on which they'd been hanging. In the center of the floor was a range. There were ovens and cold-lockers along three of the walls.

Well, there'd had to be a kitchen, now that Kowacs thought about it.

The man hidden there picked the right time to wave his hand from behind the range that sheltered him—a moment after the Marines swung in, ready to blast anything that moved, but before a quick search found him and made him a certain enemy.

"Up!" Kowacs ordered. *"Now!"*

He was plump and terrified and hairless except for a wispy white brush of a moustache that he stroked with both hands despite obvious attempts to control the gesture.

"The rest of 'em, damn you!" roared Bradley, aiming his shotgun at the corner of the range from which he expected fresh targets to creep.

"It's only me!" the bald man blubbered through his hands. "I swear to God, only me, only me, only Charlie the Cook."

Sienkiewicz stepped—she didn't have to jump—to the range top. Her rifle was pointed down and the plasma gun, its barrel still quivering with heat, jounced against her belt gear.

"Clear!" she reported crisply. Charlie relaxed visibly, until he saw that Kowacs was reaching for the handle of the nearest cold-locker.

"Not me!" the civilian cried. "Charlie only does what he's told, I swear to God, no—"

Sienkiewicz saw what was in the locker and saved

Charlie's life by kicking him in the teeth an instant before Bradley's shotgun would have dealt with the matter in a more permanent way.

Heads, arms, and lower legs had been removed in the course of butchering, but there was no doubt that the hanging carcasses were human.

Kowacs stepped over to the sprawling prisoner and cradled his rifle muzzle at the base of the man's throat. "Tell me you cooked for the Weasels," he said quietly. "Just say the fucking words."

"No-no-no," Charlie said, crying and trying to spit up fragments of his broken mouth before he choked on them. "Not the Masters, never the Masters—*they* don't need cooks. And never for me, never for Charlie, Charlie just—"

"Cap'n?" Bradley said with the hint of a frown now that he'd had time to think through his impulse of a moment before. Shooting a clearly unarmed captive. . . . "The, ah—"

He tapped the side of his helmet, where the recorder was taking down everything he said or did for after-action review by the brass.

Kowacs grabbed the prisoner by the throat and lifted him to his feet. Charlie was gagging, but the Marine's blunt fingers weren't stranglingly tight. Kowacs shoved the man hard, back into the open locker.

"We'll be back for you!" he said as he slammed the door.

Someday, maybe.

Kowacs was shuddering as he ejected the partially fired magazine from his rifle and slammed in a fresh one. "Told a guy yesterday I'd seen everything the Weasels could do to human beings," he muttered to his companions. "Guess I was wrong."

Though he didn't suppose he ought to blame this

on the Khalia. They just happened to have been around as role models.

"One *more!*" Sienkiewicz said with false brightness as her boots crashed to the floor and she followed Bradley into the hallway again.

The squad from Second Platoon had been busy enough to leave a sharp fog of propellant and explosive residues as they shot their way into the sleeping rooms on the opposite side of the corridor. They hadn't turned up any additional kills, but they were covering Kowacs' back as he'd ordered, so he didn't have any complaints.

He and his non-coms poised at the third door in this section. It jerked open from the inside while he and Sienkiewicz took up the slack on their triggers.

Neither of the rifles fired. Bradley, startled, blasted a round from his shotgun into the opening and the edge of the door.

The airfoil load chewed a scallop from the thick wood panel and tore swirls in the smoky air of the room beyond.

"*Don't shoot!*" screamed a voice from behind the doorframe, safe from the accidental shot. "I'm unarmed! I'm a prisoner!"

Kowacs kicked the door hard as he went in, slamming it back against the man speaking and throwing off his aim if he were lying about being unarmed. The room was an office, almost as large as the kitchen, with wooden filing cabinets and a desk—

Which Sienkiewicz sprayed with a half magazine, because nobody'd spoken from *there*, and anybody in concealment was fair game. Splinters flew away from the shots like startled birds, but there was no cry of pain.

Starships or no, the Khalia weren't high tech by human standards. In a human installation, even back in the sticks, there'd have been a computer data bank.

Here, data meant marks on paper; and the paper was burning in several of the open file drawers. The air was chokingly hot and smoky, but it takes a long time to destroy files when they're in hard copy.

The man half-hidden by the door stepped aside, his hands covering his face where Kowacs had smashed him with the panel.

He didn't wear a red sleeve, but there was a tag of fabric smoldering on one of the burning drawers.

What had the bastard thought he was going to gain by destroying the records?

Kowacs was reaching toward the prisoner when the man said, "You idiots! Do you know who I am?"

He lowered his hands and they did know, all three of them, without replaying the hologram loaded into their helmet memories. Except for the freshly cut lip and bloody nose, the Honorable Thomas Forberry hadn't changed much after all.

"Out," Kowacs said.

Forberry thought the Marine meant him as well as the non-coms. Kowacs jabbed the civilian in the chest with his rifle when he started to follow them.

"Sir?" said the sergeant doubtfully.

Kowacs slammed the door behind him. The latch was firm, though smoke drifted out of the gouge next to the jamb.

"They'll wipe the chips," Kowacs said.

"Sir, we *can't* wipe the recorders," Bradley begged. "Sir, it's been tried!"

"We won't have to," Kowacs said. He nodded to Sienkiewicz, lifting the plasma weapon with its one remaining charge. "We'll leave it for the brass to cover this one up."

And they all flattened against the wall as Sienkiewicz set the muzzle of the big weapon against the hole in the door of the camp administrator's office.

THE DANCER IN THE FLAMES

The flames writhing out of the ashtray were an eyeball-licking orange. For an instant Lt Schaydin was sure that the image dancing in them was that of the girl he had burned alive in Cambodia, six months before. But no, not quite; though the other's face had been of Gallic cast too.

The two enlisted men had turned at the sound of the officer brushing back the poncho curtain which divided his tent from the rear compartment of the command track. Radios were built into the right wall of the vehicle above a narrow counter. On that counter rested the CQ's clipboard and a cheap glass ashtray, full of flame. The men within—Skip Sloane, who drove the command track and was now Charge of Quarters, and the medic Evens—had been watching the fire when Schaydin looked in. It was to that ten-inch flame which the lieutenant's eyes were drawn as well.

He stared at her calves and up the swell of the hips which tucked in at a waist that thrust toward him. She looked straight at Schaydin then and her mouth

pursed to call. Above the image hung the black ripples
of smoke which were her hair. Abruptly the flame
shrank to a wavering needle and blinked out. The
compartment was lighted only by the instrument dials,
pitch dark after the orange glare. The air was sharp
with the residue of the flame; but more than that
caused Schaydin's chest to constrict. He remembered
he had called out some joke as he touched the flamethrower's trigger and set a loop of napalm through
the window of the hooch they were supposed to
destroy. The Cambodian girl must have been hiding
in the thatch or among the bags of rice. She had been
all ablaze as she leaped into the open, shrieking and
twisting like a dervish until she died. But this tiny
image had not screamed, it had really spoke. It/She
had said—

"How did you do that?" Schaydin gasped.

The enlisted men glanced at each other, but their
commander did not seem angry, only—strange.
Sloane held up a 20-ounce block of C-4, plastic explosive. Sweat rolled down the driver's chest and beer
gut. He wore no shirt since the radios heated the
command vehicle even in the relative coolness of the
Vietnamese night. "You take a bit of C-4, sir," Sloane
said. His hairy thumb and forefinger gouged out an
acorn-sized chunk of the white explosive. Another
piece had already been removed. "It takes a shock to
make it blow up. If you just touch a match to it in
the open, it burns. Like that."

Sloane handed the pellet to Schaydin, who stood
with a dazed look on his face. The C-4 had the consis-
tency of nougat, but it was much denser. "We ought
'a air the place out, though," the driver continued.
"The fumes don't do anybody much good."

"But how did you get it to look like a woman?"
Schaydin demanded. "I could see her right there, her
face, her eyes . . . and she was saying. . . ."

Evens reached past the lieutenant and flapped the poncho curtain to stir the dissipating tendrils of smoke. "C-4 makes a pretty flame," the stocky medic said, "but you don't want to get the stuff in your system. We used to have a mascot, a little puppy. She ate part of a block and went pure-ass crazy. Seeing things. She'd back into a corner and snap and bark like a bear was after her. . . . Middle of that afternoon she went haring out over the berm, yapping to beat Hell. We never did see her again."

The medic looked away from his CO, then added, "Don't think you ought to breathe the fumes, either. Hard to tell what it might make you see. Don't think I want to burn any more C-4, even if it does make the damnedest shadows I ever hope to see."

The lieutenant opened his mouth to protest, to insist that he had seen the image the instant he pushed the curtain aside; but he caught his men's expressions. His mind seemed to be working normally again. "You guys just saw a—fire?"

"That's all there was to see," said Evens. "Look, it's late, I better go rack out." Sloane nodded, tossing him the part block of explosive. The medic edged past Schaydin, into the tent and the still night beyond.

"Time for a guard check," Sloane said awkwardly and reseated himself before the microphone. One by one the heavyset man began calling the vehicles sited around the circular berm. The tracks replied with the quiet negative reports that showed someone was awake in each turret. The CQ did not look up at his commander, but when Schaydin stepped back from the compartment and turned away, he heard a rustle. Sloane had pulled the poncho closed.

Schaydin sat down on the edge of his bunk, staring at the morsel of explosive. He saw instead the girl he had glimpsed in the flame. She had danced with her body, writhing sinuously like a belly dancer as her breasts heaved against the fire's translucence. Schaydin couldn't have been mistaken, the girl had been as real as—the Cambodian girl he had burned. And this girl's expression was so alive, her fire-bright eyes glinting with arrogant demand. *What had the Cambodian girl been crying? But her eyes were dulled by the clinging napalm....*

The pellet of C-4 came into focus as Schaydin's fingers rotated it. All right, there was a simple way to see whether his mind had been playing tricks on him.

Schaydin set the ball of explosive on top of a minican, the sealed steel ammunition box prized as luggage by men in armored units. C-4 burned at over 1000 degrees, the lieutenant remembered, but it would burn briefly enough that only the paint would scorch. The flame of Schaydin's cigarette lighter wavered away from the white pellet and heated the case in his hand. Then a tiny spark and a flicker of orange winked through the yellow naphtha flare. Schaydin jerked his lighter away and shut it. Fire loomed up from the *plastique*. Its hissing filled the tent just as the roar of an incoming rocket does an encampment.

And the dancer was there again.

The engineer platoon ran a generator which powered lights all over the firebase through makeshift lines of commo wire. Left-handed and without looking at it, Schaydin jerked away the wire to his tent's lightbulb. The sputtering fire brightened in the darkness, and in it the girl's features were as sharp as if a cameo carven in ruddy stone. But the mouth moved and the dancer called to Schaydin over the fire-noise, "Viens ici! Viens a Marie!" Schaydin had studied French as an undergraduate in divinity school, enough to recognize that the tones were not quite those of modern French; but it was clear that the dancer was calling him to her. His body tensed with the impossible desire to obey. Sweat rimmed all the stark lines of his muscles.

Then the flame and the girl were gone together, though afterimages of both danced across Schaydin's eyes. The lieutenant sat in the dark for some time, oblivious to the half-movement he might have glimpsed through a chink in the poncho. The CQ turned back to his microphone, frowning at what he had watched.

Schaydin was more withdrawn than usual in the morning, but if any of his fellow officers noticed it, they put it down to the lieutenant's natural anxiety about his position. The next days would determine whether Schaydin would be promoted to captain and take on for the rest of his tour the slot he now held in place of the wounded Captain Fuller. Otherwise, Schaydin would have to give up the company to another officer and return to Third Platoon. Schaydin had thought of little else during his previous week of command, but today it barely occurred to him. His mind had been drifting in the unreality of South-East Asia; now it had found an anchorage somewhere else in time and space.

The thin lieutenant spent most of the day in his tent, with the orange sidewalls rolled up to make its roof an awning. The First Sergeant was stationed permanently in the Regiment's base camp at Di An, running an establishment with almost as many troops as there were in the field. In Viet Nam, even in a combat unit, a majority of the troops were noncombatants. Bellew, the Field First, was on R&R in Taiwan, so an unusual amount of the company's day-to-day affairs should have fallen on the commander himself.

Today Schaydin sloughed them, answering the most pressing questions distractedly and without particular interest. His eyes strayed often to his minican, where the paint had bubbled and cracked away in a circle the size of a fifty-cent piece.

She had seemed short, though he could not be sure since the image had been less than a foot tall when the flames leapt their highest. Not plump, exactly, for that implied fat and the dancer had been all rippling muscularity; but she had been a stocky girl, an athlete rather than a houri. And yet Schaydin had never before seen a woman so seductively passionate, so radiant with desire. Every time Schaydin thought of the dancer's eyes, his groin tightened; and he thought of her eyes almost constantly.

Come to me. . . . Come to Marie. . . .

The activities of the firebase went on as usual, ignoring Schaydin just as he did them. Second Platoon and some vehicles from Headquarters Company bellowed off on a Medcap to a village ten kilometers down Route 13. There the medics would dispense antibiotics and bandages to the mildly ill. The troops would also goggle at ravaged figures whom not even Johns Hopkins could have aided: a child whose legs had been amputated three years past by a directional mine; a thirty-year-old man with elephantiasis of the scrotum, walking bowlegged because of the bulk of his cantaloupe-sized testicles. . . .

Chinook helicopters brought in fuel and ammunition resupply in cargo nets swinging beneath their bellies. Schaydin did not notice their howling approach; the syncopated chop of their twin rotors as they hovered; the bustle of men and vehicles heading toward the steel-plank pad to pick up the goods. The lieutenant sat impassively in his tent even when the howitzer battery fired, though the hogs were lofting some of their shells to maximum range. The muzzle blasts raised doughnuts of dust that enveloped the whole base. Schaydin's mind's eye was on a dancing girl, not men in baggy green fatigues; the roar he heard was that of a crowd far away, watching the dancer ... and even the dust in Schaydin's nostrils did not smell like the pulverized laterite of Tay Ninh Province.

"Time for the officers' meeting, sir," Sloane murmured.

Schaydin continued to sit like a thin, nervous Buddha in a lawn chair.

"Sir," the driver repeated loudly, "they just buzzed from the TOC. It's already 1500 hours."

"Oh, right," muttered the lieutenant dizzily. He shook his head and stood, then ran his fingertips abstractedly over the blackened minican. "Right."

The Tactical Operations Center was merely a trio of command vehicles around a large tent in the middle of the firebase. Schaydin had forgotten to carry his lawn chair with him. He pulled up a box which had held mortar shells and sat facing the acetate-covered map with its crayoned unit symbols. The afternoon rain started, plunging sheets of water that made the canvas jounce like a drumhead. It sounded like an angry crowd.

The Civil Affairs Officer and the lieutenant from the military intelligence detachment shared a presentation on the results of the Medcap. They proved that zero could be divided in half to fill twenty minutes. Then the Operations Officer described F Troop's morning sweep. It had turned up two old bunkers and some cartridge cases, but no signs of recent occupation. The sector was quiet.

The balding S-3 switched to discussing the operation planned in two days. When he directed a question to Schaydin, the lieutenant continued to rock silently on his box, his eyes open but fixed on nothing in the tent.

"Schaydin!" the squadron commander snarled. "Stop sitting there with your finger up your butt and pay attention!"

"Yes, sir!" Schaydin's face flushed hot and his whole body tingled, as if he had just been roused from a dead faint. "Would you please repeat the question, sir?"

The meeting lasted another ten minutes, until the rain stopped. Schaydin absorbed every pointless detail with febrile acuteness. His flesh still tingled.

After Colonel Brookings dismissed his officers into the clearing skies, Schaydin wandered toward the far side of the defensive berm instead of going directly to his tent. He followed the path behind one of the self-propelled howitzers, avoiding the pile of white cloth bags stuffed with propellant powder. The charges were packed in segments. For short range shelling, some of the segments were torn off and thrown away as these had been. Soon the powder would be carried outside the perimeter and burned.

Burned. A roaring, sparking column of orange flame, and in it—

Schaydin cursed. He was sweating again.

Three ringing explosions sounded near at hand. The noise had been a facet of the background before the rain as well, Schaydin remembered. He walked toward the source of the sounds, one of First Platoon's tanks. It had been backed carefully away from the berm, shedding its right tread onto the ground, straight as a tow line between the vehicle and the earthen wall. Four men hunched behind a trailer some yards from the tank. One of them, naked to the waist, held a detonator in his hand. The trooper saw Schaydin approaching and called, "Stand back, sir. We're blowing out torsion bars."

The lieutenant stopped, watching. The trooper

nodded and slapped closed the scissors handle of the detonator. Smoke and another clanging explosion sprang from among the tank's road wheels. The enlisted men straightened. "That's got it," one of them murmured. Schaydin walked to them, trying to remember the name of the tall man with the detonator, the tank commander of this vehicle.

"What's going on, Emmett?" Schaydin asked.

None of the enlisted men saluted. "Emery, sir," the TC corrected. "Our tank had six torsion bars broke, so she steered and rode like a truck with square wheels. Back in the World they've got machines to drift out torsion bars, but here we're just using a couple ounces of C-4 to crack each one loose." The tall non-com pointed at the block of explosive dropped on the ground beside him. Its green sandwich backing had been peeled away from both sides, and half the doughy white *plastique* had been pinched off. Several copper blasting caps lay on the ground beside the C-4.

Emery ignored the lieutenant's sudden pallor. He stopped paying attention to Schaydin entirely since it was obvious that the officer was not about to help with the job. "Come on, snakes," Emery said, "we got a lot to do before sundown."

The crewmen scrambled to their fifty-ton mount, hulking and rusted and more temperamentally fragile than any but the men responsible for such monsters will ever know. Schaydin's staring eyes followed them as he himself bent at the knees and touched the block of C-4. Its smooth outer wrapper was cool to his fingers. Without looking at the explosive, Schaydin slid it into a side pocket of his fatigue trousers. He walked swiftly back to his tent.

Tropic sunset is as swift as it is brilliant. It crams all the reds and ochres and magentas of the temperate zones into a few minutes which the night then swallows. But the darkness, though it would be sudden, was hours away; and Schaydin's pulsing memory would not let him wait hours.

Sloane was radio watch this afternoon. The driver sat on the tailgate of the command vehicle with his feet on the frame of his cot. He was talking to the staff sergeant who would take over as CQ at 2000 hours. They fell silent when Schaydin appeared.

"Go ahead, Skip, get yourself some supper," the lieutenant said stiffly. "I'll take the radio for a while."

"S'okay, sire, Walsh here spelled me," Sloane said. He pointed at the paper plate with remnants of beef and creamed potatoes, sitting on his footlocker. "Go ahead and eat yourself."

"I said I'd take the radio!" Schaydin snapped. He was trembling, though he did not realize it. Sloane glanced very quickly at his commander, then to the startled sergeant. The driver lowered his feet from the cot and squeezed back so that Schaydin could enter the track. The two enlisted men were whispering together at the open end of the tent when their lieutenant drew the poncho shut, closing off the rest of the world.

It was dim in the solid-walled vehicle, dimmer yet when Schaydin unplugged the desk lamp. Radio dials gleamed and reflected from the formica counter, chinks of light seeped in past the curtain. But it would serve, would serve. . . .

The texture of the C-4 steadied Schaydin's fingers as he molded it. The high sides of the ashtray made it difficult to ignite the pellet. The hot steel of the lighter seared his fingers and he cursed in teary frustration; but just before Schaydin would have had to pull away winked the spark and the orange flare—

—and in it,
the girl dancing.

Her head was flung back, the black, rippling, smokey hair flying out behind her. Schaydin heard the words again, "A Marie! Ici! Viens ici!" The radio was babbling, too, on the command frequency; but whatever it demanded was lost in the roar of the crowd. Passion, as fiercely hot as the explosive that gave it form, flashed from the girl's eyes. "Come to me!"

The flame sputtered out. Schaydin was blind to all but its afterimage.

The compartment was hot and reeking. Sweat beaded at Schaydin's hairline and on his short, black moustache. He stripped the backing away from the rest of the explosive and began to knead the whole chunk, half a pound, into a single ball.

"Battle Six to Battle One-Six," the radio repeated angrily in Colonel Brookings' voice. "Goddammit, Schaydin, report!"

The ashtray had shattered in the heat. Schaydin swept the fragments nervously to the floor, then set the lump of explosive on the blood-marked formica. A shard of clear glass winked unnoticed in the heel of his hand. He snapped his lighter to flame and it mounted, and she mounted—

—and she called. Her hands could not reach out for him but her soul did and her Hell-bright eyes. "Viens ici! Viens!"

The dancer's smooth flesh writhed with no cloak but the flame. Higher, the radio dials melting, the lizard-tongue forks of the blaze beading the aluminum roof—Schaydin stood, his ankles close together like hers. He did not reach for her, not because of the heat but because the motion would be—*wrong*. Instead he put his hands behind his back and crossed his wrists. Outside the curtain, voices snarled but the dragon-hiss of the C-4 would have drowned even a sane man's senses. She twisted, her eyes beckoning, her mouth opening to speak. Schaydin arched, bending his body

just so and—
            "Come!"
                        —and he went.

The poncho tore from Colonel Brookings' fingers and a girl plunged out of the fiery radio compartment. She was swarthy but not Vietnamese, naked except for smouldering scraps of a woolen shift. Neither Brookings nor the enlisted men could understand the French she was babbling; but her joy, despite severe burns on her feet and legs, was unmistakeable.

No one else was in the vehicle.

On October 14, 1429, the assembled villagers of Briancon, Province of Dauphine, Kingdom of France, roared in wonderment. The witch Marie de la Barthè, being burned alive at the stake, suddenly took the form of a demon with baggy green skin. The change did not aid the witch, however, for the bonds still held. Despite its writhing and unintelligible cries, the demon-shape burned as well in the fire as a girl would have.

ARCLIGHT

Grunting and snarling, the nineteen tracked vehicles of G Troop struggled into a night defensive position. From the road watched a family of impassive Cambodians. The track commander of the nearest vehicle, three-six, waved at them as his ACAV shuddered through a thirty-degree arc and prepared to back into its position in the laager. Red paint marked the track's flat aluminum sides with the name "Horny Horse" and a graphic parody of the regiment's stallion insignia. None of the stolid, flat-faced onlookers gave any sign of interest, even when the ACAV lurched sideways and began to tilt. The TC leaned out of his cupola in the middle, vainly trying to see what was the matter. Jones, the left gunner, looked out over the hole opening under the tread and waved frantically, trying to shout over the engine noise. The TC nodded and snapped to the driver through his intercom, "Whip 'er right and gun 'er, Jody, we're falling into a goddamn bunker!"

The diesel bellowed as Jody let the left clutch full

out and tramped on the foot feed. The ACAV slewed
level again with the left tread spitting mangled vegetation behind it. "Cut the engine," the TC ordered, and
in the sudden silence he shouted to the command
track in the center of the rough circle of vehicles,
"Captain Fuller! We're on a bunker complex!"

The shirtless, sweating officer dropped the can of
beer he was staring to open and grabbed his dirty M-
16. No matter what you did, clean your rifle daily and
keep it in a case, the choking dust kicked up by the
tracks inevitably crept into it at the end of a day's
move. And if they really were on a bunker complex,
the move wasn't over yet. Everybody knew what had
happened to E troop last November when they laagered on an unsuspected complex and a dozen sappers had crept out inside the NDP that night.

The hole, an irregular oval perhaps a foot along the
greater axis, looked uncompromisingly black against
the red laterite of the bare ground. Worse, the tilted
edge of a slab showed clearly at the back, proving the
cavity below was artificial. Everybody knew the dinks
had been building bunkers here in the Parrot's Beak
for twenty years and more, but the captain had never
seen a stone one before.

"Want me to frag it?" someone said. It was the
red-headed TC of the track that turned the bunker
up, Fuller saw. Casely, his name was. He held his
unauthorized .45 in one hand, cocked, and a pair of
smooth-hulled fragmentation grenades in the other.

"Gimme one of them," growled Sergeant Peacock,
reaching his huge black arm toward the younger soldier. Casely handed one of the grenades to the field
first and watched him expertly mold a pound and a
quarter stick of plastic explosive around it. The white
explosive encased all the metal except the handle and
the safety pin in a lumpy cocoon. "We'll try a bunker
buster first to see if anybody's home," the sergeant

said with satisfaction. "Better clear back." He pulled the pin.

All around the laager, men were watching what was going on beside three-six. Nobody was keeping a lookout into the jungle; but, then, the dinks didn't hit armored units in the daytime. Besides, the dozen Cambodians were still squatting in the road. Intelligence might be wrong, but the locals always knew when there was going to be trouble.

Peacock sidled closer to the hole, hunching down a little at the thought that a flat brown face might pop up out of it at the last instant, eyes glaring at him behind the sights of an A.K. He gagged and blinked, then tossed the bomb the last yard with a convulsive gesture and darted back away.

"Jesus H. Christ!" he wheezed, "Jesus H. Christ! That stinks down there like nothing on earth!"

"How's that?" Fuller snapped, nervous about anything unusual. The bunker buster went off, a hollow boom like a cherry bomb in a garbage can, only a thousand times as loud. Dirt and whizzing fragments of stone mushroomed upward, drifting mostly toward three-six and showering it for thirty seconds. The crew covered their eyes and hunched their steel pots close to their shoulders. Captain Fuller, kneeling beside the track under the unexpected rain of dirt, suddenly choked and jumped to his feet swearing. "My God," he roared, "which way's the wind blowing?" The charnel reek that oozed out of the newly opened bunker was strong and indescribably foul. The troop had found NVA buried in the jungle for months in the damp warmth, found them and dug them up to search for papers; that stench had been nothing to this one.

"Must'a been a hospital," Sergeant Peacock suggested as he edged upwind of the pit. He was covering his nose with an olive drab handkerchief.

"Jesus," he repeated, "I never smelled anything like that."

Three-six's diesel ripped back into life and brought the track upwind of the hole in a wide circle. Ten yards away, its nose pointing out toward the road beside the next vehicle over, it halted and Casely descended again. He still held his pistol. "God, look at that," he said.

When the bunker buster had blown, it lifted the roof off a narrow crypt some ten feet long and half that wide. It could not have been more than inches below the surface of the soil at any point. Relatively little of the rubble kicked up by the explosion had fallen back into the cavity, leaving it open to the eyes of the men on on its edge. Most of the litter on the floor of the crypt was of bones. All were dry, and many had been smashed to powder by the blast. One skull, whole by some mischance, goggled toward the north wall.

The idol glared back at it. It was about six feet high, cut out of streaky soapstone instead of the omnipresent laterite whose pocked roughness forms the walls and ornamentation of most Cambodian temples, even those of Angkor Wat. Though it stood on two legs, there was nothing manlike about the creature. A fanged jaw twisted into a vicious grimace, leering out over the beast's pot belly. One clawed arm rested on the paunch; the other, apparently the only casualty of the explosion, had been broken off at the shoulder and lay half covered by the gravel on the floor. The gray-on-black marking of the stone blended to give the image a lifelikeness it should not have had; Fuller blinked, half expecting blood to spurt from the severed arm. Over all lay the miasma of decay, slowly diffusing on the hot breeze.

Fuller hesitated a moment, peering over the edge. "Anybody see a door to this place?" he asked. None of the group slowly gathering on the edge of the crypt answered. The whole room had been faced with thin slabs of the same stone that formed the idol. Line after line of squiggly, decorative Cambodian writing covered their surface unintelligibly. Fragments from the roof of the crypt showed similar markings.

"That ain't no hospital," Sergeant Peacock asserted needlessly, wiping his palms on the seat of his fatigues. The light-green material darkened with sweat.

Jody Bredt, the undersized Pfc. who drove three-six, sauntered over with his gas mask in his hand. He took the war a little more seriously than most of the rest of the troop and kept his mask in the hatch with him instead of being buried in the bottom of his duffle bag. "Want me to take a look down there, Captain Fuller?" he asked importantly.

"Why don't you just put in for official tunnel rat?" his TC gibed, but the officer nodded appreciatively. "Yeah, go ahead. Be careful, for God's sake, but I think this may just have been an old temple."

Jody slipped his mask on, virtually blinding himself even in the bright sunlight. The lenses were dusty and scratched from knocking around in the track for months. A preliminary sniff had convinced him that the stench had almost dissipated, but he couldn't take the mask off now that he'd made such a production of it. Gingerly, he lowered himself over the edge. Sergeant Peacock knelt down to hold his wrist in case he slipped; there might be a mine under any of the delicately carven slabs. The gooks were clever about that sort of thing. Still, any mines down there should have gone off when the bunker buster did. He let his feet touch the ground with a little more confidence and ran his hand over the wall. "I don't see any swinging doors or anything," he reported. "Maybe they got in through the roof, huh?"

"Hell, we'll never know that now," Casely snorted. "Hey, Captain, I think the smell is pretty well gone. Let me go down there."

"Why?" Fuller grunted. "Want to take that statue back with you on R&R?"

The TC grinned. The captain knew his men pretty well. "Naw, too big. I did think one of them skulls would make kind of a nice souvenir if they don't check my hold baggage too close, though."

Fuller swore and laughed. "OK," he said, squatting down preparatory to jumping in himself, "go ahead, you found the place. But I want the rest of you guys back on your tracks. We're going to be leaving here in five, as soon as I get a look around myself."

"Hey, Red, throw me something," one of the bystanders begged Casely, but the captain waved him away peremptorily. "Go on, goddamnit, I don't want all of you hanging around here in case the dinks are out there." He hopped down into the cavity, joining Casely and the driver whose mask hung from his hand again. The air was thick but had lost the earlier noisomeness.

Casely picked up the skull he wanted for a trophy with a finger through each of the eye-sockets. When he had lifted it waist high, the bone crumbled to powder. What was left of the skull shattered unrecognizably when it hit the floor. "Goddamn," the TC swore, kicking angrily at the heap of dust, "why didn't it do that when the frag went off if it had to do it at all? Now I got my hopes up and look what happens!"

Peacock, squatting like a black Buddha on the rim of the crypt, chuckled deep in his chest. "Why, the next dink we get, you just cut his head off and dry it out. How that be, Red? Get you a nice fresh head to take back to your wife."

Casely swore again. The captain was handling another of the bones. This one was a femur, sheared off some inches short of the knee joint. If the frag hadn't done it, the damage dated from the unguessable past. The bone was almost as dry and fragile as the skull that had powdered in Casely's hands. He tossed it up to the field first, shaking his head in puzzlement. "How old do you guess that is, sarge?" he asked. "I don't think I ever saw anything that used up before."

"This old guy is still in fine shape," Jody put in, rapping the brutal idol on the nose with his gas mask. "Frag didn't hurt him hardly at all, did it?" He kicked at the broken limb lying near the statue. The others, more or less consciously, had been avoiding the idol with their eyes. If you looked too closely, the crude swirls on the thing that were supposed to represent hair seemed to move by themselves. Probably the grain of the stone.

"Goddamn," Fuller said. It was not entirely blasphemous the way he said it. "Will you look at that."

The driver's foot had shaken the broken arm, paw, whatever out of the pile of rubble in which it lay. Previously unseen was the figure of the man—it was clearly a man—held in the monster's clawed grip. The man had been sculpted only a fraction of the size of the thing holding him, some thirty inches or so from foot to where the head would have been if it hadn't been broken off by the blast. Fuller looked more closely. No, the figure had been carved that way originally, limp and headless in the idol's claws. The beast-god's leering mouth seemed to take a further, even more unpleasant dimension. Fuller stretched his arm up to Sergeant Peacock. "Sarge, give me a hand. Come on, you two, we're getting out of here."

"Think the gooks been using this as a hospital?" Jody asked, scrambling up to the surface with a boost from Casely. Jody always missed the last word and didn't have quite the intelligence to supply it himself.

"I don't know what they're doing," Fuller grunted. "If there's one bunker around here, there could be a hundred though, and I'm not sitting around to find out. I think I'll ask for a B-52·strike here. God knows, they're flattening enough empty jungle they ought to be willing to hit a spot like this."

Casely picked up a bit of the crypt's roof and tossed it in his hand. "Hey," he said, "maybe some of those locals speak English. I'd like to know what these squiggles are saying."

"You're going to have to find them to ask," Peacock said with a shrug. "They must'a took off when the bunker buster went off."

"Umm," the redhead grunted. "Well, it makes a souvenir anyway." Around the circle of vehicles engines were starting up. One of the gunners signaled Casely with the radio helmet in his hand. "Come on, Red," he shouted, "'we're moving out." Casely nodded and began jogging toward the track. He wasn't sorry to be leaving this place either. Not sorry at all.

Three-six had a full crew of four men, and so they split the guard into two-hour shifts from 2200 to 0600. The new location was a dead ringer for the one they'd just left, low jungle approaching the graveled length of Highway 13, but at least there didn't seem to be any bunkers. Or idols. Casely had last guard, a concession to his rank that meant he could get six hours sleep uninterrupted, but he couldn't seem to drop off soundly. The air was cool and misty, cloaking the tracks so closely that the Sheridan to the left in the laager was almost invisible. A good night for sappers. Casely could almost feel them creeping closer.

He glanced at his watch. Three o'clock, Jody's shift. The TC was stretched out on the closed cargo hatch of the ACAV while the two gunners slept inside on mattresses laid over the ranked ammo boxes. He should have been able to see Jody sitting in the cupola, staring out into the jungle. At first glance the driver wasn't there, and Casely sat up to make sure the little guy hadn't gone and done something unusually stupid. At the first sound of movement from behind him Jody gasped and straightened up from where he was hunched over the cupola's fifty caliber machine gun. "Jeez, Red, it's you. Jeez, you gave me a shock there!" he whispered nervously.

Casely swung himself around to lean his left side on the sloping steel of the cupola and peer out into the night. "Couldn't sleep," he muttered. The rustle of static escaping from the driver's radio helmet was comforting, mechanical.

"I think there's somebody out there," Jody blurted suddenly, waving his arm toward the mist. "I keep hearing something moving, kind of."

Something like thunder began in the far distance. It didn't seem loud until you tried to whisper over it. Unlike thunder, it didn't stop. The rustling, rumbling sound went on and on, and to the west the sky brightened intermittently with white flashes.

Jody tensed. "What the hell's that?" he stammered, his right hand already snaking for the cal fifty's charging handle. His TC chuckled and stopped him. "Christ, you are new," Casely said without malice. "This the first time you heard an Arclight?"

Jody's blank expression was evident even in the gloom. "Arclight," the TC repeated. "You know, a B-52 strike. Hell, that must be ten klicks away at least."

"Ten kilometers?" the driver said in surprise. "It scared me there for a minute."

"If there's any dinks under it, it'll scare them worse," Casely stated positively. "Wait till we go through one of the bombed areas, and you'll see. They just flatten whole swaths of the jungle, a quarter mile wide and as long as there's planes in the strike. Don't leave a thing higher than the grass, either."

He glanced at his watch again and swore. "Look, I got to get some sleep. Wake me up in half an hour, huh?"

"You don't think there's something out there, Red?"

"Hell, I don't know," the TC grunted. "Keep your eyes open and wake me up in half an hour."

There was something pressing down on them from the dark, but it might have been the mist alone. Casely drew his poncho liner closer about him and fell back into a fitful sleep. He dreamed, aimlessly at first but then of the writing-covered crypt he had stood in that afternoon. He was there again, but the roof had been replaced and the walls were miles high. The idol was waiting for him. Its soapstone jaws grinned, and its remaining arm began to reach out. The stench rolled almost tangibly from its maw.

"Jesus God!" the TC blurted. His head rang with the blow he had given it, lurching uncontrollably against the cupola to get away from his dream. Even awake, the charnel fetor lay heavily in his nostrils. "Jesus," he repeated more softly. If he'd known the sort of nightmare he was due for, he'd have spelled Jody right then at 3:15 and let the driver dream it for him.

It was still pitch dark; dawn and sunset are sudden things in the tropics. The illuminated hands of his big wristwatch were clear at five after four, though, twenty minutes after Jody should have waked him up. "Hey, turtle," he whispered, "I told you to get me up at a quarter of. You like guard so much you want to pull my shift too?"

No answer. Alarmed, Casely peered into the cupola. The light fabric of the driver's shirt showed faintly where his torso covered the receiver of the cal fifty.

Despite all his talk about hearing something in the jungle, Jody had fallen asleep.

In the guts of the ACAV, the radio hissed softly. "Come on, Jody," Casely prodded. He put his hand on the driver's shoulder. Jody's body slipped fluidly off the seat, falling through the cupola into the vehicle's interior. One of the gunners snapped awake with a startled curse and turned on his flashlight.

On the back deck of the ACAV, Casely stared at the dark wetness on his hand. For a moment he was too transfixed even to look down into the track, to look down at Jody's torso sprawling in headless obscenity.

Captain Fuller yawned, then shook his head to clear it. "Sure hope we don't have another sapper tonight," he muttered. "Christ, I'm tired."

Sergeant Peacock methodically checked the tent flap, making sure it was sealed and not leaking light from the small yellow bulbs inside. The command track's engine was on, rumbling to power the lights and the two radio sets in the track itself behind the tent. It was midnight and voices crackled as the radio operator called the roll of the vehicles around the NDP.

"Tell the truth," Fuller went on with a grin of furtive embarrassment, "I wasn't sleeping too well last night even before Casely started shouting. Had one hell of a nightmare. Christ, what a thing that was."

"I knew the gooks to do it in Korea," Peacock said, his great brown eyes guarded. "Cut a fella's head off and leave his buddy sleeping right beside him. I guess they figured the story that got around did more good than if they just killed both of 'em."

The officer shrugged impatiently, lost in his own thoughts. "The dream, I meant. You don't expect your own dreams to go back on you over here. Christ, it's not as though we don't have enough trouble with the dinks."

"We moved ten klicks today," the black said mildly, shifting his bulk on his cot. "You were probably right, figuring there was a bunker system off in the jungle where we laagered last night. They'll just be glad we moved outa their hair; they won't chase us."

Captain Fuller wasn't listening. His face was peculiarly tense, and he seemed to be straining to catch a sound from outside the tent. "Who's moving around out there, Peacock?" he said at last.

The field first blinked. "Sir?" he said. The big man stood up, thrust his head through the tent flap, holding the edges of the material close to his neck to block off the light inside. There was nothing, nothing but an evil reek that seemed to permeate the whole area. He pulled back into the tent. "Everything seems all right, sir; they got a radio going in one of the tracks, maybe that's what you heard."

"No, no," the officer denied peevishly, "it was somebody moving around. I suppose it was just somebody taking a piss. Christ, I'm too jumpy to sleep and too tired to think straight when I stay awake. God damn it, I wish July was here so I could take my R&R and forget this damn place."

"Don't let dreams bother you," Sergeant Peacock counseled quietly. "I know about dreams; I had bad dreams when I was a baby, but my momma would wake me up and tell me it was all right, that it didn't mean anything. And that's so, once you wake up. Even that one last night—"

"Look, Peacock," the captain snarled, "what I don't need is a lecture from you on how childish I'm being. Besides, what do you know what I was dreaming last night?"

"Sorry, sir," the sergeant said with impassive dignity, "I'm sure I don't know what you were dreaming about. I meant my own dream about the idol—you know, the one back at yesterday's first NDP. It was pretty bad, the thing reaching out for me and all, but I knew it was just—"

The captain was staring at him in terror, all the ruddiness seeping yellowly out of his face. "My God," Fuller whispered. "Dear God, you mean you dreamed that too?" He stood up. The cot creaked behind him and his dog tags clinked together on his bare chest. To his ears, at least, there seemed to be another sound; one from outside.

"God *damn* it!" Fuller shouted. His M-16 lay under his cot, across the double V of the head and center legs. He snatched it out and snapped back the operating rod. The bolt clacked home, chambering a round. With the rifle in his hands and not another word for the sergeant, the captain stepped through the tent flaps. The radio operator glanced through the back of the tent to see what the commotion was about. Sergeant Peacock shrugged and shook his head. Outside the tent they could hear the CO's voice shouting angrily, "All right, who the hell is—"

The voice fluted horribly into a scream, high-pitched and terrified. "My God!" the radioman blurted and jumped back to his seat in front of the equipment. Sergeant Peacock scooped up his holstered pistol and the machete beside it, his right hand brushing the light switch and plunging the tent into darkness. In the track behind him the radios winked evilly as the big noncom dived out into the night.

There was nothing to be seen. The scream had cut off as quickly as it had begun. There was an angry hiss from one of the encircling tracks as somebody sent up a parachute flare. Its chill glare showed nothing more than the black overcast had as it drifted down smokily, moving southward on the sluggish wind. There was a clatter of equipment all around the circle now, men nervously activating weapons and kicking diesels into life. "There!" somebody shouted from the southern curve of the laager. The flare, yellow now, had in its dying moments caught something lying at the edge of the jungle.

"Cover me," Peacock shouted. Pistol in hand, he ran toward the afterimage of the object. Something hard skittered underfoot, not enough to throw him. It was an M-16. He did not pause to pick it up. He pounded heavily between two tracks, out into the narrow strip between laager and jungle torn by the vehicles maneuvering there earlier in the day. He was very close to what the flare had illuminated. "Gimme some light!" the sergeant roared, heedless of the fact that it would show him up to any lurking sniper.

A five-cell flashlight beamed instantly from the nearest track. The light wobbled, then steadied when it found its target. The flat beam lay in a long oval across the thing glimpsed in the flare.

"Sarge, is that the captain?" someone shouted from the track. The radio operator must have told them who had screamed.

"No, not quite," the field first replied in a strange voice. He was looking farther out into the jungle, at the shadows leaping behind the light. "It's only his leg. No, I'm wrong—I think the rest of him's here after all. Jesus, I do hope his family knows an undertaker who likes jigsaw puzzles."

Lieutenant Worthington turned back to an angry soldier, scratching the brown hair that lay close to his scalp. On the card table in front of him were laid three sections of relief map, joined and covered by a layer of clear acetate. "Look, Casely," the officer said with ebbing patience, "I know you're shook; we're all shook. And on top of that, I've got to keep this troop running until they get a replacement for Fuller out here. But I'm not going to send the troop back south to blow up a goddamn idol just because you have bad dreams about it. Besides, look here—" he thrust the map toward the TC, stubby finger pointing a long rectangle shaded in red crayon on it—"the location is off limits since six this morning until Sunday midnight. Somebody else is operating in there, I guess, and they don't want us shooting at each other."

The redhead's hands clenched. "I'm telling you," he grated, his voice tight, "it's coming for us. First Jody, then the captain—hell, what makes you think it's going to quit when it gets Peacock and me? All of you were there."

"Captain Fuller was eaten by a tiger," the lieutenant snapped. "Now why don't you cut the crap and get back to your track?"

"Goddamn funny tiger that doesn't leave footprints—"

"So it jumped! Are you going to get out of here, or are you going back to Quan Loi under guard?" Worthington started to rise out of his lawn chair to lend his words emphasis.

For an instant it seemed the enlisted man would hit him; then Casely turned and stalked off without saluting. Well, salutes weren't common in the field anyway, the lieutenant told himself as he went back to his job of sorting out the mess the captain had left for him.

Under the tarp by the supply track, Sergeant Peacock sat at another card table sipping juice from the five-gallon container there. He looked up as Casely approached. First platoon had gotten back late from a convoy run, and a few of the men were still eating their supper nearby.

"Can't you do something about him, sarge?" the TC begged. His body, under its tan, had an unhealthy hue that the field first noted without comment. The younger man was about to crack.

"Well, I guess he's right," the Negro said without emphasis. "I know what you're thinking, it was a bad dream—"

"The same dream twice in a row!" Casely broke in, "and you had it too." He drew a cup of juice from the container, and the action seemed to steady him. "Jesus Christ, you can't tell me that's just a coincidence, not with the things that happened right when we were dreaming!"

The big noncom shrugged. "So maybe we smelled something," he agreed, "and it made us think about that stinkhole we opened up the other day. It could do that, you know. Maybe some tiger was using the place for a cave and caught the smell from it. The dream don't mean anything, that's all I'm saying. If there's a tiger roaming around, we'll shoot it the next time."

The redhead took a sip of his juice and sloshed it around in his mouth. He grinned wryly. "Sarge," he said, "I almost think you believe that. Even though you know damn well that the only chance for you and me and maybe the rest of the outfit is to blow up that idol before it gets us too. Stands to reason that if we see it dreaming with only one arm and if we blow the rest of it to smithereens, it won't be able to come for us at all."

The sergeant chuckled. "Well, you better hope you're wrong, son, 'cause they aren't going to let us go back and blow that thing up. Be a fine thing if the arvins ambushed us or we ran into a sheaf of our own one-five-fives, wouldn't it?"

"God damn it, how do you stay so calm?" the younger man exploded. Sergeant Peacock looked him up and down before answering, "Well, I tell you, son, when I was about your age in Korea, my platoon was holding a ridge that the gooks wanted real bad. They came at us with bayonets; you know those old Russian ones, seventeen inches in the blade? There was one coming right for me and I swear he was the biggest gook I ever saw, bigger than me even. I had a carbine with a thirty-round box, and I shot that son of a bitch right through the chest. I mean I shot him thirty goddamn times. And he kept coming.

"I couldn't believe it. There was blood all over the front of his uniform, and he just kept coming. I put the last shot into him from closer than I am to you, and then he stuck his goddamn bayonet all the way through my guts before he died. I said to myself, Mrs. Peacock, your favorite son isn't coming back 'cause the gooks got zombies fighting for them. But I was wrong both times. They fixed me up in Japan and had me back with the rest of the unit before the ceasefire. And that gook wasn't magic either; he was just tougher than anybody else in the world. Since then I just haven't let anything scare me—especially not magic, even when I could see it. That all went out of me when the bayonet slipped in."

Casely shook his head in resignation. "I hope to God you can say that tomorrow morning," he muttered. "And I hope to God that I'm around to hear you." He walked off in the direction of his track.

Bailey and Jones sat in front of the cupola, playing cribbage and keeping a desultory watch on the surrounding jungle. Bailey was driving now that Jody was gone; that meant that only one of the machine guns in back would be manned in a fire-fight. Christ, why should he worry about that? Casely asked himself savagely. "Hey, snake," the others greeted him. The TC nodded. He climbed into the cupola and sighted along the barrel of the cal fifty. It didn't give him the comfortable feeling it sometimes did.

"Say, Red," Jones said, keeping his eyes on his

cards, "you been looking kinda rocky. Just for tonight, Pete and I thought we'd cover for you and let you get some sleep."

"No, thanks a lot, man, but no."

"Aw, come on, Red," Bailey put in. "You're so beat you're gonna fall right off the track if you don't get some sleep. Hell, we can't have that happening to a short timer with only twenty-seven days left, can we?"

"Twenty-eight," Casely corrected automatically. God, that close to going home and this had to happen! It would have been bad enough to get zapped by the dinks now, but, hell, you figure on that. . . .

"What do you say, man?" Bailey prompted.

"Sorry, I really do appreciate it. But I'm not going to sleep tonight. I know what you're thinking, but I'm right. If it gets me, it's going to get me awake. That's how it is."

Below the TC's line of sight, Jones caught Bailey's eyes. The driver frowned and gave a shrug. "Fifteen-two, fifteen-four, and a pair for six," he counted morosely.

The sky was beautiful. Cloud streaks in the west broke the brilliant sunset into three orange blades stabbing across the heavens to bleed on a wrack of cumuli. The reflecting wedges, miles high, stood like three keystones of an arch, more stunning than any sunrise could have been. Swiftly they shrunk upward, deepened, disappeared. The same clouds that had made the display possible blocked off the moon and stars utterly. It was going to be another pitch-black night.

Jones stepped around to the cargo hatch and pulled three beers out of the cooler. He handed them up to the TC to open with the church key hanging from the side of the cupola. No pop tops in Nam. Christ, little enough ice, Casely thought as he sipped his warm Pabst. What a hell of a place to die in!

Footsteps crunched on the gravelly soil. Casely's heart jumped as he turned around to find the source of the sounds. Tiger, monster, whatever, the thing could be on you before you saw it in this darkness.

"How's it going?" Sergeant Peacock's familiar voice asked. The TC relaxed, almost able to laugh at his fright. "Not bad till you scared the crap out of me just now."

"You keep cool," the sergeant admonished. He didn't attempt to climb onto the back deck; instead, he stood beside the ACAV, his head a little below the level of its sides. Casely climbed out of the cupola and squatted down beside it to see the big Negro better.

"You could have gone back on the supply bird tonight," Peacock said, his voice low but audible to Jones and Bailey inside the track now as well as to the TC. Casely didn't care. He could live anything down, if he had more than a night or two to live. In normal tones he replied, "Didn't figure that was going to do much good, sarge. We're at least ten klicks away from where we found that thing, right?"

The field first nodded.

"Well, stands to reason that if it can follow us anyways at all, it could just as easy follow me back to Quan Loi. At least here I got a chance." His left hand reached out and patted the heavy barrel of the cal fifty, sticking more than three feet out from the cupola gunshield. "Oh, I know," the redhead went on, "the captain had a gun, and Jody was right here when it got him—but Christ, back at Quan Loi or Di An there wouldn't be a goddamn thing between me and it."

The sergeant chuckled without much humor. Casely thought he could see the outline of a machete, buckled onto the pistol belt under the massive bulge of the black's stomach. The only other time the TC could remember Peacock actually wearing the big knife was the evening they got word that the firebase was being hit by everything from one-oh-sevens on down and that the NDPs could expect their share any moment. "Hey, you want a beer?" he questioned. "It's warm, but—oh *Christ!*"

The younger man leaped back into his cupola. "What's the matter?" the sergeant demanded. Then his nostrils wrinkled.

"Flares!" the noncom shouted at the top of his lungs. "Everybody shoot up flares!"

"What the hell?" Jones blurted in confusion as he and Bailey stuck their heads up out of the cargo hatch. The bolt of the cal fifty in the cupola clanged loudly as Casely snatched back the charging handle. Across the laager somebody had heard the sergeant's bellow and obeyed enthusiastically with a pair of white star clusters. They shot up like Roman candles, drawing weird shadows with their short multiple glare and silhouetting Sergeant Peacock himself as he pounded across the dirt toward the command track. A horrible stench lay over everything.

The flares burned out. The sergeant disappeared, black into the deeper blackness. Lt. Worthington lurched into sight at the flap of the command tent, his rifle in his hand. Then the sergeant bellowed, a terrible mixture of hatred and surprise that almost drowned out the hiss of another flare going up. In the cupola of three-six, Casely cursed with effort as he swung the squealing armor around and pointed the big machine gun in across the NDP.

"Red, what in God's name are you doing?" Jones shrieked. The flare popped and began floating down on its parachute. Sergeant Peacock was between three-six and the command track. His bloated shadow writhed across the soil; neither of his feet were touching the ground. Casely pressed down the butterfly trigger with both thumbs. The shattering muzzle blast pocked the sides of the command tent as the red tracers snicked out past it. The stream of fire was whipping almost straight across the laager, a long raking burst endangering everybody in the troop as it lashed the air just over Sergeant Peacock's head. The field first was struggling titanically with nothing at all; his right hand slashed the glinting machete blade again and again across the air in front of him while his left seemed clamped on the invisible something that held and supported him.

The southern sky brightened, flickered. Not another flare, Jones realized, not thunder either as the sound shuddered toward him. Arclight, a strike on the area they had started to laager in two nights back.

All around the NDP men were shouting in confusion. The lieutenant had started running toward the field first, then collapsed gagging as he took a deep breath. Diesels rumbled, but no one else had started shooting. The barrel of Casely's machine gun was cherry red. You could watch tracers start to tumble in screaming arcs as soon as they left the burnt-out barrel, but the TC continued hosing the air. Sergeant Peacock gave a choked cry; his machete snapped, then dropped from his hand. At the same instant, the cal fifty came to the end of its belt of ammunition and stuttered into silence. The TC's despairing curses were barely audible over the rising thunder of bomb blasts raking the jungle south of them.

There was an incongruous pop from the air beside Sergeant Peacock. The field first dropped to the ground, unconscious but alive. With a smile of incredulous hope etched on his face by the last glow of the flare, Casely staggered out of his cupola. His eyes were fixed on the rippling glare in the south, and he didn't seem to notice when Jones plucked his sleeve.

"God bless the Air Force," the TC was whispering. "God bless the Air Force."

BAND OF BROTHERS

Sanger was the commando's point man this morning. Twenty meters beyond the abandoned farmhouse he walked into a Gerin killzone.

"Freeze!" ordered Rudisill, the artillery specialist; second in the six-man column and shocked out of the lethargy of a long march by the pulsing alert on his helmet display. "Sanger, your helmet's fucked. You're already in a killzone."

Coils in each helmet cooled the trooper's head and approximately half his blood supply, the next best thing to total environmental control. The refrigerant didn't prevent Duquesne's atmosphere from being a steam bath, though; nor did it do anything to lighten the commando's load of gear.

For concealment purposes, they'd been inserted by sea with ten kilometers to hike before they reached their objective. Sweat had been rolling off Rudisill's body with the effort of humping his helmet, weapons, rations—and the heavy spotting table—up and down forested ridges.

Now the sweat was cold.

"Everybody halt in place," said Captain Lermontov over the unit net. "I'm coming forward."

Lermontov's voice was more than calm; it was calming. "Sanger, you know the drill. You're safe unless you try to back up, so just stay where you are. Might be a good time to take a leak."

"I done that, sir," whispered the point man. Then, "Sir, you gonna be able to get me out?"

Commando 441 had carried out twenty-seven missions on this Christ-bitten hellhole without a fatality. The troopers of other units carried lucky charms. Four-four-one had Ivan Lermontov.

But it was going to take more than luck to pull Sanger from the trap into which his faulty equipment had dropped him.

"I don't see why not," said Captain Lermontov.

Rudisill heard the soft rustle of vegetation. The commando's leader was approaching with easy caution from his number three slot in the column, a hundred meters behind the artillery specialist.

The heads-up display on Rudisill's visor showed pulsing blips as the computer-directed elements of the Gerin killzone maneuvered for optimal position. Pretty soon they'd encircle the whole commando, not just the point man. . . .

This killzone consisted of twenty separate elements, strung in a two-kilometer line almost parallel to the commando's axis of advance. If the commando'd crossed to the left rather than the right side of the knob on the last ridge, they'd've been out of the zone's sensor range. The troopers wouldn't've known—or cared—that the killzone was in place. Now—

Each element of the killzone was a 20-centimeter sphere with sensors, magnetic lift engines, and a rudimentary control/communications computer. When a target entered the sensor range of any element, that computer alerted the other elements and the whole chain drifted closer to do maximum damage to possible following targets. Nothing would happen until the target started to move out of the zone's lethal area.

The magnetic motors had an electronic signature even in standby mode. Commando helmets could detect a killzone at twice the killzone's own fifty-meter sensor range.

Except that Sanger's helmet had malfunctioned.

The shell of each sphere was pre-fragmented ceramic, backed with high explosive. Sanger was within ten meters of one. At that range, the blast would shatter the trunk of 30-centimeter hardwoods—much less a man.

"Good work, Guns," Lermontov murmured, using straight voice instead of frequency-hopping radio as he came up behind Rudisill. "If you hadn't been looking sharp, we'd be in problems now."

That was oil, not reality. The helmet, not the artillery spotter personally, had done the work; but the words made Rudisill feel better nonetheless. "They're coming down on us, sir," he said tightly.

"Sure, that's what they do," agreed Lermontov as he paused beside Rudisill.

The captain was a man of middle height, with a gymnast's shoulders and slim hips. He'd slung his assault rifle and was punching keys on the miniature handset flexed to his helmet.

The face beneath Lermontov's raised visor looked unconcerned; a boyish lock of dark blond hair peeked out from beneath his helmet.

Lermontov smiled. "Got another job for you, Guns," he said. "Need you to tell me when I look like I'm a zone element myself."

Rudisill's rifle was aimed at the stretch of forest which concealed another of the mines drifting toward the target area. He brushed sweat from his chin with the back of his left hand and said, "Sir, you can't. These helmets won't—"

Lermontov flashed a smile that brooked no more argument than a shark's did. "Don't you worry, troop," he said flatly. "These helmets'll sit up and beg for cookies if you know how to massage 'em. Your job's just to tell me—" Lermontov concentrated on the keyboard in his left palm "—when I've got it right."

Rudisill swallowed and nodded. His visor displayed the slowly moving elements of the killzone as blue dots on the ghostly relief map overlaying the reality of the forest. As Captain Lermontov touched his keyboard, another dot sprang to life beside the artillery spotter. The new arrival was fuzzy at first, but its outline quickly sharpened to a near identity with the other twenty.

"You got it, sir," Rudisill said. "But I wish you wouldn't. . . ."

"Okay, Sanger," Lermontov said over the unit push as he stepped forward. "We're golden. Help's on the way."

The undergrowth folded behind the captain, hiding him from Rudisill after a few long, gliding strides. On Rudisill's visor, the twenty-first dot moved smoothly toward the original one at a pace swifter than that of the other drifting deathtraps.

Lermontov's helmet was matching its own output to the commo and motor signatures of a killzone element. If the emanations were close enough, the Gerin sensors would ignore Lermontov until he switched the killzone off.

If the match *wasn't* close enough, the blast would be lethal within a fifty-meter circle.

Rudisill knelt carefully so that the ground took part of the weight of his pack. He pretended to ignore the drop of sweat that trembled on the end of his nose.

The dot that was Lermontov paused briefly as it reached the point man's position. Nothing came over the commo net, but Rudisill could imagine the captain patting Sanger on the shoulder, saying a few cheerful words, and moving on toward the waiting explosive.

Rudisill could imagine it because that's more or less what had happened to him when a laser toppled a tree across his thighs. The spotting table was smashed, so he couldn't call in artillery fire. He didn't have a prayer unless somebody crawled suicidally close to the Gerin bunker and dropped a grenade through its firing slit.

Which Captain Lermontov did.

The dot that was the commando's leader merged with the almost-identical killzone element.

"Okay," said the captain's voice. "Now, everybody hug the ground for just a. . . ."

Rudisill knew he should flatten from his crouch. He couldn't bring himself to move.

The line of oncoming beads faded to blurs or vanished as their motors cut back to stand-by power. The first element of a killzone to make contact became the master link; and Captain Lermontov had just shut it down.

"There, we're golden," Lermontov said. "Let's get moving, shall we? Heatherton, come forward and take point."

Rudisill finally let his breath out as he rose to his feet. "Negative," he said. "I'll take it, sir."

He moved forward, letting his eyes scan either side and the trees above him, as though he were already the column's point man.

"Guns," Lermontov replied cautiously, "we need you to spot when we reach the hostage pen."

"We need everybody," Rudisill said. "I'm here, and we know my hardware works."

He'd reached the clearing around the farmhouse.

The inhabitants hadn't been gone for long. Chickens squabbled noisily beyond the palings of the kitchen garden, and the hog which snorted off among the trees was domestic rather than feral.

The pig's masters were probably hidden nearby. Rudisill didn't bother to try calling them out. The Dukes weren't going to come forward, weren't going to help even by dipping a gourdful of drinking water for the troops risking their lives to free Duquesne from the Gerin.

The Dukes weren't shit.

Sanger was washing down a tablet of electrolyte replacement with tasteless water from the condenser in his helmet. He was nineteen years standard and could pass for twice that age at the moment.

Sanger stood, shouldering his pack. He didn't have the spotting table, but the Multi-Application Rocket System he and the other three troopers carried was equally heavy. "Thanks, buddy," he muttered to Rudisill.

"Hell, I didn't get you assigned to Lermontov's commando," Rudisill answered, speaking in a low voice because the captain was waiting only a few meters beyond.

Lermontov had clipped the keyboard back onto his helmet. His right hand gripped his rifle again. His left index finger was tracing designs on the mottled shell of the Gerin mine. The access plate in the top of the sphere was still open.

"Good job, Cap'n," Rudisill murmured.

Lermontov shrugged. "You watch yourself on point, Guns," he said.

"Always," Rudisill said without emotion. He stepped forward into the trees, following the azimuth projected onto his visor.

There were no more Gerin minefields, but the commando found repeated evidence of human occupation.

Another farm; the prints of bare feet on trails the commando crossed but never followed; once the sound of a baby crying, tantalizingly near.

"I can feel 'em watching," said Minh, the last man in line.

"*I* better not see one," Heatherton responded. "I know damn well those shit-scared bastards're reporting to the Slime."

"None of that," Lermontov said sharply. "There's no evidence that the locals cooperate with the Gerin. They're just scared. Same as you'd be if your planet'd been run by the Slime for three generations."

"Cap'n," said Sanger, "they don't have the balls t' live nor die neither. Any of *my* kin gets that scared, I'll cut their throat and put 'em outa their mis'ry."

Rudisill panted in time with the rhythm of his boots. His pack cut him over the collarbone and the jut of his hips. He'd glued sponge from fuze containers over the points of wear, but it didn't matter. In the long run, the weight and friction were the same, and the ulcers in his flesh reopened.

"I still say," Heatherton muttered, "that if *they* ain't interested 'n saving 'emselfs from the Slime, then I'm not interested neither."

"Look," said the captain, "when we release the hostages the Gerin are holding, then maybe we'll see some changes in the local attitude. That's what Headquarters figures, anyway."

"Headquarters ain't sweatin' like pigs in the boonies," Sanger retorted.

They were climbing what Rudisill's projected map said was the last rise before they reached the target; but it was a kilometer of outcrops and heavy undergrowth, and the map was a best-estimate production anyway. Rudisill figured the Headquarters analysts must've been wrong, *again*, because if the commando were really that close to a Gerin base there'd be—

"*Freeze*," Rudisill ordered as his own body locked in place. But they were all right. . . .

"Sir," he whispered, "we've found it. I'm just about *in* the defensive ring, but they got half of it shut down so my sensors didn't pick it up till now."

"What're we talking about, Guns?" Lermontov whispered back. His voice was a phantom in the artillery spotter's earphones.

Rudisill began unfolding his spotting table. "Sir," he said, "there's a plasma battery to right and left. I can't see them, but they're live. And—"

He swallowed. "And what I thought was a boulder right here in front of me, it's concrete. It's the cap of a missile site. They're loaded for bear, but I don't think they were expecting anybody to walk in the back way."

As Rudisill spoke, he clipped the leads from his helmet onto the spotting table. He could mark targets with a lightpen, but direct input was more accurate by an order of magnitude.

The meter-square table couldn't lie flat, but it better be close enough.

"Okay," said Lermontov. "I'm coming forward—"

"Wait sir," Rudisill said.

He focused on the "boulder," which was literally close enough to spit on, and pressed the ENTER key of his helmet's pad. Then he slid a meter to the side, focused on the same point, and clicked the key again. His helmet fed the triangulated data to the spotting table.

There was a muted *zeep* from the table. The relief map projected on Rudisill's visor echoed the processed data: three red beads, the Gerin sites identified either by sight or electronic signatures; and nine yellow beads spaced equidistantly around the remainder of the calculated circle.

"All *right* . . ." Lermontov murmured as he watched

the same beads on his own-display. "And you've got them . . . ?"

"Yessir," the artillery spotter said. "The data's sent to Support as soon as it's calculated. They're waiting offshore to launch as soon as they get the order."

Rudisill raised himself slightly to check the terrain of the estimated—and now confirmed—Gerin camp on the spotting table. The table's data came from the same satellite radar picture as the map on Rudisill's visor, but at least the display was better.

The ridge up which the commando was climbing fell away sharply at the crest. On the other side was a valley carved by the meanderings of a considerable watercourse. The plain's vegetation was kept to a height of ten meters or less by flooding, but giant trees from the crest spread their branches over the scallop a spring had carved from the cliff face.

Water pooled beneath the cliff before gurgling on toward the river half a kilometer away. The pool was the exact center of the Gerin's defensive ring.

"Bingo," said Rudisill.

"All the sites're vertical defense, right?" Lermontov said.

"Well, the plasma guns'd be dual purpose," said the artillery spotter. "But yeah, there's likely antipersonnel stuff closer in that's shut down too."

Rudisill kept his voice steady, but he knew what the words meant. The normal way to eliminate a concealed defensive array was to take cover, spoof the system into life, and then blast the unmasked batteries with precisely aimed artillery. The other way of discovering the system was—

"Okay," said Captain Lermontov, "that means we gotta get real close. No point in our being here if we give the Slime enough warning they grease their hostages before we nail 'em, right?"

"No bloody point our bein' here," Heatherton muttered, a complaint but not an argument.

"Heatherton, Minh, Moschelitz," the captain continued. "You take positions on the cliff top. Guns, Sanger and me'll circle to the low side and penetrate as close as we need to spot the Slime inner ring.

"Remember," Lermontov added, "take it easy."

His voice honed itself to just a hint of edge, reminding them all that he knew they were hard men—but Ivan Lermontov was the hardest of them all, and he *would* be obeyed. "The first the Slime knows we're here is when Guns' salvo takes out all their defenses. If anybody shoots before then, he's responsible for the failure of the mission and the death of a hundred fifty civilian hostages."

Softly again: "Understood?"

"*Roger,*" whispered five simultaneous voices across the commo net.

"Then let's move."

The other method of discovering a shut-down defensive array was damned dangerous. Maybe a little safer than jumping on a live grenade, but real bloody similar.

Not that Rudisill was going to argue with the captain.

Even shut down, the elements of an anti-personnel defense system could be detected if you got within a couple meters. The danger was that if the Gerin had the inner defenses under observation, they could bring their weapons live while the human troops were right in front of them.

But then, if you figured to die in bed, you didn't volunteer for a commando.

It took Lermontov's three-man section over an hour to slink around to the opposite side of the Gerin base. Their circuit confirmed the locations of four more batteries, but the outer ring defenses weren't really a threat. Even though the heavy plasma weapons could be put under manual control to fire on ground targets, there'd be a lock-out to prevent them from shooting toward the base itself. The whole commando was by now within the outer defended area.

The trees on the valley floor had soft, pulpy boles. They grew closely together. Rudisill knew that every time he brushed one, the fan of leaves ten meters above him waved like a flag toward any of the Slime which happened to be watching.

Air didn't move among the dense trunks. Rudisill prayed there was enough breeze above the low canopy to conceal the foliage he moved in the broader patterns of nature.

His right hand was cramping. He deliberately took it off the grip of his rifle and flexed it, working fatigue poisons out of the muscles.

"Sir?" said Heatherton. "We're in position. I want to scope a look."

"Okay," said Lermontov. "Optics only."

Non-emissive viewing through the long, fiber-optics lens each trooper carried was safe enough. Laser ranging or using long-wave radar to pierce a curtain of vegetation might give useful information, but they'd be almost certain to arouse the Slime defenses.

Rudisill settled in place and spread his spotting table again. He switched his visor to play the take from Heatherton's periscope at full intensity. He could've crawled through the vegetation with Heatherton's data displayed as ghost images, the way the relief map had been; but the commando wasn't in a real hurry, and Rudisill wanted a good look at the lion before he stuck his head in its mouth.

The picture wasn't razor sharp, but it was damned good for an image picked up by a 1-millimeter lens, piped down several meters of glass cable, digitized—

and finally transmitted to Rudisill's helmet over a spread of frequencies.

It was good enough to kill by.

There were two Gerin in the spring-fed pool below the cliff. From Heatherton's near-vertical angle, they looked like short-limbed octopuses—or blots of slime that somebody'd stepped on.

That would happen real soon.

There was an armored transporter under camouflage netting, forty meters down the stream which gurgled over the lip of the pool. It was only a six-place vehicle, but its forward cupola held a plasma cannon.

A third Slime sat on the transporter's entrance ramp. Its tentacles waved idly in the water flowing to either side of the vehicle's plenum-chamber skirts.

Rudisill keyed in the vehicle as an artillery target. The spotting table whined happily.

"All *right*," whispered Sanger.

The analysts had been right for a change.

There was a cave in the cliff directly beneath Heatherton. The gate at its mouth was invisible from this angle until another Gerin opened it. Shadows displayed the pattern of bars.

The guard was letting a pair of naked humans out of the cave. Commando 441 had the first sight of the hostages it was supposed to rescue.

Rudisill couldn't figure the byplay at the gate. The Slime had seemed to fondle the prisoners' necks before letting them run clumsily toward the plain, carrying tools and baskets.

Then Captain Lermontov said, "'Okay, they're wearing collars. Explosives with radio detonators and anti-tamper locks, sure as hell. The Slime let 'em supplement their rations, but they make sure they come back."

"They give 'em knives, too," Sanger noted.

"Those may be trowels," the captain said.

"I'd open up a Slime with a trowel," Sanger retorted. "So'd they, if they had balls."

The hostages trotted into the forest; Heatherton's periscope gave only brief further flashes of them. They were operating at some distance from one another. They seemed to be digging and putting the results into their baskets.

The gate shut. The Slime guarding it remained in the alcove, barely visible in the strip of shade beneath the cliff face.

"Okay," said Lermontov. "We've got the right place. Let's move up and find the inner defenses."

"Sir, I don't think we better do that," Rudisill said. "We're already inside three hundred meters. The paradigms on my spotting table, they don't include one for anti-personnel arrays on less than a three-hundred meter radius."

Nobody said anything for a moment. On Rudisill's visor, a Gerin rose from the pool with a splash. For a moment there were three of the ugly beasts within spitting distance of one another. Then one of the initial pair slipped deeper into the water and disappeared.

"Look, maybe they don't *have* an inner ring here," Sanger suggested.

"Unlikely," Lermontov said flatly, though he'd have liked to believe that as much as the others would. "The heavy weapons are too extensive for them not to have light stuff as well. They've just hidden it too well for us."

"Sir," said Rudisill. "We don't have a choice. Let's move back 'n I'll send in a drone. If we try anything without nailing the anti-personnel shit, we cut our throats 'n the hostages' too."

"Okay . . ." Lermontov said, but the word was a placeholder while he thought, not agreement. "This is what we'll do. The hostages themselves will have a notion where the defensive ring is hidden. We—"

"Maybe not," the artillery spotter interjected. "They maybe were brought here after the—"

"Chances are," Lermontov went on, "they'll know."

He didn't raise his voice, but his tone shut Rudisill up instantly. "All we need is one element to figure the whole array, right?"

"Ah," said Rudisill. "Two'd be better. But yeah, one'll give us a point and the radius. Chances are there'll be only one paradigm to match. If it's regular."

The Slime at the back of the transporter squirmed inside. A moment later, he or another Gerin reappeared with a food bar wrapped in one tentacle.

Slime worked in groups of three. That meant the vehicle's turret was probably manned.

"The outer defenses were regular?"

"Yessir," Rudisill admitted. "Like they'd asked a computer to lay it out."

Which they probably had. The Gerin had an accountant's taste for precision.

"Okay," Lermontov repeated. "We'll ask a hostage where the inner defenses are—or how they're camouflaged, whatever it takes for us to locate an element. Then we're golden."

"Aw, shit, Cap'n," Sanger whispered. "Aw, shit. I don't like this shit."

"It's the only way we're going to get the hostages out alive," said Captain Lermontov. "So that's the way we'll do it. All right?"

"Yessir," said Sanger. Rudisill's mouth was too dry for him to comment, even if he'd wanted to do so.

"Guns," the captain continued, "one of the Dukes seems to be coming your way. Stay where you are while Sanger and me move in from behind her. Let me do the talking if possible."

"Roger," Sanger said. Rudisill either spoke the word or thought it while his mouth poised to scream.

He had too much imagination. It was all right when shit started to happen and there was nothing to do but react to the terror that stalked in with blast and fury. But for times when he had to wait and *know* how much could go wrong with a plan . . . for times like this, Rudisill had too much imagination.

The soft dirt wasn't perfectly regular. He edged sideways into a low patch and flattened, wishing he were back in the base camp, or up on top of the cliff, or any damn place else in the world.

The hostage's tool echoed against a root with a hollow *chock! chock! chock!* Bare feet shuffled closer to Rudisill's hiding place.

He caught a glimpse of leg among the narrow trunks. The skin was the pasty white of a cave creature's.

The hostage stepped into plain sight, five meters away. She didn't see Rudisill. His helmet and uniform took on the mottling of his surroundings with the perfection of a chameleon's hide; and anyway, the hostage was looking for fruiting bodies like the dozen or so she already carried in her basket.

She was about fifteen years old and stark naked except for the metal collar. Her body was as filthy and scrawny as that of an alley cat.

Sanger and Captain Lermontov slipped out of the trees just behind her and moved in from either side.

The girl was humming something beneath her breath. She knelt by a tree two meters from Rudisill. Her eyes caught the regular outline of the spotting table.

Before the artillery spotter had time to react, the girl spun erect, kicking gritty loam back toward him.

"It's all right," said Captain Lermontov with his arms spread. "We're here to free—"

The hostage screamed. She flung her blunt-bladed machete into Lermontov's visored face, then sprinted between him and Sanger.

For a moment, Rudisill had a flash of what the girl was seeing: a trio of grim figures like monsters sprung from rotting vegetation. Camouflage made the men faceless blurs; only the arsenal of weapons they wore had firm outlines.

"*Geddown! Geddown!*" Rudisill shouted as he uncaged the red firing key on his table. The girl would warn—

"I got 'er!" Sanger cried as his hand rose. Not with a gun, because the shot would be worse than the screams. . . .

Sanger's hand was vertical. A long-bladed knife rose from it like a torch, hilt-down for a short throw. At this range, Sanger's arm would send the point pricking out above the girl's breastbone while the crossguard rapped her shoulder.

"No!" said Captain Lermontov, but words didn't matter now, not even *his* words, so he tackled the trooper.

Rudisill pressed the red key. He forced himself into the dirt, exhaling so that he'd be that much flatter when—

The first sound was the snarling roar of a backpack rocket, fired from the clifftop on Rudisill's warning. The next sound was a whine, *through* the damp soil and then above it, as the Gerin anti-personnel array deployed.

Gerin lasers were firing even before the MARS warhead's blast and the rippling secondary explosions of fuel and ammunition aboard the Slime transporter.

The commando hadn't been able to locate the inner ring defenses because the elements had been buried deep in the ground. Three meters *behind* where Rudisill cowered, a thick post thrust from the soil like a cylindrical toadstool. Its high-energy laser scythed through treetrunks in bursts of fire and live steam.

Rudisill's helmet went black, saving his vision from the blue-white dazzle a centimeter above his head. He poked his rifle backward like a huge pistol and fired blindly while Hell roared and ravened above him. The bare skin of his hands and throat crinkled.

Far around the circuit, a plasma weapon started to pulse skyward. Then the artillery support Rudisill had summoned burst overheard.

Rudisill's rifle had anti-personnel ammunition up, but a lucky round snapped through the laser aperture. His visor cleared when the glare paused, and he had a chance to throw the switch on his magazine to armor piercing.

Rudisill's aimed shots punched the laser unit into a colander before it could rotate a replacement lens into place.

The air bursts spewed a rain of self-forging fragments. Each one struck within satellite-computed centimeters of the targets the spotting table had sent them. The circle of Gerin plasma and missile batteries, gutted by molten penetrators, blew skyward in alternate bubbles of ionized light and flattened mushrooms of flame-streaked smoke.

The spotting table was *zeep*ing again as it transmitted the coordinates of the inner defensive ring.

Rudisill twisted, loading another magazine to replace the one he'd emptied on the automatic defense unit. He had a good view of the Slime positions now, because the laser had sawed the trees down in a jumble of steam and thrashing, feathery branches.

Sanger was okay. He'd been saved—like Rudisill— by irregularities in the ground they'd scarcely have noticed while marching. Sanger was shooting toward the guard at the cave mouth. Purple blood spurted from the back of the Slime as it tried to unlock the gate and squirm for shelter.

The laser's beam of coherent light had sliced off the feet of the running hostage, then cycled back as she fell and touched her again. Her hair smoldered, and the top of her skull lay a little distance from the rest of her body.

Captain Lermontov had been on top of Sanger when the laser began to cut. Now he lay very still.

His torso was separate from his hips.

The remains of the Gerin transporter were still burning fiercely. Rudisill had targeted it for the artillery, but the fragment's impact only fanned flames which the commando's own rocket had ignited.

The men of Heatherton's section must have destroyed the automatic defenses nearest to them, because they were able to shoot instead of cowering beneath the ravening lasers. Bullets blew froth from the pool and combed Sanger's shots in a sparkling crossfire.

Rudisill heard a familiar howl in the sky. "Watch yourselves!" he warned over the unit net. "Incoming!"

He spread himself flat again. These were shells he'd summoned, but no fire was friendly if you happened to be at the point of impact.

Instead of ducking, one of Heatherton's men fired his MARS down into the pool. A geyser of water lifted, carrying with it the bodies of two Gerin. Steam puffed out around the bars of the cave and the Slime corpse which lay there shivering as bullets continued to rake it.

The world paused for the triple, low-altitude blasts of incoming shells and the hypervelocity shockwaves of the glowing spearpoints they spewed. The ground rippled like a trampoline, flinging Rudisill into the air as mud gouted thirty meters high at the point where the laser unit had been.

The inner ring of the defensive array vanished. Bits

of metal and plastic dribbled down with the columns of gritty mud the penetrators had lifted.

"Have we got 'em?" Rudisill called. "Have we got 'em all?"

Sanger was reloading his rifle. He paused in mid motion when he noticed Lermontov for the first time. Sanger was a veteran. When the shooting started, he must have rolled into position and fired by reflex, ignoring every part of the equation except what was in his sight picture. . . .

The head of a Gerin wearing an armored battlesuit rose just above the surface of the pool. It fired up at the cliff. The Slime was using what by human standards was a light cannon. Rock crumbled around the bright orange shellbursts.

Minh yelped over the radio and a rifle went flying, but there was no body in the mini-avalanche which bounced down the cliff in response to the blasts.

"They killed the captain! They killed the captain!"

Rudisill fired at the Gerin. The angle was hopelessly bad, but his bullets sparked and splattered on the rocks across the pool. The Slime ducked back beneath the surface and Heatherton, on the cliffs above it, churned the water again with a vertical burst.

Minh still had his MARS. He launched the heavy rocket into the pool while Heatherton and Moschelitz kept the Slime down with rifle fire.

Rocks and steam spewed even higher than previously, because the water level had been dropped by the first warhead. The cliff was black where water darkened the dun stone.

More steam belched from the cave. Shadowed figures moved beyond the bars. Rudisill thought he heard shouts and crying.

"They killed the captain!"

Even in an armored suit, the Gerin couldn't survive a direct MARS hit. Rudisill's left hand stung. He looked down and noticed for the first time that his left little finger was missing. The automatic laser had—

"That must've got the—" Heatherton started to say.

The Slime rose from the bubbling water of the pool and raked the cliff top again with explosive shells.

Heatherton screamed with frustration. He triggered a wild burst as he lurched back from the spray of grit and shell fragments. Rudisill fired also, nowhere near the target that ducked away anyhow, back under the water—

"I know where it's going!" Rudisill cried. "The pool connects with the cave, so the Slime gets out of the water and clear of the shockwave!"

Moschelitz fired his rifle into the pool.

There was a *thump*! as Sanger launched his MARS, the only rocket left in the commando. Its backblast slapped Rudisill like a hot, soft pillow.

The warhead detonated with a yellow glare that filled the interior of the cave. The half-open gates blew out in a tumbling arc. They splashed to the ground between Sanger and the sectioned hostage who'd tried to escape him.

The pool burped a gout of steam. No question now about it and the cave connecting. . . .

The Gerin staggered from the mouth of the cave. It was amazing that the Slime survived even wearing armor, but it'd lost its weapon in the blast.

Rudisill, Heatherton, and Moschelitz emptied their rifles into the creature. A few of the bullets spanged and ricocheted from its battlesuit, but only a few. The corpse wasn't even twitching by the time Sanger snatched up his rifle again and reloaded.

Sanger fired off his whole magazine anyway.

The silence that followed was broken only by the ringing in Rudisill's ears.

Rudisill stood up, loading a fresh magazine by reflex. The spotting table was still attached to his helmet. He jerked the leads out, careless of whether he damaged them. He walked over to Sanger and Lermontov, a few steps and a lifetime away.

Nothing moved within the cave except whorls of smoke.

Sanger cradled the captain's head in his lap. Lermontov's helmet had fallen off. His pale blue eyes were open and sightless.

Rudisill knelt and put his arm around the shoulders of the living trooper.

"The bastards," Sanger whispered. He was weeping. "The bastards. I swear I'll kill 'em all!"

Rudisill figured he meant the Slime, but when he looked toward the smoldering cave he wasn't sure.

Rudisill wasn't sure that he *cared* which Sanger meant, either.

FIREFIGHT

"Christ," Ginelli said, staring at the dusty wilderness, "if this is a sample, the next move'll be to Hell. And a firebase there'd be cooler."

Herrold lit a cigarette and poked the pack toward his subordinate. "Have one," he suggested.

"Not unless it's grass," the heavy newbie muttered. He flapped the sleeveless flak jacket away from his flesh, feeling streaks of momentary chill as sweat started from beneath the quilted nylon. "Christ, How d'you stand it?"

Herrold, rangy and big-jointed, leaned back in the dome seat and cocked one leg over the flamethrower's muzzle. Ginelli envied the track commander's build every time he looked at the taller man. His own basic training only four months before had been a ghastly round of extra physical training to sweat off pounds of his mother's pasta.

"Better get used to it," Herrold warned lazily. "This zippo always winds up at the back of the column, so we always wait to set up in the new laagers. Think about them—pretend you're a tree."

Ginelli followed his TC's finger toward the eight giant trees in the stone enclosure. It didn't help. Their tops reached a hundred feet into the air above the desolate plain, standing aloof from the activity that raised a pall of dust beside them. The shadows pooling beneath could not cool Ginelli as he squatted sun-dazzled on the deck of the flame track.

At least Colonel Boyle was just as hot where he stood directing placements from the sandbagged deck of his vehicle. Hieu stood beside him as usual. You could always recognize the interpreter at a distance because of the tiger fatigues he wore, darkly streaked with black and green. Below the two, radiomen were stringing the last of the tarpaulin passageways that joined the three command vehicles into a Tactical Operations Center. Now you could move between the blacked-out tracks in the dark; but the cool of the night seemed far away.

On the roof, Boyle pointed and said something to Hieu. The dark-skinned interpreter's nod was emphatic; the colonel spoke into his neck-slung microphone and the two vehicles ahead of the flame track grunted into motion. Herrold straightened suddenly as his radio helmet burped at him. "Seven-zero, roger," he replied.

"We movin'?" Ginelli asked, leaning closer to the TC to hear him better. Herrold flipped the switch by his left ear forward to intercom and said, "OK, Murray, they want us on the west side against that stone wall. There'll be a ground guide, so take it easy."

Murray edged the zippo forward, driving it clockwise around the circuit other tracks had clawed in the barren earth. Except for the grove within the roomy laterite enclosure, there was nothing growing closer than the rubber plantation whose rigid files marched green and silver a mile to the east. Low dikes, mostly fallen into the crumbling soil, ordered the wasteland.

Dust plumed in the far distance as a motorbike pulled out of the rubber and turned toward the firebase. Coke girls already, Ginelli thought. Even in this desert.

Whatever the region's problem was it couldn't have been with the soil itself; not if trees like the monsters behind the low wall could grow in it. Every one of the eight the massive stonework girdled was forty feet around at the base. The wrinkled bole of the central titan could have been half that again.

The zippo halted while a bridge tank roared, churning the yielding dirt as it maneuvered its frontal slope up to the coarse laterite. The ground guide, a bare-chested tanker with a beaded sweat band, dropped his arms to signal the bridge to shut down, then motioned the flame track in beside the greater bulk. Murray cut his engine and hoisted himself out of the driver's hatch.

Common sense and the colonel's orders required that everyone on a track be wearing helmet and flak jacket. Men like Murray, however, who extended their tours to four years, tended to ignore death and their officers when comfort was at stake. The driver was naked to the waist; bleached golden hairs stood out wire-like against his deep tan. "Dig out some beers, turtle," he said to Ginelli with easy arrogance. "We got time to down 'em before they start puttin' a detail together." Road dust had coated the stocky, powerful driver down to the throat, the height he projected from his hatch with the seat raised and the cover swivelled back. Years of Vietnamese sunlight had washed all color from his once-blue eyes.

An ACAV pulled up to the flame track's right, its TC nonchalant in his cupola behind the cal fifty. To Ginelli's amazement, the motorbike he had seen leaving the rubber plantation was the next vehicle in line. It was a tiny green Sachs rather than one of the omnipresent Honda 50s, and its driver was Caucasian. Murray grinned and jumped to his feet. "Crozier! Jacques!" he shouted delightedly. "What the hell are you doin' here?"

The white-shirted civilian turned his bike neatly and tucked it in on the shady side of the zippo. If any of the brass had noticed him, they made no sign. Dismounted, Crozier tilted his face up and swept his baseball cap away from a head of thinning hair. "Yes, I thought I might find you, Joe," he said. His English was slightly burred. "But anyway, I would have come just to talk again to Whites. It is grand to see you."

Herrold unlashed the shelter tarp from the load and let it thump over the side. "Let's get some shade up," he ordered.

"Jack was running a plantation for Michelin up north when we were in the A-Shau Valley," Murray explained. "He's a good dude. But why you down here, man?"

"Oh, well," the Frenchman said with a deprecating shrug. "Your defoliation, you know? A few months after your squadron pulls out, the planes come over. Poof! Plantation Seven is dead and I must be transferred. They grow peanuts there now."

Herrold laughed. "That's the nice thing about a job in this country," he said. "Always somethin' new tomorrow."

"Yeah, not so many VC here as up there," Murray agreed.

Crozier grimaced. "The VC I am able to live with. Like them? No. But I understand them, understand their, their aims. But these people around here, these Mengs—they will not work, they will not talk, only glare at you and plant enough rice for themselves. Michelin must bring in Viets to work the rubber, and even those, they do not stay because they do not like Mengs so near."

"But they're all Vietnamese, aren't they?" Ginelli asked in puzzlement. "I mean, what else could they be?"

The Frenchman chuckled, hooking his thumbs in his trouser tops. "They live in Viet Nam so they are Vietnamese, no? But you Americans have your Indians. Here are the Montagnards—we call them; the Mountaineers, you know? But the Vietnamese name for them means 'the dirty animals.' Not the same folk, no no. They were here long before the Viets came down from the North. And the Meng who live here and a few other places, they are not the same either; not as the Viets or even the Montagnards. And maybe they are older yet, so they say."

The group waited a moment in silence. Herrold opened the Mermite can that served as a cooler and began handing out beer. "Got a church key?" he asked no one in particular. Murray, the only man on the track with a knife, drew his huge Bowie and chopped ragged triangles in the tops. Tepid beer gurgled as the four men drank. Ginelli set his can down.

"Umm," he said to his TC, "how about the co-ax?"

Herrold sighed. "Yeah, we don't want the sonafabitch to jam." Joints popped as he stood and stretched his long frame.

Crozier gulped the swig of beer still in his mouth. "Indeed not," he agreed. "Not here, especially. The area has a very bad reputation."

"That a fact?" Herrold asked in mild surprise. "At the troop meetin' last night the ole man said around here it'd be pretty quiet. Not much activity on the intelligence maps."

"Activity?" the Frenchman repeated with raised eyebrows. "Who can say? The VC come through the laborers' hootches now and again, not so much here as near A-Shau, that is true. But when I first was transferred here three years ago, there were five, maybe six hundred in the village—the Mengs, you know, not the plantation lines."

"That little place back where we left the hardball?" Ginelli wondered aloud. "Jeez, there's not a dozen hootches there."

"Quite so," Crozier agreed with a grave nod of his head. "Because a battalion of Communists surrounded it one night and killed every Meng they found. Maybe twenty survived."

"Christ," Ginelli breathed in horror, but Herrold's greater experience caused his eyes to narrow in curiosity. "Why the hell?" the tall track commander asked. "I mean, I know they've got hit squads out to gun down village cops and headmen and all. But why the whole place? Were they that strong for the government?"

"The government?" the civilian echoed; he laughed. "They spat at the District Governor when he came through. But a week before the Communists came, there was firing near this very place. Communist, there is no doubt. I saw the tracers myself and they were green.

"The rest—and this is rumor only, what my foremen told me at the time before they stopped talking about it—a company, thirty men, were ambushed. Wiped out, every one of them and mutilated, ah . . . badly. How they decided that the Mengs were responsible, I do not know; but that could have been the reason they wiped out the village later."

"Umm," Herrold grunted. He crumpled his beer can and looked for a litter barrel. "Lemme get on the horn and we'll see just how the co-ax is screwing up." The can clattered into the barrel as the TC swung up on the back deck of the zippo again. The others could hear his voice as he spoke into the microphone, "Battle five-six, track seven-zero. Request clearance to test fire our Mike seven-four."

An unintelligible crackle replied from the headset a moment later. "No sir," Herrold denied, "not if we want it working tonight." He nodded at the answer. "Roger, roger." He waved. "OK," he said to his crew as he set down the radio helmet, "let's see what it's doin'."

Ginelli climbed up beside Herrold, slithering his pudgy body over the edge of the track with difficulty. Murray continued to lounge against the side of the track. "Hell," he said, "I never much liked guns anyway; you guys do your thing." Crozier stood beside his friend, interested but holding back a little from the delicacy of an uninvited guest. The machine gun had once been co-axial to the flamethrower. Now it was on a swivel welded to the top of the TC's dome. Herrold rotated it, aiming at the huge tree in the center of the grove. A ten-foot scar streaked the light trunk vertically to the ground, so he set the buckhorn sight just above it. Other troopers, warned by radio what to expect, were watching curiously.

The gun stuttered off a short burst and jammed. Empty brass tinkled off the right side of the track. Herrold swore and clicked open the receiver cover. His screwdriver pried at the stuck case until it sprang free. Slamming the cover shut, he jacked another round into the chamber.

BAM BAM BAM BAM BAM

"God *damn* it," Herrold said. "Looks like we gotta take the whole thing down."

"Or throw rocks," Ginelli suggested.

Herrold cocked a rusty eyebrow. Unlike the thick-set newbie, he had been in country long enough to have a feel for real danger. After a moment he grinned back. "Oh, we don't have to throw rocks," he said. He unslung his old submachine gun from the side of the dome. Twenty years of service had worn most of the finish off its crudely stamped metal but it still looked squat and deadly. Herrold set the wire stock to his shoulder; the burst, when he squeezed off, was ear-shattering. A line of fiercely red tracers stabbed from the muzzle and ripped an ascending curve of splintered wood up the side of the center tree.

"Naw, we're OK while the ole grease gun works," Herrold said. He laughed. "But," he added, "We better tear down the co-ax anyhow."

"Perhaps I should leave now," Crozier suggested. "It grows late and I must return to my duties."

"Hell," Murray protested, "stick around for chow at least. Your dinks'll do without babysittin' for that long."

The Frenchman pursed his lips. "He'll have to clear with the colonel," Herrold warned.

"No sweat," the driver insisted. "We'll snow him about all the local intelligence Jacques can give us. Come on, man; we'll brace him now." Crozier followed in Murray's forceful wake, an apprehensive frown still on his face.

"Say, where'd you get these?" Ginelli inquired, picking up a fat, red-nosed cartridge like those Herrold had just thumbed into his grease gun.

"The tracers?" the TC replied absently. "Oh, I found a case back in Di-An. Pretty at night and what the hell, they hit just as hard. But let's get crackin' on the co-ax."

Ginelli jumped to the ground. Herrold handed him a footlocker to serve as a table—the back deck of the zippo was too cluttered to strip the gun there—and the co-ax itself. In a few minutes they had reduced the weapon to components and begun cleaning them.

A shadow eased across the footlocker. Ginelli looked up, still holding the receiver he was brushing with a solvent-laden toothbrush. The interpreter, Hieu, had walked over from the TOC and was facing the grove. He seemed oblivious to the troopers beside him.

"Hey Hieu," the TC called. "Why the hell'd the colonel stick us here, d'ya know? We get in a firefight and these damn trees'll hide a division a VC."

Hieu looked around slowly. His features had neither the fragility of the pure Vietnamese nor the moonlike fullness of those with Chinese blood. He was a blocky face, set as ever in hard lines, mahogany in color. Hieu stepped up to the wall before answering, letting his hands run over the rough stone like two dried oak leaves.

"No time to make berm," he said at last, pointing to the bellowing Caterpillar climbing out of a trench near the TOC. The D-7A was digging in sleeping trailers for the brass rather than starting to throw up an earthen wall around the perimeter. "The wall here makes us need ti-ti berm, I show colonel."

Herrold nodded. The stone enclosure was square, about a hundred yards to a side. Though only four feet high, the ancient wall was nearly as thick and would stop anything short of an eight inch shell. But even with the work the wall would save the engineers on the west side, those trees sure played hell with the zones of fire. Seven of them looked to Herrold to be Phillipine mahoganies; God knew what the monster in the middle was; a banyan, maybe, from the creviced trunk, but the bark didn't look like the banyans he'd seen before.

"Never saw trees that big before," the TC said aloud.

Hieu looked at him again, this time with a hint of expression on his face. "Yes," he stated. "Ti-ti left when French come, now only one." His fingers toyed with the faded duck of the ammo pouch clipped to his belt. Both soldiers thought the dark man was through speaking, but Hieu's tongue flicked between his thin lips again and he continued, "Maybe three, maybe two years only, there was other. Now only this." The interpreter's voice became a hiss. "But beaucoup years before, everywhere was tree, everywhere was Meng!"

Boots scuffled in powdery dirt; Murray and the Frenchman were coming back from the TOC. Hieu lost interest in Herrold and vaulted the laterite wall gracefully. The driver and Crozier watched him stepping purposefully toward the center of the widely spaced grove as they halted beside the others.

"But who is that?" Crozier questioned sharply.

"Uh? That's Hieu, he's our interpreter," Murray grunted in surprise. "How come?"

The Frenchman frowned ... "But he is Meng, surely? I did not know that any served in the army, even that the government tried to induct them any more."

"Hell, I always heard he was from Saigon," Herrold answered. "He'd'a said if he was from here, wouldn't he?"

"What the hell's Hieu up to, anyhow?" Ginelli asked. He pointed toward the grove where the interpreter stood, facing the scarred trunk of the central tree. He couldn't see Hieu's hands from that angle, but the interpreter twitched in ritual motion beneath the fluid stripes of his fatigues.

Nobody spoke. Ginelli set one foot on the tread and lifted himself onto the flame track. Red and yellow smoke grenades hung by their safety rings inside the dome. Still lower swung a dusty pair of binoculars. Ginelli blew on the lenses before setting the glasses to his eyes and rotating the separate focus knobs. Hieu had knelt on the ground, but the trooper still could not tell what he was doing. Something else caught his eye.

"God damn," the plump newbie blurted. He leaned

over the side of the track and thrust the glasses toward Herrold, busy putting the machine gun back together. "Hey Red, take a look at the tree trunk."

Murray, Crozier, and Ginelli himself waited expectantly while the TC refocused the binoculars. Magnified, the tree increased geometrically in hideousness. Its bark was pinkish and paper thin, smoother than that of a birch over most of the bole's surface. The gouged, wrinkled appearance of the trunk was due to the underlying wood, not any irregularity in the bark that covered it.

The tall catface in front of Hieu was the trunk's only true blemish. Where the tear had puckered together in a creased, blackened seam, ragged edges of bark fluttered in the breeze. The flaps were an unhealthy color, like skin peeling away from a bad burn. Hieu's squat body hid only a third of the scar; the upper portion towered gloomily above him.

"Well, it's not much to look at," Herrold said at last. "What's the deal?"

"Where's the bullet holes?" Ginelli demanded in triumph. "You put twenty, thirty shots in it, right? Where'd they go to?"

"Son of a bitch," the TC agreed, taking another look. The co-ax should have left a tight pattern of shattered wood above the ancient scar. Except for some brownish dimples in the bark, the tree was unmarked.

"I saw splinters fly," Murray remarked.

"Goddam wood must'a swelled right over'em," Herrold suggested. "That's where I hit, all right."

"That is a very strange tree," Crozier said, speaking for the first time since his return. "There was another like it near Plantation Seven. It had almond trees around it too, though there was no wall. They call them god trees—the Viets do. The Mengs have their own word, but I do not know its meaning."

A Chinook swept over the firebase from the south, momentarily stifling conversation with the syncopated whopping of its twin rotors. It hovered just beyond the perimeter, then slowly settled in a circular dust cloud while its turbines whined enormously. Men ran to unload it.

"Chow pretty quick," Murray commented. It was nearing four o'clock. Ginelli looked away from the bird. "Don't seem right," he said. The other men looked blank. He tried to explain, "I mean, the Shithook there, jet engines and all, and that tree there being so old."

The driver snorted. "Hell, that's not old. Now back in California where they make those things"—his broad thumb indicated the banana-shaped helicopter—"they got redwoods that're really old. You don't think anything funny about that, do you?"

Ginelli gestured helplessly with his hands. Surprisingly it was Crozier, half-seated on the laterite wall, who came to his aid. "What makes you think this god tree is less old than a redwood, Joe?" he asked mildly.

Murray blinked. "Hell, redwoods're the oldest things there are. Alive, I mean."

The Frenchman laughed and repeated his deprecating shrug. "But trees are my business, you know? Now there is a pine tree in Arizona older than your California sequoias; but nobody knew it for a long time because there are not many of them and . . . nobody noticed. And here is a tree, an old one—but who knows? Maybe there are only two in the whole world left—and the other one, the one in the north, that perhaps is dead with my plantation."

"You never counted the rings or anything?" Herrold asked curiously. He had locked the barrel into the co-ax while the others were talking.

"No . . . ," Crozier admitted. His tongue touched his lips as he glanced up at the god tree, wondering how much he should say. "No," he repeated, "but I only saw the tree once while I was at Plantation Seven. It stood in the jungle, more than a mile from the rubber, and the laborers did not care that anyone should go near it. There were Mengs there, too, I was told; but only a few and they hid in the woods. Bad blood between them and my laborers, no doubt."

"Well, hell, Jacques," Murray prompted. "When *did* you see it?" Crozier still hesitated. Suddenly realizing what the problem might be, the driver said, "Hell, don't worry about *our* stomachs, fer god's sake. Unless you're squeamish, turtle?" Ginelli blushed and shook his head. Laughing, Murray went on, "Anyhow, you grow up pretty quick after you get in the field—those that live to. Tell the story, Jacques."

Crozier sighed. The glade behind him was empty. Hieu had disappeared somewhere without being noticed. "Well," he began, "it has no importance, I am sure—all this happened a hundred miles away, as you know. But. . . .

"It was not long after Michelin sent me to Indochina, in 1953 that would be. I was told of the god tree as soon as I arrived at Plantation Seven, but that was all. One of my foremen had warned me not to wander that way and I assumed, because of the Viet Minh.

"Near midnight—this was before Dien Bien Phu, you will remember—there was heavy firing not far from the plantation. I called the district garrison since for a marvel the radio was working. But of course, no one came until it was light."

Herrold and Murray nodded together in agreement. Charging into a night ambush was no way to help your buddies, not in this country. Crozier cleared his throat and went on, "It was two companies of colonial paras that came, and the colonel from the fort himself. Nothing would help but that I should guide them to where the shooting had been. A platoon had set up an ambush, so they said, but it did not call in—even for fire support. When I radioed they assumed. . . ." He shrugged expressively.

"And that is what we found. All the men, all of them dead—unforgettably. They were in the grove of that god tree, on both sides of the trail to it. Perhaps the lieutenant had thought the Viets were rallying there. The paras were well armed and did much shooting from the shells we found. But of enemies, there was no sign; and the paras had not been shot. They were torn, you know? Mutilated beyond what I could believe. But none had been shot, and their weapons lay with the bodies."

"That's crazy," Ginelli said, voicing everyone's thought. "Dinks would'a taken the guns."

Crozier shrugged. "The colonel said at last his men had been killed by some wild tribe, so savage they did not understand guns or would not use them. The Mengs, he meant. They were . . . wilder, perhaps, than the ones here but still. . . . I would not have thought there were enough of them to wipe out the platoon, waiting as it must have been."

"How *were* the men killed?" Herrold asked at last.

"Knives I think," the Frenchman replied, "short ones. Teeth I might have said; but there were really no signs that anything had fed on the bodies. Not the killers, that is. One man—"

He paused to swallow, continued. "One man I thought wore a long shirt of black. When I came closer, the flies left him. The skin was gone from his arms and chest. God alone knows what had killed him; but his face was the worst to see, and that was unmarked."

No one spoke for some time after that. Finally Murray said, "They oughta have chow on. Coming?"

Crozier spread his hands. "You are sure it is all right? I have no utensils."

"No sweat, there's paper plates. Rest'a you guys?"

"I'll be along," Herrold said. "Lemme remount the co-ax first."

"I'll do that," Ginelli offered. His face was saffron, bloodless beneath his tan. "Don't feel hungry tonight anyhow."

The track commander smiled. "You can give me a hand."

When the gun was bolted solidly back on its mount, Herrold laid a belt of ammunition on the loading tray and clicked the cover shut on it. "Ah," Ginelli mumbled, "ah, Red, don't you think it'd be a good idea to keep pressure up in the napalm tanks? I mean, there's a lotta Mengs around here and what Murray's buddy says. . . ."

"We'll make do with the co-ax," the TC replied, grinning. "You know how the couplings leak napalm with the pumps on."

"But if there's an attack?" Ginelli pleaded.

"Look, turtle," Herrold explained more sharply than before, "we're sitting on two hundred gallons 'a napalm. One spark in this track with the pressure up and we won't need no attack. OK?" Ginelli shrugged. "Well, come on to chow then," the TC suggested.

"Guess I'll stay."

"S'OK." Herrold slipped off the track and began walking toward the mess tent. He was singing softly, "We gotta get outta this place. . . ."

Crozier left just before the storm broke. The rain that had held off most of the day sheeted down at dusk. Lightning when it flared jumped from cloud-top to invisible cloud top. It back-lighted the sky.

The crewmen huddled under the inadequate tarpaulin, listening to the ragged static that was all Murray's transistor radio could pick up. Eventually he shut it off. Ginelli swore miserably. Slanting rain had started a worm of water at the head of his cot. It had finally squirmed all the way to the other end where he sat hunched against the chill wind. "Shouldn't somebody be on the track?" he asked. Regular guard shifts started at ten o'clock, but usually everybody was more or less alert until then.

"Go ahead, turtle, it's your bright idea," Murray said. Herrold frowned more seriously. "Yeah, if you're worried you might as well. . . . Look, you get up in the dome now and Murray'll trade his first shift for your second. Right?"

"Sure," the driver agreed. "Maybe this damn rain'll stop by then."

Wearing his poncho over his flak jacket, Ginelli clambered up the bow slope of the zippo. The metal sides were too slimy with rain to mount that way. Except during lightning strokes, the darkness was opaque. When it flashed, the trees stabbed into the sudden bright skies and made Ginelli think about the napalm beneath from a different aspect. Christ, those trees were the tallest things for miles, and God knew the track wasn't very far away if lightning did hit one. God, they were tall.

And they were old. Ginelli recognized the feeling he'd had ever since the flame track had nosed up to the wall to face the grove: an aura of age. The same thing he'd sensed when he was a kid and saw the Grand Canyon. There was something so old it didn't give a damn about man or anything else.

Christ! No tree was as old as that; it must be their size that made him so jumpy. Dark as it was, the dinks could be crawling closer between lightning flashes too. At least the rain was slowing down.

The hatch cover was folded back into a clamshell seat for the man on the dome. There was a fiber pillow to put over the steel, but it was soaked and Ginelli had set it on the back deck. For the first time he could remember, the thickness of his flak jacket felt good because the air was so cold. Water that slicked off the poncho or dripped from the useless flat muzzle of the flamethrower joined the drops spattering directly onto the zippo's deck. It pooled and flowed sluggishly toward the lowest point, the open driver's hatch.

The sky was starting to clear. An occasional spray fell, but the storm was over and a quarter moon shone when the broken clouds allowed it. Herrold stuck his head out from under the tarp. "How's going, man?"

Ginelli stretched some of the stiffness out of his back and began stripping off the poncho. "OK, I guess. I could use some coffee."

"Yeah. Well, hang in there till midnight and get Murray up. We're gonna rack out now."

Shadows from the treetops pooled massively about the holes. Although there was enough breeze to make the branches tremble, the trunks themselves were solid as cliffs, as solid as Time. The scar at the base of the god tree was perversely moonlit. The whole grove looked sinister in the darkness, but the scar itself was something more.

Only the half-hour routine of perimeter check kept Ginelli awake. Voices crackled around Headquarters Troop's sector until Ginelli could repeat, "Seven zero, report negative," for the last time and thankfully take off the commo helmet. His boots squelched as he dropped beside the cot where Murray snored softly, wrapped in the mottled green-brown nylon of his poncho liner. Ginelli shook him.

"Uh!" the driver grunted as he snapped awake. "Oh, right; lemme get my boots on."

One of the few clouds remaining drifted over the moon. As Murray stood upright, Ginelli thought movement flickered on the dark stone of the wall. "Hey!" the driver whispered. "What's Hieu doing out there?"

Ginelli peered into the grove without being able to see anything but the trees. "That was him goin' over the wall," Murray insisted. He held his M16 with the bolt back, ready to chamber a round if the receiver was jarred. "Look, I'm gonna check where he's going."

"Jeez, somebody'll see you and cut loose," Ginelli protested. "You can't go out there!"

Murray shook his head decisively. "Naw, it'll be OK," he said as he slipped over the wall. "Crazy," Ginelli muttered. And it suddenly struck him that a man who volunteered for three extra years of combat probably *wasn't* quite normal in the back-home sense. Licking his lips, he waited tensely in the darkness. The air had grown warmer since the rain stopped, but the plump newbie found himself shivering.

A bird fluttered among the branches of the nearest mahogany. You didn't seem to see many birds in country, not like you did back in the World. Ginelli craned his neck to get a better view, but the irregular moonlight passed only the impression of wings and drab color.

Nothing else moved within the grove. Ginelli swore miserably and shook Herrold awake. The track commander slept with his flak jacket for a pillow and, despite his attitude of nonchalance, the clumsy grease gun lay beside him on the cot. His fingers curled around its pistol grip as he awakened.

"Oh, for God's sake," he muttered when Ginelli blurted out the story. Herrold had kept his boots on, only the tops unlaced, and he quickly whipped the ties tight around his shins. "Christ, ten minutes ago?"

"Well, should I call in?" Ginelli suggested uncertainly.

"Hell," Herrold muttered, "no, I better go tell the ole man. You get back in the dome and wait for me." He hefted his submachine gun by the receiver.

Ginelli started to climb onto the track. Turning, he said, "Hey, man." Herrold paused. "Don't be too long, huh?"

"Yeah." The track commander trudged off toward the unlighted HQ tent. A bird, maybe a large bat from its erratic flight, passed over Ginelli's head at treetop level. He raised the loading cover of the co-ax to recheck the position of the linked belt of ammunition.

There was a light in the grove.

It was neither man-made nor the moon's reflection, and at first it was almost too faint to have a source at all. Ginelli gaped frozen at the huge god tree. The glow resolved into a viridescent line down the center of the scar, a strip of brightness that widened perceptably as the edges of the cicatrix drew back. The interior of the tree seemed hollow, lined with self-shining greenness to which forms clung. As Ginelli watched, a handful of the creatures lurched from the inner wall and fluttered out through the dilated scar.

Someone screamed within the laager. Ginelli whirled around. The tactical operations center was green and two-dimensional where the chill glare licked it. A man tore through the canvas passage linking the vehicles, howling and clutching at the back of his neck until he fell. A dark shape flapped away from him. The remaining blotches clinging to the green of the tree flickered outward and the scar began to close.

The cal fifty in the assault vehicle to the right suddenly began blasting tracers point blank into the shrinking green blaze. Heavy bullets that could smash through half an inch of steel ripped across the tree. It was like stabbing a sponge with ice picks. Something dropped into the ACAV's cupola from above. The shots stopped and the gunner began to bellow hoarsely.

Ginelli swivelled his co-ax onto the tree and clamped down on its underslung trigger. Nothing happened; in his panic he had forgotten to charge the gun. Sparkling muzzle flashes were erupting all across the laager. Near the TOC a man fired his M16 at a crazy angle, trying to drop one of the flying shapes. Another spiraled down behind him of its own deadly accord. His rifle continued to fire as he collapsed on top of it. It sent a last random bullet to spall a flake of aluminum from the flame track's side, a foot beneath Ginelli's exposed head.

A soldier in silhouette against the green light lunged toward the god tree's slitted portal and emptied his rifle point blank. The knife in his hand glowed green as he chopped it up and down into the edge of the scar, trying to widen the gap. "Murray!" Ginelli called. He jerked back his machine gun's operating rod but did not shoot. He could hear Murray screaming obscenities made stacatto by choppy bursts of automatic fire from behind him.

Ginelli turned his head without conscious warning. He had only enough time to drop down into the compartment as the thing swooped. Its vans, stretched batlike between arm and leg, had already slammed it upright in braking for the kill. The green glare threw its features in perfect relief against the chaos of the firebase: a body twenty inches long, deep-torsoed like a mummified pigmy; weasel teeth; slender cones perfectly formed for slaughter; a face that could have been human save for its size and the streaks of black blood that disfigured it. Tree light flashed a shadow across the hatch as the chittering creature flapped toward other prey for the moment.

Ginelli straightened slowly, peered out of the dome. There was a coldness in his spine; his whole lower body felt as though it belonged to someone else. He knew it wasn't any use, even for himself, to slam the dome hatch over his head and hope to wait the nightmare out. The driver's compartment was open; there was plenty of room between the seat and the engine firewall beside it for the killers to crawl through.

Taking a deep breath, Ginelli leaped out of the hatch. He ignored the co-ax. A shuffling step forward in a low crouch and he slid feet first through the driver's hatch. Throttle forward, both clutch levers at neutral. The starter motor whined for an instant; then the six-cylinder diesel caught, staggered, and boomed into life. An imbalance somewhere in the engine made the whole vehicle tremble.

Murray was still gouging at the base of the scar, face twisted in maniacal savagery. Chips flew every time the blade struck, letting more of the interior glare spill out. Ginelli throttled back, nerving himself to move. "Murray!" he shouted again over the lessened throb of the diesel. "Get away—dammit, get away!"

A figure oozed out of the shadows and gripped Murray by the shoulder. Perhaps the driver screamed before he recognized Hieu; if so, Ginelli's own cry masked the sound. The Meng spoke, his face distorted with triumph. As the incredulous driver stared, Hieu shouted a few syllables at the god tree in a throaty language far different from the nasal trills of Vietnamese.

The tree opened again. The edges of the scar crumpled sideways, exposing fully the green-lit interior and what stood in it now. Murray whipped around, his blade raised to slash. An arm gripped his, held the knife motionless. The thing was as tall as the opening it stood in, bipedal but utterly inhuman.

Its face was a mirror image of Hieu's own.

Murray flung himself back, but another pallid,

boneless arm encircled him and drew him into the tree. His scream was momentary, cut off when the green opening squeezed almost shut behind him and what Hieu had summoned.

The hooked moon was out again. Hieu turned and began striding toward the shattered laager. His single ammo pouch flopped open; the crude necklace around his neck was of human fingertips, dried and strung on a twist of cambium. Behind him a score of other human-appearing figures slunk out of the grove, every face identical.

Ginelli gathered his feet under him on the seat, then sprang back on top of the track. One of the winged shapes had been waiting for him, called by the mutter of the engine. It darted in from the front, banking easily around Ginelli's out-thrust arm. Ginelli tripped on the flamethrower's broad tube, fell forward bruisingly. Clawed fingers drew four bloody tracks across his forehead as the flyer missed its aim. It swept back purposefully.

Ginelli jumped into the dome hatch and snatched at the clamshell cover to close it. As the steel lid swung to, the winged man's full weight bounced it back on its hinges ringingly. Jagged teeth raked the soldier's bare right arm, making him scream in frenzy. He yanked at the hatch cover with mad strength. There was no clang as the hatch shut, but something crackled between the edges of armor plate. The brief cry of agony was higher pitched than a man's. Outside, the scar began to dilate again.

Ginelli gripped the valve and hissed with pain. Shock had numbed his right arm only momentarily. Left-handed he opened the feeds. His fingers found a switch, flicked it up, and the pump began throbbing behind him. His whole body shuddered as he swung the dome through a short arc so that the tree's blazing scar was centered in the periscope. The universal joint of the fat napalm hose creaked in protest at being moved and a drop of thickened gasoline spattered stickily on Ginelli's flak jacket.

With a cry of horrified understanding, Hieu leaped onto the stone wall between Ginelli and the tree. "You must—" was all the Meng could say before the jet of napalm caught him squarely in the chest and flung him back into the enclosure. There was no flame. The igniter had not fired.

Mumbling half-remembered fragments of a Latin prayer, Ginelli triggered the weapon again. Napalm spurted against the tree in an unobstructed black arch. The igniter banged in mid shot and the darkness boomed into a hellish red glare. The tree keened as the flame rod's giant fist smashed against it. Its outer bark shriveled and the deep, bloody surge of napalm smothered every other color. Ginelli's fiery scythe roared as he slashed it up and down the trunk. Wood began to crackle like gunfire, exploding and hurling back geysers of sparks. A puff of dry heat roiled toward the laager in the turbulent air. It was heavy with the stench of burning flesh.

A series of swift thuds warned Ginelli of flyers landing on the zippo's deck; teeth clicked on armor. Something rustled from the driver's compartment. The trooper used his stiffening right hand to switch on the interior lights. The yellow bulbs glinted from close-set eyes peering over the driver's seat. Ginelli kicked. Instead of crunching under his boot, the face gave with a terrible resiliency and the winged man continued to squirm into the TC's compartment. A sparkling chain of eyes flashed behind the first pair. The whole swarm of killers was crowding into the track.

Ginelli's only weapon was the flame itself. Instinctively he swung the nozzle to the left and depressed it, trying to hose fire into the forward hatch of his own vehicle. Instead, the frozen coupling parted. Napalm gouted from the line. The flame died with a serpentine lurch, leaving the god tree alone as a lance of fire. The track was flooding with the gummy fluid; it clung to Ginelli's chest and flak jacket before rolling off in sluggish gobbets.

Bloody faces washed black with smears of napalm, the winged men struggled toward Ginelli implacably. His mind barely functional, the soldier threw open the hatch and staggered onto the zippo's deck. Unseen, one flyer still hung in the air. It struck him in the middle of the back and catapulted him off the vehicle. Ginelli somersaulted across the dusty, flame-lit cauldron. The napalm's gluey tenacity fixed the creature firmly against Ginelli's flak jacket; its hooked claws locked into the fabric while its teeth tore his scalp.

The huge torch of the god tree crashed inward toward the laager. A flaming branch snapped with the impact and bounded high in the air before plunging down on the napalm-filled flame track. Ginelli staggered to his feet, tried to run. The zippo exploded with a hollow boom and a mushroom of flame, knocking him down again without dislodging the vengeful horror on his back.

With the last of his strength, Ginelli ripped off the unfastened flak jacket and hurled it into the air. For one glistening instant he thought the napalm-soaked nylon would land short of the pool of fire surrounding the flame track. His uncoordinated throw was high and the winged killer had time to pull one van loose as it pinwheeled. It struck the ground that way, mired by the incendiary that bloomed to consume it.

Ginelli lay on his back, no longer able to move. A shadow humped over the top of the wall: Hieu, moving very stiffly. His right hand held a cane spear. The Meng was withered like a violet whose roots had been chopped away, but he was not dead.

"You kill all, you . . . animals," he said. His voice was thick and half-choked by the napalm that had hosed him. He balanced on the wall, black against the burning wreckage of the god tree. "All . . .," he repeated, raising the spear. "Cut . . . poison . . . burn. But you—"

Herrold's grease gun slammed beside Ginelli, its muzzle blast deafening even against the background roar of the flames. A solid bar of tracers stitched redly across the Meng's chest and slapped him off the wall as a screaming ball of fire.

It was still four hours to dawn, Ginelli thought as he drifted into unconsciousness; but until then the flames would give enough light.

CONTACT!

Something shrieked over the firebase without dipping below the gray clouds. It was low and fast and sounded so much like an incoming rocket that even the man on Golf Company's portable latrine flattened instantly. Captain Holtz had knocked over the card table when he hit the dirt. He raised his head above the wreckage in time to see a bright blue flash in the far distance. The crash that rattled the jungle moments later sent everyone scrabbling again.

"Sonic boom," Major Hegsley, the fat operations officer, pontificated as he levered himself erect.

"The hell you say," Holtz muttered, poised and listening. "Paider, Bayes," he grunted at the two platoon leaders starting to pick up their bridge hands, "get to your tracks."

Then the Klaxon on the tactical operations center blatted and everyone knew Holtz had been right again. The captain kicked aside a lawn chair blocking his way to his command vehicle. The radioman scuttled forward to give his powerful commander room in front of the bank of radios. "Battle six, Battle four-six," the tanker snapped as he keyed the microphone. "Shoot." Thirty seconds of concentrated information spat out of the speaker while Holtz crayoned grid coordinates in on an acetate-covered map. "Roger, we'll get 'em." Turning to the radioman he ordered, "Second platoon stays for security here—get first and third lined up at the gate and tell Speed I'll be with him on five-two." While the enlisted man relayed the orders on the company frequency, Holtz scooped up a holstered .45 and his chicken vest and ran for his tank.

Golf Company was already moving. Most of the drivers had cranked up as soon as they heard the explosion. Within thirty seconds of the Klaxon, the diesels of all nine operable tracks were turning over while the air still slapped with closing breechblocks. Tank 52 jingled as Hauley, its driver, braked the right tread and threw the left in reverse to swing the heavy war machine out of its ready position. Holtz ran up to the left side, snapping his vest closed at the shoulder. He was one of the few men in the squadron who wore a porcelain-armored chicken vest without discomfort, despite its considerably greater weight than the usual nylon flak jacket. In fact, Holtz was built much like one of his tanks. Though he was taller than average, his breadth made him look stocky at a distance and simply gigantic close up. He wore his black hair cropped short, but a thick growth curled down his forearms and up the backs of his hands.

Speed, a weedy, freckled staff sergeant with three years' combat behind him, grasped his captain by the wrist and helped him swing up on five-two's battered fender. As frail as he looked, Speed was probably the best track commander in the company. He was due to rotate home for discharge in three days and would normally have been sent to the rear for stand-down a week before. Holtz liked working with an experienced man and had kept him in the field an extra week, but this was Speed's last day. "You wanna load today, Captain?" he asked with an easy smile. He rocked unconcernedly as Hauley put the tank in gear and sent it into line with a jerk.

Holtz smiled back but shook his head. He always rode in the track commander's position, although in a contact he could depend on Speed to fight five-two from the loader's hatch while he directed the company as a whole. Still smiling, the big officer settled heavily onto the hatch cover behind the low-mounted, fifty-caliber machine gun and slipped on his radio helmet.

"OK, listen up," he said on the company frequency, ignoring commo security as he always did when talking to his unit. He had a serene assurance that his gravelly voice was adequate identification—and that his tanks were a certain answer to any dinks who tried to stop him. His boys were as good and as deadly as any outfit in 'Nam. "Air Force claims they zapped a bird at high altitude and it wasn't one of theirs. We're going to see whose it was and keep Charlie away till C-MEC gets a team out here. Four-four leads, west on the hardball to a trail at Yankee Tango five-seven-two, three-seven-nine; flyboys think the bird went down around seventy-forty, but keep your eyes open all the way—Charlie's going to be looking too."

Holtz's track was second in line with the remaining five tanks of the first and third platoons following in single file. As each one nosed out of the firebase its TC flipped a switch. Electric motors whined to rotate the turrets 30 degrees to one side or the other and lower the muzzles of the 90mm main guns. The big cannons were always loaded, but for safety's sake they were pointed up in the air except when the tanks prowled empty countryside. Otherwise, at a twitch of the red handle beside each track commander a wall or a crowd of people would dissolve in shattered ruin.

"Well, you think we're at war with China now?" Holtz shouted to Speed over the high jangle of the treads. "Hell, I told you you didn't want to go home— what do you bet they nuked Oakland five minutes ago?" Both men laughed.

The path from the firebase to the highway was finely divided muck after three days of use. The tanks, each of them burdened with fifty tons of armor and weaponry, wallowed through it. There was nothing laughable in their awkwardness. Rather, they looked as implacably deadly as tyrannosaurs hunting in a pack. On the asphalt hardball, the seven vehicles accelerated to thirty-five miles an hour, stringing out a little. Four-four had all its left-side torsion bars broken and would not steer a straight line. The tank staggered back and forth across the narrow highway in a series of short zigzags. From the engine gratings on its back deck, a boy with a grenade launcher stared miserably back at the CO's track while the rough ride pounded his guts to jelly.

Holtz ignored him, letting his eyes flick through the vegetation to both sides of the roadway. Here along the hardball the land was in rubber, but according to the map they would have to approach the downed aircraft through broken jungle. Not the best terrain for armor, but they'd make do. Normally the tanks would have backed up an air search, but low clouds had washed the sky gray. Occasionally Holtz could hear a chopper thrumming somewhere, above him but always invisible. No air support in a contact, that was what it meant. Maybe no medevac either.

Ahead, four-four slowed. The rest of the column ground to a chattering halt behind it. Unintelligible noises hissed through Holtz's earphones. He cursed and reached down inside the turret to bring his volume up. Noise crackled louder but all sense was smothered out of it by the increased roar of static.

Four-four's TC, Greiler, spoke into the ear of his grenadier. The boy nodded and jumped off the tank, running back to five-two. He was a newbie, only a week or two in the field, and young besides. He clambered up the bow slope of the tank and nervously blurted, "Sir, Chick says he thinks this is the turn-off but he isn't sure."

As far as Holtz could tell from the map, the narrow trail beside four-four should be the one they wanted. It led south, at any rate. Hell, if the MiG was what had gone howling over the firebase earlier the flyboys were just guessing for location anyway. The overcast had already been solid and the bird could have fallen anywhere in III Corps for all anybody knew.

"Yeah, we'll try it," Holtz said into his helmet mike. No reaction from four-four. "God damn it!" the captain roared, stabbing his left arm out imperiously. Four-four obediently did a neutral steer on the hardball, rotating 90 degrees to the left as the treads spun in opposite directions. Clods of asphalt boiled up as the road's surface dissolved under incalculable stresses. "Get on the back, son." Holtz growled at the uncertain newbie. "You're our crew for now. Speed!" he demanded, "What's wrong with our goddam radio? It worked OK at the firebase."

"Isn't the radio," Speed reported immediately, speaking into his own helmet microphone. "See, the intercom works, it's something screwing up off the broadcast freeks. Suppose the dinks are jamming?"

"Crap," Holtz said.

The trail was a half-abandoned jeep route, never intended for anything the width of a tank. They could shred their way through saplings and the creepers that had slunk across the trail, of course, and their massive rubber track blocks spewed a salad of torn greenery over their fenders. But full-sized trees with trunks a foot or more thick made even the tanks turn: grunting, clattering; engines slowing, then roaring loudly for torque to slue the heavy vehicles. Holtz glanced back at the newbie to see that he was all right. The boy's steel pot was too large for him. It had tilted forward over his eyebrows, exposing a fuzz of tiny blond hairs on his neck. The kid had to be eighteen or they wouldn't have let him in the country, Holtz thought, but you sure couldn't tell it by looking at him.

A branch whanged against Holtz's own helmet and he turned around. The vegetation itself was a danger as well as a hiding place for unknown numbers of the enemy. More than one tanker had been dusted off with a twig through his eye. There were a lot of nasty surprises for a man rolling through jungle twelve feet in the air. But if you spent all your time watching for branches, you missed the dink crouched in the undergrowth with a rocket launcher—and he'd kill the hell out of you.

Sudden color in the sky ahead. Speed slapped Holtz on the left shoulder, pointing, but the CO had already seen it. The clouds covered the sky in a dismal ceiling no higher than that of a large auditorium. While both men stared, another flash stained the gray momentarily azure. There was no thunder. Too brightly colored for lightning anyway, Holtz thought. The flashes were really blue, not just white reflected from dark clouds.

"That can't be a klick from here, Chief," Speed's voice rattled. Holtz glanced at him. The sergeant's jungle boots rested on the forward rim of his hatch so that his bony knees poked high in the air. Some people let their feet dangle inside the turret, but Speed had been around too long for that. Armor was great so long as nothing penetrated it. When something did—most often a stream of molten metal blasted by the shaped explosive of a B-41 rocket—it splashed around the inner surface of what had been protection. God help the man inside then. 'Nam offered enough ways to die without looking for easy ones.

The officer squinted forward, trying to get a better idea of the brief light's location. Foliage broke the concave mirror of the clouds into a thousand swiftly dancing segments. Five-two was jouncing badly over potholes and major roots that protruded from the coarse, red soil as well.

"Hey," Speed muttered at a sudden thought. Holtz saw him drop down inside the tank. The earphones crackled as the sergeant switched on the main radio he had disconnected when background noise smothered communications. As he did so, another of the blue flashes lit up the sky. Static smashed through Holtz's phones like the main gun going off beside his head.

"Jesus Christ!" the big officer roared into the intercom. "You shorted the goddamn thing!"

White noise disappeared as Speed shut off the set again. "No, man," he protested as he popped his frame, lanky but bulbous in its nylon padding, back through the oval hatch. "That's not me—it's the lightning. All I did was turn the set on."

"That's not lightning," Holtz grunted. He shifted his pistol holster slightly so that the butt was handy for immediate use. "Hauley," he said over the intercom to the driver, "that light's maybe a hair south of the way we're headed. If you catch a trail heading off to the left, hold it up for a minute."

Speed scanned his side of the jungle with a practiced squint. Tendons stood out on his right hand as it gripped the hatch cover against the tank's erratic lurches. "Good thing the intercom's on wires," he remarked. "Otherwise we'd really be up a creek."

Holtz nodded.

On flat concrete, tanks could get up to forty-five

miles an hour, though the ride was spine-shattering if any of the torsion bars were broken. Off-road was another matter. This trail was as straight as what was basically a brush cut could be—did it lead to another section on the plantation that flanked the hardball?— but when it meandered around a heavy tree bole the tanks had to slow to a crawl to follow it. Black exhaust boiled out of the deflector plates serving four-four in place of muffler and tail pipe. The overgrown trail could hide a mine, either an old one long forgotten or a sudden improvisation by a tankkiller team that had heard Golf Company moving toward it. The bursts of light and static were certain to attract the attention of all the NVA in the neighborhood.

That was fine with Holtz. He twitched the double handgrips of his cal-fifty to be sure the gun would rotate smoothly. He wouldn't have been in Armor if he'd minded killing.

The flashes were still intermittent but seemed to come more frequently now: one or two a minute. Range was a matter of guesswork, but appreciably more of the sky lighted up at each pulse. They must be getting closer to the source. The trail was taking them straight to it after all. But how did a MiG make the sky light up that way?

Speed lifted his radio helmet to listen intently. "AK fire," he said. "Not far away either." Holtz scowled and raised his own helmet away from his ears. As he did so, the air shuddered with a dull boom that was not thunder. The deliberate bark of an AK-47 chopped out behind it, little muffled by the trees.

Speed slipped the cap from a flare and set it over the primed end of the foot-long tube. "We can't get the others on the horn," he explained. "They'll know what a red flare means."

"Charlie'll see it too," Holtz argued.

"Hell, whoever heard of a tank company sneaking up on anybody?"

The captain shrugged assent. As always before a contact, the sweat filming the inner surface of his chicken vest had chilled suddenly.

Speed rapped the base of the flare on the turret. The rocket streaked upward with a liquid *whoosh!* that took it above the cloud ceiling. Moments later the charge burst and a fierce red ball drifted down against the flickering background. Holtz keyed the scrambler mike, calling, "Battle six, Battle six; Battle four-six calling." He held one of the separate earphones under his radio helmet. The only response from it was a thunder of static and he shut it off again. Remembering the newbie on the back deck, he turned and shouted over the savage rumble of the engine, "Watch it, kid, we'll be in it up to our necks any time now."

In the tight undergrowth, the tracks had closed up to less than a dozen yards between bow slope and the deflector plates of the next ahead. Four-four cornered around a clump of three large trees left standing to the right of the trail. The tank's bent, rusted fender sawed into the bark of the outer tree, then tore free. Hauley swung five-two wider as he followed.

A rocket spurted from a grove of bamboo forty yards away where the trail jogged again. The fireball of the B-41 seemed to hang in the air just above the ground, but it moved fast enough that before Holtz's thumbs could close on his gun's butterfly trigger the rocket had burst on the bow slope of four-four.

A great splash of orange-red flame enveloped the front of the tank momentarily, looking as if a gasoline bomb had gone off. The flash took only a split second but the roar of the explosion echoed and re-echoed in the crash of heavy gunfire. Four-four shuddered to a halt. Holtz raked the bamboo with the cal-fifty, directing the machine gun with his left hand while his right groped for the turret control to swing the main gun. Beside him, Speed's lighter machine gun chewed up undergrowth to the left of the trail. He had no visible targets, but you almost never saw your enemy in the jungle.

The muzzle brake of the 90mm gun, already as low as it could be aimed, rotated onto the bamboo. A burst of light automatic fire glanced off five-two's turret from an unknown location. Holtz ignored it and tripped the red handle. The air split with a sharp crack and a flash of green. The first round was canister and it shotgunned a deadly cone of steel balls toward the unseen rocketeer, exploding bamboo into the air like a tangle of broom straw. Brass clanged in the turret as the cannon's breech sprang open automatically and flung out the empty case. Speed dropped through the reeking white powder smoke evacuated into the hull.

Holtz hadn't a chance to worry about the newbie behind him until he heard the kid's grenade launcher chunk hollowly. Only an instant later its shell burst on a tree limb not thirty feet from the tank. Wood disintegrated in a puff of black and red; dozens of segments of piano wire spanged off the armor, one of them ripping a line down the captain's blue jowl. "Not so goddam close!" Holtz shouted, just as a slap on his thigh told him Speed had reloaded the main gun.

The second rocket hissed from a thicket to the right of five-two, lighting up black-shrouded tree boles from the moment of ignition. Holtz glimpsed the Vietnamese huddled in the brush with the launching tube on his shoulder but there was no time to turn his machine gun before the B-41 exploded. The world shattered. Even the fifty tons of steel under Holtz's feet staggered as the shaped charge detonated against five-two's turret. A pencil stream of vaporized armor plate jetted through the tank. The baggy sateen of the officer's bloused fatigues burst into flame across his left calf where the metal touched it. Outside the tank the air rang with fragments of the rocket's case. Holtz, deafened by the blast, saw the newbie's mouth open to scream as the boy spun away from the jagged impacts sledging him. Somehow he still gripped his grenade launcher, but its fat aluminum barrel had flowered with torn metal as suddenly as red splotches had appeared on his flak jacket.

Holtz's radio helmet was gone, jerked off his head by the blast. Stupid with shock, the burly captain's eyes followed the wires leading down into the interior of the tank. Pooled on the floorplate was all that remained of Speed. The gaseous metal had struck him while his body was bent. The stream had entered above the collarbone and burned an exit hole through the seventh rib near the spine. The sergeant's torso, raised instantly to a temperature of over a thousand degrees, had exploded. Speed's head had not been touched. His face was turned upward, displaying its slight grin, although spatters of blood made him seem more freckled than usual.

The clouds were thickly alive with a shifting pattern of blue fire and the air hummed to a note unconnected to the rattle of gunfire all along the tank column. The third tank in line, four-six, edged forward, trying to pass Holtz's motionless vehicle on the left. A medic hopped off the deck of four-six and knelt beside the newbie's crumpled body, oblivious to the shots singing off nearby armor.

Hauley jumped out of the driver's hatch and climbed back to his commander. "Sir!" he said, gripping Holtz by the left arm.

Holtz shook himself alert. "Get us moving," he ordered in a thin voice he did not recognize. "Give four-six room to get by."

Hauley ducked forward to obey. Holtz glanced down into the interior of the track. In fury he tried to slam his fist against the hatch coaming and found he no longer had feeling in his right arm. Where the sleeve of his fatigue shirt still clung to him, it was black with blood. Nothing spurting or gushing, though. The main charge of shrapnel that should have ripped through Holtz's upper body had impacted numbingly on his chicken vest. Its porcelain plates had turned the fragments, although the outer casing of nylon was clawed to ruin.

Five-two rumbled as Hauley gunned the engine, then jerked into gear. A long burst of AK fire sounded beyond the bamboo from which the first B-41 had come. A muffled swoosh signaled another rocket from the same location. This time the target, too, was hidden in the jungle. Holtz hosed the tall grass on general principles and blamed his shock-sluggish brain for not understanding what the Vietnamese were doing.

With a howl more like an overloaded dynamo than a jet engine, a metallic cigar shape staggered up out of the jungle less than a hundred yards from five-two's bow. It was fifty feet long, blunt-ended and featureless under a cloaking blue nimbus. Flickering subliminally, the light was less bright than intense. Watching it was similar to laying a bead with an arc welder while wearing a mask of thick blue glass instead of the usual murky yellow.

As the cigar hovered, slightly nose down, another rocket streaked up at it from the launcher hidden in the bamboo. The red flare merged with the nimbus but instead of knifing in against the metal, the missile slowed and hung roaring in the air several seconds until its motor burned out. By then the nimbus had paled almost to nonexistence and the ship itself lurched a yard or two downward. Without the blinding glare Holtz could see gashes in the center section of the strange object, the result of a Communist rocket detonating nearby or some bright flyboy's proximity-fused missile. MiG, for Chrissake! Holtz swore to himself.

A brilliant flash leaped from the bow of the hovering craft. In the thunderclap that followed, the whole clump of bamboo blasted skyward as a ball of green pulp.

To Holtz's left, the cupola machine gun of four-six opened fire on the cigar. Either Roosevelt, the third tank's TC, still thought the hovering vessel was Communist or else he simply reacted to the sudden threat of its power. Brass and stripped links bounded toward Holtz's track as the slender black sent a stream of tracers thundering up at a flat angle.

The blue nimbus slashed and paled. Even as he swore, Holtz's left hand hit the lever to bring the muzzle of his main gun up with a whine. The blue-lit cigar shape swung end on to the tanks, hovering in line with the T-shaped muzzle brake of the cannon. Perhaps a hand inside the opaque hull was reaching for its weapons control, but Holtz's fingers closed on the red switch first. The ninety crashed, bucking back against its recoil stop while flame stabbed forward and sideways through the muzzle brake. Whatever the blue glow did to screen the strange craft, it was inadequate to halt the point-blank impact of a shell delivering over a hundred tons of kinetic energy. The nimbus collapsed like a shattered light bulb. For half a heartbeat the ship rocked in the air, undisturbed except for a four-inch hole in the bare metal of its bow.

The stern third of the craft disintegrated with a stunning crack and a shower of white firedrops that trailed smoke as they fell. A sphincter valve rotated in the center of the cigar. It was half opened when a second explosion wracked the vessel. Something pitched out of the opening and fell with the blazing fragments shaken from the hull. Magnesium roared blindingly as the remainder of the ship dropped out of the sky. It must have weighed more than Holtz would have guessed from the way the impact shook the jungle and threw blazing splinters up into the clouds.

The tanks were still firing but the answering chug-chug-chug of AK-47's had ceased. Holtz reached for the microphone key, found it gone with the rest of his radio helmet. His scrambler phone had not been damaged by the shaped charge, however, and the static blanket was gone. "Zipper one-three," he called desperately on the medical evacuation frequency. "Battle four-six. Get me out a dust-off bird. I've got men down. We're at Yankee Tango seven-oh, four-oh. That's Yankee Tango seven-oh, four-oh, near there. There's clear area to land a bird, but watch it, some of the trees are through the clouds."

"Stand by, Battle four-six," an impersonal voice replied. A minute later it continued, "Battle four-six? We can't get a chopper to you now, there's pea soup over the whole region. Sorry, you'll have to use what you've got to get your men to a surgeon."

"Look, we need a bird," Holtz pressed, his voice tight. "Some of these guys won't make it without medevac."

"Sorry, soldier, we're getting satellite reports as quick as they come in. The way it looks now, nobody's going to take off for seven or eight hours."

Holtz keyed off furiously. "Hauley!" he said. "C'mere."

The driver was beside him immediately, a dark-haired Pfc who moved faster than his mild expression indicated. Holtz handed him the phones and mike. "Hold for me. I want to see what's happened."

"Did you tell about the, the . . ." Hauley started. His gesture finished the thought.

"About the hole in the jungle?" Holtz queried

sarcastically. "Hell, you better forget about that right now. Whatever it was, there's not enough of it left to light your pipe." His arms levered him out of the hatch with difficulty.

"Can I—" Hauley began.

"Shut up, I can make it," his CO snapped. His left leg was cramped. It almost buckled under him as he leaped to the ground. Holding himself as erect as possible, Holtz limped over to four-six. Roosevelt hunched questioningly behind his gunshield, then jumped out of his cupola and helped the officer onto the fender.

"Quit shooting," Holtz ordered irritably as the loader sprayed a breeze-shaken sapling. "Charlie's gone home for today. Lemme use your commo," he added to the TC, "mine's gone."

He closed his eyes as he fitted on the radio helmet, hoping his double vision would clear. It didn't. Even behind closed eyelids a yellow-tinged multiple afterimage remained. The ringing in his ears was almost as bad as the static had been, but at least he could speak. "Four-six to Battle four," Holtz rasped. "Cease firing unless you've got a target, a real target."

The jungle coughed into silence. "Now, who's hurt? Four-four?"

"Zack's bad, sir." Greiler crackled back immediately. "That rocket burned right through the bow and nigh took his foot off. We got the ankle tied, but he needs a doc quick."

Half to his surprise, Holtz found that four-four's driver and the newbie blown off the back of his own track were the only serious casualties. He ignored his own arm and leg; they seemed to have stopped bleeding. Charlie had been too occupied with the damaged cigar to set a proper ambush. Vaguely, he wondered what the Vietnamese had thought they were shooting at. Borrowing the helmet from four-six's loader, the officer painfully climbed off the tank. His left leg hurt more every minute. Heavily corded muscle lay bare on the calf where the film of blood had cracked off.

Davie Womble, the medic who usually rode the back deck of four-six, was kneeling beside the newbie. He had laid his own flak jacket under the boy's head for a cushion and wrapped his chest in a poncho. "Didn't want to move him," he explained to Holtz, "but that one piece went clean through and was sucking air from both sides. He's really wasted."

The boy's face was a sickly yellow, almost the color of his fine blond hair. A glitter of steel marked the tip of a fragment which had zig-zagged shallowly across his scalp. It was so minor compared to other damage that Womble had not bothered to remove it with tweezers. Holtz said nothing. He stepped toward four-four whose loader and TC clustered around their driver. The loader, his M16 tucked under his right arm, faced out into the jungle and scanned the pulverized portion. "Hey," he said, raising his rifle. "Hey! We got one!"

"Watch it," the bloodied officer called as he drew his .45. He had to force his fingers to close around its square butt. Greiler, the track commander, was back behind his cal-fifty in seconds, leaping straight onto the high fender of his tank and scrambling up into the cupola. The loader continued to edge toward the body he saw huddled on the ground. Twenty yards from the tank he thrust his weapon out and used the flash suppressor to prod the still form.

"He's alive," the loader called. "He's—oh my God, oh my *God!*"

Holtz lumbered forward. Greiler's machine gun was live and the captain's neck crawled to think of it, hoping the TC wouldn't bump the trigger. The man on the ground wore gray coveralls of a slick, rubbery-appearing material. As he breathed, they trembled irregularly and a tear above the collarbone oozed dark fluid. His face was against the ground, hidden in shadow, but there was enough light to show Holtz that the man's outflung hand was blue. "Stretcher!" he shouted as he ran back toward the tracks.

Hauley wore a curious expression as he held out the scrambler phone. Holtz snatched and keyed it without explanation. "Battle six, Battle four-six," he called urgently.

"Battle four-six, this is Blackhorse six," the crisp voice of the regimental commander broke in unexpectedly. "What in hell is going on?"

"Umm, sir, I've got three men for a dust-off and I can't get any action out of the chopper jockeys. My boys aren't going to make it if they ride out of here on a tank. Can you—"

"Captain," the cool voice from Quan Loi interrupted, "it won't do your men any good to have a medevac bird fly into a tree in these clouds. I know how you feel, but the weather is the problem and there's nothing we can do about that. Now, what happened?"

"Look," Holtz blurted, "there's a huge goddamn clearing here. If they cruise at five hundred we can guide them in by—"

"God damn it, man, do you want to tell me what's going on or do you want to be the first captain to spend six months in Long Binh Jail?"

Holtz took a deep breath that squeezed bruised ribs against the tight armored vest. Two troopers were already carrying the blue airman back toward the tanks on a litter made of engineer stakes and a poncho. He turned his attention back to the microphone and, keeping his voice flat, said, "We took a prisoner. He's about four feet tall, light build, with a blue complexion. I guess he was part of the crew of the spaceship the Air Force shot down and we finished off.

He's breathing now, but the way he's banged up I don't think he will be long."

Only a hum from the radio. Then, "Four-six, is this some kind of joke?"

"No joke. I'll have the body back at the firebase in four, maybe three hours, and when they get a bird out you can look at him."

"Hold right where you are," the colonel crackled back. "You've got flares?"

"Roger, roger." Holtz's face regained animation and he began daubing at his red cheek with a handkerchief. "Plenty of flares, but the clouds are pretty low. We can set a pattern of trip flares on the ground, though."

"Hold there; I'm going up freek."

It was getting dark very fast. Normally Holtz would have moved his two platoons into the cleared area, but that would have meant shifting the newbie— Christ, he didn't even know the kid's name! If they'd found the captive earlier, a chopper might have already been there. Because of the intelligence value. Christ, how those rear-echelon mothers ate up intelligence value.

"Four-six? Blackhorse six."

"Roger, Blackhorse six." The captain's huge hand clamped hard on the sweat-slippery microphone.

"There'll be a bird over you in one-oh, repeat one-oh, mikes. Put some flares up when you hear it."

"Roger. Battle four-six out." On the company frequency, Holtz ordered, "Listen good, dudes, there's a dust-off bird coming by in ten. Any of you at the tail of the line hear it, don't pop a flare but tell me. We want it coming down here, not in the middle of the jungle." He took off the helmet, setting it beside him on the turret. His head still buzzed and, though he stared into the jungle over the grips of the cal-fifty, even the front sight was a blur. Ten minutes was a long time.

"I hear it!" Roosevelt called. Without waiting for Holtz's order, he fired the quadrangle of trip flares he had set. They lit brightly the area cleared by the alien's weapon. While those ground flares sizzled to full life, Greiler sent three star clusters streaking into the overcast together. The dust-off slick, casting like a coonhound, paused invisibly. As a great gray shadow it drifted down the line of tanks. Its rotor kicked the mist into billows flashing dimly.

Gracelessly yet without jerking the wounded boy, Womble and a third-platoon tanker pressed into service as stretcher-bearer rose and started toward the bird. As soon as the slick touched down, its blades set to idle, the crew chief with his Red Cross armband jumped out. Holtz and the stretcher with the newbie reached the helicopter an instant after the two nearer stretchers.

"Where's the prisoner?" the crew chief shouted over the high scream of unloaded turbines.

"Get my men aboard first," Holtz ordered briefly.

"Sorry, Captain," the air medic replied, "with our fuel load we only take two this trip and I've got orders to bring the prisoner back for sure."

"Stuff your orders! My men go out first."

The crew chief wiped sweat from the bridge of his nose; more trickled from under his commo helmet. "Sir, there's two generals and a bird colonel waiting on the pad for me; I leave that—" he shook his head at the makeshift stretcher—"that back here and it's a year in LBJ if I'm lucky. I'll take one of your—"

"They're both dying!"

"I'm sorry but . . ." The medic's voice dried up when he saw what Holtz was doing. "You can't threaten me!" he shrilled.

Holtz jacked a shell into the chamber of the .45. None of his men moved to stop him. The medic took one step forward as the big captain fired. The bullet slammed into the alien's forehead, just under the streaky gray bristles of his hairline. Fluid spattered the medic and the side of the helicopter behind him.

"There's no prisoner!" Holtz screamed over the shuddering thunder inside his skull. "There's nothing at all, do you hear? Now get my men to a hospital!"

Hauley tried to catch him as he fell, but the officer's weight pulled them both to the ground together.

The snarl of a laboring diesel brought him out of it. He was on a cot with a rolled flak jacket pillowed under his head. Someone had removed his chicken vest and bathed away the crusts of dried blood.

"Where are we?" Holtz muttered thickly. His vision had cleared and the chipped rubber of the treads beside him stood out in sharp relief.

Hauley handed his CO a paper cup of coffee laced with something bitter. "Here you go. Lieutenant Paider took over and we're gonna set up here for the night. If it clears, we'll get a chopper for you too."

"But that . . . ?" Holtz gestured at the twilit bulk of a tank twenty feet away. It grunted to a halt after neutral steering a full 360 degrees.

"That? Oh, that was four-four," Hauley said in a careless voice. "Greiler wanted to say thanks—getting both his buddies dusted off, you know. But I told him you didn't want to hear about something that didn't happen. And everybody in the company'll swear it didn't happen, whatever some chopper jockey thinks. So Greiler just moved four-four up to where the bird landed and did a neutral steer . . . on nothing at all."

"Nothing at all," Holtz repeated before drifting off. He grinned like a she-tiger gorging on her cubs' first kill.

As Our Strength Lessens

Dawn is three hours away, but the sky to the east burns orange and sulphur and deep, sullen red. The rest of my battalion fights there, forcing the Enemy's main line of resistance.

That is not my concern. I have been taken out of reserve and tasked to eliminate an Enemy outpost. The mission appears to me to be one which could have waited until our spearhead had successfully breached the enemy line, but strategic decisions are made by the colloid minds of my human superiors. So be it.

When ion discharges make the night fluoresce, they also tear holes of static in the radio communications spectrum. "... roadwh ... and suspe ..." reports one of my comrades.

Even my enhancement program is unable to decode more of the transmission than that, but I recognize the fist of the sender: *Saratoga*, part of the lead element of our main attack. His running gear has been damaged. He will have to drop out of line.

My forty-seven pairs of flint-steel roadwheels are in depot condition. Their tires of spun beryllium monocrystal, woven to deform rather than compress, all have 97% or better of their fabric unbroken. The immediate terrain is semi-arid. The briefing files inform me this is typical of the planet. My track links purr among themselves as they grind through scrub vegetation and the friable soil, carrying me to my assigned mission.

There is a cataclysmic fuel-air explosion to the east behind me. The glare is visible for 5.3 seconds, and the ground will shake for many minutes as shock waves echo through the planetary mantle.

Had my human superiors so chosen, I could be replacing *Saratoga* at the spearhead of the attack.

The rear elements of the infantry are in sight now. They look like dung beetles in their hard suits, crawling backward beneath a rain of shrapnel. I am within range of their low-power communications net. *"Hold what you got, troops,"* orders the unit's acting commander. *"Big Brother's come to help!"*

I am not Big Brother. I am *Maldon*, a Mark XXX Bolo of the 3d Battalion, Dinochrome Brigade. The lineage of our unit goes back to the 2nd South Wessex Dragoons. In 1944, we broke the last German resistance on the path to Falaise—though we traded our flimsy Cromwells against the Tigers at a ratio of six to one to do it.

The citizens do not need to know what the cost is. They need only to know that the mission has been accomplished. The battle honors welded to my turret prove that I have always accomplished my mission.

Though this task should not have been a difficult one, even for the company of infantry to whom it was originally assigned. An Enemy research facility became, because of its location, an outpost on the flank of our line as we began to drive out of the landing zone. In a breakthrough battle, infantry can do little but die in their fighting suits. A company of

them was sent to mop up the outpost in relative
safety.

Instead . . .

As I advance, I review the ongoing mission report
filed in real-time by the infantry and enhanced at
Headquarters before being downloaded to me microseconds later. My mind forms the blips of digital
information into a panorama, much as the colloid
minds of my superiors process sensory data fired into
them across nerve endings.

Vehicles brought the infantry within five kilometers
of their objective. There they disembarked for tactical
flexibility and to avoid giving the Enemy a single soft
target of considerable value.

I watch:

*The troops advance by tiny, jerky movements of the
legs of their hard suits.* My tracks, rotating in silky
precision, purr with laughter.

The concept of vertical envelopment, overflying an
enemy's lines to drop forces in his rear, ceased to be
viable with the appearance of directed-energy weapons in the 20th century. After the development of
such weapons, any target which could be seen—even
in orbit above an atmosphere—could be hit at the
speed of light.

No flying vehicle could be armored heavily enough
to withstand attack by powerful beam weapons. The
alternative was more of the grinding ground assaults
to which civilians always object because they are costly
and brutal, and to which soldiers always turn because
they succeed when finesse does not succeed.

Our forces have landed on an empty, undefended
corner of the planet. The blazing combat to the east
occurs as our forces meet those which the Enemy is
rushing into place to block us.

I am not at my accustomed place in the front line,

but the Enemy will not stop the advance of my comrades.

I watch:

The leading infantry elements have come in sight of their objective. There is something wrong with the data, because the Enemy research facility appears as a spherical flaw—an absence of information—in the transmitted images.

Light blinks from the anomaly. It is simply that, light, with the balance and intensity of the local solar output at ground level on this planet.

The infantry assume they are being attacked. They respond with lasers and projectile weapons as they take cover and unlimber heavier ordnance. Within .03 seconds of the first shot, the Enemy begins to rake the infantry positions with small arms fire.

While the battalion was in transit to our target, briefing files were downloaded into our data banks. These files, the distillation of truth and wisdom by our human superiors, state that the Enemy is scientifically far inferior to ourselves. There is no evidence that the Enemy even has a working stardrive now, though unquestionably at some past time they colonized the scores of star systems which they still inhabit.

Enemy beam weapons are admittedly very efficient. The Enemy achieves outputs from hand-held devices which our forces can duplicate only with large vehicle-mounted units. Our scientific staff still has questions regarding the power sources which feed these Enemy beam weapons.

Thus far the briefing files. I have examined the schematics of captured Enemy lasers. The schematics show no power source whatever. This is interesting, but it does not affect the certainty of our victory.

Initially, the Enemy outpost to which I have been

tasked was not using weapons more powerful than the small arms which our own infantry carry.

I watch:

The infantry is well trained. Three-man teams shoot and advance in a choreographed sequence, directing a steady volume of fire at the outpost. At the present range it is unlikely that their rifles and lasers will do serious damage. The purpose of this fire is to disrupt the Enemy's aim and morale while more effective weapons can be brought to bear. The heavy-weapons section is deploying back-pack rockets and the company's light ion cannon.

An infantryman ripple-fires his four-round rocket pack. The small missiles are self-guiding and programmed to vary their courses to the laser-cued target.

Three of the rockets curve wildly across the bleak terrain and detonate when they exhaust their fuel. They have been unable to fix on the reflected laser beam which should have provided the precise range of the target. The anomaly has absorbed the burst of coherent light so perfectly that none bounces back to be received by the missiles' homing devices. Only the first round of the sequence, directed on a line-straight track, seems to reach the target.

The missile vanishes. There is no explosion. At .03 seconds after the computed moment of impact—there is no direct evidence that the rocket actually hit its target—the Enemy outpost launches a dozen small missiles of its own. One of them destroys the ion cannon before the crew can open fire.

Puffs of dirt mark the battlefield. The infantry is using powered augers to dig in for greater protection. The Enemy outpost continues to rake the troops with rockets and small arms, oblivious of the infantry's counterfire.

Seven hours before planetfall, a human entered the

bay where we Bolos waited in our thoughts and memories. He wore the trousers of an officer's dress uniform, but he had taken off the blouse with the insignia of his rank.

The human's face and name were in my data banks. He was Major Peter Bowen, a member of the integral science staff of our invasion force. My analysis of the air Bowen exhaled indicated a blood alcohol level of .1763 parts per hundred. He moved with drunken care.

"Good evening, Third Battalion," Bowen said. He attempted a bow. He caught himself with difficulty on a bulkhead when he started to fall over. I realized that the bay was not lighted in the human-visible spectrum. Bowen had no business here with us, but he was a human and an officer. I switched on the yellow navigation lights along my fender skirts.

Bowen walked toward me. "Hello, Bolo," he said. "Do you have a name?"

I did not answer. My name was none of his concern; and anyway, it did not appear that he was really speaking to me. Humans often say meaningless things. Perhaps that is why they rule and we serve.

"None of my business, hey, buddy," said Bowen. "There's been a lot of that goin' around lately." He was not a fool, and it appeared that he was less incapacitated by drink than I had assumed.

He reached out to my treads. I thought he was steadying his drunken sway, but instead the scientist's fingers examined the spun crystal pads of a track block. "Colonel McDougal says I'm not to brief the battalion tasking officers because that's been taken care of by real experts. Colonel McDougal's a regular officer, so he oughta know, right?"

The situation shocked me. "Colonel McDougal is your direct superior, Major Bowen," I said.

"Oh, you bet McDougal's superior to me," Bowen

said in what should have been agreement but clearly was not. "He'll be the first to tell you so, the Colonel will. I'm just a civilian with a commission. Only—I figured that since I was here, maybe I ought to do my job."

"Your job is to carry out your superior's orders to the best of your ability," I replied.

Bowen chuckled. "You too," he said. His hands caressed my bow slope. My battle honors are welded to my turret, but the flint-steel of my frontal armor bears scars which tell the same story to those who can read them.

"What's your name, friend?" Bowen asked.

My name is my password, which Bowen is not authorized to know. I do not reply.

He looked at me critically. "You're Maldon," he said, "Grammercy's your tasking officer."

I am shocked. Bowen could have learned that only from Captain Grammercy himself. Why would Grammery have spoken what was his duty to conceal? It is not my duty to understand colloid minds; but I sometimes think that if I could, I would be better able carry out the tasks they set me.

"You know the poem, at least?" Bowen added.

It was several microseconds before I realized that this, though inane, was really meant as a question. "Of course," I said. All the human arts are recorded in my data banks.

"And you know that the Earl of Essex was a fool?" said Bowen. "That he threw his army away and left his lands open to pillage because of his stupidity?"

"His bodyguards were heroes!" I retorted. "They were steadfast!"

The bay echoed with my words, but Bowen did not flinch back from me. "All honor to their courage!" he snapped. I remembered that I had thought he was drunk and a disgrace to the uniform he—partly—

wore. "They took the orders of a fool. And died, which was no dishonor. *And* left their lands to be raped by Vikings, which was no honor to them or their memory, Maldon!"

The retainers of the Earl of Essex were tasked to prevent Vikings under Olaf Tryggvason from pillaging the country. The Earl withdrew his forces from a blocking position in order to bring the enemy to open battle at Maldon. His bodyguards fought heroically but were defeated.

The Earl's bodyguards failed to accomplish their mission. There is no honor in failure.

"What did you wish to tell us, Major Bowen?" I asked.

The human coughed. He looked around the bay before he replied. His eyes had adapted to the glow of my running lights.

My comrades of the 3d Battalion listened silently to the conversation. To a creature of Bowen's size, fifty-one motionless Bolos must have loomed like features of a landscape rather than objects constructed by tools in human hands.

"The accepted wisdom," Bowen said, "is that the Anceti are scientifically backward. That the race has degenerated from an advanced level of scientific ability, and that the remnants of that science are no threat to human arms."

He patted the flint-steel skirt protecting my track and roadwheels. "No serious threat to you and your friends, Maldon."

"Yes," I said, because I thought a human would have spoken . . . though there was no need to tell Bowen what he already knew was in the official briefing files.

"I don't believe the Anceti are degenerate," Bowen said. "And I *sure* don't think they're ignorant. Nobody who's turning out lasers like theirs is ignorant. They've got a flux density of ten times our best—and there's not even a hint of a power source."

"The Enemy no longer has stardrive," I said, as if I were stating a fact instead of retailing information from the briefing files. This is a technique humans use when they wish to elicit information from other humans.

"Balls!" Bowen said. He did not speak as a human and my superior. Instead, his voice had the sharpness of a cloud as it spills lightning to the ground, careless and certain of its path. "Do you believe that, Maldon? Is that the best the mind of a Bolo Mark XXX can do synthesizing data?"

I was stung. "So the briefing files stated," I replied, "And I have no information to contradict—"

"Balls!" Bowen repeated.

I said nothing.

After a moment, the scientist continued, "There's a better than 99% probability that the Anceti are reinforcing their outpost worlds under threat of our attack. How are they doing that if they don't have stardrive, Maldon?"

I reviewed my data banks. "Reconnaissance shows the strengthened facilities," I said. I already knew how Bowen was going to respond. "Reconnaissance does not show that the equipment and personnel were imported from outside the worlds on which they are now based."

"We're talking about barren rocks, some of these planets," Bowen said. His tone dripped with disgust. I choose to believe that was a human rhetorical device rather than his real opinion of my intellect. "The Anceti and their hardware didn't spring from rocks, Maldon; they were brought there. A better than 99% probability. We just don't know how."

"The briefing files are wrong," I said. I spoke aloud to show the human that I understood.

They rule and we serve. We know one truth at a time, but colloid minds believe contradictory truths or no truth at all. So be it.

There was a question that I could not resolve, no matter how I attempted to view the information at my disposal. I needed more data. So—

"Why are you telling us this, Major Bowen?" I asked.

"Because I want you to understand," the human said fiercely, "that the Anceti's science *isn't* inferior to ours, it's just different. Like the stardrive. Did you know that every one of the star systems the Anceti have colonized at some point in galactic history crossed a track some other Anceti star system occupied? Or *will* occupy!"

I reviewed my data banks. The information was of course there, but I had not analyzed it for this purpose.

"There is no indication that the Enemy has time travel, Major Bowen," I said. "Except the data you cite, which could be explained by an assumption of time travel."

"I know that, I know that," Bowen replied. His voice rose toward hysteria, but he caught himself in mid-syllable. "I don't say they have time travel, I don't *believe* they have time travel. But they've got something, Maldon. I know they've got something."

"We will accomplish our mission, Major Bowen," I said to soothe him.

Some humans hate us for our strength and our difference from them, even though they know we are the starkest bulwark against their Enemies. Most humans treat us as the tools of their wills, as is their right. But a very few humans are capable of concern for minds and personalities, though they are encased in flint-steel and ceramic rather than protoplasm.

All humans are to be protected. Some are to be cherished.

"Oh, I don't doubt you'll accomplish *your* mission, Maldon," Bowen said, letting his fingers pause at the gouge in my bow slope where an arc knife struck me a glancing blow. "But I've failed in mine."

He made the sound of laughter, but there was no humor in it. "That's why I'm drunk, you see." He cleared his throat. "Well, I was drunk. And I'll be drunk again, real soon."

"You have not failed, Major Bowen," I said. "You have corrected the faulty analysis of others."

"I haven't corrected anything, Maldon," the human said. "I can't give them a mechanism for whatever the Anceti are doing, so nobody in the task force believes me. Nobody even listens. They're too happy saying that the Anceti are a bunch of barbarians we're going to mop up without difficulties."

"We believe you, Major Bowen," I said. I spoke for all my comrades in the 3d Battalion, though they remained silent on the audio frequencies. "We will be ready to react to new tricks and weapons of the Enemy."

"That's good, Maldon," said the human. He squeezed my armor with more force than I had thought his pudgy fingers could achieve. "Because you're the guys who're going to pay the price if Colonel McDougal's wisdom is wrong."

He turned and walked back to the hatchway. "Now," he added, "I'm going to get drunk."

I wonder where Major Bowen is now. Somewhere in Command, some place as safe as any on a planet at war. Behind me, the main battle rages in a fury of shock waves and actinic radiation. It is hard fought, but the exchanges of fire are within expected parameters.

The mission to which I have been assigned, on the other hand . . .

The infantry company called in artillery support as soon as the Enemy outpost began strafing them with back-pack missiles.

I watch:

The first pair of artillery rockets streaks over the horizon.

The missiles' sustainer motors have burned out, but the bands of maneuvering jets around each armor-piercing warhead flash as they course-correct. They are targeted by triangulation from fixed points, since the outpost itself remains perfectly absorbant throughout the electro-optical band. These are probing rounds, intended to test the Enemy's anti-artillery defenses so that the main barrage can be protected by appropriate countermeasures.

The Enemy has no defenses. The shells plunge into the center of the anomaly and disappear, just as all earlier projectiles and energy beams have done. Neither these shells nor the barrage which follows has any discernible effect on the Enemy.

.03 seconds from the first warhead's calculated moment of impact, the research facility begins to bombard our attacking infantry with artillery rockets.

The Enemy is firing armor-piercing rounds. They are already at terminal velocity when they appear from the anomaly. When the warheads explode deep underground, the soil spews up and flings dug-in infantrymen flailing into air. Sometimes the hard suits protect the infantry well enough that the victims are able to crawl away under their own power.

Back-pack missiles and small arms fire from the outpost continue to rake the infantry positions. The company commander orders his troops to withdraw. 5.4 seconds later, the acting company commander calls for a Bolo to be assigned in support.

The air over the battlefield is a pall of black dust, lighted fitfully by orange flashes at its heart.

I am now within the extreme range even of small arms fired from the research facility. The Enemy does not engage me. Shells launched from the anomaly continue to pound the infantry's initial deployment area, smashing the remains of fighting suits into smaller fragments. The surviving infantry have withdrawn from the killing ground.

Friendly missiles continue to vanish into the anomaly without effect.

Thus far I have observed the outpost only through passive receptors. I take a turret-down position on the reverse slope of a hill and raise an active ranging device on a sacrificial mounting above my protective armor. Using this mast-mounted unit, I probe the anomaly with monopulse emissions on three spectra.

There is no echo from the anomaly. .03 seconds after the pulses should have ranged the target, the outpost directs small arms fire and a pair of artillery rockets at me.

The bullets and low-power laser beams are beneath my contempt. The sacrificial sensor pod is the only target I have exposed to direct fire. It is not expected to survive contact with an enemy, but the occasional hit the pod receives at this range barely scratches its surface.

As for the artillery fire—the Enemy is not dealing with defenseless infantry now. I open a micro-second window and EMP the shells, destroying their control circuitry. The ring thrusters shut off and the warheads go ballistic. Neither shell will impact within fifty meters of my present location.

.03 seconds from the moment I fried the Enemy warheads, a high-amplitude electromagnetic pulse from the anomaly meets the next of the shells raining in from friendly artillery batteries. The warhead has already made its final course corrections, so it plunges into the calculated center of the target. The electronic fuzing will probably have failed under the EMP attack, but the back-up mechanical detonators should still function.

It is impossible to tell whether the mechanical fuzes work: there is, as I have come to expect, no sign even of kinetic impact with the anomaly.

The outpost launches two more missiles and a storm of small arms fire at me. The missiles course-correct early. They will strike me even if their control circuits are destroyed.

To the east, the air continues to flash and thunder over the Enemy's main line of resistance. Casualties there are heavy but within expected parameters. My comrades will make their initial breakthrough within five hours and thirty-seven minutes, unless there is a radical change in Enemy strength.

This research facility is far from the population centers of this planet. Did the Enemy place it in so isolated a location because they realized the risk of disaster at the cutting edge of the forces they were studying desperately to meet our assault?

I know they've got something, Major Bowen told me. He was right. The real battle will not be decided along the main line but rather here.

I open antenna apertures to send peremptory signals to Command, terminating the artillery fire mission. I use spread-transmission radio—which may be blocked by war-roiled static across the electromagnetic spectrum; laser—which will be received only if all the repeaters along the transmission path have survived combat; and ground conduction, which is slow but effectively beyond jamming.

Friendly artillery has no observable effect on the outpost, and it interjects a variable into the situation.

All variables thus far appear to have benefited the Enemy.

While I deliver instructions and a report to Command, and while my mind gropes for a template which will cover my observations thus far of the Enemy's capabilities, I deal with the incoming missiles. I spin a pair of fluctuating apertures in my turret shielding. The gaps are aligned with the lifting muzzles of my infinite repeaters and in synchronous with their cyclic rate.

I fire. Pulses along the superconducting magnets in the bores of the infinite repeaters accelerate short tubes of depleted uranium—ring penetrators—to astronomical velocity. Miniature suns blaze from kinetic impact where my penetrators intersect the warheads. The missiles lose aerodynamic stability. They tumble in glowing cartwheels across the sky.

.03 seconds after I engage the warheads, a burst of hyper-velocity ring penetrators from the anomaly shreds my sacrificial sensor pod.

My capacity to store and access information is orders of magnitude beyond that of the colloid minds I serve, but even so only part of the knowledge in my data banks is available to me at any one moment. Now, while I replace the sensors and six more missiles streak toward me out of the anomaly, I hear the baritone voice of the technician replacing my port-side roadwheels during depot service seventy-four years ago.

He sings: *Get in, get out, quit muckin' about—
Drive on!*

My data processing system has mimicked a colloid mind to short-circuit my decision tree. I have been passive under attack for long enough.

I advance, blowing the hillcrest in front of me so that I do not expose my belly plates by lifting over it.

Both direct and indirect fire have battlefield virtues.

Direct fire is limited by terrain and, if the weapon is powerful enough, by the curvature of the planet itself. But, though the curving path of indirect fire can reach any target, the warheads have necessarily longer flight times and lower terminal velocities because of their trajectory. When they hit, they are less effective than direct-fire projectile weapons; and the most devastating artillery of all, directed energy weapons, can operate only in the direct-fire mode.

The worst disadvantage of direct fire weapons is that the shooter must by definition be in sight of his target. Bolos are designed to be seen by our targets and survive.

My tracks accelerate me through the cloud of pulverized rock where the hillcrest used to be. The infinite repeaters in my turret hammer the anomaly with continuous fire. I am mixing ring penetrators and high explosive in a random pattern based on cosmic ray impacts.

I hope this will confuse the Enemy defenses. The only evident effect of my tactic is that, .03 seconds from the time the first HE round should have hit the anomaly, the Enemy begins to include high-explosive rounds in the bursts which flash harmlessly against my electromagnetic shielding.

I am clear of the rock dust. I align myself with the anomaly and fire my Hellbore from its centerline hull installation.

Even *my* mass is jolted by the Hellbore's recoil. A laser-compressed thermonuclear explosion at the breech end voids a slug of ions down the axis of the bore, the only path left open. The bolt can devour mountains or split rock on planets in distant orbits.

My Hellbore has no discernible effect on the anomaly; but .03 seconds after I fire, an ion bolt smashes into me.

I am alive. For nearly a second, I am sure of nothing

else. Circuits, shut down to avoid burning out under overload, come back on line.

I have received serious injuries. My hull and running gear are essentially undamaged. Most of the anti-personnel charges along my skirts have gone off in a single white flash. This is of no importance, since it now appears vanishingly improbable that I will ever see Enemy personnel.

87% of my external communications equipment has been destroyed. Most of the antennas have vaporized, despite the shutters of flint-steel which were to protect them. I reroute circuits and rotate back-up antennas from my hull core.

My infinite repeaters were cycling when the ion bolt struck. Ions ravening through the aperture in my electromagnetic shielding destroyed both infinite repeaters, bathed the hull and wiped it clean of most external fittings, and penetrated the turret itself through one of the weapons ports. All armament and sensory installations within my turret have been fused into a metal-ceramic magma.

The turret ring is not blocked, and the drive mechanism still works. I rotate the turret so that the back instead of the hopelessly compromised frontal armor faces the anomaly.

Data clicks into a gestalt which explains the capabilities which the Enemy has demonstrated.

I brake my starboard track while continuing to accelerate with the port drive motors. My hull slews. The change in direction throws a comber of earth and rock toward the outpost. Though my size and inertia are so great that I cannot completely dodge the Enemy's second ion bolt, the suspension of soil in air dissipates much of the charge in a fireball and thunderclap. My hull shakes, but the only additional damage I receive is to some of the recently replaced communications gear.

I am transmitting my conclusions to Command via all the channels available to me. I load a message torpedo intended for communication under the most adverse conditions. This is a suitable occasion for its use.

The Hellbore discharge has disrupted the guidance systems of the artillery rockets the Enemy launched at me seconds earlier. In the momentary silence following the bolt's near miss, I release my torpedo. It streaks away to warn Command. The Enemy ignore the torpedo in the chaos of their own tumbling shells.

The Enemy is not mirroring matter. Rather, the Enemy mirrors facets of temporal reality. Our forces have seen no evidence of Enemy stardrive because for the Enemy, a planet can fill a point in space where once existed or will one day exist. The Enemy need not transit the eternal present so long as there is a congruity between Now and When.

Personnel of the research facility I have been tasked to eliminate have developed the technique still further. They are creating a special space-time in which whatever can exist, *does* exist for them so long as there is an example of the occurrence in their reality matrix.

Their tool is the anomaly that appears from outside to be a non-reflecting void. It is a tunable discontinuity in the local space-time. The staff of the research facility use this window to capture templates, copies of which are in .03 seconds shuttled into present reality and redirected at their opponents.

The research facility can already mimic the firepower of an infantry company, a battery of rocket artillery, and—because of my actions—a Mark XXX Bolo. I have only one option.

There is no cover for an object my size between me and the research facility. Though my drive motors are spinning at full power, nothing material can outrun the bolt of a Hellbore. The third discharge catches me squarely.

The shockwave blasts a doughnut from the soil around me. My turret becomes a white-hot fireball. The electromagnetic generators in the turret were damaged by the initial bolt and could not provide more than 60% of their designed screening capacity against the second direct hit. My port skirts are blasted off; several track links bind momentarily. My drive motors have enough torque to break the welds, but again I slow and skid in a jolting S-turn.

My target is a research facility. It is possible that the Enemy will not be able to develop similar capabilities anywhere else before our forces have smashed them into defeat. That is beyond my control—and outside my mission. *This* is the target I have been tasked to eliminate.

I open the necessary circuits and bypass the interlocks. A disabled Bolo is too valuable to be abandoned, so there have to be ways.

I have no offensive armament. My Hellbore is operable, but the third ion bolt welded the gunport shutters closed. A salvo of armor-piercing shells hammers my hull, lifting me and slamming me back to the ground in a red-orange cataclysm. The multiple impacts strip my starboard track.

I think of Major Bowen, and of the Saxon bodyguards striding forward to die at Maldon:

Heart grow stronger, will firmer,
Mind more composed, as our strength lessens.

The citizens do not need to know what the cost is. They need only to know that the mission has been accomplished.

My sole regret, as I initiate the scuttling sequence that will send my fusion pile critical, is that I will not be present in .03 seconds. I would like to watch as the Enemy tries to vent an omnidirectional thermonuclear explosion into their research facility.

BEST OF LUCK

A Russian-designed .51 caliber machine gun fires bullets the size of a woman's thumb. When a man catches a pair of those in his chest and throat the way Captain Warden's radioman did, his luck has run out. A gout of blood sprayed back over Curtis, next man in the column. He glimpsed open air through the RTO's middle: the hole plowed through the flailing body would have held his fist.

But there was no time to worry about the dead, no time to do anything but dive out of the line of fire. Capt Warden's feral leap had carried him in the opposite direction, out of Curtis' sight into the gloom of the rubber. Muzzle flashes flickered over the silver tree-trunks as the bunkered machine guns tore up Dog Company.

Curtis' lucky piece bit him through the shirt fabric as he slammed into the smooth earth. The only cover in the ordered plantation came from the trees themselves, and their precise arrangement left three aisles open to any hiding place. The heavy guns ripped through the darkness in short bursts from several locations; there was no way to be safe, nor even to tell from where death would strike.

Curtis had jerked back the cocking piece of his M16, but he had no target. Blind firing would only call down the attentions of the Communist gunners. He felt as naked as the lead in a Juarez floor show, terribly aware of what the big bullets would do if they hit him. He had picked up the lucky Maria Theresa dollar in Taiwan, half as a joke, half in unstated remembrance of men who had been saved when a coin or a Bible turned an enemy slug. But no coin was going to deflect a .51 cal from the straight line it would blast through him.

Red-orange light bloomed a hundred yards to Curtis' left as a gun opened up, stuttering a sheaf of lead through the trees. Curtis marked the spot. Stomach tight with fear, he swung his clumsy rifle toward the target and squeezed off a burst.

The return fire was instantaneous and from a gun to the right, unnoticed until that moment. The tree Curtis crouched beside exploded into splinters across the base, stunning impacts that the soldier felt rather than heard. He dug his fingers into the dirt, trying to drag himself still lower and screaming mentally at the pressure of the coin which kept him that much closer to the crashing bullets. The rubber tree was sagging, its twelve-inch bole sawn through by the fire, but nothing mattered to Curtis except the raving death a bullet's width above his head.

The firing stopped. Curtis clenched his fists, raised his head a fraction from the ground. A single, spiteful round banged from the first bunker. The bullet ticked the rim of Curtis' helmet, missing his flesh but snapping his head back with the force of a thrown anvil. He was out cold when the tree toppled slowly across his boots.

*   *   *

There were whispers in the darkness, but all he could see were blue and amber streaks on the inside of his mind. He tried to move, then gasped in agony as the pinioning mass shifted against his twisted ankles.

There were whispers in the darkness, and Curtis could guess what they were. Dog Company had pulled back. Now the VC were slipping through the trees, stripping the dead of their weapons and cutting the throats of the wounded. Wherever Curtis' rifle had been flung, it was beyond reach of his desperate fingers.

Something slurped richly near Curtis on his right. He turned his face toward the sound, but its origin lurked in the palpable blackness. There was a slushy, ripping noise from the same direction, settling immediately into a rhythmic gulping. Curtis squinted uselessly. The moon was full, but the clouds were as solid as steel curtains.

Two Vietnamese were approaching from his left side. The scuff of their tire-soled sandals paused momentarily in a liquid trill of speech, then resumed. A flashlight played over the ground, its narrow beam passing just short of Curtis' left hand. The gulping noise stopped.

"Ong vo?" whispered one of the VC, and the light flashed again. There was a snarl and a scream and the instant red burst of an AK-47 blazing like a flare. The radioman's body had been torn open. Gobbets of lung and entrails, dropped by the feasting thing, were scattered about the corpse. But Curtis' real terror was at what the muzzle flash caught in mid-leap—teeth glinting white against bloody crimson, the mask of a yellow-eyed beast more savage than a nightmare and utterly undeterred by the bullets punching across it. And the torso beneath the face was dressed in American jungle fatigues.

*   *   *

"Glad to have you back, Curtis," Capt Warden said. "We're way understrength, and replacements haven't been coming in fast enough. Better get your gear together now, because at 1900 hours the company's heading out on a night patrol and I want every man along."

Curtis shifted uneasily, transfixed by the saffron sclera of the captain's eyes. The driver who had picked him up at the chopper pad had filled Curtis in on what had gone on during his eight weeks in the hospital. Seventeen men had died in the first ambush. The condition of the radioman's body was blamed on the VC, of course; but that itself had contributed to rotted morale, men screaming in their sleep or squirting nervous shots off into the shadows. A month later, Warden had led another sweep. The lithe, athletic captain should have been a popular officer for his obvious willingness to share the dangers of his command; but when his second major operation ended in another disaster of bunkers and spider holes, the only emotion Dog Company could find for him was hatred. Everybody knew this area of operations was thick with VC and that it was Dog Company's business to find them. But however successful the operations were from the division commander's standpoint—the followups had netted tons of equipment and abandoned munitions—Warden's men knew that they had taken it on the chin twice in a row.

It hadn't helped that the body of Lt Schaden, killed at the captain's side in the first exchange of fire, had been recovered the next day in eerily mutilated condition. It looked, the driver whispered, as though it had been gnawed on by something.

They moved out in the brief dusk, nervous squads shrunk to the size of fire teams under the poundings they had taken. The remainder of the battalion watched Dog's departure in murmuring cliques. Curtis knew they were making bets on how many of the patrol wouldn't walk back this time. Well, a lot of people in Dog itself were wondering the same.

The company squirmed away from the base, avoiding known trails. Capt Warden had a destination, though; Curtis, again marching just behind the command group, could see the captain using a penlight to check compass and map at each of their frequent halts. The light was scarcely necessary. The mid-afternoon downpour had washed clean the sky for the full moon to blaze in. It made for easier movement through the tangles of trees and vines, but it would light up the GIs like ducks in a shooting gallery if they blundered into another VC bunker complex.

The trade dollar in Curtis' pocket flopped painfully against him. The bruise it had given him during the ambush still throbbed. It was starting to hurt more than his ankles did, but nothing would have convinced him to leave it in his locker now. He'd gotten back the last time, hadn't he? Despite the murderous cross-fire, the tree, and the . . . other. Curtis gripped his sweaty M16 tighter. Maybe it hadn't been Maria Theresa's chop-scarred face that got him through, but he wasn't missing any bets.

Because every step he took into the jungle deepened his gut-wrenching certainty that Dog Company was about to catch it again.

The captain grunted a brief order into the phone flexed to his RTO. The jungle whispered "halt" from each of the platoon leaders. Warden's face was in a patch of moonlight. His left hand cradled the compass, but he paid it no attention. Instead his lean, dominant nose lifted and visibly snuffled the still air. With a nod and a secret smile that Curtis shivered to

see, the captain spoke again into the radio to move
the company out.

Three minutes later, the first blast of shots raked
through them.

The bullet hit the breech of Curtis' rifle instead of
simply disemboweling him. The dented barrel cracked
down across both of his thighs with sledge hammer
force. His left thumb was dislocated, though his right
hand, out of the path in which the .51 cal had
snatched the rifle, only tingled. Curtis lay on his back
amazed, listening to the thump-crack of gunfire and
bullets passing overhead. He was not even screaming:
the pain was yet to come.

An American machine gun ripped a long red streak
to within six inches of Curtis' head, no less potentially
deadly for not being aimed at him. The wounded soldier fumbled open his breast pocket and clutched at
the lucky piece. It was the only action to which he
could force his punished body. The moon glared
grimly down.

Something moved near Curtis. Capt Warden, bare
headed, was snaking across the jungle floor toward
him. Warden grinned. His face slumped suddenly like
lead in a mold, shaping itself into a ghastly new form
that Curtis had seen once before. The Warden-thing's
fangs shone as it poised, then leaped—straight into a
stream of Communist fire.

A two-ounce bullet meat-axed through the thing's
chest back to front, slapping it against a tree. Curtis
giggled in relief before he realized that the creature
was rising to its knees. Fluid shock had blasted a great
crater in the flesh over its breastbone, and the lower
half of its face was coated with blood gulped out of
its own lungs. The eyes were bright yellow and horribly alive, and as Curtis stared in fascination, the gaping wound began to close. The thing took a step

toward the helpless soldier, a triumphant grimace sweeping over its distorted features.

Without conscious direction, Curtis' thumb spun the silver dollar toward the advancing creature. The half-healed wound-lips in the thing's chest seemed to suck the coin in. The scream that followed was that of an animal spindled on white-hot wire, but it ended quickly in a gurgle as dissolution set in.

The stretcher team brought Curtis out in the morning. His right hand had been dipped into the pool of foulness soaking the ground near him, and the doctors could not unclench the fist from the Maria Theresa dollar it was frozen on until after the morphine had taken hold.

THE GUARDROOM

"Three kings," said Singer, and the alarm rang to scatter the guardroom's inevitable poker game.

All four guards came alert; but it was Cohen's turn to go out, and there was that awareness too in the glances of the others toward him.

"Never learn when to back off, will you, Cohen?" said Singer, whose body was as squat and powerful as a troll's. He gestured toward the cards which Cohen, the other long-time veteran, had thrown in without displaying. "It isn't a bluff every time."

Elfen, the youngest of them when he was recruited to the four-man guard force, chuckled and said. "He'll live longer, you mean?" He had folded his cards after the draw and now slid them into the pile.

Cohen, preparing to enter the transfer chamber, said, "Game stops when the alarm sounds," with an edge of irritation. The frown that wrinkled the veteran's high forehead was probably because he was about to go operational rather than because of the gibe about his cardplaying; but the poker game was a safe subject. "I could've been holding a full house, Singer."

163

Pauli, the fourth guard, snorted and reached for the cards Cohen had thrown in. Singer froze the pile with one hand and deliberately stirred his own cards and the rest of the deck together with the other. "Give 'em hell, buddy," he said to the man in the transfer chamber.

"Sure," said Cohen, "why should they be better off than everybody else?"

Then the circuits tripped, leaving the transfer chamber empty of what the other three men knew as Cohen: a guard, as they were, of the Citadel of Arborson.

"Been a long time since anybody's tried it," said Pauli—perhaps in regret, perhaps in hidden concern for the fact that he was next up on the rotation. Only one guard could be transferred at a time, while the number of intruders were in theory limited only by the population the Earth still managed to support. . . .

Of course, that theoretical number seemed still to be decreasing.

"Yeah," Elfen said, looser than the others because he was neither facing imminent duty nor closely bonded to Cohen—Singer had brought aboard and trained both the newer guards. "Back in my day, every full moon somebody'd get together a band to break into the Citadel of Arborson. Nobody's got any balls anymore."

"They've forgotten the trick of getting in," said Singer, rifling the cards and appearing to look at them. "Not a matter of guts, just knowledge. And maybe metal."

"*We* knew how to get in, right enough," responded Elfen with a laugh. "It was just how to get out that was the problem."

Pauli grimaced toward the transfer chamber. "Some things don't change, do they?" he said.

The guardroom in Singer's imagination was momentarily infinite and featureless, a bleak expanse of dull ochre like the walls—themselves an electronic construct, as were the cards and all the other seemingly-physical objects within. Singer's massive hands shuffled cards that were as useful as they would have been if 'real' in some more material sense. "I wonder what they think they're going to find here," he remarked to the cards. "They can't have any conception of what Arborson was doing . . . of what a *scientist* was, for god's sake. Nobody in his own day believed he was more than a crank. Our day, Cohen's and mine."

"Well, so far as that goes," Elfen objected, "what do any of *us* know about Arborson—except that he's dead?"

"Do we know that?" Singer rejoined, rapping the cards on the tabletop to bring the deck into alignment. He looked up. Neither of the other guards spoke under his lowering gaze. Singer was the leader of the guardroom, in fact, if not officially. Arborson—if he were alive, rather than being dust or an electronic memory somewhere—did not involve himself in the affairs of the guards who carried out the orders he had programmed long ago.

Singer's face relented. He raised the reshuffled cards and asked in a mild voice, "Shall we play a couple of rounds of three-handed, then?"

Pauli sucked his lips and turned away. "Why don't we just wait awhile," he said, "until Cohen comes back."

So they waited, the three of them, until the alarm sounded again to indicate that Cohen would never come back.

Pauli jumped up with a curse or a prayer, headed for the transfer chamber instinctively because his eyes were shattered by tears and emotions beyond sorrow.

Pauli had been a warrior just short of thirty years old when he entered the guardroom, an advanced age that bespoke skill and toughness as clearly as did the scars overlying his body's more formal pattern of tattoos. There was a difference between the circumstances of his former life and what he was called on now to accomplish, however; and it may have been that the process itself was more a cause for his fear than was what—in addition to Cohen's body—he expected to find outside.

Singer stopped Pauli as he had earlier blocked his attempt to check the poker hand. Pauli whirled to glare at the big veteran who rose from his chair gripping the other's wrist.

"Singer, this is none of yours!" Pauli shouted. Anger had given him back composure of a sort, the hair-trigger readiness to strike, even pointlessly, here in the guardroom. "Back off and leave me go!"

"Sure, you've got the next call up," Singer said, easing his hold enough to defuse the situation without giving the smaller man a chance to make a break for the transfer chamber. "You can handle it, just like you did those calls before—hell, I trained you, didn't I? But now will you let me take care of *my* job, which a follow-up alarm damned well is?"

"What's that?" said Elfen, who had been watching the others struggle with an expression that was more nearly sexual than professional—though he was very good, no question of that, everything Arborson could wish if Arborson had desires. . . .

"I'm senior," Singer explained, using the interruption as cover to maneuver between Pauli and the chamber. "Cohen'd go if I weren't here." And very likely Cohen *would* have made the same split-second decision, had it been Singer out there on the ground; though they had not been friends during their long association, not until this moment when the association was finally terminated.

"Elfen, you're next up if there's a third call," the veteran added, an embellishment to establish the truth of what had gone before. That detail was unnecessary since Singer was already entering the transfer chamber, but it was better not to leave Pauli with the notion that his skill and courage was in doubt. God knew—but there was no god—that the kid would need skill, courage, and all his confidence the next time he did go out.

Maybe Arborson knew, since god did not.

And Singer felt his consciousness pass through the transfer chamber in a series of pin-prick intersections that ended with the breeze on his face and the light of the quarter moon by which he saw as clearly as he could have in sunlight before he became a guard at the Citadel of Arborson.

Singer stood in the first of the four external transfer booths, screened and safe from immediate detection by the intruders—barring hugely bad luck. Bad luck of one sort or another had met Cohen, though; and in any case, the guards liked to be free of the booth's constraints well before intruders were able to penetrate as far as the Citadel itself in the midst of the sprawling grounds. Cohen's failure had cost the remainder of the guard force that edge of time.

The veteran waited only a moment to be sure that there was some distance between the voices he heard and the alcove in which he was sheltered. The sounds were from far enough away that, though they were human, no words could be distinguished. Fair enough. He stepped through the black surface which was in reality an absence of light.

Singer moved quickly and, for a man of his size and bulk, very quietly; but just now, the rustle of oak leaves beneath his boots was not a matter of primary importance. He needed to learn as quickly as possible what had happened to Cohen.

Or rather, *how* it had happened.

The tell-tales in Singer's helmet indicated the external barrier had been breached almost in the center of its northern quadrant. He headed that way, knowing that Cohen would have acted to limit the incursion before he mopped it up.

He had been a rich man, Arborson, in his day, and the grounds of the Citadel were ample to sustain a population of rodents and the foxes that preyed upon them. There was not a great or as varied a number of birds as Singer would have liked, however; though god knew he'd not been a nature-boy before entering the guardroom. The migratory species were unable to leave after Arborson sealed the grounds behind the external barrier, so they died during the three years of brutal winter; and the change from parkland to increasingly dense forest had reduced the supply of seeds for the birds that required them.

There had been hummingbirds when Singer first met Dr. Arborson. Now the guard thought he missed those arrowing, hovering little forms more than anything else in life.

Since he was right-handed, Singer approached the breach clockwise to put the barrier on his left. Counterclockwise felt safer, though it was not: Singer *knew* and acted on that knowledge that nothing outside the barrier could harm him; but emotionally there was still a desire to keep his strong side to a world that was now beyond his conception.

There was a forest of sorts on the other side of the barrier. The germ plasm of plants is far more malleable than that of animal life, and the sleet of radiation had hammered the genes ancestral to the growth outside. The barrier, transparent from within, was hedged with a thousand forms that no botanist of Singer's day would have recognized.

Most of the vegetation was of stunted shapes gnarling across piles of rubble where steel reinforcements retained a dangerous level of atomic warmth even when their structural strength had been oxidized away. There was one tall tree: a pine perhaps and a conifer surely, for cones swelled at intervals from the trunk all the way from the ground to the tip three hundred feet in the air. That height was needless since the giant would have towered above its competitors for light and air at a quarter of its present majesty, but it made an ideal post from which to overlook the sprawling black dome of the Citadel's external barrier.

Perhaps that was why so many of the intrusions into the Citadel grounds were made near the giant trunk, as was this one.

The apparatus piercing the barrier was a wooden frame covered by a mesh of hand-drawn wire. It looked unbelievably crude to have been sufficient for the purpose.

Ages before, there had been men who could carry forward the equations Arborson had published—before he chose to isolate himself on an estate whose defenses were solely physical until the long morning of miniature suns vaporizing stone and steel and bodies all across the world. There were governments then, too, or their semblance, and the sophistication of even a shattered world was quite high when all its resources were marshaled. Arborson's method of withdrawal seemed to offer the one real hope that civilization could survive the holocaust it had brought on itself.

The first intrusion through the barrier had been made with a stressed-wire tube that modified the size and shape of its rhomboidal meshes. Engineers dialed-in the mesh armor so that the fourth man trying to enter was not incinerated in the heart of the barrier as his predecessors had been. He died instead with a bullet through the brain as he squirmed out of the tube. The last of that particular party had been a woman. While her body twitched on the pile of a dozen of her friends, Singer had dragged the tube completely inside the barrier, his ears ringing with the muzzle blasts of his gun.

But later attempts—some of them, at any rate—had the benefit of knowing from the beginning what size and alignment of wires would screen intruders through the barrier. The guards still had advantages over the intruders, among them the fact that ammunition from within the Citadel was trustworthy long after parties of intruders had ceased to carry firearms except for show. Even so, not all the guards had made it through the early days. Singer had, and Cohen; and Cohen's body now was sprawled with an arrow so far through the back of his neck that its barbed point must have been deep in the leaf mold against which his face was buried. His hand was outstretched toward the mesh shield that he had intended to destroy before he hunted down the intruders.

Cohen had always been one to underestimate the competition. He'd been very good, though, good enough to last this long . . . which meant that somewhere in the forest was someone even better.

The arrow itself gave the intruder away. It had slanted down from above when it struck and finished Cohen. Singer knelt, still as a stone, and quartered the treetops with his eyes the way Cohen should have done before assuming that the tube had been left unguarded. At last he found an oak trunk that was as thick above a major crotch as it was below, with a texture that was subtly wrong.

Singer peered carefully at the section of trunk, ten

feet above the ground and twenty from the point at
which Cohen lay. It was covered with inner bark, a
robe woven of cambium and fastened artfully to conceal a human figure. The watcher had held his position after he made his kill instead of rushing down in
a triumph that would have left him cold meat for an
additional opponent.

If all of them were that good, then Pauli was going
to get a chance to try his skills on them after all.

There were two choices, one of them a crossbow
bolt of Singer's own into the intruder: a clout shot at
twenty yards, but risky if the target were armored—
and wasteful if it were not. Singer backed away, even
more cautious than he had been when he made his
final approach to the site of the intrusion. When he
was well beyond risk of alarming the watcher in the
tree by casual noise, he sped back toward the Citadel
proper at a gliding lope.

Besides the watchman at the point they had
entered—and hoped to leave—the Citadel grounds,
the intruders had separated only two men as outliers.
It was a pity that they had not guarded their backtrail
closely, so that Singer could have eliminated more of
their strength before dealing with the main body.

There were something less than a dozen intruders
at the Citadel, their numbers confused by the way
they crowded around the door they were attacking.
That portal had never been satisfactorily repaired
since the afternoon that a new recruit and Spannisky,
one of the original guards, had both died before
Cohen mopped up the party of intruders.

The outliers stood twenty yards deeper in the forest, out of sight of each other and the main body.
The obvious danger of their position was lessened by
the dog each man led, huge animals with the drooping
stance of scent hunters. The hounds' noses were

intended to do what the eyes of the men could not, warn of dangers in the darkness which moonlight could only emphasize in patches through the canopy. There was little undergrowth within the Citadel grounds this late in the summer, because the over-spreading oaks absorbed most of the sunlight that could have nourished lesser vegetation.

One of the outliers stood with his back to a tree bole, stationary but too twitchingly nervous to remain unnoticed even if his hound were not casting between a pair of vole runs at the length of its short lead. The other man was pacing something less formal than a proper guard beat. He seemed to be of a mind that the dog was better able to give warning if it were allowed to roam—albeit in a twenty-yard circuit or less. The pacing man was as nervous as his fellow. He twisted his whole torso back and forth at rapid intervals, obviously terrified that something was creeping up behind him as he followed the hound.

Singer crept carefully into a position from which his exceptional night vision allowed him to see both outliers and the group battering at the Citadel with wedges and hammers besides. The leader of the intruders was huge, taller than Singer and perhaps as solidly muscular in the shoulders and chest. He wore a bark-cloth cape and over it a headdress of black fur. As Singer watched, the man turned from the doorway to the forest and called to the outliers. His fur covering was the pelt of something descended from a domestic cat, a beast that must have weighed twenty-five pounds in life. Now, its eyes replaced by bits of red glass and its jaw gaping—the skull had been retained as support—the cat glared angrily above the harsh face of the man who wore it.

The outlier with his back to the tree glowered as he shouted in reply. His fellow, the man starting at shadows as he paced behind his hound, did not respond to the leader's summons—save by spinning in almost a complete circle at the sound. Neither outlier left his post, so the call must have been meant as encouragement rather than summons. The intruders' speech was too alien for Singer to guess at the language, much less understand it.

This gang would almost certainly be able to gain entrance through the already-weakened section. That, and the way the attacking party kept itself together, gave Singer a workable strategy—though he wished, and not for the first time, that he could have a partner during operations.

But two hands would achieve what four could have made simpler. Singer circled silently through the light brush toward the outlier who kept in motion.

The dog made Singer's task easier because of the false security it gave its master. The outlier passed close to a huge oak as he made his rounds. Singer simply positioned himself behind that tree and waited with his crossbow cocked and poised in his left hand.

As the dog preceded its master down the track they had worn on previous circuits, its big head swung from side to side like a derrick loading freight. Singer, still as the trunk against which he waited, felt the dog's warm breath on his ankle as the animal moved on without taking notice.

The man himself walked by, left wrist wrapped with the end of a five-foot leash and the short spear in his right hand poised to stab. He twisted his head around to be certain there was no bogey approaching—nervousness and not expectation, so that he did not actually see the veteran guard looming behind him. Singer smiled and cut the outlier's throat with a knife whose blade the present age could not have sharpened, much less forged.

The dog turned when its master jerked the lead

reflexively. The crossbow bolt broke both spine and windpipe before the animal could bay a warning.

Beast and man collapsed, thrashing at opposite ends of the leash that still connected them. To Singer, the *bang* of the bow-cord releasing was stunningly loud; but no one else within the Citadel enclosure remarked it.

Singer had to work very quickly now, though the door—even in its present damaged state—should give him some margin. He wiped the blade of his knife carefully before sheathing it, but he ignored the blood which oozed in a bubbling seam from the outlier's throat when Singer lifted him in a fireman's carry. With the corpse's torso across the veteran's broad shoulders, one wrist and ankle gripped to keep the burden anchored, Singer set off at a lope that would bring him to another of the Citadel's entrances without being seen by the main body of intruders. The weight of the dead man made Singer more awkward, but it did not slow him significantly. He liked to feel the play of his muscles under stress.

The Citadel's doorways were unmarked against segments of the building's metal sheath, hidden except to sophisticated equipment. The current party had been guided by the damage earlier intruders had done. Without the guidance, well—the man Singer had just killed carried a stone-tipped spear, and there was not a scrap of metal on his body. It was scarcely credible that such a band could have woven the protective screen with adequate precision. Perhaps the external barrier was losing its effectiveness with the years.

Guards were not meant to worry about that, though it could be that no one else remained. Singer had a momentary vision of a tin can rusting slowly, retaining the appearance of a protective covering long after time had leached away the contents. Then the veteran's

stride took him through the portal, which slid open
at his approach as it was programmed to do.

The part of the Citadel entered through normal
doorways was a bleak warren of conduit-lined halls to
which only necessity could draw Singer. There were
a few cabinets holding special-purpose tools and
weapons beyond those of the kit a guard received
when he went operational. Most of the interior was
closed as firmly to the guards as to intruders who
managed to penetrate the outer shell of the building
by force. Singer sometimes believed that the interior
'rooms' were actually structural elements, supporting
or capping the levels of the Citadel that held whatever
reality Arborson retained. Once before, however,
when he ran past on a mission of slaughter, a blank
wall had become momentarily transparent. Singer had
glimpsed a ballroom and dazzlingly costumed humans.
Under other circumstances, he would have assumed
he was hallucinating—as perhaps he was.

None of the guards had any notion of where the
physical reality of the guardroom might be. Perhaps
it was not even part of the Citadel's structure.

The interior of the Citadel was humidity and temperature controlled, though even that could not prevent the primers of small-arms ammunition from
degrading to the point that guns were useless. The
dispenser spool of beryllium monocrystal that the
guard snatched—wire so fine that spider-silk was
coarse beside it—still had the dull gleam of flawless,
corrosion-free uniformity, however. Singer carried it
with him in his right hand as he ran down the pattern
of long hallways with the corpse jouncing on his
shoulders.

The fact that the intruders' efforts—and even their
voices—were clearly audible on the inner side of the
portal meant the guard had less time to prepare than
he had hoped. The intruders had opened a visible

crack between the door's two leaves and were now attacking the hinges. God knew whether or not folk so primitive could do real damage if they penetrated the shell of the building; but Arborson assumed they might ... or at any rate, no one yet had told the guards that the progressive collapse of civilization had made their services superfluous.

Using the knife with which he had made his kill, Singer butterflied the corpse: splitting the breast-bone the long way and then, with the body faced away from him and his knee on the spine, pulling back on the halves of the rib cage until bones cracked and the sides flapped with no tendency of their own to close over the organs trying to slip from the cavity. He strung the body from an arm-thick pipe running along the axis of the hall a few inches beneath the ceiling.

Singer's hands were slimy with blood and lymph, making the task of threading the wire through back muscles and twice around the spine even harder than the thin wire would have caused it to be. The Citadel had no washing facilities that the guard knew of, and the fact that he was working with a fresh corpse meant that an attempt to cleanse himself would be pointless in any case.

The beryllium filament had a tab on the end so that it could be tracked and handled without special equipment. The monocrystal itself was strong enough to suspend a locomotive, but the guard was very much afraid that a thread so fine would cut even the dense bone of spinal processes under the weight of the dangling corpse. The dispenser hissed as Singer used it to sever and tack-weld the loops he ran off while it automatically fused the new end of the spool into a tab.

Ordinary baling wire would have been better for the present job, thought the big man as he gently let the wire take the full burden of the dead man he had been supporting one-handed; but you use what you've got and the beryllium filament was perfectly satisfactory, despite a minuscule grating sound from the lolling corpse and a squeal from the pipe above.

That was half the job. Singer ran back in the direction by which he had entered. Along the walls quivered patches of torchlight that entered through widening cracks in the door that the intruders were forcing. The guard carried the wire dispenser and the knife which he had not had time to wipe and sheathe again. The light crossbow jounced uncocked from a spring tether on the right side of Singer's belt where it balanced the quiver of bolts on the left. He would need the missile weapon again; but for the moment, the knife would deal with anyone he met as he dashed among the trees on the next stage of his plan to preserve the Citadel—from men who might not be able to harm it, for a man who might for ages have been dead and dust.

How long had it been, anyway? The oaks within the external barrier were protected from lightning and the attendant possibility of fire, so their growth had been stunted by the dense equality of foliage and root systems. There was no way to estimate time's passage from their size. And as for the mad tangle of vegetation beyond the barrier—as well try to count the whorls of a storm cloud.

For now, time meant the minutes remaining before the intruders broke into the Citadel.

Singer tacked a loop of beryllium filament to a fitting in the hallway before he stepped out of the building again. The door closed behind him, tugging at the dispenser. Even the tolerances of the Citadel's undamaged portals were not close enough to sever the monocrystal between their surfaces. With one end anchored immovably, the guard began to wind his lengthy snare among the oaks.

He drew loops of the filament around major trunks, tightly enough that the thin beryllium cut the outer bark and kept the segments of line between trees from sagging. The wire was so fine that, if he had wanted to, Singer could have sawed through the thickest boles with a steady pressure—severing the dense wood like a block of cheddar in a cheese slicer.

The trees were not his objective, of course. He strung his line at slants varying from eighteen to sixty inches above the ground: knee-height to neck of a man bolting between the trees.

The job required extreme care for all the haste. Not even Singer could see the strung filament which hung like the disembodied edge of a razor. If he fell against it, it would slice him to the bone or beyond—and that would keep him from completing his job.

Singer found the remaining outlier no greater problem than he expected. Fear had turned to restive loneliness in the half hour during which the man had been stationed with no company but a hound that was equally bored.

The patches of torchlight which the outlier could see from where he stood, backed still against the tree, were more fleeting and diffuse than those the same fires had flung within the cracking Citadel. It was toward those torches that the intruder turned at last and craned his neck, hoping for a glimpse of his fellows—as the dog tugged its lead in renewed interest and Singer, ten feet away in a thicket of bush honeysuckle, shot the man through the base of the brain.

The hound *woofed* in interrogation, tossing its big head from the slap of the crossbow to the sprawling collapse of the dead man to whom it was still tethered. Singer cared very little about the noise, now that he had strung a ragged line across what the intruders would think was their escape route, and he would have spared the dog if he could . . . but that was not one of the options that Arborson had permitted.

The guard's powerful forearm drew back on the bow's cocking lever while the dog, its flaring nostrils filled with the scent of death, yelped and sprang against its tether. Its last jump was toward Singer, straining so hard that it dragged along the corpse that anchored it. When the hound reached the limit of its attempt and crashed back to the ground, the guard put a bolt through its chest the long way.

Singer had no idea of how many men he had killed, either before the day Arborson hired him or after. He knew that he regretted none of them as much as he did the dog whose nostrils now sprayed bright pulmonary blood across the leaves on which it died.

Even that lengthy paired slaughter of man and beast went unnoticed by the main party in the moment of its own triumph. Metal shrieked from the direction of the Citadel, now out of the veteran's sight. Singer dared not creep closer and chance his own snare, but he flattened himself belly-down on the leaf mold. At the level of the moccasins and bare legs of the intruders, Singer could see them crowding to grip the levers they had wedged between the jamb and door leaves. The locking mechanism failed with a crash. The men gave a great shout and lurched forward, some of them tumbling onto all fours.

The leader with the catskin headdress was one of those who stumbled, though only to his knees. He rose now to his full great height, holding a torch forward in his hand. The bellow of fear from his men was louder even than their triumph of moments before.

Singer took the chance he was offered and snapped a crossbow bolt between the shoulder blades of the leader thirty feet away. The big intruder pitched forward without a sound, while the men he had commanded fled from the mutilated body of the fellow they thought was on guard behind them.

Even in flight, the survivors remained fairly well bunched. They would have been cold meat for an automatic weapon, but the beryllium razor they met at approximately waist height did quite well enough for Singer's purpose.

The wire was stationary and the victims ran slower than a sword could have been swung towards its impact. Even so, the edge the men struck was supernally sharp, and it was anchored with all of the ineluctable solidity of the Earth itself. Men screamed, and those who were able snatched out to free themselves from a gossamer tenuousness that lopped off the fingers terror flung against it.

For choice, Singer would have let the men on the wire wait for an hour or more before he exposed himself, but there was the last intruder yet to deal with—the one stationed at the break in the barrier. The noise of terror and confusion should not draw the watchman from his place even if he heard it; but dangerous as it was to count on an opponent doing the *wrong* thing, it was even more foolish to assume that someone under great stress would carry out each previous order as given.

Singer's time was short. He stepped from cover with his knife ready for use and his bow cocked against possibility.

The blade was enough. None of the men on the wire were by this point any danger to the guard, and only three of them really needed the quick stroke to finish the job. The filament had no barbs, but it cut with crystalline certainty even when a victim tried to withdraw from its invisible embrace. The intruders fumbled and lurched until they bled out. The one man who tore himself free, regardless of the pain, lay sprawled a few feet closer to the Citadel than the others. Those parts of him that had been between his ribs and the cup of his pelvis now lay in a liquid tangle beneath the wire which had skidded across bone as the intruder scooped himself free.

The guard used the dispenser's cutting jaws to sever the filament when he had disposed of the men on it. For choice, he would have clipped each segment of the lethal snare he had hung ... but if Singer were to complete what was now his main task, he did not have time for those details. The irony was not lost on the guard as he strode toward the man who had led the intruders.

The leader had enough life in him to blink when Singer snatched away the catskin headdress. The man had been trying to lift himself or crawl, but his thick fingers had only marked the loam.

The brooch which held the leader's cape at the throat was an elaborate confection of garnets and bits of window glass in a matrix of bitumen. Singer unhooked it and pulled the bark-cloth garment away before he drew his bloody knife across the man's throat. A vein on the bald scalp spasmed as it emptied, and the eyes lost even the film of life they shared with the glass in the cat's sockets.

One to go.

Singer threw the cap across his shoulders and fumbled with the brooch until he had it fastened. The garment stank, but not nearly as much as did the catskin which had been, at least, imperfectly cured before it became a headdress. That mattered as little to Singer as it did to the dead man who once wore it. The guard tossed his helmet to the ground and put the catskin on instead before he set off to meet the remaining intruder.

This time when he ran through the forest, Singer did so with the deliberate intention of making noise.

He flapped through brush too green to crackle and thumped heavily against tree trunks, bellowing wordlessly. His left hand gripped the cape to keep it from opening as he ran, because that would have exposed—among other things—the bloody knife he held blade to the thumb side in the other hand.

As the veteran burst into sight of the barrier, the wire-wrapped cylinder, and Cohen's body, his attention was focused on the intruder waiting in silence for another kill. Singer could not permit the other to know that, however—not until the intruder called to what he thought was his leader, below him and foreshortened by the angle. Singer leaped, his left hand outstretched—sure that he had taken the intruder completely by surprise.

The man's bowstring slapped his bracer as he sent an arrow down at Singer's chest. The point shattered on Singer's ceramic breastplate, but the bastard was very good and the shock of his reaction almost caused the guard to miss his grip on an ankle beneath the camouflaging drapery.

Almost. Singer was very good also.

They tumbled together, the Citadel guard's mass and momentum throwing his slighter opponent like a flail to the threshing floor. Tendons or the fibula cracked in the leg Singer held, and the bow sprang loose when the intruder hit the ground. The cape that had hidden the man fluttered from the tree to which it had been fastened. Without its shrouding, the scars on the intruder's torso and arms stood out sharply. He was missing an ear and the little finger of the hand with which he fumbled for the stone knife in his sash. Even stunned by the fall, the intruder's instincts were everything Death could have wished.

Cohen had picked the wrong time to get impatient . . . but without Cohen's body on the ground for warning, Singer wasn't sure that he couldn't have made as final a mistake himself. He punched the intruder in his jaw, using not his bare hand but the dagger pommel. Bone crunched and the wiry body went loose. The chest still rose.

The framework of the cylinder through which the gang had breached the external barrier was too heavy for even Singer to muscle it fully inside. He gripped a double handful of the wire sheathing instead and pulled on it. The meshes distorted from the precise rhomboids they had been. The currents induced in the barrier's heart ravened through the material: The wooden framework burst into flame and the wires, laboriously drawn and woven, blazed in showers of white sparks in the orange wrapper of the softer fire.

Singer tossed aside the portion of the shielding he held. By the time he next saw it, the metal would have rusted to a flush on the topsoil. Even the tetrahedral bonds of the beryllium monocrystal could, given time, be oxidized. Some day the filament would crumble at a breeze or a raindrop which, like normal light, perpetrated the external barrier unimpeded. As ragged as this party of intruders had been, the Citadel itself might be dust before others gained access ... unless the barrier failed first.

And again, the guardroom might precede the remainder of Arborson's constructs to oblivion.

Singer picked up the intruder whose breath whistled through a nose broken, it seemed, when he hit the ground. The man was smaller than the corpse Singer had used to panic the others, but he was densely muscular and a fair weight. Size was valuable and Singer, a good big man himself, knew that as well as any did. The man who'd put an arrow into Cohen and missed Singer's own throat by a finger's breadth and a millisecond could afford to give a hundred pounds to just about anybody he met, though. Trained to use the weapons of the Citadel—bows better than his, blades better than his dreams, and all the other paraphernalia that remained when time overcame chemistry—the one-time intruder would become a worthy guard for Arborson or Arborson's tomb.

Singer carried the unconscious man back to the transfer booths in the cradle of his big arms, the gentleness a personal whim since he knew that the only requirement was that the subject being recruited remain alive.

The Citadel's front door still gaped, a body before it and a body dangling within. Its repair was no concern for Singer. The conditioning that Arborson's apparatus imparted to the guards locked them within certain strait parameters. Perhaps someone from a place that was not the guardroom would appear to repair the door and dispose of the intruders, men and dogs, whom Singer could not have left alive even if he had wished to do so. A division of labor: those who took care of the Citadel of Arborson . . . and those, Singer and his fellows, who took care of attempts to break into the Citadel.

The big guard stepped through the immaterial curtain hiding the transfer booths. He could scarcely remember the first time he had done so, he and the three others who had hired themselves to guard Feodor Arborson less for the wages he promised than the possibility that the eccentric genius could provide survival in a world that teetered on the brink of a millennium and the abyss.

This much Arborson had provided: survival. He had never said that he was offering life.

The intruder gave a moan that suggested returning consciousness. Singer set him down in the second of the four alcoves. There were oak leaves on the floor, and dust; and among them, a dog-tag that had been Abraham Cohen's. In the first alcove, grating slightly under Singer's feet, was another bit of nickel steel

that time had proven was not stainless. This one gave
Singer's name, his church affiliation—none then and
less than none by now—a serial number in an army
that had not existed for thousands of years, and the
medical data, which had become pointless when
Singer first stood in the transfer booth and died.

"Ready, one and two," he said aloud and felt the
disorientation, familiar by now, as the apparatus of
the Citadel scanned his being and stripped it away
from his body.

The intruder in the second alcove fell silent, though
his autonomic nervous system would keep his heart
and lungs at work for minutes or even hours. What
had been a man was brain dead, a machine running
down.

In the other booth was the form that the Citadel
had provided for Singer's soul to don like a cloak. It
could not be said to have died, because it had never
been truly alive; it was a simulacrum of humanity supplied as equipment, along with the weapons and the
armor. It would not be preserved. An equivalent, like
this one, with no more of the smells and aura of life
than a billet of firewood, would be supplied at future
need—as had happened more times than Singer
could remember.

A titmouse hopped through the light curtain which
it had learned was no real barrier. The bodies were
of no interest to the bird however. It flew out again
when its curiosity had been satisfied.

"Glad to see you, man," said Pauli to Singer, truth-
ful in that as in most things. "And who is it we've
got here?"

"Where am I?" demanded the intruder, wide-eyed
and too shocked to be hostile.

"What's your name, friend?" asked the big guard
as he turned to the newcomer who had exited the

transfer chamber just behind him. "I'm Singer, that's Pauli and—" Elfen nodded his tattooed forehead "—Elfen." Singer offered his hand, hoping the gesture would translate. Language, like his present body, was a construct to the computer of which the guards were a part, but physical actions here had no import but that which the 'watcher' supplied from his own culture.

"My name's Kruse," the wiry recruit said, "but where *am* I?"

"Where?" repeated Elfen. "You're in the guardroom, wherever that is."

Elfen picked up the cards which lay stacked where he had left them. "Do you know how to play poker, Kruse?" he asked, holding the deck to the newcomer and rifling the edges.

"*What?*"

"Oh, don't worry," Singer said tiredly. "You'll have plenty of time to learn."

THE LAST BATTALION

"Well, I'm sorry it stopped working," Senator Stone answered irritably over his shoulder, "but since the late news was one of the things I got a mountain cabin to avoid . . ."

"Well, it is strange," his wife repeated. She was as trim-bodied at fifty as she had been when he married her just after VJ Day, the first time he could think of a future after three years of flying Mustangs into hostile skies. She was still as stubborn as the WAAF he had married, too. "It was fine and then the color went off in flashes and everything got blurry. And it's getting worse, Hershal."

Stone sighed, closing a file that was long, confidential, and involved the potential expenditure of $73,000,000. The cabin's oak flooring had an unexpected tingle as he walked across it in slippers to the small TV. His feet were asleep, he thought; but could they both be? Not that it mattered. He slapped the set while Miriam waited expectantly. The screen continued to match colored pulses to the bursts of raw noise coming from the speaker. Occasionally an intelligible word or a glimpse of Dan Rather slipped through. "Some kind of interference," Stone said. He was six feet tall, with a plumpness that his well-cut suits concealed from the public but was evident in pajamas. His hair had grayed early, but it was still thick and smooth after sixty-one years, no small political asset. Stone was no charmer, but he had learned years before that a man who is honest and has the physical presence to be called forthright will be respected even if he is wrong—and there are never many candidates the voters can respect. Shrugging, he clicked the set off. "If you needed somebody to fix your TV, you should have married some tech boy," he added.

"Instead of my hotshot pilot?" Miriam laughed, stretching out an arm to her husband. She paused as she stood, and at the same moment both realized that the high-pitched keening they had associated with the television was now louder. The hardwood floor carried more of a buzz than a trembling. Miriam's smile froze into a part of her human architecture, like the ferrous curls of hair framing her face.

Earthquake? thought Stone as two strides carried him to the south door. Not in the Smokies, surely; but politics had taught him even more emphatically than combat that there were always going to be facts that surprised you, and that survivors were people who didn't pretend otherwise. He threw the door open. Whipsnake Ridge dropped southward, a sheer medley of grays formed by mist and distance. The sky should have been clear and colorless since the Moon had not yet risen, but an auroral glow was flooding from behind the cabin to paint the night with a score of strange pastels. The whine was louder, but none of the nearby trees were moving.

"Miriam," Stone began, "you'd—"

The rap of knuckles on the north door cut him off.

"I'll get it," Miriam said quickly.

"You'll stay right here!" the senator insisted, striding past her; but her swift heels rapped down the hallway just behind him.

Stone snapped on the entryway light before unlatching the door. The cabin had no windows to the north as the only view would have been the access road and a small clearing in the second-growth pine of the Ridge, a poor exchange for the vicious storms that ripped down in winter. The outside door opened into an anteroom to further insulate the cabin, and that alcove, four feet square in floor plan, was filled by two men in black uniforms.

"You will forgive the intrusion, Senator and Madame Stone," stated the foremost in a rusty voice more used to commands, "but we could not very well contact you in more normal fashion in our haste." The speaker was as tall as Stone, a slim ramrod of a man whose iron-gray hair was cropped so short as to almost be shaven beneath the band of his service hat. The dull cloth of his uniform bagged into jackboots as highly polished as his waist-belt and pistol holster. It was not the pistol, nor the long-magazined rifle the other visitor bore that struck the first real fear into Stone, though: both men wore collar insignia, the twin silver lightning-bolt runes Stone thought he had seen the last of thirty years before. They were the badge of Hitler's SS.

"May we enter?"

"You go straight to Hell!" Stone snarled. His left hand knotted itself in the nearer black shirt while reflex cocked his right for as much of a punch as desks and the poisonous atmosphere of Washington had left him. The second Nazi was as gray as the first and was built like a tank besides, but there was nothing slow about his reactions. The barrel of his rifle slammed down across Stone's forearm. Almost as part of the same motion the stock pivoted into the senator's stomach, throwing him back in a sprawl over Miriam's legs. The entranceway light haloed the huge gunman as he swung his weapon to bear on the tangle of victims almost at its muzzle.

"Lothar!" the slim German shouted.

His subordinate relaxed. "Ja, mein Oberführer," he said as he again ported his rifle.

With a smile that was not wholly one of satisfaction, the black-shirted officer said, "Senator, I am Colonel Ernst Riedel. My companion—what would you say—Master-Sergeant Lothar Mueller and I have reached a respectable age without inflicting our presence on you. I assure you that only necessity causes us to do so now."

Stone rose to his feet. Riedel did not offer a hand he knew would be refused. Miriam remained silent behind her husband, but her right arm encircled his waist. Stone looked from the men to the rifle used to club him down. It was crude, a thing of enameled metal and green-black plastic: an MP-44, built in the final days of the Third Reich. "You're real, aren't you!" the senator said. "You aren't just American slime who wanted something different from white sheets to parade in. Where do you hide, Nazi? Do you sell cars in Rio during the week and take out your uniform Sundays to look at yourself in the mirror?"

"We are real, Senator Stone," Riedel said through his tight smile. He raised his left cuff so that the motto worked on the band there showed. It read "Die Letze" in old-style letters. "We are the Last Battalion, Senator. And as for where we hide—that you will know very shortly, for we were sent to bring you there.

"Madame Stone," he went on formally, "we will have your husband back to you in days if that is possible. I assure you, on my honor as a true Aryan and before the good God and my Leader, that we mean no harm to either of you."

"Oh, I'll trust your honor," Miriam blazed. Fifteen years as a senator's wife had taught her the use of tact, but nothing would ever convince her that every situation should be borne in silence. "How many prisoners did *you* shoot in the back at Malmedy?"

For the first time, Riedel's chalky face pinched up. "It is well for you both, Madame, that Mueller does not speak English." He added, "You may trust my honor or not, as you will. But it is not in our interests alone that we have been sent to you, nor in those alone of the country you represent. If we fail, Senator, there may well in a short time be no Aryan life remaining on Earth."

His hand gestured Stone toward the door. "You will please precede us."

Without hesitation or a backward glance, Stone brushed past the two Germans. Had he looked back he would have called attention to his wife, erect and dry-eyed in the hall. He had known enough killers while he was in service to realize that Mueller's blood-lust was no pretense. The big man had been a finger's pressure away from double murder, and they would not have been his first.

The outside door opened and dragged a gasp from Stone in the rush of warmed air. Instead of the clear night sky, a convex lens of metal roofed the clearing a dozen feet over Stone's head. The size of the clearing gave the object dimension: it was a two-hundred-foot saucer resting on a central gondola and three pillarlike legs spaced halfway between the center and the rim. Through the windows of the gondola could be seen other men, both seated and standing. An incandescent light flooded stairs which extended from the gondola to the ground, but the whole scene was lighted by the burnished iridescence of the saucer itself.

Behind Stone, the Nazi officer laughed. "It is not heat so much as the eddy currents from the electromagnetic motors that make the hull plates glow so handsomely. But walk ahead, please, Senator. She glows as much on the upper side as well and we— we do not wish to attract close attention while we are grounded."

Stone's carpet slippers brushed crisply through the ankle-high grass. The dew that should have gemmed the blades had evaporated under the hot metal lid. Stone always wore slippers and pajamas when he did not expect company, but it was one hell of an outfit in which to take the surrender of a batch of Nazi holdouts in a flying saucer.

Except that Stone knew inside him that men like Riedel were not about to surrender.

"This is Dora, the largest of our experimental models," Riedel said with pride. "She is sheathed with impervium—chromium-vanadium alloy, you perhaps know. There is no limit, nearly, to the speeds at which she may be driven without losing the strength of her hull, even in the thickest of atmospheres."

Closer to the gondola, Stone could see that it rested not on wheels but on inflated rubber cushions that must have been heavily reinforced to bear the weight of the craft. There were small signs of age visible at a nearer glance, too—if Dora was experimental, it was an old experiment. The rectangular windows whose plane surfaces suggested glass or quartz instead of nonrefractive Plexiglas were fogged by tiny pits, and the stair runners appeared to be of several different materials as if there had been replacements over the years. All the men in the gondola were bald or as grayhaired as Mueller and Riedel. The colonel noticed Stone's surprise and said, "Everyone volunteered for the mission, but we Old Fighters, of course, had preference. Everyone here was of my original crew."

The man who reached through the hatch to hasten Stone up the last high step wore gray coveralls from which any insignia had long been removed, though his air of authority was evident. He was not even middle-aged. His hands were thin and gnarled, their hairs gleaming silvery against the age-dappled skin, and the bright lights within the gondola shadowed his wrinkles into a road map through eighty years. His exchange in German with Riedel was quick and querulous. The colonel did not translate for Stone's benefit, but tones and the flash of irritation in the eyes of both men explained more than the bland, "Over-Engineer Tannenberg is anxious that we be under weigh. You will please come with me to the control room. We will have time to discuss matters fully after we have lifted off."

All ice and darkness, the Nazi strode to one of the pair of latticework elevators in the center of the gondola. Flipping one of a bank of switches, toggles instead of buttons, he set the cage in smooth but squealing upward motion. Wholly fascinated, the senator stared around him.

A bell pinged each time the cage rose to another level. Through the sides, Stone saw identical masses of copper and silicon iron, suggesting the inside of a transformer rather than the computer room the craft's gleaming exterior had led him to expect. Narrow gangways threaded into the mass, and twice Stone glimpsed aged men in stained coveralls intent on their hand-held meters. There was nothing subtle in the vessel's layout. It reeked of enormous power as surely as it did of ozone and lubricant. There were eight levels above the gondola, each of them nearly identical to the others, before the cage pinged a ninth time and grated to a stop.

"Sit there, please," Riedel directed, gesturing toward a frame-backed couch that looked unpleasantly like a catafalque. Stone obeyed without comment, his eyes working quickly. They had entered a circular room fifty feet across. Its eight-foot ceiling was soundproofed metal, but the whole circumference was open to the world through crystalline panels like those of the gondola. The saucer, domed with more of a curve on the upper side than the lower, was a fountain of pale iridescence against which the grim SS runes stood out like toppling tombstones.

A dozen preoccupied men shared the control room with Stone and Riedel. Sgt. Mueller was one of them, looking no less dangerous for having put aside his rifle. The others appeared to be officers or gray-suited engineers like Tannenberg. Three of the latter clustered in front of a console far more complex than those sprouting from the deck beside the other benches. One of the men spoke urgently into a throat mike while his companions followed the quivering motions of a hundred dials apiece.

Riedel stood, arms akimbo, and snapped out a brief series of orders. The heavyset man nearest him nodded and began flipping toggles. All three of the engineers were now speaking intently in low voices. Lights dimmed in the control room, and the air began to sing above the range of audibility.

Stone felt his weight shift. Trees climbing into the night slanted and suddenly shrank downward. Stone's cabin was below, now, visible past the glowing dome of the saucer. Lone in the pool of the yard light stood Miriam, waving her clenched right fist. Then the disk tilted again and Stone was driven flat onto his bench by a vertical acceleration not experienced since he had reached the age limit and could no longer zoom-climb a Phantom during Reserve training. The sensation lasted for longer than Stone would have believed possible, and by the time it settled into the queasiness of steady forward motion, the sky had changed. It was black, but less from the absence of light than the utter lack of anything to reflect light.

Riedel was returning. "Not bad," Stone said with a trace of false condescension, "but can you outrun a Nike Zeus?"

"The Russian equivalent, yes indeed, Senator," replied the German, capping Stone's gibe. "Each couch"—his gesture disclosed rubber lips edging the top of the bench—"can enfold a man like an oyster's shell and hold him in a water suspension. For the strongest accelerations we use even a fluid breathing medium, though of course"—and Riedel frowned in concentration at the thought—"that requires time for preparation that we do not always have."

He seated himself beside Stone. The American blinked, more incredulous than angry at what seemed an obvious lie. "You expect me to believe that this— my God, it must weigh a thousand tons! *This* could outaccelerate an antimissile missile?"

Riedel nodded, delighted with the effect he had made. "Yes, yes, the power is here—is it not obvious? That was Schauberger's work, almost entirely. But to make it usable for human beings took our Engineer Tannenberg." The colonel chuckled before adding, "Have you noticed that when men of genius grow old, they become more like old women than even old women do? Tannenberg is afraid every moment we are not aloft that the Russians will catch us."

The earlier name had snagged Stone's attention. "Schauberger?" he repeated. "Sure, I remember him. In the fifties he was touting an implosion motor or some damned thing. I remember a major from Wright-Patterson telling me about it. But then nothing came of it."

"But then your FBI questioned poor Viktor with,

shall we say, a little too much enthusiasm," Riedel corrected with a tolerant smile, "and he was reported beaten to death by Chicago hoodlums. The implosion motor was only a smokescreen though, for the electromagnetic engine he had already developed for his Führer. Think of it, this craft and these mighty engines that you see filling it—able to draw fuel from the Earth, from the very fabric of space itself!"

"If that were true," Stone said carefully, "I frankly don't see why you would need me." He chose his words to deny what he feared, that the story was as solid as the steel floor beneath his feet. To admit that aloud would gratify this colonel whose arrogance only slightly increased the disgust Stone already felt for his uniform.

The implied question reminded the Nazi sickeningly of his mission. He sighed, wondering how much to tell the fellow now. Stone was the only man short of his unapproachable president who had enough power with military and political leaders to act with the necessary swiftness. Without his willing cooperation, more than the whole Plan was a ruin. "At first we were based at Kertl," Riedel began, "where the airframe had been fabricated." He was avoiding a direct answer partly in hope that it would somehow become unnecessary if he explained the background. Riedel owned to few superiors, but there was One— and of late, with age and the pressure He bore most of all of them, that One had displayed an ever-lowering acceptance of failure. "The engines arrived by train, at last, from Obersalzberg, and we worked all night to unload them before the bombers came."

Riedel laid his service cap beside him and scrabbled the fingers of his left hand through hair that for thirty-seven years had been cropped to between five and ten millimeters' length. While everything else had changed, that precision had not. "There was no time

to do what was required—you have seen the
engines—but we did it anyway. It was like shifting
mountains with a spoon to emplace them in the airframe using the equipment we had, and all the work
underground as well. But in those days the impossible
was normal, and we were Waffen-SS. The time that
we had was being bought for us with the lives of
our comrades on the front lines, fighting tanks with
hand grenades."

Of the men in the control room, only Sgt. Mueller
was openly watching Stone and Riedel; but the inat-
tention of the others was the studied sort, that of
jackals waiting for lions to end their meal. All of the
crew understood the importance of their mission.

"The final order came by courier from Berlin, an
SS major with an attaché case in the sidecar of his
motorcycle. It had been chained to his right wrist, he
told us, but the shell that killed his driver had taken
that arm off at the elbow. With teeth and one hand
he had tourniqueted himself before retrieving the
case. The orders were not those we expected, but in
the face of such dedication we could not have
refused them."

"You ran," Stone interjected flatly, knowing that
truth would twist the edged words deeper than any
emphasis he could give them.

"We took off in three hours," the German said, his
face a block of gray iron. "It was the first time, as
soon as final engine hookups had been made. All of
us were aboard, even the kitchen staff. Everything
worked. I could not believe it—five years of design
and construction, and then no flaws. But again, there
was no choice. From the air we could see British
tanks already within three kilometers and nothing but
the forest itself to slow them. Had we left fifteen
minutes later, they might have captured our base
before the demolition charges exploded."

"What you seem to be afraid to admit," Stone pressed, "is that a single plane—saucer, whatever—isn't worth a damn no matter how advanced it is." He stood, a commanding presence again now that he had recovered his poise. The mass and smooth power of the vessel made its speed a matter of only conscious awareness. "It's only a bargaining chip, to be sold to one side or the other since you can't develop it yourself. And we and the Russians both will soon have equipment in the air that will match it, so you're running out of time to deal."

"You are incorrect to assume we are alone," Riedel said, as careful as the American to avoid theatrical emphasis that would only give truth a false patina. "We escaped alone, but there were fifty-three submarines of Type XXI—no, I do not exaggerate—that could run submerged all around the world with their snorkels. They carried above 3,000 persons, couples and young people, out before the Russians captured Danzig; and in Norway they picked up . . . some who had flown by jet out of Tempelhof just at the end."

Stone licked dry lips but his voice was firm as he insisted, "Even then they couldn't go anywhere. I've heard about the money Himmler was spreading around in South America, but even so there wasn't a country there that could have hidden such a fleet without word leaking out. A fleet needs a base."

"It has one." It was time for the final hammerblow of truth. "In New Swabia, where we met them."

"Huh?" grunted Stone, surprised and uncomprehending.

"Imbecile!" snarled the Nazi, seeing all his preparation threatened by his listener's ignorance. "In Antarctica, Queen Maud Land as you and your Allies call it! Kapitan Ritscher explored it in 1937 and we have held the interior since, no matter what color the coast is painted on a pretty map. And there is one other place we have been for twenty years, my good Senator," Riedel said, loudly now and wagging his finger like a pedant's pointer, "though others seem to believe they were the first there."

He paused, breathing very rapidly. "This vessel is not limited to the atmosphere, Senator; indeed, we are above it now to all intents and purposes. We have a base on the Moon where we have manufactured a hundred ships of this design!"

But as Stone's jaw worked in stunned silence, Riedel's pride too dissolved in despair. "We had a hundred, yes," he repeated, "but the Russians have a thousand, and they are destroying us. You must help us fight them, or Aryan man is doomed."

The sky was an emptiness that would have been violet if it had color. Pits on the crystal windows prevented the stars from gaining any real body, but a slight course correction brought the Moon in sight to port. It was gibbous and the gray of fresh-cut lead. "I don't believe that," Stone insisted. "I've made it my business over the years to know about Russian strength. Our intelligence people trust me. They aren't lying to me, and notwithstanding all the nonsense my colleagues and the media like to spout, the Russians aren't fooling our people either. Besides, if the Reds had a whole fleet like this, we'd have learned about it the hard way long since. Unless there's more to détente than *I've* ever believed."

Riedel shrugged. "'When one has eliminated the impossible . . . ,'" he quoted, then paused to consider how he should continue. Stone's logic was impeccable, its only flaw being Russia's unfathomable, senseless subtlety in not showing an apparently pat hand. Riedel had not believed it at first, either, but facts were facts. "At the first reports in 1947, we thought rumors of our Dora, here, were being retailed in garbled form," he explained. "At the time, we had only the one ship—no others had been completed before the final holocaust, and the Antarctic base was not suitable for manufactures this major. It was not until we could process aluminum on the Moon that we could expand, and that was five years later.

"There were too many reports. We were very careful with Dora, you must understand; and though we had our contacts with the world outside, no one beyond the Battalion knew anything except our Plan, to control the balance when at last East and West joined in Götterdämmerung." Riedel's face gleamed with the sweat of earnestness. He brushed at his face and extended both thin hands toward Stone. "Our rocket scientists, you and the Russians had captured; but we thought all but the least word of the Diskus Projekt had been hidden. Now we began to fear that the other sightings were more than imagination, and that our secret had escaped."

"You never saw them yourselves?" Stone asked. "The other UFOs, I mean?"

"I did," Riedel said, pride warming his words. "We had completed the first disk to be built on the Moon and I was flight-testing it. Because we expected fleet maneuvers in the future, Engineer Tannenberg had coupled a locator to the engines to display other users of the spectrum—our own vessels, we intended. But as we began our first atmospheric approach—" and Riedel lived again the moments as he described them to Stone:

In a voice as wizened as his face, Tannenberg had announced, "Colonel, there is another ship within a kilometer, at five degrees to our heading and a little lower."

"Nonsense!" Riedel snapped. At thirty kilometers altitude their test craft could have encountered only

Dora, and she would have been a bright dot on their radar screen.

A bead glared suddenly against the screen's green background. It was near them, much closer than it should have been before being picked up in the radar's fifteen-second sweep. "Navigation!" he called, his temper that of a wounded bear looking for a victim. First trial of the new hull in the pressures and powerful magnetic fields of Earth was a tense enough business without having unknown vessels slip through undetected.

"S-sir," said the white-faced technician at the main radar display, "it just now appeared."

"Colonel," Sgt. Mueller said, his hair-spined forefinger pointing downward into the blue-white haze into which their craft was descending. Metal winked, a reflection with no definable color.

"It's off the screen again!" the fearful radarman was bleating, but Riedel's voice cut through his junior's without hesitation: "Attention! All crewmen to acceleration couches! Sergeant Mueller, arm the rockets and stand by." Disconnecting his throat mike, for he spoke to himself rather than his men, Riedel added, "They think to play with us, do they? Well then, we will play with them."

Only Sgt. Mueller heard, and he grinned a wolf's grin as he ran his hands over the switches of his console.

At 300 meters, the black, portless hull of the foreign disk was stark against the sky-curve beyond. It bore no marking. Both craft were steady at a little over 1800 kph, far below the capacity of Riedel's engines. This was not his Dora, though, he thought with rage. Impervium hulls were beyond their ability to forge on the Moon—or on Earth without arousing the interest of the nations who had to be lulled into forgetfulness. Aluminum was cheap, given lunar ores and abundant power, but the new hulls could not stand the friction heating of 4,000 kph or more in the atmosphere.

"Unknown craft, identify yourself," Riedel ordered in German. He was broadcasting only on eleven meters, but with a 10 kw transmitter driving his beam, even the light bulbs on the other craft would be repeating his words.

There was no response. He tried again in English, for they were over northern Canada. All his subordinates but Mueller had slipped into their clamshell couches, taking their information from the gauges slaved into the panels over their faces. Riedel started to rebuke the sergeant, then realized that with the enemy able to evade radar, only visual control could be used for the rockets.

And there seemed little doubt that the black disk was an enemy. "Does anyone aboard speak Russian?" No one answered. Besides, what did they have to discuss with the conquerors of Berlin? "Fire one, sergeant," Riedel said evenly.

Mueller's finger stroked a 20 cm rocket from the ventral weapons bay. Its hundred kilos of explosive could be wire-guided 5,000 meters, but the gap between the two ships was point-blank range.

The charge went off scarcely halfway to the black vessel.

The spurt of red on black smoke, half a second early, was a greater surprise to Riedel than the howl of air through the fragment-riddled panels before him. The missile's own fuse should not have armed at so short a distance. Something invisible surrounding the other craft had detonated the weapon while it was almost as dangerous to its user as its target, and the target was diving away. Riedel followed, ignoring for the moment the stresses to which he was subjecting his ship and his own unshielded body. Sgt. Mueller had yanked down a whole handful of switches and four guidance flares leaped together after the black craft. It wobbled under the multiple shockwave, but a beam as pale as an icteric sclera needled back from its dome. Riedel saw the hull directly in front of him boil away as the laser struck it. His instant course change bagged his cheeks and flattened his eyeballs. The black vessel did not attempt pursuit.

The executive officer in his acceleration couch had taken over when Riedel regained full consciousness. They had resumed their planned course toward Antarctica, flying below 2,500 meters because of the gashed hull. Sgt. Mueller was clenching his hands in fierce frustration. "We need something better to kill them with," he kept repeating.

"And we got it," Riedel concluded, affect raining out of his voice. "Tannenberg said his detector could easily be modified to cause a surge in other electromagnetic engines, to cause them to vaporize. For twenty-three years he was right and we hunted the Russians throughout space. There were losses, since their lasers could very quickly slit the hulls of the ships we built—not a bad weapon, lasers; we might have fitted our bases with them sooner had not Tannenberg's induced overloads left so little of their targets." He paused in an aura of satisfaction, looking out over the clean, black sky but seeing something very different. "From a pip of light the disks we destroy become great expanding balls that are all the colors of the rainbow. In atmosphere even the copper burns, so intense is the energy released."

"You bastards," Stone said with utter conviction. "I wonder if you'll find it so pretty when *they* come up with your gadget?"

"Colonel, we are closing with another vessel," broke in one of the crewmen.

"It may be ours. We were to have an escort when

we reached open sea, if the situation permitted it," Riedel replied on his throat mike. To Stone he continued, "The Russians are an ignorant people, able only to steal from their betters. In all that time they have not duplicated the weapon."

He took a deep breath, adding, "But six months ago, they found a defense against it. And since then only the few lasers for which we have been able to buy components have kept them from our bases."

"You can't be serious," Stone said. But Riedel's mind was like his body—gray and honed and rigid. He could no more accept the superiority of an "under race" than could a computer which had been misprogrammed to deny it. That quirk has caused Riedel and his men to ignore the obvious. "Look, lasers—I don't know how long we've had them, but they weren't weapons back in 1950. And this detonator screen or whatever, *we* damned well don't have it now. If—"

"Colonel! The ship is not one of ours. It is closing!"

"Couches!" Riedel ordered. He stood, pressing as he did the switch that turned Stone's bench into an enveloping cushion. "Raise your legs and lie down, Senator. The television will show you what occurs, and we will release you as soon as possible."

The hull curve, a smooth violet as Riedel strode to his station, suddenly blazed white in a meter-long knife edge. The impervium alloy held, but Dora's evasive action in response to the laser thrust hurled the slender officer to the deck. He gripped a chart table, then let skewed acceleration fling him in the direction he wanted to go. He was safely within his couch before the third zigzag snatched at him.

"Riedel," he announced, "taking command." His fingers caressed switches they knew by touch. The enemy craft was an eddy in the frozen blue swirls of Earth's magnetic fields pictured on the detector screen. Riedel set the television cameras to track the detector anomally though he would not need the picture. By the time Dora had been retrofitted with television, he was used to being guided to battle by the detector alone. And even with their surge weapon ineffective, there would still be a battle with Riedel at the controls. He knew his Dora.

The other craft was within two kilometers now. It fingered Dora's hull with another short burst, probably unaware that its target was more refractory than earlier victims. The Nazi commander's face was a grinning death's head within his couch as he cut forward thrust and flipped Dora to spin like a coin toward the icecap twenty kilometers below. The blue eddy danced around the center of the detector screen and the TV began to flash images of a black disk seeming to approach at a thousand angles. Fluid-filled membranes clamped down on every surface of Riedel's body, but still the maddening spin worked on his ear canals and the colloid of his brain itself.

The eddy was almost in the center of the detector. Riedel's fingers acted more through instinct than by conscious calculation. On the television, the spinning edge of the black vessel froze and expanded. There was a terrible, rending crash as Dora's impervium edge buzz sawed into the unknown material of her enemy's hull. A sheet of white fire enveloped both craft as the chrome-van alloy proved tougher than what it impacted. Objects vomited from the spiraling gash in the hostile craft. One of them tumbled almost against Dora, now motionless as her enemy fell away from her. The thing was momentarily alive and quite visible on the television screens. It was about nine feet tall, with four limbs that looked like ropes knotted over a thin framework. Its mouth was working and its eyes glittered fear of death through each of their facets.

"You butchers," a voice rasped through Riedel's

earphones. His anger awakened him to the fact that he still had Dora to pilot, and the anger faded when he realized it was the American who had spoken and not one of his crewmen. "It wasn't enough to fight the whole rest of the world. You Nazis had to start an interstellar war."

There was an air leak between compartments F-87 and F-88; a bulkhead had crumpled but the outer skin, though indented, was not seriously torn. Riedel touched switches. As his acceleration couch withdrew into itself, Dora plunged down as smoothly as an elevator and swiftly enough that her passengers neared the weightlessness of free fall.

"Murderers! Criminals!"

Riedel ripped out the jack of his headset. In two steps he had snapped the outside latch on Stone's couch, effectively silencing and isolating the senator. "Lieutenant Wittvogel," he ordered, "raise the base. Secrecy is no longer necessary."

"No reply, sir," the tall communications officer called across the room. "Not even to the emergency signal."

"We're within fifty kilometers," Riedel said, but he spoke under his breath. "Keep trying," he ordered.

With an atmosphere to scatter it, sunlight and its reflection from the ice below blazed through the windows. The computer installed three years earlier—a massive thing, not a sophisticated "black box"; but Dora was not a volume-starved turbojet—was guiding them back at 3,000 kph and there was no need for Riedel to stare tensely into the rippling whiteness they skimmed. Beside him stood Sgt. Mueller, as silent as a bored sentry. He had been out of his couch before his commander. When Stone had been locked in, Mueller's responsibility had ended and he had relaxed with a grin. Even so, it was his ease rather than Riedel's stark anticipation that caught the first sight of the base.

"Sir, there's something ahead there that glows!"

Riedel took instant manual control, cutting speed and raising Dora to a kilometer's altitude. They circled the glow, banked inward for observation rather than flight necessity. A hole had been blasted in the ice, four kilometers across and of a depth obscured by the boiling lake that snarled at its rim.

"The Führer," Sgt. Mueller whispered. He jackknifed and vomited across the deck plates. Lt. Wittvogel had hurled away his microphone and, like several of his fellow crewmen, was openly weeping. Riedel himself was the least visibly affected, but as he unlatched Stone's prison he muttered, "I wonder if he taught them about the Bomb, too. They were such bad fighters, no instinct for it at all . . ."

Riedel was back at the controls, following at full speed and a kilometer's altitude the brown rim of beach against gray-green water, when Stone touched his shoulder. "You're done now, aren't you?" the American said softly.

"He could have escaped. He could be at the Moon base now—perhaps they had only one bomb. He—" Riedel's throat choked him into sudden silence.

"He?" Stone echoed. His face went as white and cold as the ice below. "I fought three years for a chance to kill—that one. If these others have done that, they have my thanks. Whatever else they intend."

On the horizon was a small freighter static in the shadow of shear, snow-browed cliffs. Inshore of it were a huddle of Quonset huts set in a splotch of snow dirtied by human habitation. "I swore an oath to your wife," Riedel forced out through tight lips, "and I would prefer to keep it. But if you say another word, Senator, you will go out at a thousand meters."

The landing legs squealed while Riedel's practiced fingers brought the disk to a hover over the Quonsets. "Wohlman," the colonel ordered abruptly, and his executive officer took the controls with a nod.

"What will you do now?" Stone asked as he stepped to the elevator in anticipation of a command.

"The Moon base will need us," Riedel said, his black and silver chest separated from the American's by an invisible wall of grief.

"If it's still there. They would have hit it first, wouldn't they?"

The cage ground to a halt in the observation gondola. The four men there were tense, hands close to their sidearms. "Inform your people, Senator," Riedel said. He riffled a worn, mimeographed book, then handed it to Stone. "Our maintenance manual. Perhaps your experts can construct their own disks from it. I have nothing better to offer you here."

Men in furs were running out of the huts. A blast of dry, chill air hammered the compartment as the hatch opened and the stairway extended. "These are Argentinians. At this time of year you should have no trouble getting a swift return to your country."

"But what are you going to do?" Stone insisted, the rubberized treads warm under his feet though the wind was a knife across the rest of his body.

Riedel's eyes, colder than the ice, thrust the American down the gangway. "Do?" he repeated. "We are SS, Senator. We will continue to fight."

Dora was rising again even before the stairs had fully retracted. A dozen startled Argentinians clustered around Stone, their parka fringes blending indistinguishably with their bushy facial hair. Around them all a huge disk had been etched in the powdered snow by the radiant metal above it.

The Antarctic sky was clear, except for a speck that vanished even as Stone's eyes followed it upward.

SOMETHING HAD TO BE DONE

"He was out in the hall just a minute ago, sir," the pinched-faced WAC said, looking up from her typewriter in irritation. "You can't mistake his face."

Capt. Richmond shrugged and walked out of the busy office. Blinking in the dim marble were a dozen confused civilians, bussed in for their pre-induction physicals. No one else was in the hallway. The thick-waisted officer frowned, then thought to open the door of the men's room. "Sergeant Morzek?" he called.

Glass clinked within one of the closed stalls and a deep voice with a catch in it grumbled, "Yeah, be right with you." Richmond thought he smelled gin.

"You the other ghoul?" the voice questioned as the stall swung open. Any retort Richmond might have made withered when his eyes took in the cadaverous figure in ill-tailored greens. Platoon sergeant's chevrons on the sleeves, and below them a longer row of service stripes than the captain remembered having seen before. God, this walking corpse might have served in World War II! Most of the ribbons ranked

209

above the sergeant's breast pockets were unfamiliar, but Richmond caught the Silver Star. Even in these medal-happy days in Southeast Asia they didn't toss many of those around.

The sergeant's cheeks were hollow, his fingers grotesquely thin where they rested on top of the door or clutched the handles of his zippered AWOL bag. Where no moles squatted, his skin was as white as a convict's; but the moles were almost everywhere, hands and face, dozens and scores of them, crowing together in welted obscenity.

The sergeant laughed starkly. "Pretty, aren't I? The docs tell me I got too much sun over there and it gave me runway warts. Hell, four years is enough time for it to."

"Umm," Richmond grunted in embarrassment, edging back into the hall to have something to do. "Well, the car's in back . . . if you're ready, we can see the Lunkowskis."

"Yeah, Christ," the sergeant said, "that's what I came for, to see the Lunkowskis." He shifted his bag as he followed the captain and it clinked again.

Always before, the other man on the notification team had been a stateside officer like Richmond himself. He had heard that a few low-casualty outfits made a habit of letting whoever knew the dead man best accompany the body home, but this was his first actual experience with the practice. He hoped it would be his last.

Threading the green Ford through the heavy traffic of the city center, Richmond said, "I take it Pfc Lunkowski was one of your men?"

"Yeah, Stevie-boy was in my platoon for about three weeks," Morzek agreed with a chuckle. "Lost six men in that time and he was the last. Six out of twenty-nine, not very damn good, was it?"

"You were under heavy attack?"

"Hell, no, mostly the dinks were letting us alone for a change. We were out in the middle of War Zone C, you know, most Christ-bitten stretch of country you ever saw. No dinks, no trees—they'd all been defoliated. Not a damn thing but dust and each others company."

"Well, what did happen?" Richmond prompted impatiently. Traffic had thinned somewhat among the blocks of old buildings and he began to look for house numbers.

"Oh, mostly they just died," Morzek said. He yawned alcoholically. "Stevie, now, he got blown to hell by a grenade."

Richmond had learned when he was first assigned to notification duty not to dwell on the ways his . . . missions had died. The possibilities varied from unpleasant to ghastly. He studiously avoided saying anything more to the sergeant beside him until he found the number he wanted. "One-sixteen. This must be the Lunkowskis.' "

Morzek got out on the curb side, looking more skeletal than before in the dappled sunlight. He still held his AWOL bag.

"You can leave that in the car," Richmond suggested. "I'll lock up."

"Naw, I'll take it in," the sergeant said as he waited for Richmond to walk around the car. "You know, this is every damn thing I brought from Nam? They didn't bother to open it at Travis, just asked me what I had it in. 'A quart of gin,' I told 'em, 'but I won't have it long,' and they waved me through to make my connections. One advantage to this kind of trip."

A bell chimed far within the house when Richmond pressed the button. It was cooler than he had expected on the pine-shaded porch. Miserable as these high, dark old houses were to heat, the design made a world of sense in the summer.

A light came on inside. The stained glass window left of the door darkened and a latch snicked open. "Please to come in," invited a soft-voiced figure hidden by the dark oak panel. Morzek grinned inappropriately and led the way into the hall, brightly lighted by an electric chandelier.

"Mr. Lunkowski?" Richmond began to the wispy little man who had admitted them. "We are—"

"But yes, you are here to tell us when Stefan shall come back, are you not?" Lunkowski broke in. "Come into the sitting room, please, Anna and my daughter Rose are there."

"Ah, Mr. Lunkowski," Richmond tried to explain as he followed, all too conscious of the sardonic grin on Morzek's face, "you have been informed by telegram that Pfc Lunkowski was—"

"Was killed, yes," said the younger of the two red-haired women as she got up from the sofa. "But his body will come back to us soon, will he not? The man on the telephone said . . . ?"

She was gorgeous, Richmond thought, cool and assured, half smiling as her hair cascaded over her left shoulder like a thick copper conduit. Disconcerted as he was by the whole situation, it was a moment before he realized that Sgt. Morzek was saying, "Oh, the coffin's probably at the airport now, but there's nothing in it but a hundred and fifty pounds of gravel. Did the telegram tell you what happened to Stevie?"

"Sergeant!" Richmond shouted. "You drunken—"

"Oh, calm down, Captain," Morzek interrupted bleakly. "The Lunkowskis, they understand. They want to hear the whole story, don't they?"

"Yes." There was a touch too much sibilance in the word as it crawled from the older woman, Stafan Lunkowski's mother. Her hair was too grizzled now to have more than a touch of red in it, enough to rust the tight ringlets clinging to her skull like a helmet of mail. Without quite appreciating its importance, Richmond noticed that Mr. Lunkowski was standing in front of the room's only door.

With perfect nonchalance, Sgt. Morzek sat down on an overstuffed chair, laying his bag across his knees. "Well," he said, "there was quite a report on that one. We told them how Stevie was trying to boobytrap a white phosphorous grenade—fix it to go off as soon as some dink pulled the pin instead of four seconds later. And he goofed."

Mrs. Lunkowski's breath whistled out very softly. She said nothing. Morzek waited for further reaction before he smiled horribly and added, "He burned. A couple pounds of willie pete going blooie, well . . . it keeps burning all the way through you. Like I said, the coffin's full of gravel."

"My god, Morzek," the captain whispered. It was not the sergeant's savage grin that froze him but the icy-eyed silence of the three Lunkowskis.

"The grenade, that was real," Morzek concluded. "The rest of the report was a lie."

Rose Lunkowski reseated herself gracefully on a chair in front of the heavily draped windows. "Why don't you start at the beginning, sergeant?" she said with a thin smile that did not show her teeth. "There is much we would like to know before you are gone."

"Sure," Morzek agreed, tracing a mottled forefinger across the pigmented callosities on his face. "Not much to tell. The night after Stevie got assigned to my platoon, the dinks hit us. No big thing. Had one fellow dusted off with brass in his ankle from his machine gun blowing up, that was all. But a burst of AK fire knocked Stevie off his tank right at the start."

"What's all this about?" Richmond complained. "If he was killed by rifle fire, why say a grenade—"

"Silence!" The command crackled like heel plates on concrete.

Sgt. Morzek nodded. "Why, thank you, Mr. Lun-kowski. You see, the captain there doesn't know the bullets didn't hurt Stevie. He told us his flak jacket had stopped them. It couldn't have and it didn't. I saw it that night, before he burned it—five holes to stick your fingers through, right over the breast pocket. But Stevie was fine, not a mark on him. Well, Christ, maybe he'd had a bandolier of ammo under the jacket. I had other things to think about."

Morzek paused to glance around his audience. "All this talk, I could sure use a drink. I killed my bottle back at the Federal Building."

"You won't be long," the girl hissed in reply.

Morzek grinned. "They broke up the squadron, then," he rasped on, "gave each platoon a sector of War Zone C to cover to stir up the dinks. There's more life on the moon than there was on the stretch we patrolled. Third night out, one of the gunners died. They flew him back to Saigon for an autopsy but damned if I know what they found. Galloping malaria, we figured.

"Three nights later another guy died. Dawson on three-six . . . Christ, the names don't matter. Some time after midnight his track commander woke up, heard him moaning. We got him back to Quan Loi to a hospital, but he never came out of it. The lieutenant thought he got wasp stung on the neck—here, you know?" Morzek touched two fingers to his jugular. "Like he was allergic. Well, it happens."

"But what about Stefan?" Mrs. Lunkowski asked. "The others do not matter."

"Yes, finish it quickly, sergeant," the younger woman said, and this time Richmond did catch the flash of her teeth.

"We had a third death," Morzek said agreeably, stroking the zipper of his AWOL bag back and forth. "We were all jumpy by then. I doubled the guard, two men awake on every track. Three nights later and nobody in the platoon remembered anything from twenty-four hundred hours till Riggs' partner blinked at ten of one and found him dead.

"In the morning, one of the boys came to me. He'd seen Stevie slip over to Riggs, he said; but he was zonked out on grass and didn't think it really had happened until he woke up in the morning and saw Riggs under a poncho. By then, he was scared enough to tell the whole story. Well, we were all jumpy."

"You killed Stefan." It was not a question but a flat statement.

"Oh, hell, Lunkowski," Morzek said absently, "what does it matter who rolled the grenade into his bunk? The story got around and . . . something had to be done."

"Knowing what you know, you came here?" Mrs. Lunkowski murmured liquidly. "You must be mad."

"Naw, I'm not crazy, I'm just sick." The sergeant brushed his left hand over his forehead. "Malignant melanoma, the docs told me. Twenty-six years in the goddam army and in another week or two I'd be *warted* to death.

"Captain," he added, turning his cancerous face toward Richmond, "you better leave through the window."

"Neither of you will leave!" snarled Rose Lunkowski as she stepped toward the men.

Morzek lifted a fat gray cylinder from his bag. "Know what this is, honey?" he asked conversationally.

Richmond screamed and leaped for the window. Rose ignored him, slashing her hand out for the phosphorous grenade. Drapery wrapping the captain's body shielded him from glass and splintered window frame as he pitched out into the yard.

He was still screaming there when the blase of white fire bulged the walls of the house.

THE TANK LORDS

They were the tank lords.

The Baron had drawn up his soldiers in the courtyard, the twenty men who were not detached to his estates on the border between the Kingdom of Ganz and the Kingdom of Marshall—keeping the uneasy truce and ready to break it if the Baron so willed.

I think the King sent mercenaries in four tanks to our palace so that the Baron's will would be what the King wished it to be ... though of course we were told they were protection against Ganz and the mercenaries of the Lightning Division whom Ganz employed.

The tanks and the eight men in them were from Hammer's Slammers, and they were magnificent.

Lady Miriam and her entourage rushed back from the barred windows of the women's apartments on the second floor, squealing for effect. The tanks were so huge that the mirror-helmeted men watching from the turret hatches were nearly on a level with the upper story of the palace.

I jumped clear, but Lady Miriam bumped the chair

217

I had dragged closer to stand upon and watch the arrival over the heads of the women I served.

"Leesh!" cried the Lady, false fear of the tanks replaced by real anger at me. She slapped with her fan of painted ox-horn, cutting me across the knuckles because I had thrown a hand in front of my eyes.

I ducked low over the chair, wrestling it out of the way and protecting myself with its cushioned bulk. Sarah, the Chief Maid, rapped my shoulder with the silver-mounted brush she carried for last-minute touches to the Lady's hair. "A monkey would make a better page than you, Elisha," she said. "A gelded monkey."

But the blow was a light one, a reflexive copy of her mistress' act. Sarah was more interested in reclaiming her place among the others at the windows now that modesty and feminine sensibilities had been satisfied by the brief charade. I didn't dare slide the chair back to where I had first placed it; but by balancing on tiptoes on the carven arms, I could look down into the courtyard again.

The Baron's soldiers were mostly off-worlders themselves. They had boasted that they were better men than the mercenaries if it ever came down to cases. The fear that the women had mimed from behind stone walls seemed real enough now to the soldiers whose bluster and assault rifles were insignificant against the iridium titans which entered the courtyard at a slow walk, barely clearing the posts of gates which would have passed six men marching abreast.

Even at idle speed, the tanks roared as their fans maintained the cushions of air that slid them over the ground. Three of the Baron's men dodged back through the palace doorway, their curses inaudible over the intake whine of the approaching vehicles.

The Baron squared his powerful shoulders within

his dress cloak of scarlet, purple, and gold. I could not see his face, but the back of his neck flushed red and his left hand tugged his drooping moustache in a gesture as meaningful as the angry curses that would have accompanied it another time.

Beside him stood Wolfitz, his Chamberlain; the tallest man in the courtyard; the oldest; and, despite the weapons the others carried, the most dangerous.

When I was first gelded and sold to the Baron as his Lady's page, Wolfitz had helped me continue the studies I began when I was training for the Church. Out of his kindness, I thought, or even for his amusement ... but the Chamberlain wanted a spy, or another spy, in the women's apartments. Even when I was ten years old, I knew that death lay on that path—and life itself was all that remained to me.

I kept the secrets of all. If they thought me a fool and beat me for amusement, then that was better than the impalement which awaited a boy who was found meddling in the affairs of his betters.

The tanks sighed and lowered themselves the last finger's breadth to the ground. The courtyard, clay and gravel compacted over generations to the density of stone, crunched as the plenum-chamber skirts settled visibly into it.

The man in the turret of the nearest tank ignored the Baron and his soldiers. Instead, the reflective face shield of the tanker's helmet turned and made a slow, arrogant survey of the barred windows and the women behind them. Maids tittered; but the Lady Miriam did not, and when the tanker's face shield suddenly lifted, the mercenary's eyes and broad smile were toward the Baron's wife.

The tanks whispered and pinged as they came into balance with the surroundings which they dominated. Over those muted sounds, the man in the turret of the second tank to enter the courtyard called, "Baron

Hetziman, I'm Lieutenant Kiley and this is my number two—Sergeant Commander Grant. Our tanks have been assigned to you as a Protective Reaction Force until the peace treaty's signed."

"You do us honor," said the Baron curtly. "We trust your stay with us will be pleasant as well as short. A banquet—"

The Baron paused, and his head turned to find the object of the other tanker's attention.

The lieutenant snapped something in a language that was not ours, but the name "Grant" was distinctive in the sharp phrase.

The man in the nearest turret lifted himself out gracefully by resting his palms on the hatch coaming and swinging up his long, powerful legs without pausing for footholds until he stood atop the iridium turret. The hatch slid shut between his booted feet. His crisp moustache was sandy blond, and the eyes which he finally turned on the Baron and the formal welcoming committee were blue. "Rudy Grant at your service, Baron," he said, with even less respect in his tone than in his words.

They did not need to respect us. They were the tank lords.

"We will go down and greet our guests," said the Lady Miriam, suiting her actions to her words. Even as she turned, I was off the chair, dragging it toward the inner wall of imported polychrome plastic.

"But, Lady . . . ," said Sarah nervously. She let her voice trail off, either through lack of a firm objection or unwillingness to oppose a course on which her mistress was determined.

With coos and fluttering skirts, the women swept out the door from which the usual guard had been removed for the sake of the show in the courtyard. Lady Miriam's voice carried back: "We were to meet them at the banquet tonight. We'll just do so a little earlier."

If I had followed the women, one of them would have ordered me to stay and watch the suite—though everyone, even the tenants who farmed the plots of the home estate here, was outside watching the arrival of the tanks. Instead, I waited for the sounds to die away down the stair tower—and I slipped out the window.

Because I was in a hurry, I lost one of the brass buttons from my jacket—my everyday livery of buff; I'd be wearing the black plush jacket when I waited in attendance at the banquet tonight, so the loss didn't matter. The vertical bars were set close enough to prohibit most adults, and few of the children who could slip between them would have had enough strength to then climb the bracing strut of the roof antenna, the only safe path since the base of the West Wing was a thicket of spikes and razor ribbon.

I was on the roof coping in a matter of seconds, three quick hand-over-hand surges. The women were only beginning to file out through the doorway. Lady Miriam led them, and her hauteur and lifted chin showed she would brook no interference with her plans.

Most of the tankers had, like Grant, stepped out of their hatches, but they did not wander far. Lieutenant Kiley stood on the sloping bow of his vehicle, offering a hand which the Baron angrily refused as he mounted the steps recessed into the tank's armor.

"Do you think I'm a child?" rumbled the Baron, but only his pride forced him to touch the tank when the mercenary made a hospitable offer. None of the Baron's soldiers showed signs of wanting to look into the other vehicles. Even the Chamberlain, aloof if not afraid, stood at arm's length from the huge tank which even now trembled enough to make the setting sun quiver across the iridium hull.

Because of the Chamberlain's studied unconcern about the vehicle beside him, he was the first of the welcoming party to notice Lady Miriam striding toward Grant's tank, holding her skirts clear of the ground with dainty, bejeweled hands. Wolfitz turned to the Baron, now leaning gingerly against the curve of the turret so that he could look through the hatch while the lieutenant gestured from the other side. The Chamberlain's mouth opened to speak, then closed again deliberately.

There were matters in which he too knew better than to become involved.

One of the soldiers yelped when Lady Miriam began to mount the nearer tank. She loosed her dress in order to take the hand which Grant extended to her. The Baron glanced around and snarled an inarticulate syllable. His wife gave him a look as composed as his was suffused with rage. "After all, my dear," said the Lady Miriam coolly, "our lives are in the hands of these brave men and their amazing vehicles. Of *course* I must see how they are arranged."

She was the King's third daughter, and she spoke now as if she were herself the monarch.

"That's right, milady," said Sergeant Grant. Instead of pointing through the hatch, he slid back into the interior of his vehicle with a murmur to the Lady.

She began to follow.

I think Lady Miriam and I, alone of those on the estate, were not nervous about the tanks for their size and power. I loved them as shimmering beasts, whom no one could strike in safety. The Lady's love was saved for other subjects.

"Grant, that won't be necessary," the lieutenant called sharply—but he spoke in our language, not his own, so he must have known the words would have little effect on his subordinate.

The Baron bellowed, *"Mir—"* before his voice caught. He was not an ungovernable man, only one whose usual companions were men and women who lived or died as the Baron willed. The Lady squeezed flat the flounces of her skirt and swung her legs within the hatch ring.

"Murphy," called the Baron to his chief of soldiers. "Get up there with her." The Baron roared more often than he spoke quietly. This time his voice was not loud, but he would have shot Murphy where he stood if the soldier had hesitated before clambering up the bow of the tank.

"Vision blocks in both the turret and the driver's compartment," said Lieutenant Kiley, pointing within his tank, "give a three-sixty-degree view at any wavelength you want to punch in."

Murphy, a grizzled man who had been with the Baron a dozen years, leaned against the turret and looked down into the hatch. Past him, I could see the combs and lace of Lady Miriam's elaborate coiffure. I would have given everything I owned to be there within the tank myself—and I owned nothing but my life.

The hatch slid shut. Murphy yelped and snatched his fingers clear.

Atop the second tank, the Baron froze and his flushed cheeks turned slatey. The mercenary lieutenant touched a switch on his helmet and spoke too softly for anything but the integral microphone to hear the words.

The order must have been effective, because the hatch opened as abruptly as it has closed—startling Murphy again.

Lady Miriam rose from the turret on what must have been a power lift. Her posture was in awkward contrast to the smooth ascent, but her face was composed. The tank and its apparatus were new to the Lady, but anything that could have gone on within the shelter of the turret was a familiar experience to her.

"We have seen enough of your equipment," said the Baron to Lieutenant Kiley in the same controlled voice with which he had directed Murphy. "Rooms have been prepared for you—the guest apartments alongside mine in the East Wing, not the barracks below. Dinner will be announced—" he glanced at the sky. The sun was low enough that only the height of the tank's deck permitted the Baron to see the orb above the courtyard wall "—in two hours. Make yourselves welcome."

Lady Miriam turned and backed her way to the ground again. Only then did Sergeant Grant follow her out of the turret. The two of them were as powerful as they were arrogant—but neither a king's daughter nor a tank lord is immortal.

"Baron Hetziman," said the mercenary lieutenant. "Sir—" the modest honorific for the tension, for the rage which the Baron might be unable to control even at risk of his estates and his life. "That building, the gatehouse, appears disused. We'll doss down there, if you don't mind."

The Baron's face clouded, but that was his normal reaction to disagreement. The squat tower to the left of the gate had been used only for storage for a generation. A rusted harrow, upended to fit farther within the doorway, almost blocked access now.

The Baron squinted for a moment at the structure, craning his short neck to look past the tank from which he had just climbed down. Then he snorted and said, "Sleep in a hog byre if you choose, Lieutenant. It might be cleaner at that."

"I realize," explained Lieutenant Kiley as he slid to

the ground instead of using the steps, "that the
request sounds odd, but Colonel Hammer is concerned that commandos from Ganz or the Lightning
Division might launch an attack. The gatehouse is separated from everything but the outer wall—so if we
have to defend it, we can do so without endangering
any of your people."

The lie was a transparent one; but the mercenaries
did not have to lie at all if they wished to keep us
away from their sleeping quarters. So considered, the
statement was almost generous, and the Baron chose
to take it that way. "Wolfitz," he said offhandedly as
he stamped toward the entrance. "Organize a party
of tenants—" he gestured sharply toward the pattern
of drab garments and drab faces lining the walls of
the courtyard "—and clear the place, will you?"

The Chamberlain nodded obsequiously, but he continued to stride along at his master's heel.

The Baron turned, paused, and snarled, "Now," in
a voice as grim as the fist he clenched at his side.

"My Lord," said Wolfitz with a bow that danced
the line between brusque and dilatory. He stepped
hastily toward the soldiers who had broken their rank
in lieu of orders—a few of them toward the tanks and
their haughty crews but most back to the stone shelter
of the palace.

"You men," the Chamberlain said, making circling
motions with his hands. "Fifty of the peasants,
quickly. Everything is to be turned out of the gatehouse, thrown beyond the wall for the time being.
Now. Move them."

The women followed the Baron into the palace.
Several of the maids glanced over their shoulders, at
the tanks—at the tankers. Some of the women would
have drifted closer to meet the men in khaki uniforms,
but Lady Miriam strode head high and without
hesitation.

She had accomplished her purposes; the purposes of her entourage could wait.

I leaned from the roof ledge for almost a minute further, staring at the vehicles which were so smooth-skinned that I could see my amorphous reflection in the nearest. When the sound of women's voices echoed through the window, I squirmed back only instants before the lady reentered her apartment.

They would have beaten me because of my own excitement had they not themselves been agog with the banquet to come—and the night which would follow it.

The high-arched banquet hall was so rarely used that it was almost as unfamiliar to the Baron and his household as it was to his guests. Strings of small lights had been led up the cast-concrete beams, but nothing could really illuminate the vaulting waste of groins and coffers that formed the ceiling.

The shadows and lights trembling on flexible fastenings had the look of the night sky on the edge of an electrical storm. I gazed up at the ceiling occasionally while I waited at the wall behind Lady Miriam. I had no duties at the banquet—that was for house servants, not body servants like myself—but my presence was required for show and against the chance that the Lady would send me off with a message.

That chance was very slight. Any messages Lady Miriam had were for the second-ranking tank lord, seated to her left by custom: Sergeant-Commander Grant.

Only seven of the mercenaries were present at the moment. I saw mostly their backs as they sat at the high table, interspersed with the Lady's maids. Lieutenant Kiley was in animated conversation with the Baron to his left, but I thought the officer wished primarily to distract his host from the way Lady Miriam flirted on the other side.

A second keg of beer—estate stock; not the stuff brewed for export in huge vats—had been broached by the time the beef course followed the pork. The serving girls had been kept busy with the mugs—in large part, the molded-glass tankards of the Baron's soldiers, glowering at the lower tables, but the metal-chased crystal of the tank lords was refilled often as well.

Two of the mercenaries—drivers, separated by the oldest of Lady Miriam's maids—began arguing with increasing heat while a tall, black-haired server watched in amusement. I could hear the words, but the language was not ours. One of the men got up, struggling a little because the arms of his chair were too tight against those to either side. He walked toward his commander, rolling slightly.

Lieutenant Kiley, gesturing with his mug toward the roof peak, was saying to the Baron, "Has a certain splendor, you know. Proper lighting and it'd look like a cross between a prison and a barracks, but the way you've tricked it out is—"

The standing mercenary grumbled a short, forceful paragraph, a question or a demand, to the lieutenant who broke off his own sentence to listen.

"Ah, Baron," Kiley said, turning again to his host. "Question is, what, ah, sort of regulations would there be on my boys dating local women. That one there—" his tankard nodded toward the black-haired servant. The driver who had remained seated was caressing her thigh "—for instance?"

"Regulations?" responded the Baron in genuine surprise. "On *servants*? None, of course. Would you like me to assign a group of them for your use?"

The lieutenant grinned, giving an ironic tinge to

the courteous shake of his head. "I don't think that'll be necessary, Baron," he said.

Kiley stood up to attract his men's attention. "Open season on the servants, boys," he said, speaking clearly and in our language, so that everyone at or near the upper table would understand him. "Make your own arrangements. Nothing rough. And no less than two men together."

He sat down again and explained what the Baron already understood: "Things can happen when a fellow wanders off alone in a strange place. He can fall and knock his head in, for instance."

The two drivers were already shuffling out of the dining hall with the black-haired servant between them. One of the men gestured toward another buxom server with a pitcher of beer. She was not particularly well-favored, as men describe such things; but she was close, and she was willing—as any of the women in the hall would have been to go with the tank lords. I wondered whether the four of them would get any farther than the corridor outside.

I could not see the eyes of the maid who watched the departure of the mercenaries who had been seated beside her.

Lady Miriam watched the drivers leave also. Then she turned back to Sergeant Grant and resumed the conversation they held in voices as quiet as honey flowing from a ruptured comb.

In the bustle and shadows of the hall, I disappeared from the notice of those around me. Small and silent, wearing my best jacket of black velvet, I could have been but another patch of darkness. The two mercenaries left the hall by a side exit. I slipped through the end door behind me, unnoticed save as a momentary obstacle to the servants bringing in compotes of fruits grown locally and imported from across the stars.

My place was not here. My place was with the

tanks, now that there was no one to watch me dreaming as I caressed their iridium flanks.

The sole guard at the door to the women's apartments glowered at me, but he did not question my reason for returning to what were, after all, my living quarters. The guard at the main entrance would probably have stopped me for spite: he was on duty while others of the household feasted and drank the best quality beer.

I did not need a door to reach the courtyard and the tanks parked there.

Unshuttering the same window I had used in the morning, I squeezed between the bars and clambered to the roof along the antenna mount. I was fairly certain that I could clear the barrier of points and edges at the base of the wall beneath the women's suite, but there was no need to take that risk.

Starlight guided me along the stone gutter, jumping the pipes feeding the cistern under the palace cellars. Buildings formed three sides of the courtyard, but the north was closed by a wall and the gatehouse. There was no spiked barrier beneath the wall, so I stepped to the battlements and jumped to the ground safely.

Then I walked to the nearest tank, silently from reverence rather than in fear of being heard by someone in the palace. I circled the huge vehicle slowly, letting the tip of my left index finger slide over the metal. The iridium skin was smooth, but there were many bumps and irregularities set into the armor: sensors, lights, and strips of close-range defense projectors to meet an enemy or his missile with a blast of pellets.

The tank was sleeping but not dead. Though I could hear no sound from it, the armor quivered with inner life like that of a great tree when the wind touches its highest branches.

I touched a recessed step. The spring-loaded fairing that should have covered it was missing, torn away or shot off—perhaps on a distant planet. I climbed the bow slope, my feet finding each higher step as if they knew the way.

It was as if I were a god.

I might have attempted no more than that, than to stand on the hull with my hand touching the stubby barrel of the main gun—raised at a sixty-degree angle so that it did not threaten the palace. But the turret hatch was open and, half-convinced that I was living in a hope-induced dream, I lifted myself to look in.

"Freeze," said the man looking up at me past his pistol barrel. His voice was calm. "And then we'll talk about what you think you're doing here."

The interior of the tank was coated with sulphurous light. It was too dim to shine from the hatch, but it provided enough illumination for me to see the little man in the khaki coveralls of the tank lords. The bore of the powergun in his hand shrank from the devouring cavity it had first seemed. Even the 1 cm bore of reality would release enough energy to splash the brains from my skull, I knew.

"I wanted to see the tanks," I said, amazed that I was not afraid. All men die, even kings; what better time than this would there be for me? "They would never let me, so I sneaked away from the banquet. I—it was worth it. Whatever happens now."

"Via," said the tank lord, lowering his pistol. "You're just a kid, ain'tcha?"

I could see my image foreshortened in the vision screen behind the mercenary, my empty hands shown in daylit vividness at an angle which meant the camera must be in another of the parked tanks.

"My Lord," I said—straightening momentarily but overriding the reflex so that I could meet the mercenary's eyes. "I am sixteen."

"Right," he said, "and I'm Colonel Hammer. Now—"

"Oh Lord!" I cried, forgetting in my joy and embarrassment that someone else might hear me. My vision blurred and I rapped my knees on the iridium as I tried to genuflect. "Oh, Lord Hammer, forgive me for disturbing you!"

"Blood and *martyrs*, boy!" snapped the tank lord. A pump whirred and the seat from which, cross-legged, he questioned me rose. "Don't be an idiot! Me name's Curran and I drive this beast, is all."

The mercenary was head and shoulders out of the hatch now, watching me with a concerned expression. I blinked and straightened. When I knelt, I had almost slipped from the tank; and in a few moments, my bruises might be more painful than my present embarrassment.

"I'm sorry, Lord Curran," I said, thankful for once that I had practice in keeping my expression calm after a beating. "I have studied, I have dreamed about your tanks ever since I was placed in my present status six years ago. When you came I—I'm afraid I lost control."

"You're a little shrimp, even alongside me, ain't-cha?" said Curran reflectively.

A burst of laughter drifted across the courtyard from a window in the corridor flanking the dining hall.

"Aw, Via," the tank lord said. "Come take a look, seein's yer here anyhow."

It was not a dream. My grip on the hatch coaming made the iridium bite my fingers as I stepped into the tank at Curran's direction; and besides, I would never have dared to dream this paradise.

The tank's fighting compartment was not meant for two, but Curran was as small as he had implied and I—I had grown very little since a surgeon had fitted me to become the page of a high-born lady. There were screens, gauges, and armored conduits across all the surfaces I could see.

"Drivers'll tell ye," said Curran, "the guy back here, he's just along for the ride 'cause the tank does it all for 'em. Been known t' say that myself, but it ain't really true. Still—"

He touched the lower left corner of a screen. It had been black. Now, it became gray unmarked save by eight short orange lines radiating from the edge of a two-centimeter circle in the middle of the screen.

"Fire control," Curran said. A hemispherical switch was set into the bulkhead beneath the screen. He touched the control with an index finger, rotating it slightly. "That what the Slammers's all about, ain't we? Firepower and movement, and the tricky part—movement—the driver handles from up front. Got it?"

"Yes, My Lord," I said, trying to absorb everything around me without taking my eyes from what Curran was doing. The West Wing of the palace, guest and baronial quarters above the ground-floor barracks slid up the screen as brightly illuminated as if it were daylight.

"Now *don't* touch nothin'!" the tank lord said, the first time he had spoken harshly to me. "Got it?"

"Yes, My Lord."

"Right," said Curran, softly again. "Sorry, kid. Lieutenant'll have my ass if he sees me twiddlin' with the gun, and if we blow a hole in Central Prison here—" he gestured at the screen, though I did not understand the reference "—the Colonel'll likely shoot me hisself."

"I won't touch anything, My Lord," I reiterated.

"Yeah, well," said the mercenary. He touched a four-position toggle switch beside the hemisphere. "We just lowered the main gun, right? I won't spin the turret, 'cause they'd hear that likely inside. Matter of fact—"

Instead of demonstrating the toggle, Curran fingered the sphere again. The palace dropped off the screen and, now that I knew to expect it, I recognized the faint whine that must have been the gun itself gimbaling back up to a safe angle. Nothing within the fighting compartment moved except the image on the screen.

"So," the tanker continued, flipping the toggle to one side. An orange numeral 2 appeared in the upper left corner of the screen. "There's a selector there too—" he pointed to the pistol grip by my head, attached to the power seat which had folded up as soon as it lowered me into the tank at Curran's direction.

His finger clicked the switch to the other side—I appeared in place of 2 on the screen—and then straight up—3. "Main gun," he said, "co-ax—that's the tribarrel mounted just in front of the hatch. You musta seen it?"

I nodded, but my agreement was a lie. I had been too excited and too overloaded with wonder to notice the automatic weapon on which I might have set my hand.

"And 3," Curran went on, nodding also, "straight up—that's both guns together. Not so hard, was it? You're ready to be a tank commander now—and—" he grinned, "—with six months and a little luck, I could teach ye t' drive the little darlin' besides."

"Oh, My Lord," I whispered, uncertain whether I was speaking to God or to the man beside me. I spread my feet slightly in order to keep from falling in a fit of weakness.

"*Watch* it!" the tank lord said sharply, sliding his booted foot to block me. More gently, he added, "Don't be touching *nothing*, remember? That—" he

pointed to a pedal on the floor which I had not
noticed "—that's the foot trip. Touch it and we give
a little fireworks demonstration that nobody's gonna
be very happy about."

He snapped the toggle down to its original position;
the numeral disappeared from the screen. "Shouldn't
have it live nohow," he added.

"But—all this," I said, gesturing with my arm close
to my chest so that I would not bump any of the
close-packed apparatus. "If shooting is so easy, then
why is—*everything*—here?"

Curran smiled. "Up," he said, pointing to the hatch.
As I hesitated, he added, "I'll give you a leg-up, don't
worry about the power lift."

Flushing, sure that I was being exiled from Paradise
because I had overstepped myself—somehow—with
the last question, I jumped for the hatch coaming and
scrambled through with no need of the tanker's help.
I supposed I was crying, but I could not tell because
my eyes burned so.

"Hey, slow down, kid," called Curran as he lifted
himself with great strength but less agility. "It's just
Whichard's about due t' take over guard, and we don't
need him t' find you inside. Right?"

"Oh," I said, hunched already on the edge of the
tank's deck. I did not dare turn around for a moment.
"Of course, My Lord."

"The thing about shootin'," explained the tank lord
to my back, "ain't *how* so much's when and what.
You got all this commo and sensors that'll handle any
wavelength or take remote feeds. But *still* somebody's
gotta decide which data t' call up—and decide what
it means. And decide t' pop it er not—" I turned just
as Curran leaned over to slap the iridium barrel of
the main gun for emphasis. "Which is a mother-huge
decision for whatever's down-range, ye know."

He grinned broadly. He had a short beard, rather

sparse, which partly covered the pockmarks left by some childhood disease. "Maybe even puts tank commander up on a level with driver for tricky, right?"

His words opened a window in my mind, the frames branching and spreading into a spidery, infinite structure: responsibility, the choices that came with the power of a tank.

"Yes, My Lord," I whispered.

"Now, you better get back t' whatever civvies do," Curran said, a suggestion that would be snarled out as an order if I hesitated. "And *don't* be shootin' off yer mouth about t'night, right?"

"No, My Lord," I said as I jumped to the ground. Tie-beams between the wall and the masonry gatehouse would let me climb back to the path I had followed to get here.

"And thank you," I added, but varied emotions choked the words into a mumble.

I thought the women might already have returned, but I listened for a moment, clinging to the bars, and heard nothing. Even so I climbed in the end window. It was more difficult to scramble down without the aid of the antenna brace, but a free-standing wardrobe put that window in a sort of alcove.

I didn't know what would happen if the women saw me slipping in and out through the bars. There would be a beating—there was a beating whenever an occasion offered. That didn't matter, but it was possible that Lady Miriam would also have the openings cross-barred too straitly for even my slight form to pass.

I would have returned to the banquet hall, but female voices were already greeting the guard outside the door. I had only enough time to smooth the plush of my jacket with Sarah's hairbrush before they swept in, all of them together and their mistress in the lead as usual.

By standing against a color-washed wall panel, I was able to pass unnoticed for some minutes of the excited babble without being guilty of "hiding" with the severe flogging that would surely entail. By the time Lady Miriam called, "Leesh? *Elisha!*" in a querulous voice, no one else could have sworn that I hadn't entered the apartment with the rest of the entourage.

"Yes, My Lady?" I said, stepping forward.

Several of the women were drifting off in pairs to help one another out of their formal costumes and coiffures. There would be a banquet every night that the tank lords remained—providing occupation to fill the otherwise featureless lives of the maids and their mistress.

That was time consuming, even if they did not become more involved than public occasion required.

"Leesh," said Lady Miriam, moderating her voice unexpectedly. I was prepared for a blow, ready to accept it unflinchingly unless it were aimed at my eyes and even then to dodge as little as possible so as not to stir up a worse beating.

"Elisha," the Lady continued in a honeyed tone— then, switching back to acid sharpness and looking at her Chief Maid, she said, "Sarah, what *are* all these women doing here? Don't they have rooms of their own?"

Women who still dallied in the suite's common room—several of the lower-ranking stored their garments here in chests and clothes presses—scurried for their sleeping quarters while Sarah hectored them, arms akimbo.

"I need you to carry a message for me, Leesh," explained Lady Miriam softly. "To one of our guests. You—you do know, don't you, boy, which suite was cleared for use by our guests?"

"Yes, My Lady," I said, keeping my face blank. "The end suite of the East Wing, where the King slept last year. But I thought—"

"Don't think," said Sarah, rapping me with the brush which she carried on all but formal occasions. "And don't interrupt milady."

"Yes, My Lady," I said, bowing and rising.

"I don't want you to *go* there, boy," said the Lady with an edge of irritation. "If Sergeant Grant has any questions, I want you to point the rooms out to him— from the courtyard."

She paused and touched her full lips with her tongue while her fingers played with the fan. "Yes," she said at last, then continued, "I want you to tell Sergeant Grant oh-four hundred and to answer any questions he may have."

Lady Miriam looked up again, and though her voice remained mild, her eyes were hard as knife points. "Oh. And Leesh? This is business which the Baron does not wish to be known. Speak to Sergeant Grant in private. And never speak to anyone else about it— even to the Baron if he tries to trick you into an admission."

"Yes, My Lady," I said bowing.

I understood what the Baron would do to a page who brought him that news—and how he would send a message back to his wife, to the king's daughter whom he dared not impale in person.

Sarah's shrieked order carried me past the guard at the women's apartment, while Lady Miriam's signet was my pass into the courtyard after normal hours. The soldier there on guard was muzzy with drink. I might have been able to slip unnoticed by the hall alcove in which he sheltered.

I skipped across the gravel-in-clay surface of the courtyard, afraid to pause to touch the tanks again when I knew Lady Miriam would be peering from her window. Perhaps on the way back . . . but no, she would be as intent on hearing how the message was received as she was anxious to know that it had been delivered. I would ignore the tanks—

"*Freeze*, buddy!" snarled someone from the turret of the tank I had just run past.

I stumbled with shock and my will to obey. Catching my balance, I turned slowly—to the triple muzzles of the weapon mounted on the cupola, not a pistol as Lord Curran had pointed. The man who spoke wore a shielded helmet, but there would not have been enough light to recognize him anyway.

"Please, My Lord," I said. "I have a message for Sergeant-Commander Grant?"

"From who?" the mercenary demanded. I knew now that Lieutenant Kiley had been serious about protecting from intrusion the quarters allotted to his men.

"My Lord, I . . ." I said and found no way to proceed.

"Yeah, Via," the tank lord agreed in a relaxed tone. "None a' my affair." He touched the side of his helmet and spoke softly.

The gatehouse door opened with a spill of light and the tall, broad-shouldered silhouette of Sergeant Grant. Like the mercenary on guard in the tank, he wore a communications helmet.

Grant slipped his face shield down, and for a moment my own exposed skin tingled—or my mind *thought* it perceived a tingle—as the tank lord's equipment scanned me.

"C'mon, then," he grunted, gesturing me toward the recessed angle of the building and the gate leaves. "We'll step around the corner and talk."

There was a trill of feminine laughter from the upper story of the gatehouse: a servant named Maria, whose hoots of joy were unmistakable. Lieutenant Kiley leaned his head and torso from the window above us and shouted to Grant, his voice and his anger recognizable even though the words themselves were not.

The sergeant paused, clenching his left fist and reaching for me with his right because I happened to be closest to him. I poised to run—survive this first, then worry about what Lady Miriam would say—but the tank lord caught himself, raised his shield, and called to his superior in a tone on the safe side of insolent, "All right, all right. I'll stay right here where Cermak can see me from the tank."

Apparently Grant had remembered Lady Miriam also, for he spoke in our language so that I—and the principal for whom I acted—would understand the situation.

Lieutenant Kiley banged his shutters closed.

Grant stared for a moment at Cermak until the guard understood and dropped back into the interior of his vehicle. We could still be observed through the marvelous vision blocks, but we had the miminal privacy needed for me to deliver my message.

"Lady Miriam," I said softly, "says oh-four hundred."

I waited for the tank lord to ask me for directions. His breath and sweat exuded sour echoes of the strong estate ale.

"Won't go," the tank lord replied unexpectedly. "I'll be clear at oh-three *to* oh-four." He paused before adding, "You tell her, kid, she better not be playin' games. Nobody plays prick-tease with *this* boy and likes what they get for it."

"Yes, My Lord," I said, skipping backward because I had the feeling that this man would grab me and shake me to emphasize his point.

I would not deliver his threat. My best small hope

for safety at the end of this affair required that Lady Miriam believe I was ignorant of what was going on, and a small hope it was.

That *was* a slim hope anyway.

"Well, go on, then," the tank lord said.

He strode back within the gatehouse, catlike in his grace and lethality, while I ran to tell my mistress of the revised time.

An hour's pleasure seemed a little thing against the risk of two lives—and my own.

My "room" was what had been the back staircase before it was blocked to convert the second floor of the West Wing into the women's apartment. The dank cylinder was furnished only with the original stone stair treads and whatever my mistress and her maids had chosen to store there over the years. I normally slept on a chair in the common room, creeping back to my designated space before dawn.

Tonight I slept *beneath* one of the large chairs in a corner; not hidden, exactly, but not visible without a search.

The two women were quiet enough to have slipped past someone who was not poised to hear them as I was, and the tiny flashlight the leader carried threw a beam so tight that it could scarcely have helped them see their way. But the perfume they wore— imported, expensive, and overpowering—was more startling than a shout.

They paused at the door. The latch rattled like a tocsin though the hinges did not squeal.

The soldier on guard, warned and perhaps awakened by the latch, stopped them before they could leave the apartment. The glowlamp in the sconce beside the door emphasized the ruddy anger on his face.

Sarah's voice, low but cutting, said, "Keep silent,

my man, or it will be the worse for you." She thrust a gleam of gold toward the guard, not payment but a richly-chased signet ring, and went on, "Lady Miriam knows and approves. Keep still and you'll have no cause to regret this night. Otherwise . . ."

The guard's face was not blank, but emotions chased themselves across it too quickly for his mood to be read. Suddenly he reached out and harshly squeezed the Chief Maid's breast. Sarah gasped, and the man snarled, "What've they got that *I* don't, tell me, huh? You're *all* whores, that's all you are!"

The second woman was almost hidden from the soldier by the Chief Maid and the panel of the half-opened door. I could see a shimmer of light as her hand rose, though I could not tell whether it was a blade or a gun barrel.

The guard flung his hand down from Sarah and turned away. "Go on, then," he grumbled. "What do I care? Go *on*, sluts."

The weapon disappeared, unused and unseen, into the folds of an ample skirt, and the two women left the suite with only the whisper of felt slippers. They were heavily veiled and wore garments coarser than any I had seen on the Chief Maid before—but Lady Miriam was as recognizable in the grace of her walk as Sarah was for her voice.

The women left the door ajar to keep the latch from rattling again, and the guard did not at first pull it to. I listened for further moments against the chance that another maid would come from her room or that the Lady would rush back, driven by fear or conscience—though I hadn't seen either state control her in the past.

I was poised to squeeze between the window-bars again, barefoot for secrecy and a better grip, when I heard the hum of static as the guard switched his belt radio live. There was silence as he keyed it, then his low voice saying, "They've left, sir. They're on their way toward the banquet hall."

There was another pause and a radio voice too thin for me to hear more than the fact of it. The guard said, "Yes, Chamberlain," and clicked off the radio.

He latched the door.

I was out through the bars in one movement and well up the antenna brace before any of the maids could have entered the common room to investigate the noise.

I knew where the women were going, but not whether the Chamberlain would stop them on the way past the banquet hall or the Baron's personal suite at the head of East Wing. The fastest, safest way for me to cross the roof of the banquet hall was twenty feet up the side, where the builders' forms had left a flat, thirty-centimeter path in the otherwise sloping concrete.

Instead, I decided to pick my way along the trash-filled stone gutter just above the windows of the corridor on the courtyard side. I could say that my life—my chance of life—depended on knowing what was going on . . . and it did depend on that. But crawling through the starlit darkness, spying on my betters, was also the only way I had of asserting myself. The need to assert myself had become unexpectedly pressing since Lord Curran had showed me the tank, and since I had experienced what a man *could* be.

There was movement across the courtyard as I reached the vertical extension of the load-bearing wall that separated the West Wing from the banquet hall. I ducked beneath the stone coping, but the activity had nothing to do with me. The gatehouse door had opened and, as I peered through dark-adapted eyes, the mercenary on guard in a tank exchanged with the man who had just stepped out of the building.

The tank lords talked briefly. Then the gatehouse door shut behind the guard who had been relieved while his replacement climbed into the turret of the vehicle parked near the West Wing—Sergeant Grant's tank. I clambered over the wall extension and stepped carefully along the gutter, regretting now that I had not worn shoes for protection. I heard nothing from the corridor below, although the casements were pivoted outward to catch any breeze that would relieve the summer stillness.

Gravel crunched in the courtyard as the tank lord on guard slid from his vehicle and began to stride toward the end of the East Wing.

He was across the courtyard from me—faceless behind the shield of his commo helmet and at best only a shadow against the stone of the wall behind him. But the man was Sergeant Grant beyond question, abandoning his post for the most personal of reasons.

I continued, reaching the East Wing as the tank lord disappeared among the stone finials of the outside staircase at the wing's far end. The guest suites had their own entrance, more formally ornamented than the doorways serving the estate's own needs. The portal was guarded only when the suites were in use—and then most often by a mixed force of the Baron's soldiers and those of the guests.

That was not a formality. The guest who would entrust his life solely to the Baron's goodwill was a fool.

A corridor much like that flanking the banquet hall ran along the courtyard side of the guest suites. It was closed by a cross-wall and door, separating the guests from the Baron's private apartment, but the door was locked and not guarded.

Lady Miriam kept a copy of the door's microchip key under the plush lining of her jewel box. I had found it but left it there, needless to me so long as I could slip through window grates.

The individual guest suites were locked also, but as I lowered myself from the gutter to a window ledge I heard a door snick closed. The sound was minuscule, but it had a crispness that echoed in the lightless hall.

Skirts rustled softly against the stone, and Sarah gave a gentle, troubled sigh as she settled herself to await her mistress.

I waited on the ledge, wondering if I should climb back to the roof—or even return to my own room. The Chamberlain had not blocked the assignation, and there was no sign of an alarm. The soldiers, barracked on the ground floor of this wing, would have been clearly audible had they been aroused.

Then I did hear something—or feel it. There had been motion, the ghost of motion, on the other side of the door closing the corridor. Someone had entered or left the Baron's apartment, and I had heard them through the open windows.

It could have been one of the Baron's current favorites—girls from the estate, the younger and more vulnerable, the better. They generally used the little door and staircase on the outer perimeter of the palace—where a guard *was* stationed against the possibility that an axe-wielding relative would follow the lucky child.

I lifted myself back to the roof with particular care, so that I would not disturb the Chief Maid waiting in the hallway. Then I followed the gutter back to the portion of roof over the Baron's apartments.

I knew the wait would be less than an hour, the length of Sergeant Grant's guard duty, but it did not occur to me that the interval would be as brief as it actually was. I had scarcely settled myself again to wait when I thought I heard a door unlatch in the guest suites. That could have been imagination or

Sarah, deciding to wait in a room instead of the corridor; but moments later the helmeted tank lord paused on the outside staircase.

By taking the risk of leaning over the roof coping, I could see Lord Grant and a woman embracing on the landing before the big mercenary strode back across the courtyard toward the tank where he was supposed to be on guard. Desire had not waited on its accomplishment, and mutual fear had prevented the sort of dalliance after the event that the women dwelt on so lovingly in the privacy of their apartment . . . while Leesh, the Lady's page and no man, listened of necessity.

The women's slippers made no sound in the corridor, but their dresses brushed one another to the door which clicked and sighed as it let them out of the guest apartments and into the portion of the East Wing reserved to the Baron.

I expected shouts, then; screams, even gunfire as the Baron and Wolfitz confronted Lady Miriam. There was no sound except for skirts continuing to whisper their way up the hall, returning to the women's apartment. I stood up to follow, disappointed despite the fact that bloody chaos in the palace would endanger everyone—and me, the usual scapegoat for frustrations, most of all.

The Baron said in a tight voice at the window directly beneath me, "Give me the goggles, Wolfitz," and surprise almost made me fall.

The strap of a pair of night-vision goggles rustled over the Baron's grizzled head. Their frames clucked against the stone sash as my master bent forward with the unfamiliar headgear.

For a moment, I was too frightened to breathe. If he leaned out and turned his head, he would see me poised like a terrified gargoyle above him. Any move

I made—even flattening myself behind the wall coping—risked a sound and disaster.

"You're right," said the Baron in a voice that would have been normal if it had any emotion behind it. There was another sound of something hard against the sash, a metallic clink this time.

"*No*, My Lord!" said the Chamberlain in a voice more forceful than I dreamed any underling would use to the Baron. Wolfitz must have been seizing the nettle firmly, certain that hesitation or uncertainty meant the end of more than his plans. "If you shoot him now, the others will blast everything around them to glowing slag."

"Wolfitz," said the Baron, breathing hard. They had been struggling. The flare-mouthed mob gun from the Baron's nightstand—scarcely a threat to Sergeant Grant across the courtyard—extended from the window opening, but the Chamberlain's bony hand was on the Baron's wrist. "If you tell me I must let those arrogant outworlders pleasure *my* wife in *my* palace, I will kill you."

He sounded like an architect discussing a possible staircase curve.

"There's a better way, My Lord," said the Chamberlain. His voice was breathy also, but I thought exertion was less to account for that than was the risk he took. "We'll be ready the next time the—outworlder gives us the opportunity. We'll take him in, in the crime; but quietly so that the others aren't aroused."

"Idiot!" snarled the Baron, himself again in all his arrogant certainty. Their hands and the gun disappeared from the window ledge. The tableau was the vestige of an event the men needed each other too much to remember. "No matter what we do with the body, the others will blame us. Blame *me*."

His voice took a dangerous coloration as he added, "Is that what you had in mind, Chamberlain?"

Wolfitz said calmly, "The remainder of the platoon here will be captured—or killed, it doesn't matter—by the mercenaries of the Lightning Division, who will also protect us from reaction by King Adrian and Colonel Hammer."

"But . . ." said the Baron, the word a placeholder for the connected thought which did not form in his mind after all.

"The King of Ganz won't hesitate an instant if you offer him your fealty," the Chamberlain continued, letting the words display their own strength instead of speaking loudly in a fashion his master might take as badgering.

The Baron still held the mob gun, and his temper was doubtful at the best of times.

"The mercenaries of the Lightning Division," continued Wolfitz with his quiet voice and persuasive ideas, "will accept any risk in order to capture four tanks undamaged. The value of that equipment is beyond any profit the Lightning Division dreamed of earning when they were hired by Ganz."

"But . . ." the Baron repeated in an awestruck voice. "The truce?"

"A matter for the kings to dispute," said the Chamberlain offhandedly. "But Adrian will find little support among his remaining barons if you were forced into your change of allegiance. When the troops he billeted on you raped and murdered Lady Miriam, that is."

"How quickly can you make the arrangements?" asked the Baron. I had difficulty in following the words: not because they were soft, but because he growled them like a beast.

"The delay," Wolfitz replied judiciously, and I could imagine him lacing his long fingers together and staring at them, "will be for the next opportunity your—Lady Miriam and her lover give us, I shouldn't imagine that will be longer than tomorrow night."

The Baron's teeth grated like nutshells being ground against stone.

"We'll have to use couriers, of course," Wolfitz added. "The likelihood of the Slammers intercepting any other form of communication is too high. . . . But all Ganz and its mercenaries have to do is ready a force to dash here and defend the palace before Hammer can react. Since these tanks *are* the forward picket, and they'll be unmanned while Sergeant Grant is—otherwise occupied—the Lightning Division will have almost an hour before an alarm can be given. Ample time, I'm sure."

"Chamberlain," the Baron said in a voice from which amazement had washed all the anger. "You think of everything. See to it."

"Yes, My Lord," said Wolfitz humbly.

The tall Chamberlain *did* think of everything, or very nearly; but he'd had much longer to plan than the Baron thought. I wondered how long Wolfitz had waited for an opportunity like this one; and what payment he had arranged to receive from the King of Ganz if he changed the Baron's allegiance?

A door slammed closed, the Baron returning to his suite and his current child-mistress. Chamberlain Wolfitz's rooms adjoined his master's, but my ears followed his footsteps to the staircase at the head of the wing.

By the time I had returned to the West Wing and was starting down the antenna brace, a pair of the Baron's soldiers had climbed into a truck and gone rattling off into the night. It was an unusual event but not especially remarkable: the road they took led off to one of the Baron's outlying estates.

But the road led to the border with Ganz, also; and

I had no doubt as to where the couriers' message would be received.

The tank lords spent most of the next day busy with their vehicles. A squad of the Baron's soldiers kept at a distance the tenants and house servants who gawked while the khaki-clad tankers crawled through access plates and handed fan motors to their fellows. The bustle racks welded to the back of each turret held replacement parts as well as the crew's personal belongings.

It was hard to imagine that objects as huge and powerful as the tanks would need repair. I had to remember that they were not ingots of iridium but vastly complicated assemblages of parts—each of which could break, and eight of which were human.

I glanced occasionally at the tanks and the lordly men who ruled and serviced them. I had no excuse to take me beyond the women's apartment during daylight.

Excitement roused the women early, but there was little pretense of getting on with their lace-making. They dressed, changed, primped—argued over rights to one bit of clothing or another—and primarily, they talked.

Lady Miriam was less a part of the gossip than usual, but she was the most fastidious of all about the way she would look at the night's banquet.

The tank lords bathed at the wellhead in the court-yard like so many herdsmen. The women watched hungrily, edging forward despite the scandalized demands of one of the older maids that they at least stand back in the room where their attention would be less blatant.

Curran's muscles were knotted, his skin swarthy. Sergeant Grant could have passed for a god—or at least a man of half his real age. When he looked up at the women's apartments, he smiled.

The truck returned in late afternoon, carrying the two soldiers and a third man in civilian clothes who could have been—but was not—the manager of one of the outlying estates. The civilian was closeted with the Baron for half an hour before he climbed back into the truck. He, Wolfitz, and the Baron gripped one another's forearms in leave-taking; then the vehicle returned the way it had come.

The tank lord on guard paid less attention to the truck than he had to the column of steam-driven produce vans, chuffing toward the nearest rail terminus.

The banquet was less hectic than that of the first night, but the glitter had been replaced by a fog of hostility now that the newness had worn off. The Baron's soldiers were more openly angry that Hammer's men picked and chose—food at the high table and women in the corridor or the servants' quarters below.

The Slammers, for their part, had seen enough of the estate to be contemptuous of its isolation, of its low technology—and of the folk who lived on it. And yet—I had talked with Lord Curran and listened to the others as well. The tank lords were men like those of the barony. They had walked on far worlds and had been placed in charge of instruments as sophisticated as any in the human galaxy—but they were not sophisticated *men*, only powerful ones.

Sergeant-Commander Grant, for instance, made the child's mistake of thinking his power to destroy conferred on him a sort of personal immortality.

The Baron ate and drank in a sullen reverie, deaf to the lieutenant's attempts at conversation and as blind to Lady Miriam on his left as she was to him. The Chamberlain was seated among the soldiers because there were more guests than maids of honor. He watched the activities at the high table unobtrusively, keeping his own counsel and betraying his nervousness only by the fact that none of the food he picked at seemed to go down his throat.

I was tempted to slip out to the tanks, because Lord Curran was on duty again during the banquet. His absence must have been his own choice; a dislike for the food or the society perhaps . . . but more probably, from what I had seen in the little man when we talked, a fear of large, formal gatherings.

It would have been nice to talk to Lord Curran again, and blissful to have the controls of the huge tank again within my hands. But if I were caught then, I might not be able to slip free later in the night—and I would rather have died than missed that chance.

The Baron hunched over his ale when Lieutenant Kiley gathered his men to return to the gatehouse. They did not march well in unison, not even by comparison with the Baron's soldiers when they drilled in the courtyard.

The skills and the purpose of the tank lords lay elsewhere.

Lady Miriam rose when the tankers fell in. She swept from the banquet hall regally as befit her birth, dressed in amber silk from Terra and topazes of ancient cut from our own world. She did not look behind her to see that her maids followed and I brought up the rear . . . but she did glance aside once at the formation of tank lords.

She would be dressed no better than a servant later that night, and she wanted to be sure that Sergeant Grant had a view of her full splendor to keep in mind when next they met in darkness.

The soldier who had guarded the women's apartments the night before was on duty when the Chief Maid led her mistress out again. There was no repetition of the previous night's dangerous byplay this time. The guard was subdued, or frightened; or, just possibly, biding his time because he was aware of what was going to come.

I followed, more familiar with my route this time and too pumped with excitement to show the greater care I knew was necessary tonight, when there would be many besides myself to watch, to listen.

But I was alone on the roof, and the others, so certain of what *they* knew and expected, paid no attention to the part of the world which lay beyond their immediate interest.

Sergeant Grant sauntered as he left the vehicle where he was supposed to stay on guard. As he neared the staircase to the guest suites, his stride lengthened and his pace picked up. There was nothing of nervousness in his manner; only the anticipation of a man focused on sex to the extinction of all other considerations.

I was afraid that Wolfitz would spring his trap before I was close enough to follow what occurred. A more reasonable fear would have been that I would stumble into the middle of the event.

Neither danger came about. I reached the gutter over the guest corridor and waited, breathing through my mouth alone so that I wouldn't make any noise. The blood that pounded through my ears deafened me for a moment, but there was nothing to fear. Voices murmured, Sarah and Sergeant Grant, and the door that had waited ajar for the tank lord clicked to shut the suite.

Four of the Baron's soldiers mounted the outside steps, as quietly as their boots permitted. There were faint sounds, clothing and one muted clink of metal, from the corridor on the Baron's side of the door.

All day I'd been telling myself that there was no safe way I could climb down and watch the events through a window. I climbed down, finding enough purchase for my fingers and toes where weathering had rounded the corners of stone blocks. Getting back to the roof would be more difficult, unless I risked gripping an out-swung casement for support.

Unless I dropped, bullet-riddled, to the ground.

I rested a toe on a window ledge and peeked around the stone toward the door of the suite the lovers had used on their first assignation. I could see nothing—

Until the corridor blazed with silent light.

Sarah's face was white, dazzling with direct reflection of the high-intensity floods at either end of the hallway. Her mouth opened and froze, a statue of a scream but without the sound that fear or self-preservation choked in her throat.

Feet, softly but many of them, shuffled over the stone flags toward the Chief Maid. Her head jerked from one side to the other, but her body did not move. The illumination was pinning her to the door where she kept watch.

The lights spilled through the corridor windows, but their effect was surprisingly slight in the open air: highlights on the parked tanks; a faint wash of outline, not color, over the stones of the wall and gatehouse; and a distorted shadowplay on the ground itself, men and weapons twisting as they advanced toward the trapped maid from both sides.

There was no sign of interest from the gatehouse. Even if the tank lords were awake to notice the lights, what happened at night in the palace was no affair of theirs.

Three of perhaps a dozen of the Baron's soldiers stepped within my angle of vision. Two carried rifles; the third was Murphy with a chip recorder, the spidery wands of its audio and video pick-ups retracted because of the press of men standing nearby.

Sarah swallowed. She closed her mouth, but her

eyes stared toward the infinite distance beyond this world. The gold signet she clutched was a drop from the sun's heart in the floodlights.

The Baron stepped close to the woman. He took the ring with his left hand, looked at it, and passed it to the stooped, stone-faced figure of the Chamberlain.

"Move her out of the way," said the Baron in a husky whisper.

One of the soldiers stuck the muzzle of his assault rifle under the chin of the Chief Maid, pointing upward. With his other hand, the man gripped Sarah's shoulder and guided her away from the door panel.

Wolfitz looked at his master, nodded, and set a magnetic key on the lock. Then he too stepped clear.

The Baron stood at the door with his back to me. He wore body armor, but he can't have thought it would protect him against the Slammer's powergun. Murphy was at the Baron's side, the recorder's central light glaring back from the door panel, and another soldier poised with his hand on the latch.

The Baron slammed the door inward with his foot. I do not think I have ever seen a man move as fast as Sergeant Grant did then.

The door opened on a servants' alcove, not the guest rooms themselves, but the furnishings there were sufficient to the lovers' need. Lady Miriam had lifted her skirts. She was standing, leaning slightly backwards, with her buttocks braced against the bed-frame. She screamed, her eyes blank reflections of the sudden light.

Sergeant-Commander Grant still wore his helmet. He had slung his belt and holstered pistol over the bedpost when he unsealed the lower flap of his uniform coveralls, but he was turning with the pistol in his hand before the Baron got off the first round with his mob gun.

Aerofoils, spread from the flaring muzzle by asymmetric

thrust, spattered the lovers and a two-meter circle on the wall beyond them.

The tank lord's chest was in bloody tatters and there was a brain-deep gash between his eyebrows, but his body and the powergun followed through with the motion reflex had begun.

The Baron's weapon chunked twice more. Lady Miriam flopped over the footboard and lay thrashing on the bare springs, spurting blood from narrow wounds that her clothing did not cover. Individual projectiles from the mob gun had little stopping power, but they bled out a victim's life like so many knife blades.

When the Baron shot the third time, his gun was within a meter of what had been the tank lord's face. Sergeant Grant's body staggered backward and fell, the powergun unfired but still gripped in the mercenary's right hand.

"Call the Lightning Division," said the Baron harshly as he turned. His face, except where it was freckled by fresh blood, was as pale as I had ever seen it. "It's time."

Wolfitz lifted a communicator, short range but keyed to the main transmitter, and spoke briefly. There was no need for communications security now. The man who should have intercepted and evaluated the short message was dead in a smear of his own wastes and body fluids.

The smell of the mob gun's propellant clung chokingly to the back of my throat, among the more familiar slaughterhouse odors. Lady Miriam's breath whistled, and the bedsprings squeaked beneath her uncontrolled motions.

"Shut that off," said the Baron to Murphy. The recorder's pool of light shrank into shadow within the alcove.

The Baron turned and fired once more, into the tank lord's groin.

"Make sure the others don't leave the gatehouse till Ganz's mercenaries are here to deal with them," said the Baron negligently. He looked at the gun in his hand. Strong lights turned the heat and propellant residues rising from its barrel into shadows on the wall beyond.

"Marksmen are ready, My Lord," said the Chamberlain.

The Baron skittered his mob gun down the hall. He strode toward the rooms of his own apartment.

It must have been easier to climb back to the roof than I had feared. I have no memory of it, of the stress on fingertips and toes or the pain in my muscles as they lifted the body which they had supported for what seemed (after the fact) to have been hours. Minutes only, of course; but instead of serial memory of what had happened, my brain was filled with too many frozen pictures of details for all of them to fit within the real timeframe.

The plan that I had made for this moment lay so deep that I executed it by reflex, though my brain roiled.

Executed it by instinct, perhaps; the instinct of flight, the instinct to power.

In the corridor, Wolfitz and Murphy were arguing in low voices about what should be done about the mess.

Soldiers had taken up positions in the windowed corridor flanking the banquet hall. More of the Baron's men, released from trapping Lady Miriam and her lover, were joining their fellows with words too soft for me to understand. I crossed the steeply-pitched roof on the higher catwalk, for speed and from fear that the men at the windows might hear me.

There were no soldiers on the roof itself. The wall

coping might hide even a full-sized man if he lay flat, but the narrow gutter between wall and roof was an impossible position from which to shoot at targets across the courtyard.

The corridor windows on the courtyard side were not true firing slits like those of all the palace's outer walls. Nonetheless, men shooting from corners of the windows could shelter their bodies behind stone thick enough to stop bolts from the Slammers' personal weapons. The sleet of bullets from twenty assault rifles would turn anyone sprinting from the gatehouse door or the pair of second-floor windows into offal like that which had been Sergeant Grant.

The tank lords were not immortal.

There was commotion in the women's apartments when I crossed them. Momentarily a light fanned the shadow of the window bars across the courtyard and the gray curves of Sergeant Grant's tank. A male voice cursed harshly. A lamp casing crunched, and from the returned darkness came a blow and a woman's cry.

Some of the Baron's soldiers were taking positions in the West Wing. Unless the surviving tank lords could blow a gap in the thick outer wall of the gate-house, they had no exit until the Lightning Division arrived with enough firepower to sweep them up at will.

But I could get in, with a warning that would come in time for them to summon aid from Colonel Hammer himself. They would be in debt for my warning, owing me their lives, their tanks, and their honor.

Surely the tank lords could find a place for a servant willing to go with them anywhere?

The battlements of the wall closing the north side of the courtyard formed my pathway to the roof of the gatehouse. Grass and brush grew there in ragged clumps. Cracks between stones had trapped dust, seeds, and moisture during a generation of neglect. I crawled along, on my belly, tearing my black velvet jacket.

Eyes focused on the gatehouse door and windows were certain to wander: to the sky; to fellows slouching over their weapons; to the wall connecting the gatehouse to the West Wing. If I stayed flat, I merged with the stone . . . but shrubs could quiver in the wrong pattern, and the Baron's light-amplifying goggles might be worn by one of the watching soldiers.

It had seemed simpler when I planned it; but it was necessary in any event, even if I died in a burst of gunfire.

The roof of the gatehouse was reinforced concrete, slightly domed, and as proof against indirect fire as the stone walls were against small arms. There was no roof entrance, but there was a capped flue for the stove that had once heated the guard quarters. I'd squirmed my way through that hole once before.

Four years before.

The roof of the gatehouse was a meter higher than the wall on which I lay, an easy jump but one which put me in silhouette against the stars. I reached up, feeling along the concrete edge less for a grip than for reassurance. I was afraid to leave the wall because my body was telling itself that the stone it pressed was safety.

If the Baron's men shot me now, it would warn the tank lords in time to save them. I owed them that, for the glimpses of freedom Curran had showed me in the turret of a tank.

I vaulted onto the smooth concrete and rolled, a shadow in the night to any of the watchers who might have seen me. Once I was *on* the gatehouse, I was safe because of the flat dome that shrugged off rain and projectiles. The flue was near the north edge of the structure, hidden from the eyes and guns waiting elsewhere in the palace.

I'd grown only slightly since I was twelve and beginning to explore the palace in which I expected to die. The flue hadn't offered much margin, but my need wasn't as great then, either.

I'd never needed *anything* as much as I needed to get into the gatehouse now.

The metal smoke pipe had rusted and blown down decades before. The wooden cap, fashioned to close the hole to rain, hadn't been maintained. It crumbled in my hands when I lifted it away, soggy wood with only flecks remaining of the stucco which had been applied to seal the cap into place.

The flue was as narrow as the gap between window bars, and because it was round, I didn't have the luxury of turning sideways. So be it.

If my shoulders fit, my hips would follow. I extended my right arm and reached down through the hole as far as I could. The flue was as empty as it was dark. Flakes of rust made mouselike patterings as my touch dislodged them. The passageway curved smoothly, but it had no sharp-angled shot trap as far down as I could feel from outside.

I couldn't reach the lower opening. The roof was built thick enough to stop heavy shells. At least the slimy surface of the concrete tube would make the job easier.

I lowered my head into the flue with the pit of my extended right arm pressed as firmly as I could against the lip of the opening. The cast concrete brought an electric chill through the sweat-soaked velvet of my jerkin, reminding me—now that it was too late—that I could have stripped off the garment to gain another millimeter's tolerance.

It was too late, even though all but my head and one arm were outside. If I stopped now, I would never have the courage to go on again.

The air in the flue was dank, because even now in

late Summer the concrete sweated and the cap prevented condensate from evaporating. The sound of my fear-lengthened breaths did not echo from the end of a closed tube, and not even panic could convince me that the air was stale and would suffocate me. I slid farther down; down to the *real* point of no return.

By leading with my head and one arm, I was able to tip my collarbone endwise for what would have been a relatively easy fit within the flue if my ribs and spine did not have to follow after. The concrete caught the tip of my left shoulder and the ribs beneath my right armpit—let me flex forward minutely on the play in my skin and the velvet—and held me.

I would have screamed, but the constriction of my ribs was too tight. My legs kicked in the air above the gatehouse, unable to thrust me down for lack of purchase. My right arm flopped in the tube, battering my knuckles and fingertips against unyielding concrete.

I could die here, and no one would know.

Memory of the tank and the windows of choice expanding infinitely above even Leesh, the Lady's page, flashed before me and cooled my body like rain on a stove. My muscles relaxed and I could breathe again—though carefully, and though the veins of my head were distending with blood trapped by my present posture.

Instead of flapping vainly, my right palm and elbow locked on opposite sides of the curving passage. I breathed as deeply as I could, then let it out as I kicked my legs up where gravity, at least, could help.

My right arm pulled while my left tried to clamp itself within my rib cage. Cloth tore, skin tore, and my torso slipped fully within the flue, lubricated by blood as well as condensate.

If I had been upright, I might have blacked out momentarily with the release of tension. Inverted, I could only gasp and feel my face and scalp burn with the flush that darkened them. The length of a hand farther and my pelvis scraped. My fingers had a grip on the lower edge of the flue, and I pulled like a cork extracting itself from a wine bottle. My being, body and mind, was so focused on its task that I was equally unmoved by losing my trousers—dragged off on the lip of the flue—and the fact that my hand was free.

The concrete burned my left ear when my right arm thrust my torso down with real handhold for the first time. My shoulders slid free and the rest of my body tumbled out of the tube which had seemed to grip it tightly until that instant.

The light that blazed in my face was meant to blind me, but I was already stunned—more by the effort than the floor which I'd hit an instant before. Someone laid the muzzle of a powergun against my left ear. The dense iridium felt cool and good on my damaged skin.

"Where's Sergeant Grant?" said Lieutenant Kiley, a meter to the side of the light source.

I squinted away from the beam. There was an open bedroll beneath me, but I think I was too limp when I dropped from the flue to be injured by bare stone. Three of the tank lords were in the room with me. The bulbous commo helmets they wore explained how the lieutenant already knew something had happened to the guard. The others would be on the ground floor, poised.

The guns pointed at me were no surprise.

"He slipped into the palace to see Lady Miriam," I said, amazed that my voice did not break in a throat so dry. "The Baron killed them, both, and he's summoned the Lightning Division to capture you and your tanks. You have to call for help at once or they'll be here."

"Blood and martyrs," said the man with the gun at my ear, Lord Curran, and he stepped between me and the dazzling light. "Douse that, Sparky. The kid's all right."

The tank lord with the light dimmed it to a glow and said, "Which *we* bloody well ain't."

Lieutenant Kiley moved to a window and peeked through a crack in the shutter, down into the courtyard.

"But . . ." I said. I would have gotten up but Curran's hand kept me below the possible line of fire. I'd tripped the mercenaries' alarms during my approach, awakened them—enough to save them, surely. "You have your helmets?" I went on. "You can call your colonel?"

"That bastard Grant," the lieutenant said in the same emotionless, diamond-hard voice he had used in questioning me. "He slaved all the vehicle transceivers to his own helmet so Command Central wouldn't wake *me* if they called while he was—out fucking around."

"Via," said Lord Curran, holstering his pistol and grimacing at his hands as he flexed them together. "I'll go. Get a couple more guns up these windows—" he gestured with jerks of his forehead "—for cover."

"It's my platoon," Kiley said, stepping away from the window but keeping his back to the others of us in the room. "Via, *Via!*"

"Look, sir," Curran insisted with his voice rising and wobbling like that of a dog fighting a choke collar. "I was his bloody driver, I'll—"

"*You* weren't the fuck-up!" Lieutenant Kiley snarled as he turned. "This one comes with the rank, trooper, so shut your—"

"I'll go, My Lords," I said, the squeal of my voice

lifting it through the hoarse anger of grown men arguing over a chance to die.

They paused and the third lord, Sparky, thumbed the light up and back by reflex. I pointed to the flue. "That way. But you'll have to tell me what to do then."

Lord Curran handed me a disk the size of a thumbnail. He must have taken it from his pocket when he planned to sprint for the tanks himself. "Lay it on the hatch—anywhere on the metal. Inside, t' the right a' the main screen—"

"Curran, *knot* it, will you?" the lieutenant demanded in peevish amazement. "We can't—"

"*I* don't want my ass blown away, Lieutenant," said the trooper with the light—which pointed toward the officer suddenly, though the pistol in Sparky's other hand was lifted idly toward the ceiling. "Anyhow, kid's got a better chance'n you do. Or me."

Lieutenant Kiley looked from one of his men to the other, then stared at me with eyes that could have melted rock. "The main screen is on the forward wall of the fighting compartment," he said flatly. "That is—"

"He's used it, Lieutenant," said Lord Curran. "He knows where it is." The little mercenary had drawn his pistol again and was checking the loads for the second time since I fell into the midst of these angry, nervous men.

Kiley looked at his subordinate, then continued to me, "The commo screen is the small one to the immediate right of the main screen, and it has an alphanumeric keypad beneath it. The screen will have a numeral two or a numeral three on it when you enter, depending whether it's set to feed another tank or to Grant's helmet."

He paused, wet his lips. His voice was bare of affect, but in his fear he was unable to sort out the minimum data that my task required. The mercenary officer realized that he was wandering, but that only added to the pressure which already ground him from all sides.

"Push numeral one on the keypad," Lieutenant Kiley went on, articulating very carefully. "The numeral on the visor should change to one. That's all you need to do—the transceiver will be cleared for normal operation, and we'll do the rest from here." He touched his helmet with the barrel of his powergun, a gesture so controlled that the iridium did not clink on the thermoplastic.

"I'll need," I said, looking up at the flue, "a platform—tables or boxes."

"We'll lift you," said Lieutenant Kiley, "and we'll cover you as best we can. Better take that shirt off now and make the squeeze easier."

"No, My Lord," I said, rising against the back wall—out of sight, though within a possible line of fire. I stretched my muscles, wincing as tags of skin broke loose from the fabric to which blood had glued them. "It's dark-colored, so I'll need it to get to the tank. I, I'll use—"

I shuddered and almost fell; as I spoke, I visualized what I had just offered to do—and it terrified me.

"Kid—" said Lord Curran, catching me; though I was all right again, just a brief fit.

"I'll use my trousers also," I said. "They're at the other—"

"Via!" snapped Lord Sparky, pointing with the light which he had dimmed to a yellow glow that was scarcely a beam. "What *happened* t' you?"

"I was a servant in the women's apartments," I said. "I'll go now, if you'll help me. I must hurry."

Lord Curran and Lieutenant Kiley lifted me. Their hands were moist by contrast with the pebbled finish of their helmets, brushing my bare thighs. I could think only of how my nakedness had just humiliated me before the tank lords.

It was good to think of that, because my body eased itself into the flue without conscious direction and my mind was too full of old anger to freeze me with coming fears.

Going up was initially simpler than worming my way down the tube had been. With the firm fulcrum of Lieutenant Kiley's shoulders beneath me, my legs levered my ribs and shoulder past the point at which they caught on the concrete.

Someone started to shove me farther with his hands.

"No!" I shouted, the distorted echo unintelligible even to me and barely heard in the room below. Someone understood, though, and the hands locked instead into a platform against which my feet could push in the cautious increments which the narrow passage required.

Sliding up the tube, the concrete hurt everywhere it rubbed me. The rush of blood to my head must have dulled the pain when I crawled downward. My right arm now had no strength and my legs, as the knees cramped themselves within the flue, could no longer thrust with any strength.

For a moment, the touch of the tank lord's lifted hands left my soles. I was wedged too tightly to slip back, but I could no more have climbed higher in the flue than I could have shattered the concrete that trapped me. Above, partly blocked by my loosely waving arm, was a dim circle of the sky.

Hands gripped my feet and shoved upward with a firm, inexorable pressure that was now my only chance of success. Lord Curran, standing on his leader's shoulders, lifted me until my hand reached the outer lip. With a burst of hysterical strength, I dragged the rest of my body free.

It took me almost a minute to put my trousers on. The time was not wasted. If I had tried to jump down to the wall without resting, my muscles would have let me tumble all the way into the courtyard—probably with enough noise to bring an immediate storm of gunfire from the Baron's soldiers.

The light within the gatehouse must have been visible as glimmers through the same cracks in the shutters which the tank lords used to desperately survey their position. That meant the Baron's men would be even more alert ... but also, that their attention would be focused even more firmly on the second-floor windows—rather than on the wall adjacent to the gatehouse.

No one shot at me as I crawled backwards from the roof, pressing myself against the concrete and then stone hard enough to scrape skin that had not been touched by the flue.

The key to the tank hatches was in my mouth, the only place from which I could not lose it—while I lived.

My knees and elbows were bloody from the flue already, but the open sky was a relief as I wormed my way across the top of the wall. The moments I had been stuck in a concrete tube more strait than a coffin convinced me that there were worse deaths than a bullet.

Or even than by torture, unless the Baron decided to bury me alive.

I paused on my belly where the wall mated with the corner of the West Wing. I knew there were gunmen waiting at the windows a few meters away. They could not see me, but they might well hear the thump of my feet on the courtyard's compacted surface.

There was no better place to descend. Climbing up to the roofs of the palace would only delay my danger, while the greater danger rushed forward on the air cushion vehicles of the Lightning Division.

Taking a deep breath, I rolled over the rim of the wall. I dangled a moment before my strained arms let me fall the remaining two meters earlier than I had intended to. The sound my feet, then fingertips, made on the ground was not loud even to my fearful senses. There was no response from the windows above me— and no shots from the East Wing or the banquet hall, from which I was an easy target for any soldier who chanced to stare at the shadowed corner in which I poised.

I was six meters from the nearest tank—Lord Curran's tank, the tank from which Sergeant Grant had surveyed the women's apartments. Crawling was pointless—the gunmen were above me. I considered sprinting, but the sudden movement would have tripped the peripheral vision of eyes turned toward the gatehouse.

I strolled out of the corner, so frightened that I could not be sure my joints would not spill me to the ground because they had become rubbery.

One step, two steps, three steps, four—

"Hey!" someone shouted behind me, and seven powerguns raked the women's apartments with cyan lightning.

Because I was now so close to the tank, only soldiers in the West Wing could see me. The covering fire sent them ducking while glass shattered, fabrics burned, and flakes spalled away from the face of the stone itself. I heard screams from within, and not all of the throats were female.

A dozen or more automatic rifles—the soldiers elsewhere in the palace—opened fire on the gatehouse with a sound like wasps in a steel drum. I jumped to the bow slope of the tank, trusting my bare feet to grip the metal without delay for the steps set into the iridium.

A bolt from a powergun struck the turret a centimeter from where my hand slapped it. I screamed with dazzled surprise at the glowing dimple in the metal and the droplets that spattered my bare skin.

Only the tank lords' first volley had been aimed. When they ducked away from the inevitable return fire, they continued to shoot with only their gun muzzles lifted above the protecting stone. The bolts which scattered across the courtyard at random did a good job of frightening the Baron's men away from accurate shooting, but that randomness had almost killed me.

As it was, the shock of being fired at by a friend made me drop the hatch key. The circular field-induction chip clicked twice on its way to disappear in the dark courtyard.

The hatch opened. The key had bounced the first time on the cover.

I went through the opening head first, too frightened by the shots to swing my feet over the coaming in normal fashion. At least one soldier saw what was happening, because his bullets raked the air around my legs for the moment they waved. His tracers were green sparks; and when I fell safely within, more bullets disintegrated against the dense armor about me.

The seat, though folded, gashed my forehead with a corner and came near enough to stunning me with pain that I screamed in panic when I saw there was no commo screen where the lieutenant had said it would be. The saffron glow of instruments was cold mockery.

I spun. The main screen was behind me, just where it should have been, and the small commo screen—reading 3—was beside it. I had turned around when I tumbled through the hatch.

My finger stabbed at the keypad, hit 1 and 2

together. A slash replaced the 3—and then 1, as I got control of my hand again and touched the correct key. Electronics whirred softly in the belly of the great tank.

The West Wing slid up the main screen as I palmed the control. There was a 1 in the corner of the main screen also.

My world was the whole universe in the hush of my mind. I pressed the firing pedal as my hand rotated the turret counterclockwise.

The tribarrel's mechanism whined as it cycled and the bolts thumped, expanding the air on their way to their target; but when the blue-green flickers of released energy struck stone, the night and the facade of the women's apartments shattered. Stones the size of a man's head were blasted from the wall, striking my tank and the other palace buildings with the violence of the impacts.

My tank.

I touched the selector toggle. The numeral 2 shone orange in the upper corner of the screen which the lofty mass of the banquet hall slid to fill.

"Kid!" shouted speakers somewhere in the tank with me. *"Kid!"*

My bare toes rocked the firing pedal forward and the world burst away from the axis of the main gun.

The turret hatch was open because I didn't know how to close it. The tribarrel whipped the air of the courtyard, spinning hot vortices smoky from fires the guns had set and poisoned by ozone and gases from the cartridge matrices.

The 20 cm main gun sucked all the lesser whorls along the path of its bolt, then exploded them in a cataclysm that lifted the end of the banquet hall ten meters before dropping it back as rubble.

My screen blacked out the discharge, but even the multiple reflections that flashed through the turret hatch were blinding. There was a gout of burning stone. Torque had shattered the arched concrete roof when it lifted, but many of the reinforcing rods still held so that slabs danced together as they tumbled inward.

Riflemen had continued to fire while the tribarrel raked toward them. The 20 cm bolt silenced everything but its own echoes. Servants would have broken down the outside doors minutes before. The surviving soldiers followed them now, throwing away weapons unless they forgot them in their hands.

The screen to my left was a panorama through the vision blocks while the orange pips on the main screen provided the targeting array. Men, tank lords in khaki, jumped aboard the other tanks. Two of them ran toward me in the vehicle farthest from the gatehouse.

Only the west gable of the banquet hall had collapsed. The powergun had no penetration, so the roof panel on the palace's outer side had been damaged only by stresses transmitted by the panel that took the bolt. Even on the courtyard side, the reinforced concrete still held its shape five meters from where the bolt struck, though fractured and askew.

The tiny figure of the Baron was running toward me from the entrance.

I couldn't see him on the main screen because it was centered on the guns' point of impact. I shouted in surprise, frightened back into slavery by that man even when shrunken to a doll in a panorama.

My left hand dialed the main screen down and across, so that the center of the Baron's broad chest was ringed with sighting pips. He raised his mob gun as he ran, and his mouth bellowed a curse or a challenge.

The Baron was not afraid of me or of anything else. But he had been *born* to the options that power gives.

My foot stroked the firing pedal.

One of the mercenaries who had just leaped to the tank's back deck gave a shout as the world became ozone and a cyan flash. Part of the servants' quarters beneath the banquet hall caught fire around the three-meter cavity blasted by the gun.

The Baron's disembodied right leg thrashed once on the ground. Other than that, he had vanished from the vision blocks.

Lieutenant Kiley came through the hatch, feet first but otherwise with as little ceremony as I had shown. He shoved me hard against the turret wall while he rocked the gun switch down to safe. The orange numeral blanked from the screen.

"In the *Lord's* name, kid!" the big officer demanded while his left hand still pressed me back. "Who told you to do *that*?"

"Lieutenant," said Lord Curran, leaning over the hatch opening but continuing to scan the courtyard. His pistol was in his hand, muzzle lifted, while air trembled away from the hot metal. "We'd best get a move on unless you figure t' fight a reinforced battalion alone till the supports get here."

"Well, get in and *drive*, curse you!" the lieutenant shouted. The words relaxed his body and he released me. "*No*, I don't want to wait around here alone for the Lightning Division!"

"Lieutenant," said the driver, unaffected by his superior's anger, "we're down a man. You ride your blower. Kid'll be all right alone with me till we join up with the colonel and come back t' kick ass."

Lieutenant Kiley's face became very still. "Yeah, get in and drive," he said mildly, gripping the hatch coaming to lift himself out without bothering to use the power seat.

The driver vanished but his boots scuffed on the armor as he scurried for his own hatch. "Gimme your bloody key," he shouted back.

Instead of replying at once, the lieutenant looked down at me. "Sorry I got a little shook, kid," he said. "You did pretty good for a new recruit." Then he muscled himself up and out into the night.

The drive fans of other tanks were already roaring when ours began to whine up to speed. The great vehicle shifted greasily around me, then began to turn slowly on its axis. Fourth in line, we maneuvered through the courtyard gate while the draft from our fans lifted flames out of the palace windows.

We are the tank lords.

THE END

The Red Shift Lounge was the sort of bar where people left their uniforms back in their billet, so the sergeant who entered wearing dress whites and a chest full of medal ribbons attracted the instant attention of the bartender and the half dozen customers.

The unit patch on the sergeant's left shoulder was a black shrunken head on a white field, encircled by the words 121st MARINE REACTION COMPANY. The patch peeped out beneath a stole of weasel tails, trophies of ten or a dozen Khalians.

The Red Shift was part of the huge complex of Artificial Staging Area Zebra, where if you weren't military or a military dependent, you were worse. Everybody in the lounge this evening, including the bartender, was military: the two men in a booth were clearly officers; the two men and the woman drinking beer at a table were just as clearly enlisted; and the stocky fellow at the far end of bar could have been anything except a civilian.

But no uniforms meant no insignia, no questions

about who had the right to go find a mattress with who . . . no salutes.

And none of the problems that occurred when somebody figured a couple hot landings gave him the *right* not to salute some rear-echelon officer.

But down-time etiquette didn't matter when the guy in uniform was a sergeant from the Headhunters, the unit that had ended the war between the Alliance of Planets and the Khalia.

The War between Civilization and Weasels.

"Whiskey," ordered the sergeant in a raspy, angry voice.

"I thought," said one of the officers in diffident but nonetheless clearly audible tones, "that the One-Twenty-first shipped out today on the *Dalriada* at eighteen hundred hours."

The clock behind the bartender showed 1837 in tasteful blue numerals that blended with the dado lighting.

"For debriefing on Earth," the officer continued.

"And the parades, of course," his companion added.

The sergeant leaned his back against the bar. Something metallic in his sleeve rang when his left arm touched the dense, walnut-grained plastic. "I couldn't stomach that," he said. "Wanna make something of it?"

"Another beer," said the stocky man at the other end of the bar. His voice was mushy. The bartender ignored him.

"No, I don't," said the officer. "I don't suppose I would even if I were on duty."

"Bartender," called his companion. "I'll pay for that whiskey. As a matter of fact, sergeant, would you like to—"

He paused. The first officer was already sliding out of the booth, carrying his drink. "Would you mind if we joined you?" his companion said, getting up and heading for the bar before he completed the question.

"Naw, I'm glad for the company," the sergeant said. "I just couldn't take—I mean, *peace* with the weasels? We had 'em where we wanted 'em, by the balls. We shoulda kept going till this—" he tugged at his weasel-tail stole "—was the only kinda weasel there was!"

"I'm proud to meet a member of the Headhunt-ers," said the first officer. "My name's Howes—" he stuck out his hand "—and my friend here is, ah, Mr. Lewis."

Beyond any question, the two men were Com-manders or even Captains Howes and Lewis when they were in uniform.

"Sergeant Oaklin Bradley," the Headhunter said, shaking hands with both officers. "Sorry if I got a little short . . . but 'cha know, it tears the guts outa a real fighting man to think that we're going to quit while there's still weasels alive."

The bartender put the whiskey on the bar. Brad-ley's back was to him. The bartender continued to hold the glass for fear the Headhunter would bump it over.

"You were there at the surrender, I suppose?" Howes said as he picked up the whiskey and gave it to Bradley.

The woman, an overweight "blonde" in a tank top, got up from the table and made her way to the bar. She was dead drunk—but familiar enough with the condition to be able to function that way.

"Aw, Babs," said one of her companions.

Earlier, the trio at the table had been having a discussion in loud, drunken whispers. Just as Sergeant Bradley entered the lounge, Babs had mumblingly agreed to go down on both enlisted men in an equip-ment storage room near the Red Shift.

If her companions were unhappy about losing the

entertainment they'd planned for the evening, it didn't prevent them from joining her and the two officers in the semicircle around the uniformed hero at the bar.

"Oh, yeah," Bradley said. "I was there, all right." He'd waited to speak until chairlegs had stopped scraping and everyone was close enough to hear easily. "We landed right in the middle of the weasel Presidential Palace or whatever. . . ."

"High Council Chambers," Lewis murmured.

"Yes, yes, I'd heard that," Howes said. His eyes were greedy as they rested on Bradley's fringe of weasel tails. "The Khalians worship strength, so just reaching their capital put the Alliance on top of their dominance pyramid."

The man at the end of the bar stared into his empty mug, turning it slowly and carefully as if to make sense of his distorted reflection in the bottom.

"We killed so many of 'em you could float a battleship in the blood," Bradley said, licking his lips. "Never felt so good about anything in my life. We blew our way into the very fucking center of the place, caught all the weasel brass with their pants down . . . and Cap'n Kowacs, he said we had to let 'em surrender instead a burning 'em all the way we shoulda done."

Bradley tossed down his liquor in a quick, angry motion, then slapped the empty glass on the bar. Babs shifted closer so that one of her heavy breasts lay against the Headhunter's biceps.

"Well, it did end the war," Lewis said, examining his fingernails and looking vaguely embarrassed for disagreeing with the hero.

"*That* part of the war!" Howes retorted sharply. "There's still whoever it was behind the Khalians to begin with."

The bartender refilled the whiskey glass.

The Headhunter at the bar of the Red Shift Lounge remembered....

In the belly of the Dropship K435, Captain Miklos Kowacs squinted to focus on the image of their target. His holographic display stayed rock-steady as they dived toward the huge Khalian complex, but Kowacs' own eyes and brain vibrated like dessert gelatine.

Speed through an atmosphere meant turbulence, and the lord knew that to survive the Headhunters were going to need speed as well as electronics that spoofed the Identification: Friend or Foe signal from the weasel fortress.

Every second Marine in the three line platoons carried a man-portable rocket launcher. "Man-portable" because men were carrying them, not because they were light or handy. Most of the Marines who didn't have launchers lugged three-packs of reloads.

The rockets were to disable the missile launchers of the Khalian base. Even when that job was done, the Headhunters wouldn't have to go underground after the weasels: three of the Marines were strapped under 30-kilo tanks of DPD gas—

Which was designed to sink through the tunnels of a Khalian burrow and kill every living thing that breathed it.

There'd been plenty of room aboard the Attack Transport *Dalriada,* the K435's mothership, but the Headhunters were over-equipped to fit comfortably ftbonto the dropship itself. Marines squatted shoulder to shoulder, bumping one another and cursing bitterly....

Knowing, among other things, that the weight and bulk of the rockets which the mission required meant that they'd had to leave behind the body armor which they'd otherwise have been wearing during an assault like this.

Of course personal armor wouldn't matter a damn if the ship bit the big one while they were all aboard her.

The units aboard the *Dalriada*'s other seven dropships had normal missions: land on the fringe of a defended area and attack. The 121st was different. Last time out, the Headhunters had captured a Khalian courier vessel; now the whole company was shoe-horned into a secret weapon that pretended to *be* a weasel ship, telling the target not to fire on them as they raced down to cut Khalian throats.

There were various ways the local weasels could configure their IFF. Faint lines across Kowacs' holo-gram display recorded the burning tracks of the first two drones sent ahead of K435. At the third try, the fortress hadn't fired, so Operations was betting that K435 could get in untouched if it sent the same IFF response as that last drone.

Operations bet a single hundred-Marine chip. The Headhunters were betting their lives.

"... seconds to touchdown!" the flight deck warned. A break in transmission erased the figure, but if they were *seconds* close, K435 was well within the defended envelope.

"Wait for it!" bellowed Sergeant Bradley over the unit frequency as he saw inexperienced troopers rise to jump out before the dropship landed.

No missile explosion, no hammering flares from autoloading plasma weapons. They were all going to live—

Until the weasel ground personnel got done with them. That was fine. Weasels were what the Head-hunters had come to meet.

Too many new Marines on this drop. There'd been too fucking many casualties in the Bullseye operation. . . .

Kowacs felt a minuscule lift in K435's bow as the

shock of the vessel's approach was reflected from the ground. An instant later, the braking motors fired at full thrust and hammered the rows of squatting Head-hunters down against the deck plating.

"*Now!*" Kowacs, Bradley, and all four platoon leaders shouted as explosive bolts blew away the dropship's hatches and the 121st Marine Reaction Company, the Headhunters, lurched into action.

The world was bright and hot and smelled like brown flames.

An orbital-defense missile roared up from its launcher as the Marines shook themselves out onto the flat roof of the fortress. The sound of the three-tonne missile going supersonic just above the launch tube was ear-splitting.

A Headhunter fired her hand-held rocket launcher while she was still abroad K435. Backblast made that a dangerous trick—but this wasn't a desk job, and starting to shoot instantly was a pretty good response to the shock of landing and the missile launch.

The weasel missile tube was built into the fabric of the fortress. The small Marine round guided for the center of the opening, then fired a self-forging fragment straight down the tube's throat. Even if the armor-piercer didn't penetrate the launcher cap while the next anti-orbital round was being loaded, it was almost certain to jam the cap in place and prevent the weasels from using that tube again.

The weasel fortress was a jumble of huge flat boxes, with point-defense plasma weapons inset at each corner and heavy missile batteries buried deep in their cores. K435 was supposed to have landed on the high-est of the twenty to twenty-five cast-concrete prisms, but that hadn't worked out: a box to the west over-looked the one on which the Headhunters were deploying, and the weasel plasma guns could depress

at any instant to sweep the whole company to a glowing memory.

"Delta, check 220 degrees," Kowacs ordered his
Weapons Platoon. His helmet's artificial intelligence
put him at the top of the pyramid of lieutenants
assigning sectors and sergeants high-lighting specific
targets for the Marines of their squad. "Clear the
high—"

There was a deafening crash and a blast of static—
a plasma discharge radiated all across the radio-
frequency spectrum.

Corporal Sienkiewicz stood beside Kowacs because
her strength and ruthlessness made her the best bodyguard he could find in a company of strong, ruthless
Marines. She'd just fired her hand-carried plasma
weapon, a heavy tube that looked delicate against her
husky two-meter frame.

A Khalian gun position vanished; then the whole
top edge of the concrete prism stuttered with dazzling
plasma bursts and long tendrils of quicklime burned
from the concrete and spewing away in white-hot tendrils. Delta had its own belt-fed plasma weapons set
up on tripods, and they didn't need Kowacs' orders
to tell them it was everybody's ass if they didn't nail
the close-in defenses before some weasel brought the
guns under manual control.

The noise of plasma weapons, rockets and rocket
warheads made it hard for Kowacs to think, much
less hear any of the message traffic on his earphones.
Although Kowacs' helmet damped the worst of the
racket, shockwaves slapped the skin of his face and
hands like huge, hot raindrops.

Squad leaders with echo-location gear were using
the noise to map all the surfaces of the Khalian fortress. When holographic images on a sergeant's helmet visor indicated a missile tube in his squad's

sector, he relayed the target to a Marine with a rocket launcher.

The Headhunters' top-attack rockets ripped and snapped all across the concrete jumble. Occasionally a blast of smoky yellow flame indicated that one of the big Khalian missiles had blown up within its launcher.

But the Khalians weren't shooting any more.

Kowacs turned around so that his unaided eyes could confirm that his visor display already insisted. Through the skeletal ribs of K435 and across the fortress, as well as on his side of the landing vessel, nobody was firing except Kowacs' own Marines.

Missiles didn't rise to engage the ships in orbit. Plasma weapons didn't chew themselves new firing slits to that they could bear on the Marine landing force. . . .

Unbefuckinglievable.

There was a momentary lull in the gunfire as the rest of the Headhunters realized the same thing. Then Sergeant Bradley screamed, "Door opening!" on the primary unit push, and three rockets streaked simultaneously toward the northwest corner of the block on which the marines had landed.

The leaves of the hidden steel trapdoor rang like bells as they flew apart under the impact of the self-forging fragments. There were swatches of fur in the blast debris also.

"Double it!" Kowacs ordered, but there were already three more rockets in the air and three more sharp explosions over the sally-port, chopping weasels into cat's meat before their counterattack had time to get under way.

Kowacs was more agile than most of the Headhunters because he was burdened only with his personal weapons. He began running toward the shattered trapdoor, shouting, "Gas carriers to me!"

"You'd've thought the rocket blasts would've kept

the weasels down for at least a few minutes. More furry, yellow-fanged heads popped out of the sally-port even before Kowacs got out the last syllable of his order.

He shot as he ran, spraying the area with a dozen ricochets for every bullet that counted—but ammo was cheap, and at least a dozen other Headhunters were firing along with their captain. The vivid white fireball of a plasma burst hid the target momentarily; Sie had saved back one charge for an emergency like this.

The weasels had been waving something.

More weasels rose out of the half-molten pit where the trapdoor had been. They vanished in a maelstrom of bullets and grenade fragments.

Kowacs paused twenty meters from the sally-port to reload. A Marine with one of the green-painted gas cylinders caught up with him. Sienkiewicz was giving the fellow a hand with his load.

More weasels leaped from the fortress. Kowacs aimed but didn't fire. Other Marines ripped the fresh targets into gobbets of bloody flesh.

The weasels were waving white flags.

"Cease fire!" Kowacs shouted. Still more weasels were coming up. "Cease fire!"

There were ten or a dozen unarmed Khalians in the next group, all of them waving white flags. Some were females.

A Headhunter fired his assault rifle. One of the tripod-mounted plasma weapons vaporized the weasels with three bolts.

More weasels came up from the crater.

"Cease fire!" Kowacs screamed as he ran forward, facing his marines as he put his body between them and the Khalians.

Facing most of his Marines, because Sie was on one side of him and Sergeant Bradley was on the other. Both non-coms were cursing their captain, but not so bitterly as Kowacs cursed himself and the command responsibility that made him do *this* when he should've been shooting weasels.

Nobody shot. Nobody spoke. Kowacs' panting breath roared behind the constriction of his visor.

Kowacs slowly turned to face the weasels again. His lungs were burning. He flipped his visor out of the way, though that left him without the heads-up display if he needed it.

There were twelve Khalians. They stood on the lip of the crater, waving their small square flags. Each weasel had its nose pointed high in the air, baring the white fur of its throat. Their muzzles were wrinkling, but Kowacs didn't know whether that was a facial expression or just a reaction to the stench of blast residues and death.

Miklos Kowacs had killed hundreds of weasels during his Marine career. He'd never before spent this long looking at a living one.

"Helmet," he said, "translate Khalian."

He splayed the fingers of his left hand, the hand that didn't hold a fully-loaded automatic rifle, in the direction of the weasels. "You!" he said. "Which of you's the leader?" as the speaker on top of his helmet barked the question in weaseltalk.

None of the Khalians wore clothing or ornamentation. The one on the left end of the line lowered his nose so that he could see ahead of himself, stepped forward, and chattered something that the translation program in Kowacs' helmet rendered as, "Are you Fleet Marines? You *are* Fleet Marines."

"Answer me!" Kowacs shouted. "Are you in charge?" The concrete seemed to ripple. It was solid, but Nick Kowacs wasn't solid just now. . . .

"We wish to surrender to Fleet Marines," the weasel

said. He was about a meter forty tall, mid-breastbone level to Kowacs. "Are you Fleet Marines?"

"Goddam," Bradley whispered, his scarred left hand wringing the foregrip of the shotgun he pointed.

"You bet," said Nick Kowacs. His brain was echoing with screams and other memories and screams. "We're the Headhunters, we're the best." *Weasels never surrendered.* "You want to surrender this whole fortress?"

"That too," said the weasel. "You are fighters whom we respect. Come below with us to receive our surrender, Fleet Marine."

Sienkiewicz laughed.

"Bullshit," Kowacs said flatly. "You tell your people to come on out, one at a time, and we'll see about surrender."

"Please," barked the weasel. "You must come into the Council Chamber to take our surrender."

"Bullshit!" Kowacs repeated.

He risked a glance over his shoulder. The three Marines with gas cylinders, kneeling under the weight of their loads, were in the front rank of waiting troops. "Look, get your people up here, or—"

The Khalians had no equipment, but they had been born with tusks and sharp, retractile claws. "Then I have failed," the speaker of the group said. He raised a forepaw and tore his own throat out.

"—almighty!" Bradley blurted as Kowacs choked off his own inarticulate grunt. The weasel thrashed on the seared concrete, gushing arterial blood from four deep slashes. The furry corpse was still twitching when a second Khalian stepped forward.

"Come into the Council Chamber with us, Fleet Marine," the new envoy said. "Only from there can the surrender be broadcast to all."

"No!" shouted Sergeant Bradley. The weasel raised his paw; sunlight winked on the clawtips.

"Yes!" shouted Captain Miklos Kowacs, feeling the ground shiver like the dying weasel before him.

"Ah, sir?" said one of the Marines carrying a gas cylinder. "*All* of us?"

Lieutenant Mandricard, the senior platoon leader, had faced his platoon around to cover the Headhunters' rear while the rest of the Marines were shooting weasel pop-ups. He glanced over his shoulder at the company commander.

Kowacs pointed a finger at Mandricard and said over the general push, "Gamma Six, you're in charge here until I get back, right? If that's not in—" *how long?* "—six zero minutes, finish the job."

He nodded toward the gas cylinders. And smiled like a cobra.

"Sir," said Bradley, "we can't do this."

Kowacs looked at him. "I gotta do it, Top," he said.

"Hold one," said Corporal Sienkiewicz. She'd unharnessed one of the gas carriers and was now—

Godalmighty! She was molding a wad of contact-fuzed blasting putty onto the tank of gas. If she dropped the heavy cylinder, the charge would rupture it and flood the whole area with DPD!

"Right," Sienkiewicz said as she examined her handiwork. "Now we're ready to go down."

Bradley swore coldly, checked his shotgun, and said, "Yeah, let's get this dumb-ass shit over with."

Kowacs hadn't told Sie and the sergeant to accompany him; but he knew they wouldn't accept an order to stay behind. "G—" he said to the Khalian envoy. His voice broke. "Go on, then."

The eleven surviving weasels scrambled into the blasted entrance. Kowacs strode after them.

"I'll lead," said Sienkiewicz.

"Like hell you will," Kowacs snapped as his rigid arm blocked his bodyguard's attempt to push past.

The entrance was a stinking pit. A crowd of weasels,

all of them carrying flags, filled the floor below. The metal staircase had been destroyed by the first volley of rockets; since then, the Khalians had been scrambling up wooden poles to reach the roof and their deaths.

Shattered poles, corpses, and charred white scraps of cloth covered the concrete floor on which living weasels pushed and chittered in a cacaphony that the translation program couldn't handle.

"Back!" barked the Khalian envoy, raising both his clawed forepaws in symbolic threat. "To the Council Chamber!"

The Khalian mob surged down the hallway like a shockwave travelling through a viscous fluid. There were lights some distance away, but the Headhunters' blasts had destroyed the nearest fixtures.

Kowacs looked down, grimaced, and dropped. His boots skidded on the slimy floor.

"Watch—" he said to his companions, but Sie was already swinging herself down. Her right hand gripped the edge of the roof while her left arm cradled her lethal burden like a baby.

Bradley must've thought the same thing, because he said, "Hope the little bastid don't burp," as he followed into the Khalian fortress.

"Come this way!" ordered the envoy as though he and not the Headhunters were armed. The weasels' demonstrated willingness to die made them very hard to control.

Pretty much the same was true of Marines in the reaction companies too, of course.

The ceiling was so low that Kowacs, stocky rather than tall, brushed his helmet until he hunched over. He expected to hear Sie cursing, but the big woman didn't say a word. She was probably concentrating so that she didn't drop the bomb in her arms and end all this before—

Before it was supposed to end. Not necessarily different from the way it was going to end anyway.

The hallway curved. For a moment, Kowacs' helmet picked up the crisp commands of Gamma Six as Mandricard put the Headhunters in as much of a posture of defense as the featureless roof permitted. Reception faded to static, then nothing at all.

They came to a bank of wire-fronted elevators and a crowd of waiting Khalians. "Come with me," the envoy said as he stepped into the nearest cage.

The cage was small and low; three humans in battlegear and a Khalian filled it uncomfortably. As the elevator started to descend, Kowacs saw a horde of weasels pushing into the remaining cages.

Bradley began to shake. The muzzle of his gun wobbled through tight arcs. "It stinks . . ." he mumbled. "It *stinks.*"

He was right, of course. The air circulating in the Khalian burrow smelled of Khalians, and that was a stench worse than death to a man like Bradley, who'd seen what the weasels left of his little daughter on Tanjug . . .

Or to a man like Nick Kowacs, whose family had been on Gravely when the weasels landed there.

Kowacs shivered. "Top!" he said harshly. "Snap out of it. You're not going claustrophobic on me now."

Bradley took off his helmet and squeezed his bald, scarred scalp with his left hand. His eyes were shut. "It's not the fuckin' tunnels," he said. "Not the tunnels. All these weasels . . . I just, I wanna—"

Bradley's fingertips left broad white dimples on his skin when he took his hand away. The weasel envoy watched the sergeant with bright black eyes.

No one spoke again until the cage stopped and the Khalian repeated, "Come with me," as his paw clashed the door open.

Kowacs couldn't guess how deep in the earth they

were now. There was a sea of fur and tusks and chittering weasel voices outside the elevator. Many of this
crowd wore ornaments of brass and leather, but
Kowacs didn't see any weapons.

He stepped out behind the envoy, watching the
passageway clear before them and wondering if the
Khalians would close in again behind the three
humans.

It didn't matter. They were *in* this, he and Top and
Sie, as far as they could get already. At least the tunnel ceiling was high enough for humans, even the
corporal with her burden of death.

The envoy led through an arched doorway. The
chamber within was huge even by human standards.

The chamber was full of Khalians.

The smell and sound and visual impact stopped
Kowacs in his tracks. One of his men bumped him
from behind.

Kowacs closed his eyes and rubbed them hard with
the back of his left wrist. That made it worse. When
he didn't see the room filled with weasels, his mind
quivered over the memory of his mother, her gnawed
corpse thick with the musk of the furry monsters
that had—

"*No!*" Kowacs screamed. The distant walls gave
back the echo, cushioned by the soft susurrus of
breathing mammals. There was no other sound.

He opened his eyes.

A group of Khalians was coming forward from the
crowd. There were twenty or more of them. They
wore jewelry and robes patterned with soft, natural
colors.

They were very old. Some hobbled, and even those
weasels who were able to walk erect had grizzled fur
and noticeably worn tusks.

Weasels don't wear clothing. . . .

There was a great sigh from the assembled company.

The aged Khalians gripped their robes and tore them apart in ragged, ritual motions. Some of them were mewling; their facial fur was wet with tears. They fell to the floor and began writhing forward, their throats and bellies bared to the Marines.

The weasel in the center of the groveling line gave a series of broken, high-pitched barks. The voice of Kowacs' helmet translated, "Khalia surrenders to you, warriors of the Fleet Marines. We are your subjects, your slaves, to use as you wish."

Come to the Council Chamber, the weasel envoy had said. *The High Council of Khalia. They weren't surrendering this fortress—*

"Khalia surrenders—"

They were surrendering the whole Khalian race!

"—to you, warriors of the—"

Bradley's shotgun crashed. Its airfoil charge was designed to spread widely, even at point-blank range. The load sawed through the chest of the Khalian speaker like so many miniature razors. The weasel's tusked jaws continued to open and close, but nothing came out except drops of bloody spittle.

The aged Khalian nearest the dead one began to chant, "We are your slaves, warriors of the Fleet Marines. Use us as you will. We—"

Sergeant Bradley's face was that of a grinning skull. He'd dropped his helmet in the elevator cage. There was no reason left behind his glazing eyes. "You'll die," he said in a sing-song voice, "you'll all—"

He fired again. His charge splashed the skull of the corpse.

"—die, every fucking—"

Kowacs gripped the shotgun barrel with his left hand. The metal burned him. He couldn't lift the muzzle against Bradley's hysterical grip.

"Put it down, Top!" he ordered.

The moaning of the crowd was louder. Waves of

Khalian musk blended sickeningly with powder smoke.

"—are your subjects, your—"

Bradley fired into the dead weasel's groin.

"—weasel in the fucking uni—"

"Down!" Kowacs screamed and touched the muzzle of his assault rifle to Bradley's temple where a wisp of hair grew in the midst of pink scar tissue. Kowacs' vision tunnelled down to nothing but the hairs and the black metal and the flash that would—

There was a hollow *thunk.*

Bradley released the shotgun as he fell forward unconscious. Sienkiewicz looked at her captain with empty eyes. There was a splotch of blood on the green metal of the gas cylinder and a matching pressure cut on the back of Bradley's skull, but the sergeant would be all right as soon as he came around. . . .

"On behalf of the Alliance of Planets," Kowacs said in a quavering voice, "I accept your surrender."

He covered his eyes with his broad left hand. He shouldn't have done that, because that made him remember his mother and he began to vomit.

"Hey, Sergeant Bradley," said one of the enlisted men in the Red Shift Lounge, "let *me* get 'cha the next drink."

The man in whites toyed with his stole of Khalian tails. "We shoulda kept killin' 'em till everybody had a weasel-skin blanket!" he said. "We shoulda—"

Somebody came into the bar; somebody so big that even Sergeant Bradley looked up.

The newcomer, a woman in coveralls, squinted into the dim lounge. She glanced at the group around Bradley, then ignored them. When she saw the stocky man at the far end of the bar, she strode forward.

The sudden smile made her almost attractive.

Bradley's hand closed on his fresh drink. "If there's

still one weasel left in the universe," he said, "that's too many."

"Sar'nt?" murmured the drunken blond. "Why'n't you'n me, we go somewhur?"

"Hey, cap'n" said the big woman to the man at the far end of the bar. "Good t' see you."

"Go 'way, Sie," he replied, staring into his mug. "You'll lose your rank if you miss lift."

"Fuck my rank," she said. Everyone in the lounge was looking at them. "Besides," she added, "Commander Goldstein says the *Dalriada*'s engines 're broke down till we get you aboard. Sir."

She laid the man's right arm over her shoulders, gripped him around the back with her left hand, and lifted him in a packstrap carry. He was even bigger than he'd looked hunched over the bar, a blocky anvil of a man with no-colored eyes.

"You're always gettin' me outa places I shouldn't a got into, Sie," the man said.

His legs moved as the woman maneuvered him toward the door, but she supported almost all of his weight. "Worse places 'n this, sir," she replied.

"They weren't worse than now, Sie," he said. "Trust me."

As the pair of them started to shuffle past the group near the door, the woman's eyes focused on the uniformed man. She stopped. The man she held braced himself with a lopsided grin and said, "I'm okay now, Sie."

"Who the hell are you?" the big woman demanded of the man wearing the Headhunter uniform.

"What's it to you?" he snarled back.

"This is Sergeant Bradley of the 121st Marine Reaction Company," said one of the enlisted men, drunkenly pompous.

"Like hell he is," the big woman said. Her arms

were free now. "Top's searching bars down the Strip the other direction, lookin' for Cap'n Kowacs, here."

Kowacs continued to grin. His face was as terrible as a hedge of bayonets.

The group around "Sergeant Bradley" backed away as though he had suddenly grown an extra head.

The imposter in uniform tried to run. Sienkiewicz grabbed him by the throat from beyond. "Thought you'd be a big hero, did ya? Some clerk from Personnel, gonna be a hero now it's safe t' be a hero?"

The imposter twisted around. A quick-release catch *snicked*, shooting the knife from his left sleeve into his palm.

Sienkiewicz closed her right hand over the imposter's grip on his knife hilt. She twisted. Bones broke.

The knife came away from the hand of her keening victim. Sie slammed the point down into the bar top, driving it deep into the dense plastic before she twisted again and snapped the blade.

"Big hero . . ." she whispered. Her expression was that of nothing human. She gripped the weasel-tail stole and said, "How much did these cost 'cha, hero?" as she tore the trophies away and flung them behind her.

The bartender's finger was poised over the red emergency button that would summon the Shore Police. He didn't push it.

Sienkiewicz' grip on the imposter's throat was turning the man's face purple. Nobody moved to stop her. Her right hand stripped off the uniform sleeve with its Headhunter insignia and tossed it after the stole.

Then, still using the power of only one arm, she hurled the imposter into a back booth also. Bone and plastic cracked at the heavy impact.

"I'm okay, Sie," Kowacs repeated, but he let his corporal put her arm back around him again.

As the two Headhunters left the Red Shift Lounge,

one of the enlisted men muttered, "You lying scum," and drove his heel into the ribs of the fallen man.

Kowacs found that if he concentrated he could walk almost normally. There was a lot of traffic this close to the docking hub, but other pedestrians made way good-naturedly for the pair of big Marines.

"Sie," Kowacs said, "I used to daydream, you know? Me an old man, my beard down t' my belt, y'know? And this little girl, she comes up t' me and she says, 'Great Grandaddy, what did you do in the Weasel War?'"

"Careful of the bollard here, sir," Sienkiewicz murmured. "There'll be a shuttle in a couple minutes."

"And I'd say to her," Kowacs continued, his voice rising, "Well, sweetheart—I survived.'"

He started to sob. Sienkiewicz held him tightly. The people already standing at the shuttle point edged away.

"But I never thought I *would* survive, Sie!" Kowacs blubbered. "I never thought I would!"

"Easy, sir. We'll get you bunked down in a minute."

Kowacs looked up, his red eyes meeting Sienkiewicz' concern. "And you know the funny thing, Sie," he said. "I don't think I did survive."

"Easy. . . ."

"Without weasels t' kill, I don't think there's any Nick Kowacs alive."

The Way We Die

Seems like the rain falls harder since we crossed the line from War Zone C. Harder and more regular—start about 1700 after we laager up for the night, then rain like a son of a bitch for the next two hours. In Cambodia they don't hold the command meetings at 1900 any more, they just wait for the rain to stop. Then Lieutenant Brown with his big eight-track recorder pops out of the hatch of Two-zero—that's the platoon's only Sheridan now—and walks over to the command track in the center of the laager.

The rain sure comes down, don't it? Oh, you get used to it after you've been in-country a while. Some other time I might strip and shower in it. Not right now.

It was bright sun this morning when Flip died.

Looked like we were really going places when they let us cross the border, you know? Really going to get COSVN and end this fucking war. Maybe we got close at Snuol, I dunno. That's the only time the dinks dug in and fought back. Other than that, it's all been mines and automatic ambushes. Mines from them and AAs from us.

At Snuol the dinks got two tracks and we got four fifty-one cals. We got Lieutenant Brown, too.

Lieutenant Golightly, the old platoon leader, was dusted off with some shrapnel from a B-40 in him. The rocket hit his Sheridan when it was already stopped and everybody was bailing out of it; woulda been a bad scene otherwise.

Ever see a Sheridan burn? Naw, you're too green.

The Colonel's bird brought Lieutenant Brown in that night. Lieutenant Golightly had been pretty popular, but I don't know that put anybody against Lieutenant Brown.

Flip 'n me watched Brown get off the chopper with both hands full of gear, ducking low because of the blades. He was a little fella, slim in the waist but with broad shoulders for his size. No kid, either. He looked pretty near thirty. Word is he made staff sergeant before going to OCS. Red hair and a moustache he started growing just after getting in-country; it still looked ragged.

"Hey, lookit that, snake!" Flip said to me. "Sprouting hair like that, he'll be a good dude."

Bad guess, that.

The first thing Brown said to us was, "My gear's on the pad. A couple you guys carry it over to my Sheridan."

As he started to walk off I said, "Ah, which one, El-Tee? We combat-lossed Two-two this morning, that was Lieutenant Golightly's track. There's Two-zero and Two-one left."

"Either one, dammit," he says. "Just get my gear under cover before it starts raining again." And he walks off toward the command track.

Flip and me looked at each other, then lugged the gear over to Two-zero. I was track commander for Two-one, 'n Flip was my driver. Neither of us figured we wanted to share the car with the new el-tee after all.

A Sheridan's bigger than an ACAV but it doesn't have as much room inside. An ACAV's just an aluminum box on treads. The TC's got a cal fifty in his cupola, and there's two swivel-mounted M60 machine guns for the rest of the crew. With only machine gun ammo and personal gear inside, there's room enough for all three of the guys who aren't pulling guard to rack out at the same time.

Sheridans're tanks. The hull is aluminum, sure, but it's got a big steel turret in the middle with a one-five-two millimeter main gun.

That gun's the worst thing about a Sheridan, worse 'n the unarmored belly that nearly rubs the ground. Some bright boy figured out that the brass case holding the gunpowder takes up a lot of room. If you make the case so it burns, you could hold thirty shells in a Sheridan instead of maybe twenty.

Only the bright boy didn't figure out what might happened to them thirty bare charges if something started a fire in the turret. If a B-40 hit the hull, for instance, or if you ran over a mine big enough to punch a hole through that little thin floorplate, or if somebody screwed up and set off a grenade inside the hull.

Ever see a Sheridan burn?

With all them big shells inside, there's not room for much else. Our gear goes in the bustle rack, the mesh trough around the back of the turret. Since it's out in the wet, you can't just carry your socks in a duffle bag. You either put your gear in empty ammo cans or you might as well leave it back at Quan Loi for all the good it'll do you in the field.

Lieutenant Brown didn't have more in his duffle bag than'd fit in the two Minicans Lieutenant Golightly left behind, but there was this big eight-track tape recorder besides. It was a beauty, about $400 worth, but a hell of a thing to bring to Cambodia. It weighed near thirty pounds, and it was a good foot and a half square.

We set the recorder on the front slope of Two-zero while we broke the news to the crew that they were the new el-tee's track.

We'd thought maybe the new guy'd want to ride an ACAV instead. There's six ACAVs and three Sheridan's in a platoon—full strength; we were already down to five and two—so the platoon leader's got a choice. Sheridans have the firepower, which is nice; but a lotta guys wouldn't ride on one for a bet.

It takes a while to get used to all that bare gunpowder down below you. A lotta things don't seem important after you been in-country a while, though.

Flip started screwing with the recorder while we waited for Lieutenant Brown to come back. Nothing happened when he pushed the buttons.

"Hey, snake," I told him. "This thing don't have batteries. You gotta plug it into the wall."

Brown came up beside us then, so fast I didn't know he was there until he grabbed Flip by the shoulder and spun him around. "What do you think you're doing, soldier?" he says.

"Hey, steady on, El-Tee," Flip said. "We were just looking—"

Brown pushed Flip back against the track. I'd never seen an officer get so mad before. "Listen, punk!" he shouts. "I'm not 'hey,' I'm not 'el-tee.' I'm 'sir' or I'm 'Lieutenant Brown,' and that's what you'll call me every time. Is that understood?"

"Sure, Lieutenant Brown," Flip mumbled.

Flip was pretty surprised, even more 'n the rest of us. He was always a little runt, even back home in High Point when we were kids. Flip never got into fights, just acted easy-going and didn't believe that anybody really wanted to start something. He was the last guy in the world to get jumped like that.

Brown walked back to the command track. He took the recorder with him. Thought we might still want to mess with it, I guess.

We didn't say much after he left.

I had my own run-in with the man a couple days later.

We'd found a trail through the jungle. It didn't seem to get much use, but you never can tell how Charlie'll try to slip the next load of rockets south. Like I say, after Snuol, it's all been mines and automatic ambushes. We radioed back to troop headquarters, and the CO told us set up an AA.

Brown had never seen a real automatic ambush. He watched close while we strung the tripwire and placed the Claymore mines at intervals along the trail. If some dink comes di-di bopping into the tripwire, all the mines go off at once.

There's two pounds of C4 explosive in each Claymore. That blows a charge of BBs out across the trail like a big shotgun. When a dozen go off, KABAM! You've got everybody for fifty yards from the tripwire lying right there for you in the morning.

"Pretty slick, huh?" I said to Lieutenant Brown.

He grunted. "They told us at training school how it was done."

Newbie school, he meant.

"You know there's enough C4 in those Claymores to blow an ACAV clean over on its back?" I said. "That's just what the dinks'd do with it if they spotted the AA before they hit the tripwire. So we got a trick to fix that."

I took the doctored frag out of my pocket. I'd already unscrewed the time fuze and replaced it with the igniter pistol from a demolition set. That way when the handle of the grenade flies up, instead of starting a five-second fuze, it goes bang right away.

This was sorta my job. The rest of the platoon backed off.

I knelt down and used my bayonet to dig a fist-size hole for the frag. I put the last claymore over it, setting the spikes in tight so the mine'd hold down the handle of the grenade after I pulled the pin. Then if the dink tried to lift the Claymore, the grenade'd blow him to hell with a silly expression on his face.

Brown looked funny when he saw what I was doing. Then he put out his hand and said, "You aren't going to boobytrap that, are you?"

"Sure," I told him. "We always do it this way. Sometimes we just set an ammo can full of rocks beside the trail with one of these—" I tapped the frag "—under it. Look, if you get nervous, you can move back with the other guys, but the fact I'm still here proves I never stepped on my dick doin' it yet."

Brown didn't laugh. He got so red in the face I couldn't hardly see the freckles. The two bandoliers of ammo for his M16 rustled as he took a breath.

"Put that goddam grenade back in your pocket," he says. "The first thing you do at troop is put the time fuze back in it like it's supposed to be. And you never—*never*—think of boobytrapping an automatic ambush again."

"But sir," I says, "it keeps the dinks—"

He cut me off. "Don't argue with me, shithead!" he snarls. "What's going to happen when you want to take them down in the morning? Or don't you know you can't leave AAs set up more than overnight?"

I was getting pissed too. "Up here there aren't any friendlies walking around," I said. "Anybody steps into an AA had it coming to him. There's no point in setting 'em up every night and taking 'em down every morning for fear some papa-san'll drive his buffalo into one of 'em."

"One more word!" he shouts. "One more word and you got six months in Long Binh Jail to wonder where your stripes went to. Want to try me, soldier?"

I mighta popped him—I'm not like Flip—but he'd've had my ass in the LBJ and no mistake. I just looked away and set up the remaining mine over the hole that should've had the frag in it. Back at the NDP, I put a regular fuze back in the grenade, but I kept the igniter pistol.

I didn't figure Brown'd last forever. I mean, he's flat-assed crazy.

Well, I guess you could say anybody is, after a while out here, but. . . .

Anyway, it don't mean nothin'.

Even Captain Richie, he got pissed off about the way Brown is with his recorder. It's got an adapter so he runs it off the Sheridan's batteries. He built a bracket for it inside the turret. If you climbed onto Two-zero when he wasn't there, he'd come nosing around in a couple minutes to make sure you weren't fucking with his toy. And every night he takes it with him to the command meeting.

Except for the drivers, nobody rides inside a track over here, especially if it's a Sheridan. And in this troop we don't fight the main gun except when we're pulling perimeter security back at the firebase and there's a dirt berm to keep B-40s outa the hull.

The loader's got a machine gun welded to the top of the turret. He sits on the hatch cover—some guys have regular seats welded there—and doesn't have a foot inside the track while we're moving. The TC, that's me, has a cal fifty in the cupola. There the red handle to fight the main gun, too, but that's one shot only: nobody expects the loader to be inside the hull until things've quieted down again.

So the recorder sitting on top of the ammo didn't really matter in a firefight; only you would've figured a guy like Brown to think so if somebody else did it.

Last night . . .

I guess last night was what really sprung it.

We had regular guard shifts on Two-one. Me first because I'm TC; Chico and Billy, the loader and the back deck gunner, second and third; and Flip last because that's the second-best slot and he's got next most time in-country after me.

It was about 1930. I was up in the cupola, looking out at the jungle beyond my machine gun, and Flip sat on the turret beside me, smoking a joint. It was the regular kind, the Cambodian filtertips. They come in packs of twenty-five with a picture of a marijuana plant on the front and a lot of the squiggles that pass for writing in Cambodia. It didn't matter, you see, because there was no way the dinks were going to hit us that night, and Flip had last guard anyway.

Besides, a guy's got a right to do his thing.

We heard boots on the gravel. Flip spun the jay out into the dark.

I don't know why he did it, Christ, all the officers know we blow grass and don't make a big thing about it, but it was a good thing this time.

Lieutenant Brown jumps up on the back deck of the track, still holding his recorder, and yells, "Which of you sons of bitches is smoking pot? Come on, goddammit! You think I don't know the smell?"

"Pot, sir?" says Flip all innocent like, and the el-tee takes him by the shoulder.

"Don't do that!" I said. Flip's my buddy.

Brown let got of Flip then. He knew what'd happen if he didn't, with the whole crew there to swear that he'd hit me first. There's a few things the army don't let officers do to enlisted men.

"Cooney and Bowles, huh?" Brown said, real quiet.

"Okay, boy, for now. But I'm watching, you see? I'm going to *have* your asses, and you better believe it. Walk straight, son. Walk very straight."

He jumped down from the track then and went back the way he'd come. I waited until he'd scrunched out of sight and said, "Throw the rest of your joints right out after that one, Flip."

"Shit, man, he's gone."

"Throw it away, snake," I said, meaning it. "He's gonna be back inside of five with the CO, and they'll shake the whole track down. Get clean fast."

Sure enough, Brown and Captain Richie came over a few minutes later. I don't blame the CO, he didn't have much choice after Lieutenant Brown bitched to him. But he'd've burned us sure if he'd caught us holding.

I didn't kid myself that this was the last shakedown we'd be seeing, either. Not until Lieutenant Brown left or he caught us on something.

This morning we had a minesweep, down a stretch of Route 13 south of where we laagered. Billy and the back-deck gunner from Two-zero were out in front with the mine detectors, swinging the long booms from side to side to cover all the gravel road. I don't think either of them really knew how to use the detectors, but it didn't much matter since the dinks don't use steel-cased mines any more.

Nowadays the dinks fill a concrete shell with C4 from our Claymores and fit a wooden pressure plate. The only metal is the copper in the detonator. If you've got your detector tuned fine enough to pick *that* up, the headphones squeal like a hung-up cat every time you swing over a scrap of barbwire laying in the gravel. You just trust to luck and hope you'll see if there's traces of fresh digging.

Or that some mama-san in a cyclo will roll over the mine before you do.

We were lead track, right behind the sweepers with our turret cocked to the right and the tube of the main gun depressed. The five ACAVs followed at pretty close intervals with their cal fifties aimed left and right alternately, so that if something started we could spray both sides of the road right away.

Not that we expected anything to happen.

Two-zero with Lieutenant Brown in the cupola brought up the rear.

When you're working behind minesweeps you have to move by fits and starts. While we were stopped waiting for the sweeps to get far enough ahead of us again, Flip called back from his hatch, "Hey Chico, want to drive for a while?"

Chico didn't mind changing. He took the controls, and Flip hopped up onto the loader's hatch. He pulled his head close and I took off my commo helmet so I could hear him over the whine of the diesel.

"Look what I got from a coke girl," he says, and he shows me another pack of jays.

"Goddammit, Flip, I told you to stay clean," I said, mad now and a little scared. I didn't think Lieutenant Brown'd shake us down on a minesweep, but he sure as hell might as soon as we got back to troop. *He* knew the coke girls sold grass too.

"No sweat," Flip said. "I'll give 'em to Shorty on Six-six to hold for me as soon as we get turned around. But I'm gonna smoke one now, whatever that mother-fucker says."

I shrugged and said, "It's your ass."

Flip dropped down inside the turret and lit up where nobody but me could see him. The sweetish smoke started drifting back, and I wondered if Brown would catch a whiff at the end of the column. Anyway, it was that bastard's own fault that Flip was blowing grass on duty.

"Hey, snake," Flip yelled so I could hear him. "This is good stuff. Want a drag?"

I shook my head. I figured to stay clean until Brown got the CO pissed off enough to transfer him off all our backs.

The sweeps were forty yards ahead of us again and Chico eased in the clutches. That's when we hit the mine.

It was a big one. It went off right behind the driver's compartment, lifting up the front end of the Sheridan and blowing Chico clean out into the road. That maybe saved his life, 'cause the ammo caught fire then.

When a Sheridan burns it goes *whoosh* with jets of red flame shooting up twenty feet into the sky from all three hatches like searchlights. I was already rolling clear when the flame boomed up past me. It blistered me right through my jungle fatigues.

Flip didn't have a chance, not even time to scream, down in the turret with them shells all around him. I was looking at him right as the mine went off, the joint halfway to his lips and a big easy smile for me.

When a Sheridan burns there's nothing you can do but watch. The flames kept roaring out of the hatches for five minutes. The turret settled through the aluminum hull until it rested on the treads.

There were half a dozen smoke grenades inside my cupola. When they cooked off, puffs of red and yellow and violet smoke burped out of the glare.

Nothing exploded. We didn't carry any HE rounds.

The dustoff bird had landed before the fire was out. It took off with Chico, he was pretty shook up.

There wasn't anything wrong with me. As for Flip, the track'll cool off in a day or two and we'll see what's left then. Flip won't care.

I'm driving six-three now, until we get a replacement Sheridan. Sure, I'll TC another Sheridan. It don't mean nothing. You get used to a lot of things after you been in-country a while.

Lieutenant Brown's got a Grateful Dead tape on. You can hear it coming out of the hatches of Two-zero. Funny taste for a lifer. The way he's got the recorder bracketed against the turret, there's a space about the size of your fist behind it. You know, about the size of a grenade.

The rain's stopping. Pretty soon Lieutenant Brown'll pick up his recorder to head for the command meeting.

Ever see a Sheridan burn? Keep watching Two-zero.

AFTERWORD:
ONE WAR LATER

I'm not a pacifist, but anyone who's read my fiction knows that I regard wars as about the worst thing that can happen to the people who fight them. I really thought when I wrote the introduction to the original form of this collection that the United States might never again be directly involved in a full-scale war.

More fool me, I suppose. There we go with the Gulf War and over a million troops involved. A tremendous military victory at very slight cost in terms of U.S. personnel casualties.

We'll get back to that last point shortly.

As wars go, the Gulf War has a lot to recommend it. Perhaps most startling to a Viet Nam vet is the fact that the high-tech hardware generally worked. More important though less surprising is that our military high command behaved professionally this time also.

I say "less surprising" because most of the Gulf War generals had been company and battalion officers in Viet Nam. That didn't necessarily make them brilliant, but it made it unlikely that they would permit themselves to be micromanaged by idiots the way their predecessors were micromanaged by Lyndon Johnson and Robert S. MacNamara.

Because of hardware that worked for a change and professionalism at all levels of our military, our forces achieved their goals in an amazingly short time. Granted, some Monday-morning quarterbacks claim that different goals should have been set. Maybe so, but that takes nothing away from the success of our military in doing what it *was* told to do.

Some of the media have expressed the notion that the Iraqis weren't really a dangerous enemy. That isn't what Iran, a country with twice the population, came to believe during the war between them that lasted for most of the 1980s. To a considerable extent the second-guessers are really claiming that Third Worlders can't fight. Very few Viet Nam vets would agree. Nor Korean War vets. Nor Afghan War vets, for that matter. A lot of things look easy once somebody else has done them.

Direct U.S. casualties were a matter of hundreds—many of them caused by our own weaponry because the advance was too rapid for perfect coordination among its elements. Statistically, more troops would have been killed during the period of the Gulf War had they been at stateside bases where cars and booze were available instead of being bunkered in a country that bans alcohol. Young American men and women face a lot of lethal risks that don't involve being shot at by a uniformed enemy. Even as it was, the friend of mine who was killed during Desert Shield was a non-battle casualty.

For a soldier on our side, the Gulf War was as close to perfect as a war gets. Which leads us to the other 20,000 casualties: the veterans suffering from Gulf War syndrome.

In another remarkable example of people having learned something from the Vietnam War, Congress is in the process of compensating those suffering from Gulf War syndrome even though experts aren't any more sure of what causes it than they were of the illnesses Nam vets claim were caused by Agent Orange. The government's attitude toward Nam vets was that if government doctors couldn't determine a mechanism to cause the vets' problems, the problems didn't exist. For the government bureaucrats involved, that was absolutely true: the problems didn't exist, for them.

The symptoms of Gulf War syndrome are various and unrelated. They include fatigue, rashes, gastrointestinal and respiratory disorders, and muscle pain. The even more varied causes suggested include Iraqi chemical and biological weapons (which the U.S. government claims weren't used), countermeasures against chemical and biological weapons (which *even* the U.S. government admits were administered in haste and ignorance), desert fungus, and about anything else you want to name. The U.S. Army is worried enough about the U-238 shot used in our tanks' main guns that vehicles hit by friendly fire are quarantined in Charleston as potential radiation hazards.

The important thing to me is that this time nobody is denying that we've got a lot of sick soldiers on our hands, nor that their problems are somehow related to them having been in a war zone.

That—service in a war zone—is really the only common denominator among the sufferers. I noted in the introduction that war demands behavior patterns which by the standards of civilian life are insane. Without getting too mystical, I think most people (and certainly most doctors) will agree that mental state has a great deal to do with physical health.

If you believe the stress of an office or a production

line can cause ulcers, migraines, hives—think about spending six months in a bunker waiting for somebody faceless to kill you.

And join me in hoping that we won't have to put more of our young men and women into insane situations any time soon.

Dave Drake
Chatham County, NC